REVENGE, SERVED ROYAL

Also by Celeste Connally

All's Fair in Love and Treachery

Act Like a Lady, Think Like a Lord

REVENGE, SERVED ROYAL

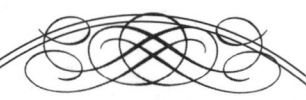

CELESTE CONNALLY

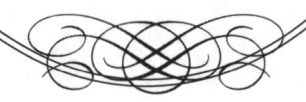

MINOTAUR BOOKS
NEW YORK

This is a work of fiction. All of the characters, organizations, and events portrayed in this novel are either products of the author's imagination or are used fictitiously.

First published in the United States by Minotaur Books, an imprint of St. Martin's Publishing Group

EU Representative: Macmillan Publishers Ireland Ltd, 1st Floor, The Liffey Trust Centre, 117–126 Sheriff Street Upper, Dublin 1, DO1 YC43

REVENGE, SERVED ROYAL. Copyright © 2025 by Stephanie Celeste Perkins. All rights reserved. Printed in the United States of America. For information, address St. Martin's Publishing Group, 120 Broadway, New York, NY 10271.

www.minotaurbooks.com

Designed by Meryl Sussman Levavi

Map by Liane Payne

The Library of Congress Cataloging-in-Publication Data is available upon request.

ISBN 978-1-250-38739-4 (hardcover)
ISBN 978-1-250-38740-0 (ebook)

The publisher of this book does not authorize the use or reproduction of any part of this book in any manner for the purpose of training artificial intelligence technologies or systems. The publisher of this book expressly reserves this book from the Text and Data Mining exception in accordance with Article 4(3) of the European Union Digital Single Market Directive 2019/790.

Our books may be purchased in bulk for specialty retail/wholesale, literacy, corporate/premium, educational, and subscription box use. Please contact MacmillanSpecialMarkets@macmillan.com.

First Edition: 2025

10 9 8 7 6 5 4 3 2 1

*In memory of Katherine Myers Sabom—
my dear, wonderful friend,
and a light in all of her friends' lives.
Until we have chips and salsa again, Kogie.*

Windsor Castle, 1815

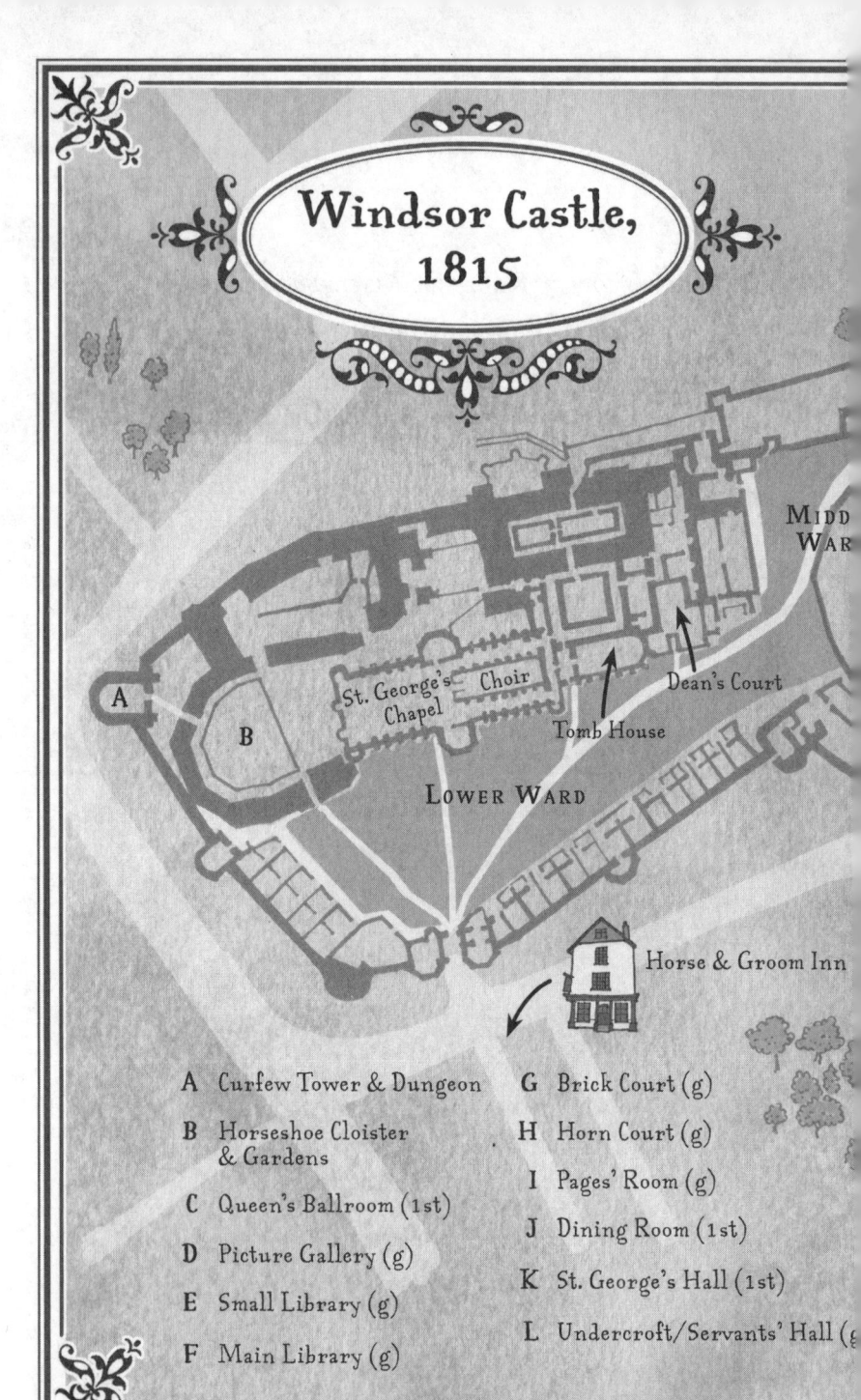

MIDDLE WARD

St. George's Chapel — Choir

Tomb House

Dean's Court

LOWER WARD

Horse & Groom Inn

- **A** Curfew Tower & Dungeon
- **B** Horseshoe Cloister & Gardens
- **C** Queen's Ballroom (1st)
- **D** Picture Gallery (g)
- **E** Small Library (g)
- **F** Main Library (g)
- **G** Brick Court (g)
- **H** Horn Court (g)
- **I** Pages' Room (g)
- **J** Dining Room (1st)
- **K** St. George's Hall (1st)
- **L** Undercroft/Servants' Hall (g)

Windsor Castle

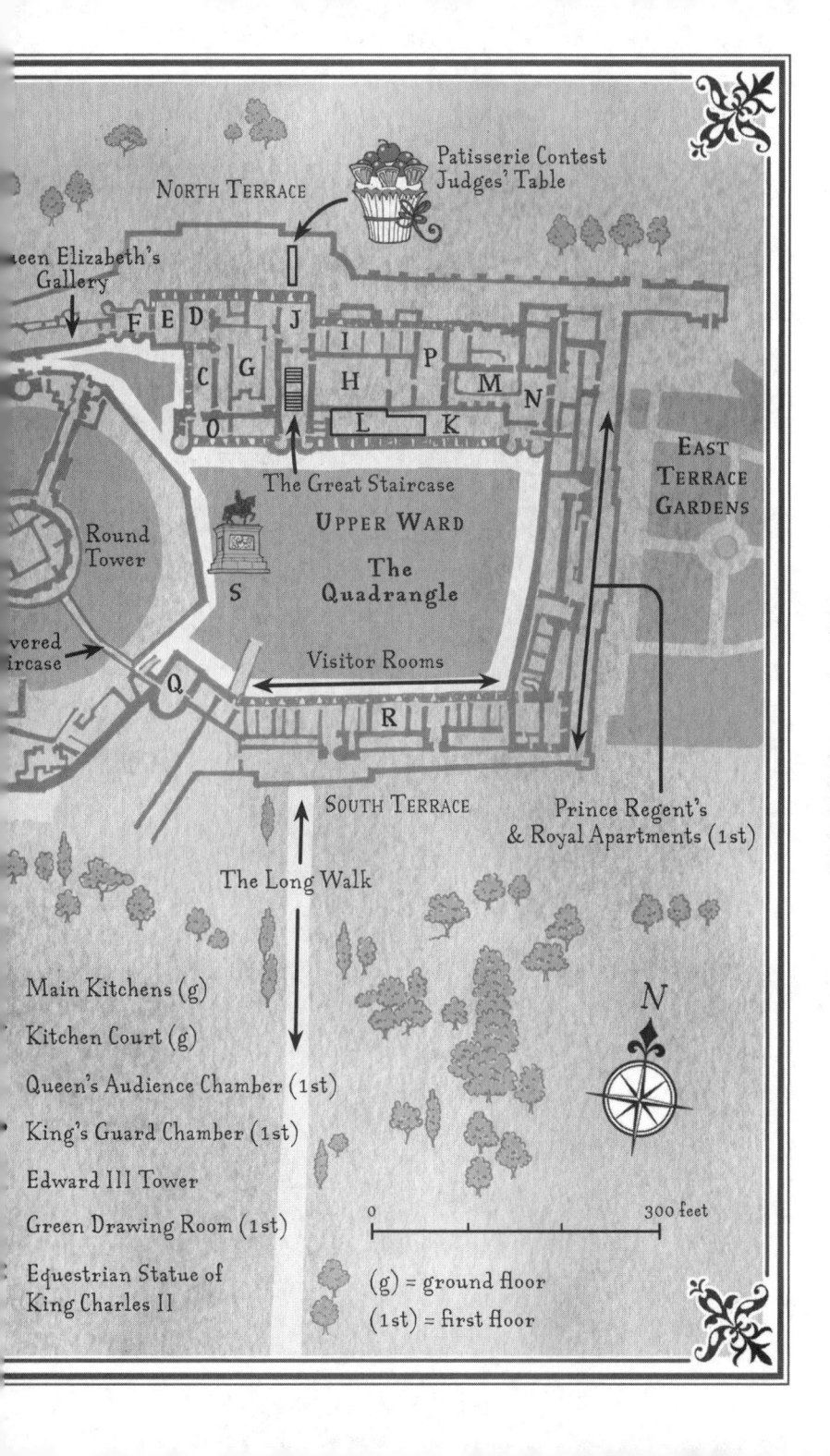

- North Terrace
- Patisserie Contest Judges' Table
- Queen Elizabeth's Gallery
- The Great Staircase
- Upper Ward
- The Quadrangle
- Round Tower
- Covered Staircase
- East Terrace Gardens
- Visitor Rooms
- Prince Regent's & Royal Apartments (1st)
- South Terrace
- The Long Walk

- Main Kitchens (g)
- Kitchen Court (g)
- Queen's Audience Chamber (1st)
- King's Guard Chamber (1st)
- Edward III Tower
- Green Drawing Room (1st)
- Equestrian Statue of King Charles II

(g) = ground floor
(1st) = first floor

0 — 300 feet

N

ONE

Sunday, 20 August 1815
Forsyth House
Berkeley Square, London

MRS. BING COWERED IN THE CORNER OF THE FORSYTH HOUSE kitchens, using her long wooden spoon like a saber, jabbing wildly at anyone who attempted to approach her.

"Stay back!" she cried in a shaking voice. "You shall not force me to go!"

With the last parry that had a wide-eyed kitchen maid leaping backward, a crumpled piece of paper slipped from Mrs. Bing's hand and wafted to the floor.

Mrs. Ruddle, who always exhibited the stoic countenance of a respected housekeeper, now radiated disapproval at witnessing what she considered needless histrionic behavior.

"Mrs. Bing, you must take hold of yourself," she hissed. "How could you behave this way in front of her ladyship? It is unseemly." Yet she, too, was rebuffed by a thrust of Mrs. Bing's rapier-like wooden spoon.

Lady Petra Forsyth, her ladyship in question, decided it was time to intervene.

"Mrs. Bing, I am sorry to see you so out of sorts. Pray tell, whatever is the matter?"

Her gentle tone only caused the normally stalwart cook's lower lip to tremble further. Mrs. Bing's soft brown eyes filled with tears, and her ever-calm voice rose up another octave, causing Sable, the sleek brown pointing dog sitting at Petra's feet, to tilt her head first one way, then the other.

"But my l-l-lady, I do not know. What could they want with me? I cannot think on what I could have done!"

"Well, then let us see, shall we?" With a word from Petra uttered in Gaelic, Sable trotted forward and picked up the crumpled paper, bringing it back with a gently wagging tail, which then began to beat twice as fast.

Petra knew exactly who would make her dog react that way. The sound of bootheels coming to a stop in the doorway behind her made her certain, as did her cook's reaction.

"Mr. Shawcross. I do beg your pardon, sir," Mrs. Bing said on a shaky breath, her hands flying to her mob cap, which had gone lopsided over her normally neat, dark chignon that was just beginning to show a strand or two of silver. At present, with tendrils coming loose, and her cheeks now blushing the same color as the merry flames beneath a set of three chickens on a spit, Mrs. Bing looked like the windswept, fresh-faced girl she must have been when she was growing up on the Devon coast.

"Nonsense, Mrs. Bing," came Duncan's cheerful reply. "You are never in the wrong in this kitchen so far as I have ever witnessed, and as such, never need to beg my pardon."

This kindness was too much for Mrs. Bing. She pulled her apron up to cover her face, which had flushed an additional shade of red, and let out a strangled sob.

Petra whirled to give an exasperated look to the tall, roguish-looking man with hair the color of dark molasses and decidedly naughty green eyes that crinkled at the edges at the sight of her. She pointed over his shoulder.

"And you may go back whence you came, Duncan Shawcross. I will not have you disrupting Mrs. Bing's kitchen even more than it is at present." She lowered her voice, not that it could be heard above Mrs. Bing's noisy keens. "You know your compliments have her in a flutter at the best of times. Normally, it is quite adorable, I agree. But you are rather making things worse at present."

Petra narrowed her eyes, seeing how Duncan's were dancing with merriment as he made for the nearby stoneware jar that held a fresh batch of Mrs. Bing's ginger biscuits. Swiftly, she moved to block his access, holding up the crumpled paper. "And as it was you who brought this offending letter that has caused the unsettling of my household, you may leave without a biscuit."

A flash of white teeth, more so than most because he did not partake of tobacco like other men, and Duncan gave one of his cheeky bows.

"My apologies, my lady," he said, his eyes lingering a moment too long on her mouth, as if he might lean in and give her lower lip a bite in the same manner he would his favorite biscuit. Then he added in a whisper, "Especially for being quite adorable." With an elegant tip of his head to the four other women present, he turned on his heel, with Sable bounding after him.

Petra rolled her eyes at his retreating back, knowing she would turn to find Mrs. Bing and the kitchen maid both further in a state, and Mrs. Ruddle with the edges around her stern mouth softening despite herself.

And Annie—by thunder, the lips of her lady's maid would be twitching with the desire to giggle, though Petra knew it was only the combination of Duncan being his most charming along with the sense of ridiculousness permeating the kitchen that could have accomplished such a feat.

Yet, if Petra caught Annie's eye, all would be lost. Neither would be able to keep a serious countenance, and Mrs. Bing would likely drop to the flagstone floor in a puddle of blubbering tears if she thought either was laughing at her expense. And that, for a number of reasons, the topmost being her respect for her cook, could never happen.

"Right," she said, and began to smooth out the paper without yet facing the others to allow them time to collect themselves. For despite the fact that Forsyth House was run by Lady Petra on a small complement of loyal servants who were made to be comfortable in Petra's presence, they remained ever mindful of the fact that Lady Petra was the daughter of the fifth Earl of Holbrook. That she was a goddaughter to the Duchess of Hillmorton, and a favorite of both Her Grace and the duke. And that only a couple of months earlier, in late June, Petra had saved the life of Prince Frederick, the King and Queen's second son, earning the favor of Her Majesty and the entire royal family.

What was more, proud women they all were, these servants of Forsyth House. Proud of their work, of their station, and of their ability to successfully run such a large house with such a small contingency when most houses of this size required twice as many, if not more. They were proud of their connection to the House of Forsyth, the earl, and Lady Petra herself, too.

And since Petra had scandalized London society by announcing that she would never marry—and lately had become wrapped up in adventures that could have taken her life and tarnished the Forsyth name—she constantly reminded herself of her own luck to have these women in her household. Thus, she would take whatever bad news was contained on this fine stationery without judgment toward Mrs. Bing.

The worried frown that had been slowly building on her face eased as she took in the words written in a very fine hand indeed. And then the crest that was recognizable to every person in London, whether or not they were able to read the words themselves. She spun round, delight in her voice.

"But Mrs. Bing, what is causing you such vexation? This is wonderful news. You have been invited to Windsor Castle in a fortnight's time by Her Majesty herself." Petra scanned the wording again, her smile growing. "Oh, how wonderful. It is a patisserie competition for the most talented bakers of the ton."

Mrs. Bing appeared little comforted by this revelation, however. Petra thus hastened to explain, but not before asking the kitchen maid to bring tea and slices of currant-studded pound cake for all.

"All this invitation means is that, should you wish it, you would spend a week at Windsor Castle competing with nine other cooks in a baking competition—as a diverting exercise, and nothing more."

"But I read something about being blinded, my lady." Mrs. Bing clutched her wooden spoon to her chest as if it would protect her. "Is that to be my fate should my bakes not be considered worthy?"

Hurriedly, Petra reread the invitation, then had to curl her toes tightly to keep from smiling.

"I am happy to say that is not the case at all, Mrs. Bing. It is merely a *blind competition*, meaning when the judges taste the competitors' entries, they do so without knowing who made what biscuit, or fairy cake, loaf of bread, or what have you. That way it is judged solely on the taste, and looks, and not on the cook herself, or the house from which she comes."

"A most fair way of doing things, is it not, Mrs. Bing?" said Mrs. Ruddle with one of her rare, if brief, encouraging smiles. But Mrs. Bing's eyes were still wide as saucers, so Petra continued.

"There will be other events going on as well, all to help celebrate Their Majesties' upcoming fifty-fourth wedding anniversary. If you win the patisserie contest, you will earn the right to brag that which we all know, that you are the best cook in all of London and much of the reason why my dinner parties are always a coveted invitation."

"And if I should lose, my lady?" she asked in a terrified whisper.

"If you should happen *not* to win, Mrs. Bing, it means nothing,"

Petra said with a blithe shrug. "Not to me, and not to all of us here at Forsyth House." She tapped her chin thoughtfully with a finger. "Though it is possible the earl might use it as leverage in attempting to convince you to move out to Suffolk and Buckfields and cook for him there. For you know he is always attempting to poach you from me, the rascal."

This caused Mrs. Bing to emit a short, girlish giggle, for having the Earl of Holbrook brag to all and sundry about her cooking was almost better than any honor the Queen could bestow on her.

Fiddling with the handle of her teacup with an expression of studied nonchalance, Mrs. Bing then said, "And if I should like the challenge?" She pursed her lips, narrowing them into the middle distance, and into her past. "I often competed in the village fetes when I were a girl, my lady. And I always earned the top ribbon with my cakes and biscuits."

"Well, then," Petra said, "we would be cheering you on from Forsyth House, would we not?"

This earned vociferous affirmations from the others in the room, teasing a pleased flush from Mrs. Bing's cheeks. A moment later, there was the sound of dog nails clicking on the floor as Sable trotted back into the kitchen and laid her head in Petra's lap.

"She brought you something, my lady," the kitchen maid said. "It looks like the same type of invitation what Mrs. Bing received."

Indeed, in Sable's mouth was another envelope. Petra took it, saying, "I wonder who else has been invited?" And then her eyebrows rose when she turned it over and saw written upon it, *The Honorable Lady Petra Forsyth*.

She turned to see Duncan once more in the doorway, leaning against the doorframe, and gave him a narrow look. "You know something."

He shrugged one well-muscled shoulder, more visible as he was in shirtsleeves and a waistcoat, but he did not even bother to hide a grin. She slid her fingers beneath the wax seal, read the invitation, and felt a bit of the overwhelmed sensation Mrs. Bing had a few moments earlier.

"Heavens. I have been asked by Her Majesty to be one of five judges for the patisserie competition." Then excitement surged through her. An entire week in the luxury of Windsor Castle, eating biscuits and fairy cakes? Yes, *indeed*.

Duncan had handed Annie a scroll, explaining it to be a copy of all the planned events, and that similar, much larger scrolls would be hanging inside Windsor Castle for all participants to see.

"Lady Caroline will also be a judge," Annie said excitedly as she read. "And Miss Lottie will do a demonstration with her dogs, and Miss Frances of her apothecary skills. There are several other women doing demonstrations, from music to needlepoint—oh, and even a woman who studies the stars. She will be giving a lecture."

When the others crowded around to read the scroll, Petra exchanged a secret smile with Duncan, who had his own set of stars tattooed on his chest, right above his heart—five small ones in the shape of the constellation Cassiopeia, mimicking the smattering of freckles across Petra's nose.

"And there will be a tilting contest, a ball on the final evening—we must go to the modiste today for a lovely new gown, my lady—and more lectures throughout the week. And look, do, for one lecturer is Sir Rufus Pomeroy, the former royal chef. He will speak on the history of British cuisine, as well as being a patisserie judge along with two other gentlemen, Lady Caroline, and you, my lady."

Petra clapped her hands together. "Oh, Chef Rufus! Or, *Sir* Rufus, I should correctly say, as he was granted a knighthood for his service to the royal family. How wonderful it will be to see him again. It has been, goodness, twenty years now. He has become such a celebrity in recent years that I do not know if he will even recognize me. Though I could not fault him—I was but a child of four when we last saw each other."

"I have no doubt that Sir Rufus will know you in an instant, my lady," said Mrs. Ruddle kindly. Then she explained for the confused-looking kitchen maid that the retired royal chef had once worked at Buckfields for the earl and late countess. "He left the earl's employ in late 1795 to work in His Majesty's kitchens. He later began writing cookery books, and became so famous and wealthy from them that he was able to leave service. In 1811, if I am not mistaken."

Petra smiled fondly at the memory of the chef, though her mind's portrait of him was quite fuzzy indeed as she was so young when last in his company. She mostly recalled a smiling round face and a sturdy build that was a bit shorter than her own papa, which would put Sir Rufus several inches shorter than Duncan. She did not know his current age, but felt him likely to be somewhere near his sixtieth decade.

What she did know was that Sir Rufus now traveled about Great Britain and was often feted at the best houses in the kingdom. He was known for disliking London, however, which was in large part why she had never crossed paths with him in the years since he had left service. All in all, it did not surprise her that his cookbooks had become so popular. Yet she was content to remember him from her early childhood.

"Sir Rufus was always so kind to me. He often made me my favorite shortbread and had it sent up to the nursery, too, even when my nursemaid told him not to."

"He was a favorite of the late countess as well," Mrs. Ruddle said, and Mrs. Bing nodded in agreement.

"Indeed," Petra said. "It pleases me greatly that the cake he created and called La Bella Contessa in her honor is still made in the Buckfields kitchens and served on special occasions. In fact, Sir Rufus—when we simply called him Chef—promised the earl he would never give another soul the recipe."

Though she had lost her mother before she could even walk, Petra had always felt close to her when her favorite dishes were served. And similar to her mama, Petra particularly favored La Bella Contessa. It consisted of seven thin layers of cinnamon-spiced chocolate cake almost floating between slender bands of icing flavored with chocolate, crushed walnuts, and a touch more cinnamon. The whole cake was then covered in a shiny coating of chocolate mixed with cream, and the cake's top was decorated with a line of crushed walnuts that had been first glazed with honey, cinnamon, and sugar.

Of course, Petra had no idea how to go about making this cake, but she knew its ingredients by heart as she still had a copy of the original recipe.

Duncan, his hand already in the stoneware jar and pulling out two ginger biscuits, was saying, "I shall be there as well—representing Hillmorton House, of course—in a fencing exhibition and riding in the tilting contest." Just before biting into one of the biscuits, he added with a waggle of his eyebrows, "And do you know who the judge is to be in the final round of the patisserie contest? None other than the current royal cook, Monsieur Chef Antonin Carême."

This news elicited delighted gasps. The handsome chef from France had come under the notice of all of England recently, and especially of Annie when she met him two months earlier in the servants' hall of Buckingham House. Annie had charmed the Frenchman so much that he had gifted her his recipe for *pain ordinaire*, a rather delicious, if simple, everyday bread.

"Oh, Mrs. Bing," breathed Annie. "You will adore Chef Carême—but possibly you may not wish to tell him you improved upon his *pain ordinaire*. You know how impassioned those Frenchmen can become."

Mrs. Bing sniffed and picked up her wooden spoon again as if about to sheathe a saber. A certain canny look came into her eyes as she straightened her shoulders. "I will not tell him—I will show him. No Frenchman will outdo me when it comes to baking."

"Brava, Mrs. Bing!" Duncan said heartily, making her cheeks pinken once more.

Holding up her teacup to Mrs. Bing in a sort of toast, Petra said, "Well, Mrs. Bing, it seems you and I shall be representing Forsyth House at Windsor Castle in a fortnight's time, and I say every other house represented should quake in their boots!"

"Huzzah!" cried out Mrs. Bing, and she raised her cup, too, as everyone else cried out, "May they quake in their boots!"

TWO

Monday, 4 September 1815
Day one of the royal celebrations
Windsor Castle
Windsor, Berkshire

ANNIE LIFTED A DRESS FROM ONE OF PETRA'S TRUNKS, SHOOK it out with such force that it caused a snapping sound, made a dissatisfied noise, and laid it on a nearby chaise longue. Then repeated the process as Petra looked on.

"We have been at Windsor but two hours, Annie, and yet it is six times I have watched you show such great annoyance at the state of my dresses. I have begun to worry you shall grow hoarse from all the angry-goose noises coming from your throat. It is rather unlike you, especially because you pack with such care. Is something the matter?"

"Nothing at all, my lady," Annie said primly.

Petra swung her feet down from the window seat she had been occupying, and laid her copy of *Camilla* to one side. Her hands clasped casually behind her back, she strolled over to where Annie was now fiercely shaking out a riding habit in an emerald green with dark blue embroidery in a floral pattern about the collar, cuffs, and each button.

"Normally, I do despise my riding habits, as you well know, but I rather like this one," Petra said, keeping her tone mild.

"That is because you designed it specially with hidden breeches beneath," Annie returned. Indeed, as she grabbed a clothing brush and whisked the habit over to the sofa, the unbuttoned skirt flew open at the middle seam to reveal buckskin breeches in the same dark blue. It was an ingenious design, if Petra might say so herself. All she had to do was unbutton the skirt and then secure each side safely to hooks hidden beneath a bow at the small of her back.

"Mm, yes. It goes well with the saddle Duncan had made for me, too."

It was a very ladylike sidesaddle, of course, but with an extra stirrup leather and stirrup conveniently tucked away inside a saddlebag. Should she be able to without causing a scandal, Petra could simply extract the extra stirrup and attach it before swinging her right leg up and over her horse's neck to go from sidesaddle to astride. She had practiced time and time again during her last trip to Buckfields, with Duncan timing her. Between unbuttoning her riding skirt and attaching her stirrup, she could go from riding like a lady to riding like a gentleman in under two minutes.

But that was neither here nor there at the moment. It was Annie's mood she needed to unbutton, especially when she watched Annie all but attack her riding habit with the clothing brush.

"Has someone belowstairs upset you, Annie? For there shall no doubt be personalities here to test even those with the most patient temperament..."

"Everyone has been most accommodating," Annie replied, though her gently pointed chin seemed to tighten all the same.

"It is not Charles, is it?" Petra then asked. "You seemed delighted when Duncan asked if Charles might serve as his valet this week, even if means we all must remember to call him Foyle now as befitting his new status. He has not become insufferable, has he? Charles—or rather *Foyle*, that is—not Duncan." Her lips quirked up. "Though one could be forgiven for thinking it was Duncan whom I meant. He can be quite the frustrating creature when he so chooses."

"It is not Foyle, thank you, my lady. He is truly pleased to be here, and I am grateful to Mr. Shawcross for asking him." Annie had said this with a brief smile, but a moment later, a vertical line formed between her eyes and she went back to treating Petra's dresses as if they had personally offended her.

"Well, it cannot be Mrs. Bing," Petra said, still with determined lightness. "For you yourself told me she was overjoyed when she saw the kitchens and learned how the patisserie contest would progress."

"Yes, she is terribly excited for it all to begin," Annie said, setting aside the riding habit and snatching up Petra's new short corset.

"Only I cannot partake of any of the fun," Petra continued, feigning a pout. "Nor may Lady Caroline, Sir Rufus, Lord Wadley-Bates, and Sir Franklin, for that matter. As judges, we are not allowed in the kitchens or the preparation area. In fact, I am quite surprised they did not put us at Frogmore House with all of the guest lecturers."

"Indeed, my lady," Annie said, but it was clear she was giving a rote reply as she inspected the corset, adjusting one of the small blue bows at the straps so that it lay flat.

Petra thought about doing something silly, like jumping onto the bed and making a comic show of performing some of the defensive kicks and punches she had been learning as of late until Annie came out of her moody reverie. Instead, she placed her hands on her hips and aimed for a direct approach when yet another dress was shaken out with undue force.

"Annie, are you going to tell me what has you in such a state of vexation?"

Yet there came a knock at her door, and Annie rushed so quickly to answer it that a curled strand of chestnut hair flew back from her temple.

It was Mrs. Daley, the head housekeeper at Windsor Castle. She bobbed a quick curtsy, and came straight to the point.

"Do you have everything you need, my lady? Yes? Splendid. Her Majesty instructed you are to be next door to your particular friend and His Majesty's cousin, Lady Caroline Markingham-Smythe. She arrived not long ago."

"Pray tell, did I hear my name?" came a familiar voice, tinged with amusement.

Petra poked her head out of the door to see Caroline walking down the corridor, her glossy dark hair and silk day dress both in the latest fashion and setting off her tall form, long neck, and clear brown eyes.

"Do continue, Mrs. Daley," said Caroline. "You have known me long enough to know I would not require you to come to my door and repeat everything you are about to tell Lady Petra when I am standing right here. The corridor is rather unconventional, of course, but I shan't tell my royal cousins if you won't."

The housekeeper inclined her head, suppressing a grin in a way that spoke of an indulgent familiarity with Caroline's cheekiness. Then she began by indicating the two rooms across the hall and explaining that Her Majesty was still determining which ladies of rank would be situated in each.

"There are nearly one hundred and fifty invited to stay here at the castle, but the total number of invitees over the course of the event is over five hundred. Naturally, many will be at the other two royal residences within Windsor Great Park. This includes guests at the Royal Lodge, who are mostly unmarried gentlemen competing in various events." A prim tone came into the housekeeper's voice. "Her Majesty feels the nearly four miles to and from the castle grounds will be an excellent reminder that they are to remember the rules of propriety."

"I rather think Her Majesty is expecting too much of a trifling four miles, Mrs. Daley," Caroline drawled.

The housekeeper looked momentarily shocked, then her expression gave back over to measured merriment.

"I understand your ladyship's husband was to join us for one day to participate in the swimming race at Virginia Water Lake," she said. "But, alas, he was called away with his duties to the navy. If I may say so, 'tis a shame, my lady. I do enjoy seeing Captain Smythe."

"As do I," Caroline agreed, a smile coming easily to her lips. "Though my captain did tell me he recommended a replacement to Her Majesty for the swim, to which she graciously agreed. Did Lord Whitfield accept the invitation?"

Caroline's countenance was of such studied curiosity that Petra nearly laughed, for Whitfield had happily confirmed the news days earlier in her own drawing room, with Caroline beaming at his side.

For Mrs. Daley's part, as the royal housekeeper whose job lent her to overhearing society's gossip, the subtle gleam in her eyes said she wasn't fooled regarding the true connection between Caroline and Whitfield. Yet no hint of censure entered her voice as she confirmed Whitfield's presence on Thursday and returned to her explanations.

"Those staying at Frogmore House are guest lecturers and those giving demonstrations, with very few staying more than a night or two as London is such an easy distance," she explained.

This included Petra's and Caroline's dear friends Lottie Reed and Frances Bardwell, both of whom would be presenting later in the week. They, however, had been invited to stay for the ball that culminated the celebrations of Their Majesties' fifty-fourth wedding anniversary. The ball, Mrs. Daley said, delight briefly showing on her face, would have closer to a thousand in attendance.

"Now then," she continued, "your ladyships' presence is requested with the other guests in the main library at seven o'clock for a welcome by Her Majesty, the Queen, and His Royal Highness, the Prince Regent."

Petra's lips twitched at how Mrs. Daley eyed Caroline, who briefly attempted innocence.

"What? Oh, very well, I promise I shall be there on time."

"*I promise* I shall have her there on time, Mrs. Daley," Petra said, and received a theatrically scandalized look from her dearest friend.

"Excellent," said Mrs. Daley with satisfaction. "Supper is then at eight in St. George's Hall, but as this week is intended to be one of celebration and enjoyment, only tonight and the ball on the last evening will require full evening dress. All other meals will be taken at your leisure in the dining room—or in your rooms, if you so choose."

She then gestured down the hallway, eastward of Petra's room.

"Then in the middle of this wing is the Green Drawing Room, which may be used by all guests at any time for a bit of respite. However, tea each afternoon will be held in the main library and the small library, which connect to each other, and are on the ground floor of the north wing."

"I shall be Lady Petra's faithful guide to the castle," said Caroline, then lowered her voice to sotto voce, "including the secret passageways, yes, Mrs. D.?"

"Lady Caroline!" Mrs. Daley admonished, but her eyes positively danced. Glancing at Petra with an approving look that indicated she knew of Petra's recent adventures, too, she added, "Though I think her ladyship has earned the right."

Exchanging a grin with Caroline, Petra then checked the watch pinned to her dress. "Why, it is almost four o'clock now."

Mrs. Daley nodded. "And so I shall leave you two to enjoy touring the castle. If anything is needed from the kitchens, please ring for Tilly, your hall maid." And with a curtsy, she moved on.

Caroline hastened to link her arm with Petra's.

"Come with me, dearest, for we have but an hour before we must return to dress for tonight's supper. Let us go to the Green Drawing Room first, where I know we can view the list of events for tomorrow. There will be a company of funambulists performing and I must know where and when. Did you know the men do so in nothing more than the tightest of breeches?"

Petra only had time for one swift glance back at Annie before Caroline pulled her along into the corridor. Worryingly, Annie was still clutching one of Petra's dresses, the crease still between her hazel eyes, and Petra was determined to discover the cause of it.

THREE

"I THOUGHT YOU KNEW A SECRET PASSAGEWAY OR A SHORTCUT," Petra said, panting slightly as she leaned up against the wall inside the small library.

Caroline unfurled the fan hanging from her wrist and waved it with alacrity at her face.

"It would have helped if you had reminded me to use one *before* we all but sprinted across Windsor Castle, not after." She shook her fan admonishingly at Petra. "Though if you had not insisted on knowing the best way to the stables earlier, we would have been back in our rooms at a more respectable time. One and a quarter hours for my lady's maid to ready me for the evening? Why, it was positively barbaric."

"Oh, something savage, to be sure," Petra said, fighting a grin as she smoothed the skirt of her dress, which was a shade darker than the apricot hue of her bodice and sleeves and embroidered in the blackwork style with flowering vines. "Though Annie did not find the task so difficult with me."

Annie, in fact, had been so decidedly cheerful when dressing Petra for the evening that it was almost more worrying than her previous dark mood—but there had once more been no time to press her upon the matter.

"Do not look so unrepentant," Caroline chided. "We were forced to dash down the stairs in the south wing, across the entire width of the Quadrangle, and through the picture gallery here in the north wing, only to be informed by that footman"—she jabbed her fan at the liveried footman standing just outside the library, who glanced over nervously—"that Her Majesty and the Prince have not yet arrived. All because of your obsession with horses. Do you deny it?"

Petra laughed, grabbed her friend's hand, and turned her in the opposite direction. "I have no wish to deny it. Now, let us take a brief turn about the library. Have I told you yet how becoming your dress is? You wear purple so well, and your diamond and amethyst necklace is stunning. A gift from Lord Whitfield?"

"It is indeed, and you are now forgiven," Caroline purred, flouncing out her skirts so the sheer overlay briefly floated over the striped purple silk beneath.

They strolled about, debating the size of the so-called small library—settling on more than forty feet long and half that in width—and deciding it was well designed and quite cozy with its intricately paneled ceiling, plush reading armchairs, and tables filled with interesting pieces of antiquity. And, of course, all the lovely shelves filled to the brim with leather-bound books, their titles in glowing gold leaf inviting readers to investigate further.

Walking through a set of carved-wood doors, they then reached the main library, which was more than twice the size of the first one, just as beautiful and opulent, and teeming with guests.

Petra stopped at a bank of windows, finding the clouds were still visible in the twilight, as if a painter had daubed soft streaks of vermilion and ocher at their edges. She gazed out over the North Terrace, the walkway overlooking Windsor Park that had been built by King Henry VIII, then greatly improved upon by his resourceful daughter Elizabeth.

"Oh, look, it is the patisserie contestants. They appear to be practicing for the first round of judging tomorrow."

Ten cooks, verifiable by their white aprons, neckerchiefs, and slightly pointed white caps, came into view, led by a cook from the royal kitchens wearing the distinctive blue-gray that was coming to be known as Windsor blue. While all the baking preparations would be done in the large, open-air courtyard next to the kitchens called, fittingly, Kitchen Court, the actual contest where Petra and her fellow judges would taste each bake was to be held on the North Terrace. Unless, of course, the weather should turn inclement, whereby another large courtyard known as Horn Court would then serve as the contest location.

Mrs. Bing, whom Petra could recognize easily due to the dark chignon at the back of her head and her tendency for holding one shoulder a little higher than the other, stood proudly in line. Even from the window, it was evident Mrs. Bing was smiling and laughing with the other participants. Petra felt a wash of contentment at the sight of her cook so obviously enjoying herself.

Now if only she could feel the same regarding Annie's happiness at being at Windsor.

"Lady Petra, Lady Caroline, there you are!"

Whirling around, they were surrounded in a trice by a group of their fellow guests.

"We insist that you offer explanations as to how the judging of the patisserie contest will commence," one very upright woman Petra knew as Lady Norworthy said in a commanding voice while holding a lorgnette up to her eyes by its mother-of-pearl handle. A moment later, someone ushered two more judges into the circle.

The first was Lord Wadley-Bates. Fatherly in age, portly in build, and genial in nature, he had sired seven children and was the London-based publisher of cookery and gardening books. He proudly asserted that he had tasted every dish in every book he'd ever published. As such, he had proclaimed himself an expert in the tasting of nearly every type of English sweet and baked good one could make.

"As my wife remained in London and cannot agree, I submit my figure as proof!" He patted his stomach, making everyone laugh.

The other gentleman, with a hooked nose and nary but a few wisps of fair hair covering his otherwise bald pate, was Sir Franklin

Haverstock. His fortune had been made in Northumberland in the milling of self-rising flour and he, too, declared himself an expert on baked goods.

"As so many use the very flour I sell, I am known for baking, and eating, every sweet recipe in the cookery books his lordship publishes," he said, with a nod to his fellow judge. "In fact, I've oft been told I could write one of my own!"

Lord Wadley-Bates guffawed, slapping Sir Franklin on the shoulder in his mirth. Pitching forward momentarily from the blow, Sir Franklin glowered as he straightened before giving in to something resembling a self-deprecating smile.

"And you shall no doubt be meeting Sir Rufus Pomeroy quite soon, for he is our fifth judge," said Lord Wadley-Bates, looking about at the assembled faces. "His cookery books are responsible for so much of my publishing house's success and I look forward to his excellent commentary on each of the bakes put forward by the fine cooks here this week."

There were satisfied nods all around, and then one diminutive countess spoke up.

"I did not know that a total of ten cooks were invited," she said. "How will you ever reduce the number? And how will there ever be enough room in the kitchens for all to . . ." She hesitated, plainly unclear on how her own cook managed to produce any meals at all, much less desserts. "Well, for all to do whatever it is they do in the kitchens. Surely there are not enough ovens, or what have you."

When it seemed all eyes were on Petra for this knowledge, she smiled and explained.

"The baking contest begins tomorrow and runs for five days, with the final bake to conclude on Saturday, the day of Their Majesties' ball. Each day, we shall be judging the entrants at three o'clock."

"Teatime, if you will," interjected Caroline, "for we all know it is the best time of day for something sweet." This was met with enthusiastic agreement.

"For the first round, the cooks all arrived with biscuits they have already made," Petra continued. "This allows them to begin creating their entries for day two straight away. The ovens are shared, you understand, with every cook having an allotted time. Each of the first four days, two cooks are eliminated, until we have only two contestants left for the last day of baking. Thus, on the fifth day, which is Saturday, the final two cooks will compete for the honor of being named the best baker in England."

When a viscount asked what the first biscuit to be judged was, Sir Franklin replied, "The humble Shrewsbury cake, my lord." And seeing the viscount looking as if he would scoff, Sir Franklin was quick to defend the choice. "True, it is little more than a flat biscuit made of butter, sugar, eggs, flour, and a bit of mace, cinnamon, or similar, but that is precisely what makes them so difficult to perfect."

"I quite agree, Sir Franklin," said Lord Wadley-Bates. "Even the smallest change in amount of one or more ingredients can make quite the difference. As does baking time. They are harder to make than one might expect!"

Caroline addressed the viscount with one of her disarming smiles. "Indeed, I should like you to try to make such a simple recipe and have them taste as wonderful as these ten bakers will prove them to be, my lord."

The viscount held up his hands in surrender. "I can see these contestants have stalwart and clever judges, so I shall keep my thoughts to myself and let them decide who earns the title."

A smooth, French-accented voice then came from behind the group.

"Ah, yes, but the final winner shall be determined by me."

The crowd turned and parted to find a handsome man with hair the color of roasted chestnuts, even darker eyes, and a gently clefted chin. He wore a double-breasted coat of stark white over dark pantaloons and black Hessian boots. His eyes radiated confidence and passion, and so many women drew in a breath at the sight of him that it sounded like a brief windstorm had erupted in the Windsor Castle library. He gave a small smile and then a polite bow in recognition of it.

"I have come to introduce myself, my lords, *mesdames et messieurs*. I am Chef Antonin Carême, and it is my honor to welcome you to Windsor Castle for *le concours de pâtisserie*—the baking contest, no? And to begin what will be a week of many delights, I have prepared a little treat. Not enough to spoil the appetite for tonight's supper, no! Simply an *amuse-gueule*, a little amusement for the mouth."

He turned sideways, and a series of footmen carrying silver platters walked in and stood in a line. Their trays contained small plates, each holding a plum-sized pastry bun that was split in two halves and filled with a thick, custard-like filling.

"I call them *choux à la crème*," Chef Carême said, looking around, his eyes stopping on Petra to linger just a moment more than the others. "They are a profiterole made of delicate pastry, which I then fill with vanilla *crème de pâtisserie*. This is my own recipe I have perfected. Please, enjoy."

As the guests hurried to the footmen to take a plate, the chef met Petra's eyes once more in a way that made her think, *Heavens*, before he turned and strode out of the library.

"It is a good thing Shawcross is still inspecting the fencing venue," Caroline said in her ear, "for that handsome Frenchman does not know the art of subtlety. I think it is a good thing he will be in the kitchens most of this week."

"And I think you should stop teasing me," Petra said on a laugh.

"I heard the Prince is rather unhappy with Chef Carême," Caroline continued, unabated. "For the Frenchman loathes our English weather and wishes to return to his fair country. When I was lunching earlier with Her Majesty, Prinny arrived and complained that the chef was threatening to leave as soon as the contest was over."

Petra recalled the past June, when she sat in the Queen's private breakfast room in Buckingham House and first heard of the talented Chef Carême—as well has his desire to leave England. "Mm, yes. I believe Her Majesty shares that displeasure."

Caroline playfully arched an eyebrow. "Maybe I should suggest to my royal cousins that if Lady Petra were to speak with the chef in her excellent French then he might be inclined to stay?"

"If you do not stop," Petra retorted, "I will suggest to Her Majesty that it is you who needs censuring. Now, let us try these *choux à la crème*—I daresay that sounds much more elegant than 'cream puffs.'" And, within moments, their smiles turned rapturous when they bit into the pastry. A little moan was in the back of Petra's throat, in fact, when Caroline nudged her.

"Stop lusting over your *chou*, dearest, for a green-eyed pirate is heading your way, with a handsome older gentleman in tow. I, however, shall use their arrival to go make my hellos to the Duchess of Hillmorton." She gave a surreptitious wink as she moved away. "*Do* try not to have another man flirt with you in the space of five minutes put together, will you?"

Four

Petra looked up to find Duncan in her sights. He in fact was looking a bit piratical with his dark, wavy hair windswept, and wearing only shirtsleeves and a paisley waistcoat in shades of green that did extraordinary things to the already mesmerizing color of his eyes.

Though not a single woman cast anything more than appreciative glances at his lack of a tailcoat, one blustery naval captain remarked upon his state of undress with distaste. Duncan, however, charmingly explained that during the testing of a set of light cavalry sabers for a weaponry demonstration, his opponent accidentally sliced a button from his coat.

"And swiftly, Mr. Shawcross returned the favor," said the older man in jovial tones, holding out his arms to display his own shirtsleeves, eliciting laughs from those around them.

A moment later, both men were shielded from view as two valets arrived, each with a tailcoat neatly folded over one forearm. Charles was the taller and darker of the two. Duncan, of course, addressed him by his surname.

"Well done, Foyle. I thank you for your speediness," he said as Petra's footman helped him shrug into the tailcoat. "My lady," Charles said, with smiling blue eyes and a bow of his head.

"Good evening, Foyle," she replied, and if possible, he stood straighter. Yet his eyes cut briefly sideways when the other man addressed his own valet.

"*Not now, Beecham,*" the man hissed. "Help me on with my coat and be gone."

"Of course, sir," Beecham said through gritted teeth. The shocking hint of insolence caused Petra to glance his way and take in auburn hair and a jaw clenched tight. A moment later, the valet then gave a stiff bow and took his leave, striding after Charles out of the library.

"Now, Lady Petra," Duncan began, and she returned her gaze to his, finding him tilting his head toward the other man still adjusting his coat lapels. "I should like to introduce you to a gentleman who has been wishing to make your acquaintance for some time."

Curious, Petra finally had a proper look at the man. She found him to be of slim build and average height with a full head of white hair, ruddy cheeks, and bright gray eyes that widened briefly before pinching with his smile, sending deep starbursts of lines onto his temples. A smile came to her own face as well.

"I should have said 'renew' the acquaintance, as I see she recognizes you without my introduction, Sir Rufus," Duncan said genially.

"Ah, Lady Petra," the older man exclaimed, which he followed by giving a very gentlemanly bow. "The last time I saw you at Buckfields, you were but a little girl with ribbons in your curls"—his eyes twinkled with merriment—"and always with at least one scrape upon your knee when you snuck away from your nursemaid and came to the kitchens in search of something sweet. Truly, I am most delighted to make your acquaintance again, as well as be a patisserie judge alongside you." A brief tremble of emotion then came to his lips. "If I may say so, you have grown up splendidly. You look so much like your late mama."

Petra beamed. "You may indeed say so, as it is the best of compliments. It is I who am honored to see you again, *Sir* Rufus," she replied, emphasizing his honorific with a warmth that made his eyes dance. "And may I congratulate you on all your success as the author of cookery books. My own Mrs. Bing at Forsyth House tells me she simply could not do without her copy of *The Accomplished English Cook*."

Sir Rufus chuckled. "Then I suppose it is a good thing that we are blindly judging the contest, for if I knew which bake was hers, I would have to give her full marks for that laudation alone."

"I see I am not needed here," Duncan said with a grin before turning to Sir Rufus. "I recall you raving over the Frenchman's *choux à la crème* and I do believe that platter of them I see are calling out to me. Do forgive me, but I think I shall answer."

He offered to fetch Sir Rufus a plate of the pastries, but the chef waved off the notion, his hand going to his stomach as if he was minding his waistline. Duncan grinned and bowed briefly to Petra. She watched him walk off, always willing to admire the decided V shape of his back, beginning from his broad shoulders down to his slim hips and beyond.

Remembering herself, Petra then smiled up at Sir Rufus, only to find him staring over her shoulder, his cheeks having rapidly paled.

"Sir Rufus? Are you well?" Petra asked.

She turned her head, just catching a bright flash of color before it whisked out of sight behind a trio of gentlemen.

In fact, there were spots of color everywhere within the easily a dozen or so people milling about in front of the bookshelves. This included the Duchess of Hillmorton wearing a necklace festooned with dazzling aquamarines, Caroline in her dress of lively amethyst purple, and Lord Wadley-Bates, whose straining waistcoat held more than one shade of citrus-hued orange. Even Sir Franklin's waistcoat, though mostly brown, was accented with stripes the color of bluebells. Yet not one of them even glanced their way.

"Did you know, Lady Petra," Sir Rufus said, loud enough to recapture her attention, "after my lecture tomorrow regarding the history of British cuisine, I shall be presenting the entirety of my recipes to Her Majesty? They will become part of the royal collection. Her Majesty tells me they will be put into a permanent display within the castle's Round Tower, which is in the process of becoming an archive."

At Petra's congratulations, Sir Rufus looked to have regained his composure. Indeed, so much so that he nearly preened.

"Yes, it has been a dream of mine to make my full scale of recipes not just into another cookery book, but into a grand collection. In fact, several of my most famous dishes are ones I developed whilst in the employment of the earl, at Buckfields. Would you care to see my collection before they go on display?"

"I would be delighted," Petra said. To be able to speak privately with the chef who had been so kind to her as a child, and possibly hear some recollections of her late mother at the same time? She would happily pore over recipes with him for such an opportunity.

"Splendid!" exhorted Sir Rufus. "I shall be finalizing the order in which I will present them tomorrow morning. I always rise from my bed before the cock crows, and even more so with each day, it seems. Mr. Shawcross assured me you were not averse to awakening early. Thus, might you meet me before the other guests in the castle awaken? Possibly by half seven, in the small library?"

Petra was about to request half past eight at the earliest, for Her Majesty's dinner tonight would no doubt go until one in the morning, if not longer. She did enjoy witnessing the morning hours, but she should like to sleep in a bit after such festivities as well. Yet her lips had barely parted when a recognizable, plummy voice made them both turn toward the windows.

"Sir Rufus! Come here and explain to the duke why I insist upon serving a claret with roast venison! He favors white wine, the peasant!"

It was the Prince Regent, having clearly arrived before his mama. He was motioning impatiently with one arm, a *choux à la crème* in his hand dropping a dollop of pastry cream onto the Axminster carpet. Duncan and his grandfather, the Duke of Hillmorton, were standing next to him, and both Shawcross men looked politely amused by the Prince, as was required.

Sir Rufus, his gray eyes having turned stony at the sight of the Prince and the duke, turned back to Petra. He met her gaze with a curiously impelling look. "I beg of you not to be late."

And then he was moving away, leaving her blinking after him until a viscountess who kept thoroughbreds at the Earl of Holbrook's stables greeted her and a pleasant few minutes were spent discussing her racehorses. Finally, a liveried steward came striding toward the center of the room. Using a ceremonial walking stick, he gave three brisk taps upon the floor.

It seemed the Queen had finally arrived. The first night was about to begin.

"And thus, to begin our week of merriment, learning, and gastronomic delights," said Queen Charlotte after a mercifully short welcome speech, "I direct you first to the windows facing the Round Tower for a delightful surprise."

Already standing near one of the windows, Petra was suddenly swarmed by her fellow guests when she heard someone say her name. Looking up, she found a beautiful woman some fifteen years her senior with familiar speckled blue eyes and nearly black hair cropped short in the *à la Titus* fashion, her curls coming forward to frame her face. It was a countenance Petra had not seen in a six-month at least, and all thoughts of Sir Rufus instantly vanished.

"Aunt Ophelia!" she exclaimed as she rushed into her aunt's arms and heard the heartwarmingly familiar cry of "Petra, my love!"

There was only time for a brief, happy embrace before shouts of "Ohhh!" and "Look there!" had Petra and her aunt pulling apart to look out the windows onto the torchlit courtyard formed in the triangular space between King John's Tower, the Round Tower, and Queen Elizabeth's Gallery.

Petra hid a giggle behind her hand, for it was Caroline's dream come true. A group of funambulists, all men—and all wearing breeches so tight that even the term "inexpressibles" did not do them justice—began performing feats of stunning acrobatic moves, including one who walked a tightrope stretching from a window in the Round Tower all the way to another in the indoor walking gallery once used by the Virgin Queen herself.

As the crowd watched, entranced, Petra turned with a smile to her aunt, Lady Ophelia, the widowed Viscountess Throckmorton.

She was the fifth Earl of Holbrook's half sister, and the product of the fourth earl's second marriage, which was why Lady Ophelia, at not quite forty years of age, was not only much younger than Petra's papa, but also dark of hair and with a tall, slim build. If it were not for inheriting the Forsyth blue eyes, her aunt could have passed for Caroline's relation more than Petra's.

"I could not be more delighted to see you, Aunt Ophelia, but why did you not write to let me know you would be here at Windsor this week?"

She said this even as she glanced about for Duncan in order to call him over, knowing he would be as happy to see her aunt as she was. Petra spied him near the tea table, having a laugh with his grandfather as they each ate a second cream puff. A few feet away was Sir Rufus, now looking quite recovered and conversing with a handsome, fair-haired man whom Petra had heard called Major Carlson.

Aunt Ophelia, too, was gazing thoughtfully in the direction of the major and Sir Rufus, then linked her arm with Petra's as they hung back by the windows.

"Darling, I've only just arrived after a long and arduous trip from Yorkshire, but I wanted to surprise you. I was shocked to receive Her Majesty's invitation, I must say. She insisted that I come, writing that it has been far too long since I was anywhere near London."

Her aunt gave a cheerful shrug that made a tinkling sound of the little glass beads sewn onto the edges of her diaphanous shawl. As per usual it was vivid in color, this time in an eye-watering hue of green that still managed to look fashionable over her white dress shot through with silver threads. Further complementing her outfit was a Forsyth family heirloom around the second finger of her right hand: a stunning gold ring, its setting made to look like vines holding up a cabochon of lapis lazuli the size of a quail egg. She waved her hand in an airy gesture as she continued, making the blue and gold tones blur together prettily.

"Yet as she once handpicked me to marry dear Prinny, I suppose she still has a soft spot for me. Thus, here I am!"

"What?" Petra exclaimed through startled laughter. "You were once courted by Prince George? How did you never say?"

"Oh, it was but the *briefest* of moments." Aunt Ophelia leaned in, her eyes twinkling with mischief, as her voice lowered to something barely audible. "And not a moment I ever wished to relive, for he once took the liberty of kissing me, and it was rather like one's lips meeting with those of a gasping toad." She chuckled, her voice returning to a normal level as her blue eyes wandered to land on the Prince, then hastily returned to Petra before he caught her stare. "It was so very long ago to be considered ancient history. There was never any bad blood—not that I knew of, I assure you."

Petra was about to insist she elucidate further, but her aunt's whole face had lit after spying someone over Petra's shoulder.

"Lady Caroline, there you are, darling! I have been waiting to see you. Did you know I was placed in the room across from the both of you? I was warned of a draft, but I told the housekeeper I am hale and hearty and I care not." She glanced between Caroline and Petra with a wide smile. "Oh yes, we three shall have a lovely time."

FIVE

Within a few minutes, Petra, Caroline, and Aunt Ophelia had claimed a Chesterfield sofa and were so engrossed in exchanging the latest news that they started when the Queen's voice rang out.

"And if you like to talk so much, Lady Petra, then I believe you should come to the middle of the library and help Mr. Wyatt display his maps."

"What is happening?" Petra asked out of the side of her mouth, rising slowly from the sofa.

"It seems we have been rude," whispered her aunt, her laughing blue eyes going to a gentleman standing in the middle of the library and holding several large placards containing architectural drawings. "For that is the renowned architect Jeffry Wyatt, and I believe he was attempting to give a lecture."

"I call on you, too, Major Carlson," the Queen trilled, though this time with a tinge of humor. "Whilst I expect you are interviewing every fellow landowner about the rearing of his pigs, no doubt you will also find Mr. Wyatt's lecture quite illuminating."

"Indeed, Your Majesty, my apologies," said the major amiably as he began walking toward the architect, a slight limp in his right leg with every step.

"The major is a gentleman farmer?" Petra asked curiously. Though assuredly a respectable profession, it was not likely to earn him an invitation from the Queen.

Aunt Ophelia gave the smallest shrug. Caroline, though, whipped open her fan and spoke from behind it as Petra took the moment to stall by removing her reticule from her wrist and pulling up her gloves.

"No, dearest, he is the Prince's personal solicitor and quite the eligible specimen—though he is also the second son of a baron. Sadly, Lord Carlson—one of Prinny's closest comrades—died in 1813. He took his own life in despair after his eldest son and heir died at the Battle of Salamanca the year prior, and his wife not long before that. Prinny was devastated, yet he kept the major on despite the Carlson name having been tarnished as a result. The major himself was wounded in battle several years ago, after which he began rising through the ranks of those who study the law." Caroline canted her head thoughtfully as she peered over her fan to take in the major's lean frame. "He has forgone his father's title, saying it should have been his brother's, and seems to have retained a bit of melancholy about him since then, the poor, handsome, charming man."

"Lady Caroline, your summaries of a person never fail to be thorough, concise, and exceptionally socially informative all at the same time," said Aunt Ophelia.

"Thank you—it is a wonder Her Majesty has not made me one of her intelligence officers," replied Caroline with such sincerity that Petra could not help but grin as she hurried to the middle of the room. The major returned her smile in an easy manner and they each accepted three placards from Mr. Wyatt.

The architect then proceeded to give a rather interesting lecture on how Windsor Castle had gone from a wooden structure built at the command of William of Normandy in 1066 to the expansive, crenellated stone castle that was undeniably King George III's most magnificent and impressive residence.

Throughout the discussion, Petra and Major Carlson walked through the library holding renderings of the castle as it developed from medieval times, through the reigns of King Henry

VIII and Queen Elizabeth—who was responsible for paving the North Terrace walkway—and finished with the Restoration and into the reigns of the first Hanoverian kings. Encouraged by the lively atmosphere, they even became a bit theatric when displaying their placards, much to the amusement of the assembled guests.

After Mr. Wyatt took his bow and the clapping had died down, Her Majesty then instructed Lady Caroline to join Petra at the front of the room and read out the list of events happening for the next day. This included the most celebrated London modiste to display the latest fashions for ladies, an expert to give a lecture on farming techniques, and two famous pugilists to have a boxing match out on the Quadrangle.

"And for those ladies interested in cookery," Petra read out, "Sir Rufus Pomeroy, former royal chef to Their Majesties, will give a guided tour of the royal kitchens." She paused, cutting her eyes in question to Queen Charlotte, who seemed to read her thoughts.

"Do not be concerned that he is breaking my rule that judges may not be in the kitchens, Lady Petra," Her Majesty drawled. "The tour has been scheduled for eleven o'clock, when the patisserie contests are at their midday meal."

Grinning, Petra searched the crowd for Sir Rufus's face, expecting to see him beaming proudly, but instead discovered him in the back of the room, staring into the middle distance. Only when one gentleman clapped him on the shoulder did he seem to return to himself, accepting the applause with a gracious bow.

Caroline then began reading out the last part of the itinerary, explaining there would be several events to be held on the grounds or in the Great Park for the villagers of Windsor to attend, including a competition for best pig, heifer, draft horse, and working dog.

The crowd clapped their approval, and then, led by the Queen and the Prince Regent, moved like a great bejeweled wave of silk and wool finery upstairs to St. George's Hall.

The feast was course after course of the most delicious dishes, all prepared by Chef Carême and his kitchen staff. One of the many highlights, in Petra's opinion, was the dessert table, which in its center held a *pièce montée*—a sculpture made entirely of spun sugar, marzipan, and colored sugar icing. The chef had crafted a small but marvelously exact replica of the castle's Round Tower sitting atop its tree-dotted motte and complete with its two exterior staircases and the British flag waving atop the battlements. Flanking the sugar sculpture were two ornate cake stands holding aloft six layers of violet-flavored mousse tinted in alternating shades of lavender and royal purple. And every last inch of the dessert table then held silver cups full of trifle. Guests were encouraged to take one out to the East Terrace gardens and enjoy their pudding of almond biscuits soaked in wine and nestled between layers of custard and Chantilly cream while an orchestra accompanied a dazzling show of fireworks.

As the guests began to file out, cups of trifle in hand, the Prince of Wales called out to Petra. She approached with a smile and a curtsy.

"I require you to do something for me, Lady Petra," he said in his manner of speaking that always managed to sound a bit petulant. "It seems Chef Carême wishes to leave my employ."

"That would be a shame indeed, Your Royal Highness," she said dutifully.

"Yes, it would, and I am most unhappy," he said, his lips pushing forward into a pout. "But I understand Carême, who is nevertheless rather talented, has taken quite a liking to *you*."

She went to protest this—while silently chastising Caroline for saying such things—but was cut off.

"No, I have no doubt it is the truth. You are quite comely, Lady Petra. If I were not married already . . ."

Thankfully, the Prince was looking over her head and did not catch her eyes momentarily widen in horror as he continued.

"And thus, I should like you to convince Chef Carême to stay on, for at least another two years. Yes, I demand he pledge to stay another two years at least, and train six—no, eight—chefs whilst he is here. I wish for all my chefs to cook in the French manner. Would you not agree that is best, Lady Petra? Will you convince Carême to stay on in the royal household? Yes? Excellent. Then I expect a favorable response before the ball in five days' time."

Actually, Petra had not been given the chance to form a word. The Prince had agreed for her and then walked off, patting his rotund belly as he snapped at a footman to bring him two cups of trifle.

Yet, she had to laugh at the absurdity of the moment. It seemed she had now been charged with a quest that she already knew was unlikely to succeed, with Carême so strongly wishing to return to his country. At least she had already been set another task that would give her the perfect opportunity to speak with him.

It had happened earlier when she overheard the Queen speaking with the Duchess of Hillmorton. Her Majesty was cross that Chef Carême did not wish to host Sir Rufus and ten ladies for the scheduled tour of the kitchens. It seemed Carême, while taking no issues with Sir Rufus in general, felt the very idea of a tour was beneath his dignity, regardless of the fact that the kitchens were so large they could easily accommodate a group of onlookers.

Upon catching sight of Petra, the Queen had called her over.

"Lady Petra, I shall put you in charge of making certain the two chefs—both old and new—do not end up like so many rutting stags and let their egos get in the way of my guests having an enjoyable time. You will attend the tour with the group, and find some way to charmingly intervene should there be any issues. I understand the ladies who wish to attend will meet in the Green Drawing Room tomorrow at a quarter to eleven."

"It would be my honor, Your Majesty," Petra said.

Now, full of excellent food and warmed by three glasses of wine, she wandered out onto the East Terrace, where she found Duncan waiting for her with two silver cups of trifle. It was a gloriously perfect evening, made more so with a show of fireworks and music. She and Duncan stood side by side beneath the canopy of a glorious oak. They ate their trifles, and shared a sweet, lingering kiss when everyone else had their head tipped back to the show of exploding lights in the sky.

SIX

Tuesday, 5 September 1815
Day two of the royal celebrations

I CONFESS I DO NOT KNOW IF I HAVE EVER HAD A NIGHT I ENJOYED more, Petra thought as she walked sleepily through the nearly silent castle the next morning. The sun was just rising, enough to show the day would begin with fluffy white clouds drifting across a blue September sky.

All in all, she had talked and laughed so much the night before that the muscles in her jaw had become sore. And she had eaten and drunk so much that she was comfortably sleepy by the time she swayed, still a bit tipsy, to her bedchamber, arm in arm with Aunt Ophelia and Caroline, just after one in the morning. There she found Annie's usual temperate spirits seemingly restored, and Petra was a bit ashamed to feel grateful, for she had been too tired to do anything more than undress and slip into bed.

Still, before she had known it, Annie was gently shaking her awake, saying, "I am sorry you must leave your bed, my lady, but we must get you dressed to meet with Sir Rufus."

Now, as she passed through the picture gallery, Petra thought of how Annie had uncharacteristic dark circles under her eyes, which only appeared after a severe lack of sleep. Nevertheless, Annie had displayed her usual thoughtful competency, making certain Petra had toast and marmalade, plus a strong cup of tea mixed with a touch of headache powder to ease her slightly throbbing head. In return, Petra had insisted Annie nap until she returned, saying there was no need for a chaperone with Sir Rufus and his valet.

Yet a frown touched Petra's lips. Did Annie even reply? She could not recall. Instead, Annie had bustled about, helping Petra into a dress of rose-hued heavy silk and hastily pinning her curls into a simple chignon.

I feel as if Annie had even managed to open the bedchamber door and usher me out into the hall whilst fastening my necklace at the same time, Petra thought, fingering the string of oval-cut peridots touching her throat.

With her dress making a gentle swishing noise as she made her way through the castle, Petra rubbed her arms in the cold stone hallways. Yet the very sight of the stone—the scratches and gentle dips from thousands of feet just like hers—made her mind stray a bit to muse on all Windsor Castle had seen over the centuries.

Just as the architect, Mr. Wyatt, had explained last night, the castle had stood in one form or another since 1066, and, oh, the events it had seen. Entering the picture gallery, Petra's eyes went immediately to a battle scene depicting the First Barons' War in the thirteenth century, and she could imagine the yells of men as they clashed with King John's soldiers on these very grounds. It made her think on the women who came afterward, hunting for their husbands, sons, and brothers, and finding them felled.

She imagined these women dropping to their knees—yet she felt they would have emitted keening wails, not frightened screams.

Why was it, then, that a scream was ringing in her ears?

She paused, before lifting her skirts and running the last twenty steps of the long picture gallery, pushing open the door into the small library, hearing another scream even as she did.

In the dim morning light coming through the windows, a young maidservant cowered a few feet away, against the bookcases. Upon seeing Petra, she let out a terrified yelp, and her broom clattered to the ground as she pointed a shaking finger toward the center of the room.

"My lady! Murder! Sir Rufus 'as been murdered!"

It was true. Sir Rufus Pomeroy was dead.

Sprawled supine upon the carpet, his gray eyes were open, bulging out in grotesque fashion even as they stared fixedly at the library's paneled ceiling. Around his body, dozens of pages containing his recipes were strewn, like the petals of a daisy flung out from an uncaring hand.

And standing over him, breathing hard while tugging at what looked to be a length of black silk about the great chef's neck, was his own valet.

His name came to Petra's tongue just as she remembered it being angrily hissed the previous evening.

"*Beecham?* What the devil did you do?"

The valet stilled, then lifted his head. Auburn hair flopped down over his forehead, half concealing his eyes, which looked both terrified and dangerous. A muscle pulsed in his cheek, emphasizing a sharply angled jawline. And then he leapt into a sprint, like a greyhound sighting its quarry—and the prey was evidently she.

The housemaid screamed, and it somehow made Petra react, grabbing the broom from the floor. When Beecham, at full stride, came close, she stepped back, dropped into a crouch, and swung the long wooden pole in a low arc. It made contact just above his ankles with a resounding thwack.

Beecham cried out as he tripped, his arms flailing as he sailed in the air for a moment, then his temple struck the edge of a side table before he landed with a heavy thud on the library floor.

Petra, in addition to many childhood years of wrestling with Duncan, now had training to rely upon. Dropping the broom, she leapt upon the valet's back, pinning him with her knees, as she cried out to the housemaid, "Your apron, girl! Give me your apron!"

The girl, while wailing in terror, managed to do as she was told as Petra yanked Beecham's hands behind his back. Then she used the apron strings to bind his wrists.

Then she realized she needn't have been so frantic. Beecham was out cold.

Nevertheless, she instructed the whimpering housemaid to bring her one of the tasseled tiebacks off of the green velvet curtains, which she used to tightly bind Beecham's ankles together.

Panting and inwardly cursing her corset, Petra staggered to her feet and went to pick up the broom again. But a gasp from behind her had her whirling toward the library doors, this time accidentally wielding the broom's sorghum rushes instead of the pole.

"Annie!" she breathed, lowering her impromptu weapon. "You frightened me."

"*I* frightened *you*, my lady?" Annie squeaked, hazel eyes wide and one hand out to fend off the broom. "I heard such screaming. Are you well, my lady? I found a footman to send for Mr. Shawcross. Whatever has happened here?" She bobbed her head around Petra's shoulder in an effort to better see who was tied up on the ground. "Were you attacked by this man?"

"I am well, and you did just what was needed by sending for Duncan."

Petra, still breathing a bit hard, gestured grimly toward the middle of the library.

"I am quite sorry to say that Sir Rufus Pomeroy has been murdered. He was strangled by his valet. And when Beecham here attempted to attack me and make his escape, I felled him." She looked down to see that the valet was still unconscious, then eyed Annie. "How did you know to follow me?"

Annie was staring. Not at the sadly gruesome sight of Sir Rufus, but instead down at the valet. She then unnecessarily held out her other arm, over which was a neatly folded tartan shawl in muted greens, pinks, and grays, and her voice sounded far away, almost like she might swoon.

"I realized you had forgotten your shawl, my lady."

Petra frowned. Annie had one of the strongest constitutions she had ever known, yet was looking uncharacteristically faint.

"Annie, are you unwell?" she asked, but it was another whimper that made her turn.

The terrified maidservant still cowered in the corner. Petra moved between her and the body of Sir Rufus.

"What is your name, girl?" she snapped. She disliked taking such a tone with any servant, but in cases such as these, it was best for directing the girl's concentration away from the horrible sight of murder.

"M-Marta, my lady," came the girl's shaky voice as she gripped the skirts of her Windsor-blue cotton dress.

"You have been very brave, Marta," she said, keeping her tone brisk. "Tell me, what did you witness?"

The girl seemed to shrink back against the wall even further, answering in something just above a whisper.

"I came in to tidy the small library like I's told ta by Mrs. Daley, my lady. It's me job every morning. I walked in, and began me sweepin', and then I looked over and 'bout jumped outta me skin, I did."

She pointed a shaking finger to the unconscious valet still lying prone on the floor, his hands tied behind his back with the strings from Marta's own apron, and his ankles tied with a tasseled velvet curtain tieback.

"I saw 'im yankin' on Sir Rufus's neck with that black ribbon! I saw 'im kill Sir Rufus!"

"And did you see or hear anything else? Did you witness any confrontation between the two men?" Petra asked, giving the girl a narrow-eyed look to indicate that no untruths would be tolerated.

Marta shook her head emphatically, strands of fair hair coming loose from beneath her mob cap. "No, my lady. The valet were done killin' Sir Rufus when I came in. After that, all's I remember was screamin' until you rushed in."

Petra gave another glance to Sir Rufus, suppressing a shudder as she noted the way his tongue was lolling out of one side of his mouth.

"Are you the only servant in this part of the castle?" she asked, and Marta nodded.

"The others are long gone from tidyin' these rooms, my lady," she said. Her eyes strayed to the clock upon the mantel. "By an hour or more, I'd say. I always follow after them to do one more sweepin' and dustin'."

When pressed, Marta could confirm the other servants had finished cleaning as she'd seen them in the servants' hall before making her way to the small library. Yes, quite calm they all were; none had looked as if they'd witnessed anything amiss.

Petra nodded, and knew what she needed to do next. Holding out the broom to the girl, she tilted her head toward the doors.

"Marta, you will go and find Mrs. Daley. You will keep your composure and tell Mrs. Daley I am requesting that she come to the small library at once. But you will speak to no one else about what you have seen here in the meantime. Do you understand? Have I your pledge?"

Marta nodded vigorously as she bobbed a curtsy and was positively fleeing the room before Petra could even finish saying, "Good, now make haste."

She pulled the library doors closed, locking them as she glanced over to find her lady's maid chewing on her bottom lip. Annie kept looking back at the body of Sir Rufus, then down at Beecham, each movement producing deeper worry lines between her eyes.

"I agree with the emotions I see on your countenance; it is most worrying," Petra said, feeling dismay and sadness welling up within her. "Poor Sir Rufus! But you are not as frightened as young Marta, are you? If so, whilst I could not fault you, if your stomach should be feeling turned, I would ask that you return to our chambers so as to not complicate matters further."

But Annie did not answer. On the ground, Beecham was finally stirring, groaning as he moved his head. Blood was coming from his lip and nose, but it did not appear to be serious. Yet when he tried to move his arms and could not, that was when he began thrashing.

As soon as he had twitched, Petra strode to a nearby table that held several objects of antiquity. One was an iron horseman's mace, a weapon about the length of a riding crop and not much wider. The handle and an arrow-like flange on the opposite end were made of agate, with a truly wicked steel spike at the very tip. It was ceremonial in nature, yes, but she could not help but think it would have made for a much easier way to kill Sir Rufus.

"You will cease your struggling, Mr. Beecham," she said coldly. "For you are trussed like a guinea fowl and will not so easily get out of it. Should you manage to do so, however, I am quite willing to bash you over the head with this mace."

With a growling yell, Beecham had managed to roll halfway over, but he stopped at seeing Petra smacking her palm with the weapon's spiked flange.

"My lady," he panted. "I did not kill him. I swear it."

"And yet we have a witness that says you did, sir," Petra replied.

"No," he said, wincing as he struggled. "The maid, she did not see what she thought, my lady. I swear it!" Fear came into his voice. "Please, hear me out, my lady. I did not kill Sir Rufus."

"You had best be quiet, Mr. Beecham," Petra said. "Mr. Shawcross, one of the Queen's intelligence officers, is on his way, and will likely call upon the Coldstream Regiment of Foot Guards. You will no doubt be questioned then and afterward taken to the Tower of—"

She stopped when Annie stepped to her side, looking down at the valet as she released a shuddering breath.

"I should like to hear what he has to say, my lady, if I may. Before Mr. Shawcross arrives."

Lying on his side, one of Beecham's eyes was already starting to blacken. With a wince, his gaze swiveled from Petra to Annie, widening in apprehension.

"Whyever for?" Petra asked, perplexed.

Annie was still staring down at the valet. Her face, before so pale, had hardened.

"Because, my lady, Mr. Beecham is my brother, and I should like to hear from his own lips why he committed such a heinous act. Especially since the last time I saw him I risked my position, and your trust, to allow him to keep his freedom."

SEVEN

"I do not understand," Petra said, swiveling to face her lady's maid. "Your surname is Robertson, not Beecham. I know you have a younger brother—Oliver, yes?—but he is with the navy, is he not? I recall you saying he enlisted as a lad, not long after you arrived at Buckfields to become my lady's maid."

Yet even as she said it, she could see the similarities between Annie and the valet known as Beecham. The same reddish cast to their hair, the same stubborn chin and heart-shaped face. And both had clear hazel eyes with little flecks of darker green.

"He *was* in the navy, my lady," Annie replied, disappointment heavy in her voice, "but did not take to the sea, so he worked in the dockyards at Plymouth for a time. Then at those in Woolwich, and later at Portsmouth. He has had several professions, and is always moving on, never staying anywhere very long. Beecham was my mother's maiden name. I insisted Oliver take it and start anew as a different man when I did not report him to the Earl of Holbrook."

"The earl?" Petra repeated, startled. "What does my papa have to do with this?"

Annie was still staring down into her brother's eyes, however.

"Do forgive me, for I shall explain all to you, my lady. And you may deal with me as you see fit. But at the moment, I should like to hear Oliver's confession. For he knows he cannot tell me an untruth and get away with such nonsense."

Annie glanced at the watch fastened to her dress, which was

a heavy cotton in a moss-colored chintz. When she addressed her brother, her tone was one of the coldest winter's day.

"I have already sent a footman for Mr. Shawcross. I was told he was out on a ride, but was expected back soon. I would wager we have but ten minutes or less before he arrives." She paused, then added, "Oliver, Mr. Shawcross will be much less gentle with you than my lady or I. So you best speak before you are made to do so."

Petra glanced beneath her lashes at Annie. They both knew that Duncan preferred a nonviolent approach to interrogation, unless absolutely necessary. So why try to frighten Oliver?

She had always known Annie was close with her family. And as the oldest sibling of four, Annie had always felt a strong obligation to make certain her two sisters and brother were healthy, and of a good mind and heart. Annie had seen to it that they were all educated, using the wages she earned as Petra's lady's maid, even when her parents were scarcely able to afford to do more than feed and clothe their children.

With these thoughts, Petra felt as if she might understand. Seeing Oliver turn out wild was as awful as if he were her own child, for Annie felt herself as much a parent to him as a sister. Annie was heartbroken, and for that, Petra became rather cross. For no one had the right to upset Annie without suffering consequences.

"All right, then," she said. "Help me to assist your brother in sitting up, and then he will explain himself—or I will use the steel point of this mace on his twiddle-diddles until he does." She pointed the steel weapon to the area between Beecham's legs for extra effect.

Both Annie and Oliver briefly looked agog at her as he was helped into a sitting position, and if she'd had any doubts they were siblings, they were well and truly gone. Despite Oliver's now split lip and rapidly bruising cheek and eye, their expressions were nearly identical.

"Now, let us make certain he is facing poor Sir Rufus, so he can see what horrible thing he has wrought," Petra said.

Oliver looked over to where Sir Rufus lay on the floor, the length of black silk ribbon still wrapped about the chef's neck.

"But I did not," Oliver insisted. "I did not kill him, my lady. Annie, you must believe me."

"I believed you the previous time, Oliver," Annie snapped. "And the one before that. Yet look where I stand now. Finding you not having returned to the navy as you promised, but as the valet to a great man. You did not even write to tell me—or warn me that you would be here. No, I had to find out when I came face-to-face with you in the servants' hall. And in doing so, I had to lie to Mr. Foyle, who knew something was wrong as soon as I saw you."

She leaned down and shook an admonishing finger in her brother's face.

"What is more, I hear you have been pestering Sir Rufus about something. Replying in an insolent manner when he speaks to you, and embarrassing him in front of Her Majesty's guests. I am ashamed of you, I am."

Annie spun around, her fist held to her mouth as if to stop herself from crying.

So, Oliver was the reason Annie had been so out of sorts. The ne'er-do-well brother had returned, and Annie had been worried about just what Oliver might do or say. It was quite likely she was also concerned that Oliver's actions would reflect negatively on her, and likely on Petra.

They will not, Petra thought fiercely. *And I will make certain Annie knows this. But right now it is important to understand what happened.*

"You say you did not kill Sir Rufus, Mr. Beecham," Petra said, adding, "For I shall use the name you are called here, at this castle, so as to keep your link to Annie a secret until which time she chooses to explain that you are her relation."

Surprisingly, this declaration made Oliver blanch, almost as if she really had struck him. He looked down, as if speech was eluding him. Petra had little sympathy for him, though. Not when he had caused Annie so much distress—and not to mention what it seemed he had done to Sir Rufus.

"Time is getting on, Mr. Beecham," she said. "Whatever you have to say to us, please say it now."

Oliver cleared his throat, and shifted his broad shoulders. It was then Petra realized how big he was, even though he was sitting down, with his hands still tied behind his back. He was nearly as tall and well-muscled as Duncan—and had her mind fully grasped this when he had come charging at her, she might not have had the nerve to attempt to fell him. She was glad now that she hadn't had much time to think, and had just done.

"It is true, sister, I have indeed been pestering Sir Rufus," he said, clearly speaking to Annie. "But it is because he has not paid me my wages in a three-month. We arrived here at Windsor Castle last week and I have been lucky enough to get food and drink as his valet whilst we have been in residence. But we were to leave for Buckinghamshire as soon as Her Majesty's celebrations were over, and I would be Sir Rufus's sole servant. I would be footman, butler, and valet, and he had not paid me in some time."

He looked up at Annie imploringly, but she had not yet turned back around. Petra tapped her foot impatiently, and Oliver hurried to continue.

"And there is another reason. Whilst I loathed being on a ship, I enjoyed preparing meals. After last seeing you, sister, I worked at a public house, where I met Sir Rufus in the spring of 1813. He took me on to be both his valet and his apprentice chef. I've become quite a good one, too, even creating recipes for the Duke of Rutland's household, and that of the Princess Mary, yet I did not get paid a single farthing. He promised me he would, and he did not. He has not even crafted a recipe of his own in some time, in fact."

A spark of anger flared in his eyes.

"What is more, he did not give me credit for my recipes. Both the duke and the princess believe the dishes to be the work of Sir Rufus, and not of Chef Oliver Robertson." He gritted his teeth, glancing at his sister's rigid back, and said reluctantly, "Oliver Beecham, I mean, of course."

Annie finally whirled around, her hands on her hips.

"I care not, Oliver. If Sir Rufus put his time and energies into training you—which is something many young chefs would have given their eyeteeth for—then it is the experience you gain that is your payment. In my opinion, he owed you nothing." She closed the gap between them and glared fiercely down at him. "I expect you had debts, and that is the real reason why you needed the wages he owes you. Would I be correct?"

Oliver did not answer, but cast his eyes downward again. Annie looked like she might burst into tears, yet whether they were of frustration or sadness—or both—Petra could not quite discern.

"It is time you tell us what happened here with Sir Rufus," Petra said, resuming the use of her commanding voice. "And I should like the truth as much as Annie."

"Yes, my lady," Oliver replied dully, then began by explaining that, despite sleeping in Sir Rufus's dressing room, to be nearby for his morning duties, he had not heard his employer awaken, dress, or leave his chambers.

"If he rang for me, I did not hear the bell." He looked up at Petra. "Sir Rufus did not arrive to his bedchamber until half two this morning. And he was gone again by the time I awoke at a quarter to seven, having finally slept after cleaning the shirt and trousers he'd worn at supper, laying out his attire for today, and preparing his daily stomach tonic. I was full tired, I was."

"And when you finally pulled your lazy bones out of bed?" Annie said, her arms crossed over her chest.

"Well, I rushed into his bedchamber ready to make my apologies, and found he was gone. I knew he was coming here to the small library with all his recipes, of course. He'd left them out last night, tied with that"—using his battered chin, he jutted it toward Sir Rufus, his voice quieting for a moment—"with that black silk ribbon. I'm not even certain how he obtained it. He normally uses a leather case he had made specially."

Petra waved this off. "You must arrive at the point, Beecham. Mr. Shawcross will no doubt be here directly. What do you say happened next?"

Oliver's eyes widened at the mention of Duncan, and his words came quickly.

"You should know, Sir Rufus had been anxious recently—and especially since yesterday, when all the guests arrived. He was worried about some he would meet again."

"Preposterous," Annie retorted. "Sir Rufus was quite highly regarded. Do not invent stories, Oliver."

"But I am not, sister," he implored, shaking his head, then wincing at the pain it caused him. "Sir Rufus was not as well-liked as you might think, and he does not get along with everyone. In fact, he argued with no less than five people yesterday. Three gentlemen, and two ladies, they were. And earlier, I heard Sir Rufus laughing and speaking with another person—though I know not if it were a gentleman or a lady. He said he had something that more than one person wanted, and he had hidden it within the castle."

"That sounds like all your stories, Oliver," Annie said, leaning over so that her face was just a foot or so from her brother's, her expression thunderous. "Always with just enough to make you sound as if you could indeed be innocent, but not enough to provide proof."

Once more she whirled around. For a moment, Petra thought this a rather childish reaction, but she saw Annie's eyelashes truly glistening with tears. It was plain that Annie did not wish for Oliver to see her crying—most likely because he would know he was having an effect on her heart. Petra stepped sideways just enough to shield Annie from her brother's view.

"We shall return to what you said in a moment, Beecham," she said. "For now, tell us what happened after you discovered Sir Rufus had left his bedchamber."

Oliver was attempting to see around Petra to his sister, but when Petra smacked the horseman's mace in her palm once more, he complied.

"I knew he would want coffee, so I went to the kitchens to fetch it, along with a rack of toast. It is about all he can stomach on mornings after a heavy meal. Especially in recent months. Too many years of rich food, he said. I placed the tray on that small table, next to the chair where I expected to find him sitting."

Once more, Oliver used his chin to point in the direction of where the body of Sir Rufus lay. Petra had not noticed it at first as the table was low and partially hidden by the armchair. By craning her neck, however, she could see a Wedgwood teapot and the accouterments of a simple breakfast tray.

"As the kitchens were busy, it was going near half seven when I arrived here, and I was careful to watch how I went with a pot of hot coffee." Oliver smiled wryly. "I'm more accomplished as a cook than a footman, I'm afraid."

To this, Annie gave a small irritated huff, but still did not turn around. Oliver, however, was staring into the quite recent past and either did not hear his sister, or did not wish to defend his skills.

"I found him, on the ground . . . like that," Oliver said quietly. "Strangled, he was. It had clearly just happened, for he was still as warm to the touch as any living person."

Petra could not help but note that Oliver's face had paled. He looked up at Petra with eyes wide and guileless as he all but whispered his next words.

"I felt . . . I felt that if I could just get the ribbon off his neck, maybe Sir Rufus would breathe again." Urgency crept back into his voice. "I kept trying and trying, my lady, but it was knotted. I was so determined, I did not even notice when the housemaid came in the room. I do not think I even realized she was screaming until your ladyship rushed in."

For a moment, all three were silent. Then Petra said, "All right, if that is your story—"

"It is the truth, my lady!" Oliver shouted.

Annie whirled and cuffed him on the ear. "You will not raise your voice to Lady Petra, Oliver."

Like the younger brother he was, Oliver shrank away with a look that was more hurt than frightened.

"I apologize, my lady," he said. "But my story is the honest truth."

All three of them seemed to crane their ears toward the doors at the same time. The tramping of bootheels—several sets—was coming at a clip. Duncan and, very likely, some of the Coldstream Guards were in the picture gallery and would be here at any moment.

Oliver looked to his sister.

"You must believe me, Annie. Please," he begged.

Annie did not answer, but her eyes were vacillating between anger and worry.

"Tell me their names, Mr. Beecham," Petra said, laying the horseman's mace back on the table where she found it.

Oliver's eyes swiveled her way, and it was clear he did not know whom she meant.

"The three gentlemen and two ladies with whom Sir Rufus argued. I cannot promise I can help you, but I will at least interview those involved."

Oliver gulped, his Adam's apple bobbing in dramatic fashion.

"Do you see, my lady? He cannot answer because he was not being truthful," Annie said, but with no joy at being correct in her voice.

"I do not think so," Petra said thoughtfully, watching Oliver's face carefully. "I think he is frightened. Of speaking the names of those he saw." When he lowered his gaze to his knees, Petra felt she might have discovered the issue after all.

The sound of men coming closer was echoing outside the small library's doors. Oliver's head whipped toward the entrance; his forehead was perspiring now. Annie dropped down to her knees beside her brother, her bond with Oliver momentarily overriding her anger.

"Oliver, you may trust my lady Petra. Tell us their names."

"But I do not know if the arguments meant anything. I simply cannot be certain," Oliver said. Defeat now threaded his voice. "I also only recognized two of the voices—one lady and one gentleman. But all are members of the aristocracy—it was clear from hearing them speak. Thus, I do not know if it will matter, despite what I saw and heard."

"Then did you see anything else, Beecham?" Petra pointed emphatically toward the place upon the library floor where the chef who had once been so kind to her now lay. "Was there anything you can think of that may have led to Sir Rufus having his life taken in such a horrible, violent manner? You must know something."

Oliver shook his head even as he seemed to think back.

"His debts—I do not know what they were, or how much, but it is most obvious he had them. He was too private by half about such things. I was never allowed to see his ledgers. I was only allowed to assist him in the kitchen. Nevertheless, I never saw anything of significance. In his bedchamber, all he had were his old recipes, ready to present to Her Majesty."

There was banging at the library's oak doors.

"Lady Petra?" called Duncan.

"Mr. Beecham," Petra urged. "Tell me anything you can about the five people with whom he argued—and the sixth person who knows Sir Rufus hid something, too. I shall endeavor to interview them with great care, that I promise you."

This pledge seemed to help, for Oliver nodded and spoke quickly.

"I could not tell you anything about the sixth person," he said, "Of the others, two of the men, I knew them not. From what I heard, though, the first nearly came to blows with Sir Rufus, and the second broke down in tears." He paused, adding, "And the two ladies—please forgive me, your ladyship, but one of them was your aunt, Lady Ophelia. I did not recognize the second. Regardless, he rowed quite fiercely with both."

Petra's brows knitted at hearing her aunt's name, and Annie drew in a shocked breath, yet they all started as the door banged again, with Duncan's calls growing more insistent.

"Lady Petra! Annie! Unlock the door so that I know you are both unhurt, or I shall break it down!"

"Annie, please unlock the doors," Petra said before she took a step closer to Oliver and urged, "Who is the third gentleman, Mr. Beecham? The one you recognized."

"Oliver, for once do not hold your tongue," Annie hissed, but in desperation, even as she began turning the key in the lock. A moment later, Duncan was shouldering his way into the library, followed by several men dressed in the scarlet uniforms of Windsor's famous Coldstream Guards, and the commotion nearly drowned out Oliver's quavering words.

"His Royal Highness, Prince George. He threatened to kill Sir Rufus, my lady."

EIGHT

THERE WAS LITTLE PETRA COULD DO FOR OLIVER BEECHAM IN the face of such damning evidence. Especially as Marta, the young maidservant, had come across Duncan and the guards before reaching Mrs. Daley, rushing to him with the news of the murder before reluctantly returning to the library to confirm what she had witnessed.

After checking Sir Rufus for a pulse and finding none, Duncan shook his head with pity then looked toward the girl, saying, "And you claim to have proof, miss?"

To this, Marta had stepped forward, pointed a shaking finger at Oliver, her eyes wild and filled with fear, as she issued her condemnation.

"That's 'im, sir! I saw 'im pullin' on that piece of black silk, chokin' the last bit of life out of Sir Rufus. A madman 'e is! A murderin' madman!"

"Is what the girl says true to the best of your knowledge, Lady Petra?" Duncan asked calmly, as two of the guards hauled Oliver roughly to his feet, eyeing both the apron strings binding the valet's wrists, and the tasseled rope around his ankles. They glanced at Petra in surprise that was quickly cloaked in disinterest.

Whether or not she would have liked it, she would not be credited with capturing Beecham, that much was clear.

Charles, who had come running in behind the guards, went immediately to Annie and gently pulled her away from the fray. There were bright spots of pink upon her cheeks, but Petra also could see her eyes were two shades brighter from distress as she stared at her brother. Charles spoke into Annie's ear, but she merely shook her head once before shifting her gaze to Petra. There was pleading in her eyes as Petra gave Duncan her attention.

"I have spoken to Mr. Beecham, and he claims he was attempting to untie the length of silk from Sir Rufus's neck," she said. "That someone else did this horrible act, and he was trying to save Sir Rufus."

Another Coldstream Guard, a tall one with broad shoulders, straight brown hair, and a square jawline, who had watched idly as the first two had pulled Oliver up, now spoke.

"Forgive me, my lady, but that is not what Mr. Shawcross asked." The man did not look as if he really wished for her forgiveness, though. Especially when he said, "He requested to know if what this housemaid said were true. And I should like to hear the answer as well."

When a muscle pulsed in Duncan's jaw, but he did not rebuke the guard, Petra understood that this man must have significant authority within the castle, possibly that outstripped Duncan's. This seemed the likely scenario when she finally noticed a row of medals upon his tunic. Be that as it may, she did not care for the man or his manners straight off.

"And your name, sir?" she replied coolly.

"Colonel Wolston, my lady," he said, and only then did he offer her a bow. When she did not curtsy in return, he added, "I am the highest-ranking officer of the Coldstream Guards here at Windsor Castle, as well as the castle's constable, with the full authority to act in the Prince Regent's stead in matters concerning the safety of His Royal Highness."

"And what of Her Majesty's safety?" Petra returned, lifting an eyebrow.

"Our beloved Queen is always first in the Prince's thoughts, and therefore is first in mine as well, my lady," Wolston replied silkily. "All that I do is for the protection of the entire royal family."

"As it should be, Colonel," Petra replied, her silvery tone matching his.

Wolston's upper lip twitched slightly, as if he might smirk. "Now, if you would be so kind as to answer Mr. Shawcross's question, Lady Petra," he said instead.

"Indeed, my lady," Duncan said, stepping forward just enough that her eyes were drawn to his own. "The castle is waking up in earnest and we do not wish to bring undue distress upon the royal family's guests when we transport the body. Thus, time is of the essence." He then glanced briefly at Oliver. "If you have evidence of this man's innocence, or guilt, you must speak."

Until now, Oliver had been standing quietly, staring in a shocked manner somewhere left of Petra's feet. Now he raised eyes swirling with hope to her. Petra did not need to look over her shoulder to know that Annie's eyes were likely looking at her in the same way.

She fumed for a moment that her own hands were tied, even if proverbially, but there was naught she could say but the truth.

"I have no evidence either way, sir," she said.

Wolston grinned mirthlessly, then snapped, "Search him."

As if waiting for the cue the way a hunting dog did to fetch a downed bird, one of the guards took to pulling out every pocket in Oliver's well-cut black trousers, waistcoat, and jacket. He was so quick that Oliver barely had time to look aghast or jerk against the other guard standing behind him, still holding his tied wrists in a viselike grip.

Petra had seen Teddy pick a man's pocket like that once, when she had required it of him. Nimble fingers, he had told her with his sun-bright grin and golden curls flopping down over his forehead, were a necessity for those sleeping rough on the streets.

Not seconds later, the guard was lifting something out of Oliver's waistcoat between his first two fingers. He then handed it with the tiniest upward curve of his lips over to Wolston.

"What do we have here?" Wolston drawled, holding up a small brass key of about two inches in length. "This certainly would not work the door of your, or your late master's, bedchamber. Or the armoires or desks within the rooms, for that matter."

"It is not mine, sir. I do not know how it came to be in my waistcoat," Oliver retorted with some indignation.

"Is that so?" said Wolston, disbelief rampant in his voice. "Then I must inform you that Sir Rufus spoke with me last night, after the dinner. He said that he wished to report a theft. Of a brass key that fits a lock to a small safe that the Prince Regent allowed him to use whilst working here at the castle. Sir Rufus said he kept some valuables in it." Wolston tossed the key up in the air, and caught it handily. "I would wager that, if I used this key, I would find the safe had been emptied. By you, Beecham."

"What?" blustered Oliver. "I have never stolen from Sir Rufus. And I did not kill him. I swear it. I did not even know Sir Rufus had the use of a safe here."

At that point, he began to truly struggle against his guard. Without so much as a warning, the other guard with the nimble fingers threw his fist into Oliver's stomach. The valet all but folded in half, coughing and gasping for air. In the doorway, Marta the maidservant let out a squeak, her fingers steepling over her mouth.

Petra glanced back at Annie, who was standing half behind Charles. It appeared as if she was allowing Charles to shield her from the proceedings, but Petra knew better. What little could be seen of Annie's face was stricken, and she was trying to hide it from everyone present.

Petra caught Duncan's eye, then glanced quickly to Marta, then back to Annie, letting her face speak a request her lips could not. Though his expression briefly registered confusion—for Annie looking distressed was an unusual sight indeed—Petra could have kissed him for how quickly he took her meaning and did not hesitate in acting.

"Foyle," Duncan said, his voice calm but commanding. "Please escort Annie and Marta away from these proceedings. Find Mrs. Daley and have her give Marta some tea and cake, and send some to Lady Petra's chambers as well. I shall need to speak with her ladyship and take down what she witnessed first."

Annie looked as if she wished to protest, but Petra said, "Do not worry yourself. I shall do my duty here and return to my rooms forthwith. Please do not wait for me to take some tea and cake for yourself, though. It will be good for the shock we have all experienced here."

"Yes, my lady," Annie said quietly. Eyes down, she kept to Charles's side as he collected Marta at the doorway before closing the doors behind him. Briefly, Oliver raised haunted eyes to his sister's back, then dropped them just as quickly. If nothing else, he was respecting his sister's wishes that their connection to one another was not discovered.

Should she consider this a point in Oliver's favor? Petra knew not as she faced the castle's highest-ranking Guardsman.

NINE

Colonel Wolston was rolling the brass key between his fingers, calm as he pleased.

"I would have liked you to go with your lady's maid, my lady," he said. "It is unseemly for you to be here alone without a companion, even if you have declared yourself a spinster." And before Petra found her words, he added, "Plus, you must rest before your first round of the baking contest today, and you shall sadly be down one judge. It is quite important to Her Majesty that you choose the best baker wisely. Thus, you must ensure that you do not overtax yourself with this terrible business."

"I do not think I need rest to taste Shrewsbury cakes, Colonel," Petra returned.

She would be damned before she would mention that she had also agreed to attend the kitchen tour and demonstration happening later this morning—even as she recalled with a pang that it had been Sir Rufus who had arranged for it in the first place. Would it still happen? And would the contest need a replacement judge? Both remained to be seen. For now, she continued to unwaveringly meet Wolston's gaze.

He responded by giving her another incline of his head, then gestured to the body of Sir Rufus.

"Nevertheless, it must be most distressing for you to see such an unpleasant sight, or be in the room with the ruffian who killed the man who was once your own family's chef." He turned cold eyes onto Oliver, yet still addressed Petra. "In fact, we would not like you to be subjected to this coward Beecham for any longer than you already have. We shall take him now, and question him more thoroughly, away from your gentle sensibilities."

"From my gentle... You jest, Colonel," Petra said loudly and derisively over Duncan's own scoff. "And there is no need to take Beecham just yet."

But Wolston had nodded to his guards, and each one roughly took one of Oliver's upper arms, turning him to face the library doors. One had already produced a knife and sliced through the apron strings, while a third guard had done the same with the curtain tieback. Before Petra could make any significant protest other than exhorting "I say!" Wolston had slipped shackles over Oliver's wrists, which remained behind his back, and locked the irons into place with the expert turning of a key into the barrel lock.

"You must believe me," Oliver had reverted to repeating, looking from Wolston to Duncan and back again. "I told Lady Petra and she believes me. I did not kill Sir Rufus! I tried to save him, I did!"

"We shall see about that," Wolston said, and gave his guards another nod, telling them, "Send men to collect the body of Sir Rufus. Tell them to make haste."

The guards then shoved Oliver forward, and it seemed one angled him so that his shoulder slammed into the frame of the library door.

Duncan took two steps forward, looking as if he would intervene, but Wolston stepped in his path as the guards hauled Oliver out of the library as easily as if he were a weakened lamb and not a wide-shouldered man in the peak of health.

"You have no authority here, Shawcross," Wolston said, giving the key a flip once more and catching it without breaking eye contact with Duncan. "Do not cross lines that you would wish you had not."

"I only think that you should treat the man with some respect, as well as the right to be considered innocent until excellent proof of his guilt exists," Duncan replied, with what Petra knew was deceptive mildness.

Wolston's sneer was so brief, Petra was not wholly certain she had seen it. "You cannot assume Beecham is not guilty because your Lady Petra chose to be soft on him."

"And you should not assume that is how I conduct myself," Duncan returned, his teeth bared in a smile. "Ever."

Yet Wolston seemed unaffected. Instead, he inclined his head once more to Petra.

"Do forgive me, your ladyship, but it is the truth. Shawcross here knows little of the facts, except that you appear to believe Beecham. And instead of taking stock of what the witness said"—he gestured toward the sad portrait that was Sir Rufus's body with his recipes strewn about him—"Shawcross chose to trust *you*. It is not the way one properly investigates a murder, being tame with a suspect who was all but caught in the act of taking a life, simply because a lovely but gently bred woman looks at one with such pleading azure eyes."

A very rude reply was on Petra's lips as her eyes narrowed, but she bit it back at the last heartbeat. Wolston was baiting her, and Duncan. She only hoped she could continue to take the high road. Especially since Wolston had pocketed the brass key and was now strolling over to view poor Sir Rufus.

Wolston was just near enough that she could stick out a foot and trip him. His clearly once-broken nose would be damaged again when it landed upon the small table he was passing. Or she could make a grab for his thumb, which he was using to brush at a spot on his chin, and pull it backward so bloody hard that he would . . .

"You see, your ladyship," Wolston said, interrupting her vengeful thoughts, "I know that valet well by now, after having associated with him for the past week."

He then paused, as if assessing the body was now his only

desire in life. Petra nearly laughed, thinking even a terrible play-actor could do better.

Instead, she said with great evenness, "Since it is evident you should like to tell me, Colonel, how did you find Mr. Beecham?" She clasped her hands behind her back and followed Wolston so that she stood inches from his shoulder as they both looked down at the quite pitiable sight of Sir Rufus. She then sent him a brief, serene smile. "Oh, no, do not distress yourself, Colonel. I have seen much worse than a strangled man, I assure you."

Duncan had moved around the other side so that he faced Petra and Wolston. He looked down upon the body, too, his green eyes raking over every inch of the scene as well.

"It is quite true, Wolston," he said almost lazily. "But do be good enough to answer her ladyship's question and tell us about Beecham."

He then looked up, meeting the colonel's eyes steadily, a hardness coming into his voice.

"For whilst your authority might supersede mine at the moment, Her Majesty will wish me to know all the facts so that I may make decisions regarding her security *outside of* Windsor Castle, and indeed beyond. And the security of the Prince Regent and the rest of the royal family as well. For I am in charge of their safety throughout the whole of England, and Her Majesty is quite aware I take my duties with the utmost seriousness."

Petra turned and blinked innocently up at Wolston, who had not missed the faint growl beneath Duncan's politely uttered words. A flush of red was creeping up Wolston's neck that rather clashed with his vibrant uniform. Still, after a moment that exuded anger, he gave a nod of acceptance and briefly flashed his teeth in a smug grin.

"Quite so, Shawcross. Then I shall leave it to you to relay this tragic news to Her Majesty and the Prince Regent. We shall withhold any announcement to the castle guests until you have had that pleasure. Why, I shall even assist by sending one of my men to alert Her Majesty that you are requesting an immediate audience."

Wolston called out, and another guard walked smartly into the library, then raced out again once given his orders.

Petra could tell Duncan was groaning inwardly. Had the situation been different, she would have laughed at his expense. He had set his foot into that particular muck all on his own.

Stepping away from Petra to walk around the body, Wolston gave his opinions on Oliver with the firmness of one who is confident in what they know.

"Beecham is a gambler, with debts to some here in the castle that far outweigh whatever wages he is—or, was—earning from Sir Rufus. I know he was becoming desperate for money to pay some of my men what he owed them. He even tried to borrow money off of me but two days ago. His request was denied."

Wolston bent down to examine Sir Rufus's neck, and the length of black silk. Pulling a small knife from within his tunic, he swiftly cut the ribbon away, allowing Petra to finally see that it was about an inch wide, with edges that had been carefully, almost beautifully sewn to keep them from fraying. Nevertheless, the mark it had left around Sir Rufus's neck was ghastly, but Wolston merely tsked.

"Yes, indeed, strangled. Would you not agree, Shawcross?"

"I would," stated Duncan tersely. But before he could add anything further, Wolston had returned to the subject of Oliver's character.

"Beecham also has seduced one parlormaid and one of the kitchen girls in his short time here, leaving both in floods of tears. The kitchen girl walked in on him with the parlormaid, who was enthusiastically riding St. George, as it were." He glanced up at Petra at this, adding, "Pardon me for speaking so crudely, my lady."

"I do believe I am unaffected," Petra replied dryly.

"Ah, of course," Wolston said softly, and glanced between Petra and Duncan, making it clear he knew she was no spinster when it came to giving away her feminine favors to the illegitimate, half-Scottish grandson of the Duke of Hillmorton. He was only lucky that Duncan had stooped to riffle through some of the recipes strewn about the carpet and did not hear. Wolston smirked and continued.

"I can tell you that Beecham is also insolent, believes himself to be better than his station, and often skulked about the kitchens, asking the cooks to taste dishes whenever Sir Rufus was working on his contribution to Her Majesty's royal collection."

Duncan surreptitiously rolled his eyes at this. Wolston then came back around to stand beside Petra.

"And certainly not the least, but the last thing I shall say at present before I must away to question the cowardly valet, is about what I witnessed three weeks ago. I delivered the invitation to these celebrations to Sir Rufus's house in Buckinghamshire myself. Sir Rufus answered the door, showing himself to have a black eye and sore ribs. He told me that his valet, in a fit of rage that his wages would not be increased, attacked him. 'I thought Beecham would kill me' were Sir Rufus's exact words. Rather telling, do you not think?"

A rap sounded on the door, and at Wolston's urging, a group of men entered bearing a canvas litter for carrying the body of Sir Rufus.

Without giving time for any other questions, Wolston bowed to Petra and gave a curt nod Duncan's way.

"Now, if your ladyship and Shawcross will excuse me, I have a prisoner to interrogate."

TEN

At the west end of the Queen's Audience Chamber, by the fire, Queen Charlotte turned around when Petra approached, holding a stack of Sir Rufus's recipes, with Duncan at her side.

Her Majesty was wearing an exquisitely embroidered ankle-length pelisse of pale blue sarsenet, though the double flounce of French lace and a hint of cambric muslin peeking out from the walking coat's hem allowed Petra to deduce it had been selected not because the Queen desired a brisk morning stroll, but because it easily covered her morning dress. Gold combs then held the queen's silver hair in an attractively simple arrangement, and her blue-topaz earrings seemed to wink playfully as a shaft of morning light shot through the window. Her tawny eyes were narrowed, however, and a bit too much powder on her face further emphasized the level of her discontent, having settled into the frown lines bracketing her pursed mouth.

The bells in St. George's Chapel had just rung the nine o'clock hour as Petra made her curtsy, marking one and one-half hours since she had discovered poor Sir Rufus, dead on the library floor. Since the discovery of Annie's brother here at Windsor Castle, and the vexing knowledge that there was a murderer amongst the nearly one hundred and fifty guests currently within its walls.

Whether it was one of the guests Oliver claimed had argued with Sir Rufus, she and Duncan had agreed that remained to be seen. However, Petra only had time to tell Duncan that Oliver had recognized the Prince Regent's voice before the Guardsman who had been sent to request a private audience with the Queen arrived back at the library. The guard had then remained within earshot until Petra had entered the audience chamber alongside Duncan, keeping her from informing him that Aunt Ophelia's voice had also been recognized.

Even so, Petra could not help but feel a small sense of relief. It would give her time to speak privately with her aunt first.

Yet she suddenly felt a sense of urgency in the matter as she watched the Queen lifting a shawl the color of bluebells from a nearby chair, draping it over her shoulders. Petra was recalling the previous evening in the main library, when Sir Rufus's face had paled with the sight of someone, or something, that troubled him. How she had followed his gaze and watched as a flash of bright color vanished into the crowd.

Petra now realized that what she had seen was her aunt's vivid green shawl.

A wash of dread came over her, but it was set aside at the sight of her cross-looking monarch.

"Well?" snapped the Queen. "Why am I being bothered at such an early hour of the morning? I was told it was important. Enough that you have requested a private audience with me. I have been hastily dressed for the moment, and I do not care for looking anything less than my best. I have not even had my breakfast yet, and that will not do. Explain yourselves."

Duncan put his hands behind his back. "Your Majesty, I shall let Lady Petra have that honor, for it was she who discovered the . . . ah, issue."

Queen Charlotte's lips ticked upward. "Throwing her to the proverbial wolf, are you, Mr. Shawcross?"

Repressing a grin, Petra blinked guilelessly up at Duncan, whose reply came without a moment's hesitation.

"Your Majesty, I have learned that as much as I would like Lady Petra to lean on me for protection, she is quite capable in nearly every situation without me," he said, the burr of his Scottish mother tongue warmer than her own tartan shawl that she'd thrown on for the trek through the castle.

"And, I must add that I would never dream of likening Your Majesty to a wolf," Duncan said, his accent softening almost into a lilt. "Instead, you remind me of the graceful and quite beautiful snow leopards I witnessed during my brief time in Russia. The most intelligent eyes, and such a glossy silver coat. They are quite stealthy . . . until they pounce. Though I am told their prey suffers only but a moment."

"And I was told I might have to suffer your silver tongue, Mr. Shawcross," replied the Queen, but a little flutter in her powdered cheeks belied her amusement. She then eyed Petra. "Well? What say you? Why have I been dragged from my bed?" Her eyes slitted further even as one gray eyebrow quirked upward. "You two are not here to beg for my approval to marry, are you?"

"What?" Petra said, thoroughly startled. Then she hastily cleared her throat. "I do beg your pardon, Your Majesty. What I mean to say is no, we are not intending to marry." She cast a glance toward Duncan to see his own dryly amused expression as he carefully studied the floor. "It is something else, I am afraid. Something entirely tragic."

The Queen moved to settle upon a small sofa. "Is that so? Well, go on. I cannot agree with you if you do not explain the circumstances."

Petra nodded. "Of course, Your Majesty. I regret to inform you that I discovered the death of Sir Rufus Pomeroy this morning. In the small library."

The Queen's eyes widened in genuine surprise.

"Sir Rufus has died? Well . . . this is dreadful indeed. Yes, it is most sad. Though I am not certain it required rousing me from my bed, especially as he only went a few months earlier than he expected."

When both Petra and Duncan glanced at each other, both clearly taken aback, Her Majesty tsked.

"Did he not tell you, Lady Petra? It was a secret few knew, I suppose—even the Prince Regent was unaware—but there is no reason to keep it now. He was afflicted with cancer. No, I do not know which kind. But when he heard you were invited, I thought he might confess it."

She picked up a small golden bell with a black enameled handle. "I will send my steward to speak with Sir Rufus's valet, and all necessary arrangements will be made. And there will simply have to be four judges for the patisserie contest instead of five."

She went to ring the bell, but Petra took a hasty step forward, receiving an arched eyebrow as she did.

"That is very kind of you, Your Majesty, but I'm afraid I had good reason to insist upon a private audience with you at such an hour," Petra said. "You see, it was very clear Sir Rufus did not expire of some natural cause—or of his cancer."

"No?" said the Queen, though it seemed she was already losing interest as her eyes began roaming over a small collection of snuff boxes on a nearby table.

"I am afraid not, Ma'am," Petra said. "I regret having to say it, but Sir Rufus was murdered. In fact, it cannot be denied that he was strangled."

In the short period before Wolston's men took the body of Sir Rufus away, Duncan had managed to check for evidence of poison or any other signs of lethal damage. There had been nothing except for a swollen wrist and fingernail scratches on his neck. Was the former caused during an attempt to lash out at his killer, and the latter as he struggled against the ribbon tightening around his neck?

The Queen's head had snapped up. She was fairly vibrating with anger. "*Murdered?* In my castle? How dare someone disrespect my home in this manner! Who was the blackhearted evildoer? I shall have him executed forthwith!"

Petra let her voice become soothing, as Duncan had earlier. "I do agree whoever has done this has been as disrespectful of Your Majesty as they were of the life of poor Sir Rufus," she began.

"Yes, yes, of course that is what I meant," the Queen replied peevishly.

"I had no doubt, Ma'am," Petra said. "You see, we have someone in custody. Sir Rufus's valet, in fact. Colonel Wolston is interviewing him as we speak. The colonel is quite convinced he has his man, but Mr. Shawcross and I are not wholly certain that Mr. Beecham—that is, the valet—is the guilty party."

Before she finished speaking, the doors to the Queen's Privy Chamber at the far end of the room had opened and the Prince Regent strode in. He, too, looked to have been hastily dressed, with his thick neck and multiple chins looking more pronounced due to a simple cravat instead of being somewhat hidden by his usual high, stiff collars. He seemed two levels more cross than his venerable mama.

Petra and Duncan had barely finished their greetings when Prince George growled, "You say that Wolston thinks this ruffian is guilty, Shawcross?"

"He does indeed, Sir, but Lady Petra and I cannot—"

"Yes, yes, I heard what Lady Petra said," the Prince said, brushing a lock of graying dark hair from his forehead, "but if Wolston says this rogue is guilty of killing Sir Rufus, then I am inclined to believe him. He has been the constable here at Windsor for five years now, and has never put us wrong." He turned to his mother. "I say, that was quick, Mama. Wolston is to be commended."

"Mm, indeed," murmured the Queen with a nod, her tone rather more dry than jubilant.

The Prince did not seem to notice and looked rather delighted at such a swift outcome.

"If that is the case, then I am glad the perpetrator has been caught. I'll order Wolston to send . . . Beecham, is it? . . . to the dungeon in Curfew Tower, to be hanged in three days' time."

Petra felt her mouth form into a shocked O, then quickly pressed her lips together. She went to step forward to plead for leniency for Annie's brother, but caught a sharp glance from the Queen and stopped.

Her Majesty then turned on her sofa to give her son a fond look—one that the Prince clearly believed by his satisfied smile, but Petra assuredly did not.

"My dearest," began the Queen. "Your decisiveness is most admirable, as usual. Quite reminds me of your dear papa. However, this is a week of celebrations, and it will already be dampened by the tragic passing of our esteemed chef who served the royal household so well for fifteen years. Would you not consider holding off on pronouncing the valet's sentence whilst we mourn Sir Rufus, and then allow the events that have already been planned for the week to continue without such a pall hanging over them?"

Briefly, she gestured toward the windows, in the direction of the Quadrangle.

"Why, in three days' time, that will be your venue for the tilt. With both Colonel Wolston and Mr. Shawcross scheduled to participate in the jousting—and competing for not just the glory, but also your condescension. A hanging would quite interrupt what is sure to be a day filled with cheers in your honor, would it not?"

The Prince set his chin in defiance, his lips forming into a childish pout. Petra held her breath as the Queen made a show of gently smoothing down her pelisse. And then the Prince's countenance cleared.

"Yes, you are right, Mama. I should not like to spoil the celebrations, much less my tilting contest. It shall be such fun." He lifted his chin, looking resolved. "Shawcross, tell Colonel Wolston he is to send the valet to Curfew Tower in the Lower Ward, but I will hold off on pronouncing his sentence for one week, until the Monday after our guests return home. Wolston is to refrain from allowing talk of the hanging to permeate the celebrations." The Prince then turned to go, but spoke over his shoulder: "And Lady Petra?"

"Yes, Your Highness?" she replied.

"You will not allow this to distract your mind from the task which I set you, yes?"

"Indeed, I shall not, Sir."

The Prince had not truly waited for her reply. Yet he stopped again and spun back to face Petra and Duncan.

"In fact, I would like to hold off on Sir Rufus's exact cause of death until then as well. For the week, all our guests shall know is that the great and talented Sir Rufus Pomeroy experienced an accident of some sort and died. He was looking quite unwell yesterday. Maybe say he fell ill and expired."

The Queen said, "We may also simply speak the truth, that Sir Rufus was dying anyway of a cancer. It was to be a secret until after the celebrations, but, well . . ."

The Prince's blue eyes widened for a long moment as he digested this news, but swiftly his expression returned to one of impatience.

"Whatever you choose, we shall not make a fuss and ruin my—I mean His Majesty and Her Majesty's joyous anniversary celebrations. Are my wishes understood?"

"Yes, Your Highness. Thank you," Duncan said.

"Good, now go, Shawcross, and alert Wolston and his men."

Duncan bowed and was gone through the east doors before the Prince had strolled back through those on the opposite end.

Petra, still holding the stack of recipes, was left standing in front of the Queen, who was looking decidedly pleased with herself.

"If I may say so, you were quite impressive, Your Majesty," Petra said, grinning when it was clear from the queen's amused countenance that she would not object to seeing it.

"One must know how and when to be pliant, Lady Petra," she said of her gentle directing of her son. "Do not forget that a woman's strength is sometimes the most powerful when she takes a softer approach." With a mild frown, she said, "I have been deliberate in giving you and Shawcross time to investigate, and prove either your hunches correct, or Wolston's. Do not waste time in determining other suspects, too, as I am assuming you are intending to do."

She rose from her sofa, all amusement gone.

"And do not make me, or my son, look the fool."

"No, indeed, Your Majesty. And I thank you. Mr. Shawcross and I shall endeavor to deserve your kind efforts." Holding out the stack of papers, she said, "These are Sir Rufus's recipes. He had been sorting them in the library but they, ah, became rather strewn about. I cannot see that they are in any order at all."

The Queen waved over a footman. "I shall have someone sort them before they go into my collections." Petra handed over the stack, knowing she was being dismissed. She curtsied, but the Queen was already moving in the opposite direction, toward the door to her privy chamber.

Though as she watched the Queen go, Petra bit her lip. If what Oliver Beecham had said was correct, the Prince Regent was already one of her suspects.

And by the way the Prince was willing to have Oliver hanged without any true proof of guilt? Well, it might just be bloody difficult to keep her promise that Prince George would not end up looking exceptionally foolish.

ELEVEN

Charles was out of breath by the time he caught up with Petra, just a few steps from the hallway that would lead to her bedchamber.

"Mr. Shawcross relayed the Prince's orders to Colonel Wolston, my lady. The Coldstream Guards will keep their silence on the manner of Sir Rufus's death until otherwise directed. Her Majesty's guests will be told that Sir Rufus, after suffering from cancer, sadly passed after feeling ill the night before. It will be explained that the valet, Mr. Beecham, was sent back to Buckinghamshire to alert Sir Rufus's solicitor and prepare for a funeral."

"That will have to do for now, then," Petra said.

"Didn't like it much, the colonel," Charles continued with a brief look of distaste. "Said that there were already too many who knew, especially when the Guardsmen went rushing through the castle, and with Marta unlikely to hold her tongue. I went directly to speak with Mrs. Daley—who I was told to confide in—and she says she will help keep the girl out of trouble."

"Well done," Petra said. "We will just have to contain the news as best we can. And the colonel may lump it regardless."

To her mulish tone, Charles's dark blue eyes briefly brightened with humor, but then his whole countenance turned somber.

"My lady," he said. "I confess I am rather worried about Annie. She told me who Mr. Beecham is to her, that he is her brother. If I am being honest, I had wondered if he might be a relation with how similar I noted they looked at times. Still, I do not know how she will take it if Beecham is found guilty."

He looked so miserable for Annie that it only made Petra more determined to know the truth.

"Mr. Shawcross and I will do everything we can to uncover other suspects, and then we will work even harder to understand what is, and what is not, the truth in hopes of exonerating Mr. Beecham. I give you my word."

She wondered if Annie had confessed to Charles about there already being five suspects—even if three had yet to be named—but his expression indicated he was none the wiser.

"And no matter what," she continued, "we will stand by Annie and help her in any way we can, yes?"

Charles was already nodding vigorously. "Without a doubt, my lady. And I shall do whatever is needed to assist you and Mr. Shawcross—who bade me to tell you that he returned to the small library and searched for any signs that Beecham had worn gloves and removed them. Just in case, one understands. But no gloves were found."

"Thank you, Foyle," she said, giving him a smile.

His shoulders straightened proudly with hearing his surname, and Petra felt she might end up losing Charles to his new life as a valet. He seemed to have taken to the job with great pride. And if that be the case, she would wish him well—and hope that it might be Duncan who hired him.

"What next, my lady?" he asked.

Petra was thinking on the fact that Oliver Beecham had heard five people rowing with Sir Rufus. Knowing the Prince was one of the five was vexing enough, so she was trying hard not to concentrate on Aunt Ophelia being another one named.

And then she recalled Oliver saying Sir Rufus spoke with a sixth person, and told that person that he, Sir Rufus, had hidden something that one or more of the others wanted. That it was hidden somewhere in the castle.

Yet Windsor Castle had nearly a thousand rooms in all—plus no telling how many nooks and secret places in which to conceal an item. How would she ever begin to narrow that number down? Much less be able to search the vast majority of His Majesty's residence without any number of guests, servants, and the Coldstream Guards seeing her?

Not to mention a murderer. *Blast.*

Pulling in a steadying breath, she reminded herself that she had people here at the castle she could trust. Duncan and Annie, of course. And Charles, too, who was looking at her with the expression of one who had faith in her to know the next step. It occurred to her she also had Caroline and Duncan's grandmama, the Duchess of Hillmorton, on her side. Without a doubt she could rule both out as potential suspects.

The duchess, of course, was so well known that it would be unlikely Oliver would not have recognized her voice. And Caroline had never made the acquaintance of Sir Rufus prior to last night, when Petra herself had introduced the two not long before the supper had commenced. Naturally, Sir Rufus had been thoroughly charmed, and had promised to give Caroline the recipe for his famous lemon shortbread that had been a staple at Windsor, but perfected during his time working at Buckfields so long ago.

For the first time after seeing Sir Rufus's life taken in such a horrid manner, Petra allowed herself to think on what else had been lost. That a man responsible for the culinary delights of many in England was now gone. Truly, it was a sad day indeed, and there was a small part of her that was glad she had not seen Sir Rufus since she was a little girl. Her heavy heart was therefore not made worse for better knowing him, and thus she could better concentrate on finding his killer.

Charles was still waiting patiently for her to speak, and it was then that an idea came to mind. She glanced about to make certain they were still alone.

"Do you know if Beecham has yet been taken to Curfew Tower?"

"I can find out, my lady," said Charles. "If he has not, what would you like me to do?"

Petra considered the time. "I am due to begin my judging duties at the patisserie contest at three o'clock this afternoon. I wish to speak with Beecham, but without Colonel Wolston or any other guards knowing. Do you believe you could determine if that were possible?"

Charles nodded. "The colonel knows I am assisting Mr. Shawcross and thus, I may move about the castle a bit more freely. I shall see what I can discover about Beecham's whereabouts."

When he had left, Petra finally entered the corridor that held her chambers, and three others. The rooms next to hers were Caroline's, then across the hall were those of Aunt Ophelia. The fourth was currently still unoccupied. Petra was musing on who might be placed there when the hall maid, called Tilly, came out of her aunt's bedchamber carrying a breakfast tray.

Toast crumbs and a half-empty crystal pot of marmalade were noted along with a teapot and a teacup containing the dregs of black China tea, telling Petra that her aunt had taken her preferred morning nourishment. A fresh pot of tea would likely have just been delivered, with her aunt sipping on a cup as she wrote in her diary of the night before. If she were not wearing a white silk robe with feathers about the wrists and neckline, Petra would be aghast. Aunt Ophelia did not let the sartorial side down even when alone in her boudoir, and Petra adored her for it.

She went to knock upon her aunt's door, but it was Tilly's voice she heard from down the corridor.

"I'm afraid Lady Ophelia is not in her rooms, my lady," she said.

"She isn't?" Petra returned blankly, glancing at the breakfast tray.

"Well, she was, of course," the girl said, her eyes guileless and smiling, "but she left some time ago. When, my lady? Well, I brought this tray to her at a quarter to six, I did. Lady Ophelia seemed a bit out of sorts, if I may be so bold as to say so. She was out of bed, dressed, and pacing about her bedchamber. Seemed quite happy to see her breakfast, though. Poured herself some tea even as I were setting the tray down and ate her toast quickly. Nearly finished by the time I cleared away the whisky glasses, and then she called out to her maid that she felt the need for a walk."

"She did?" Petra asked blankly. "At such an early hour?"

"Oh, I were quite surprised, too, my lady," said Tilly. "I don't see fine ladies out walking about the castle, or anywhere, come to think of it, before ten or eleven o'clock. Lady Ophelia's lady's maid didn't seem to think it so odd, though. Replied in French, she did. Sounded quite elegant."

"Mm, yes, Geraldine does indeed speak very prettily," Petra said, though she suppressed a sigh as she did so.

Ten years ago, when Aunt Ophelia had become widowed, Geraldine had already been rather lax at her duties. And the intervening years had not shown any improvement. It seemed Aunt Ophelia kept the woman around because Geraldine's French sensibilities meant that she encouraged her mistress's venturesome sense of style and equally lively outlook on life.

Briskly, Petra rapped on her aunt's door, and then entered, calling out, "Geraldine? Are you here?"

After a moment, her aunt's lady's maid silently appeared. She was about thirty, but her bland expression and sharply planed features made her look a bit formidable, even though her black hair was curled quite fashionably. She gave a curtsy, then looked expectantly at Petra without an offer of assistance.

"Do you know where Lady Ophelia is at present, Geraldine? Or when she will return here to her chambers?"

And, as Petra suspected might happen, it was a fool's errand to ask—and she quickly realized inquiring about any interactions with Sir Rufus would be even sillier. For Geraldine responded in the way she had always done, whether Aunt Ophelia was innocently walking in the gardens with her two wolfhounds or engaging in vigorous amorous congress with the bachelor vicar from the next village—with each one as likely to happen as the other, as Petra had discovered herself long ago.

Geraldine lifted her shoulder in a very Gallic shrug and said, "Ah, but my Lady Ophelia, she tells me all she wishes me to know, and that is all I need to know, *ce n'est pas?*"

To be fair, Annie might respond in much the same way to inquiries about Petra's life—though in the King's English, of course. The difference was, Annie protected Petra and her secrets with the force of a Coldstream Guard, while Geraldine was little inclined to make such an effort.

Though in this moment, when Aunt Ophelia had been named as a possible murder suspect—and had been proven to be in castle parts unknown at the time of the murder itself—Geraldine's laissez-faire attitude was quite unhelpful indeed.

"Please tell my aunt that I should like to speak with her as soon as possible," Petra said finally, adding, "it is quite important."

Once more in the hallway, Petra checked her watch again. It was a quarter to ten, and she was more than a little peckish. Besides, it would be no use trying to find her aunt in a castle as big as Windsor. Why, Aunt Ophelia could be out walking on the Long Walk or in the parklands, even. But there was a possibility she might take a second, more substantial, breakfast after her perambulations. Petra decided to make her way to the dining room in hopes of finding her aunt there.

Yet before she did, there was another equally important conversation to have, and there was no use in putting it off. She crossed the hall and turned the knob to her own bedchamber door.

TWELVE

Petra found Annie standing by the wardrobe, wringing her hands, worry etched all over her face.

"What news of my brother, my lady?" she asked in a whisper.

Petra explained all that had happened without mincing words. "The Queen has duly guided the Prince into giving Duncan and me the week to sort out the truth. If Oliver is innocent, I promise we will do our utmost to prove it."

Annie nodded, silent tears filling her eyes. She did not attempt to wipe them away.

"Regarding what you said about not confessing something Oliver did to the earl," Petra then said. "How did you mean?"

Shame flooded Annie's face.

"It will only make things worse for Oliver, my lady," she said. "And for me as well, I suppose. I will have deserved it if you turn me out, but I do not wish for anything to further make my brother look guilty."

Petra walked over to the sofa, and insisted Annie sit down as well.

"I think it would be better if you simply told me all." And as gently as she could, she added, "Now, please, Annie."

After a long hesitation, Annie began speaking.

"Do you recall our visit to Buckfields when I discovered the tenant farmer who been robbed and beaten to death?"

Petra nodded. "It was during that very mild spate of weather we had in December of 1812. You were returning from visiting your parents when you found the farmer. You ran to Buckfields to fetch the earl, and I insisted on coming back to the farmer's house with you. You said you'd seen a gypsy escaping into the woods as you walked the path alongside the farmer's property." She blinked in surprise. "Do not tell me it was Oliver you saw."

"Yes, and no, my lady." Annie pulled a handkerchief from her pocket and dabbed at her eyes. "Oliver had recently left yet another occupation as an assistant gamekeeper, and was staying with our mother and father. I did not know this when I went to visit them, for he had just arrived. I stayed most of the day with my dear parents, my sisters, and Oliver, but he left about an hour before me. To visit the alehouse in the village of Holbrook."

"And the fastest way to the village is to use the path that would take him by the farmer's house," Petra mused.

"That is true, my lady. As I mentioned, I left barely an hour later, and took the same path. And when I saw the farmer, lying a few feet from his doorway, I also heard someone in his house. I picked up a nearby rake to defend myself and then looked through the window." Her voice became choked. "I saw my brother, going through the farmer's things."

Petra could not help it. She gasped a little.

"Oliver—he killed the farmer? There was no gypsy?"

Annie, who had been worrying the edge of her handkerchief, now stopped and looked into Petra's face.

"My brother swears there was a man, my lady. Oliver told me it was he who scared off the intruder who killed the farmer and stole the poor man's possessions. As he tells it, Oliver surmised the farmer caught the man stealing, and the man then took the first weapon he could find and bashed the farmer until he was dead."

"Should I guess that you chose to believe Oliver's tale and let him go instead of bringing him to the earl to let the facts be weighed properly?" Petra asked after digesting what she had heard. "Thus, whilst it is possible that Oliver was telling the truth, you also could have given a thief and a murderer—even one who is your brother—his freedom?"

Annie's eyes were welled again, but she nodded. "You now know the truth, and I am so terribly sorry, my lady." She went to stand, her voice thick with emotion. "I will collect my things and go."

But Petra laid a hand on Annie's arm.

"You most certainly will not."

Fear shot through Annie's eyes. "Will you send me to Curfew Tower as well, my lady?"

Removing her hand, Petra would only say, "First of all, I should like you to tell me one thing about that day. When you saw Oliver, did he look like he did this morning? After I felled him, I mean. Was either of his eyes blackened? His nose or lips bloodied?"

Brows knitting, Annie shook her head. "No, my lady. His face was quite clean. Our mother insisted he scrub himself in the bath after arriving home that morning."

Petra was silent for a moment, then spoke with grim resignation.

"Annie, you should have confided in me. We should have gone together to speak with the earl."

Hanging her head, Annie agreed, and whispered another apology.

"Yet I understand why you allowed Oliver to leave," Petra said. A relieved sigh then issued from her lips. "And it was quite clear that neither Oliver nor you took stock of the farmer's injuries before you made your hasty decisions."

Annie cautiously looked up. "How do you mean, my lady?"

"Well, the farmer fought with whomever killed him," Petra explained. "Do you not recall seeing the evidence? His knuckles were bloody, and a bit swollen. To me, it looked as if he had broken one of his fingers, too—but I never asked for confirmation of such. If Oliver had fought him, Annie, there would have been evidence. Blood or scrapes or bruises on his face. Or his body, and his clothing."

Hope was springing in Annie's eyes, and Petra felt she knew the feeling well.

"I could not look at the poor farmer once I led the earl and his men back to the scene," Annie said wonderingly. "Yet there was no blood anywhere on Oliver, my lady. I swear it. He looked as fresh as he did when he'd left our father's home."

"Then, whilst he may have been attempting to loot the farmer's house—"

Annie hurried to finish the thought. "Even if he was planning on it, he had nothing on his person. I checked his coat and pockets more thoroughly than that guard did earlier." Then her voice went weak with guilt. "Oh . . . I now think it may be possible he was telling the truth that day."

"I expect that, after so many years of hearing his stories and helping him out of his mischiefs, you had learned to mistrust him first," Petra said gently. Then she stood and held out her hands.

"Will you stay, Annie? For you must know I would never send you to any tower, even if Oliver had been guilty."

Annie's face broke into a watery smile and she clutched Petra's hands tightly. "Do you mean it? Of course I shall stay." Her lips trembled again. "But what if Oliver is guilty this time?"

Yet something about telling this story had made Petra go back over what she had witnessed this morning.

"I do not think he is," she said slowly. "I did not notice it when we were first interrogating him, but when the guards cut the apron strings from his wrists and then put the irons on him, he did this." Petra put her wrists together behind her back and splayed her fingers.

"I do not understand," Annie said.

"His hands," Petra said excitedly. "His palms were a bit pink, but if he had been pulling that hard upon a piece of black silk—which is quite slippery, you know—and had to pull hard enough to choke a fully grown man to death, his palms and fingers would be reddened. They might even contain blisters or cuts from the effort. But Oliver's were free of blemishes."

Annie's grin lit up the room, but Petra was quick to insert caution. "I cannot rightly be certain as I only saw them for a moment. Though it did not occur to me at the time to ask Duncan, you understand. It is possible he noticed a different state of Oliver's hands."

Annie put her own together as if in prayer. "Oh, I do hope you are correct, my lady. No matter what, he is my brother, and I do love him. I know he is a good man, he just needs to practice allowing that side of him to come out."

Petra nodded, but still encouraged caution. "No one understands the feeling of hoping someone is good more than I do," she said, thinking of how she had been led to distrust Duncan just a few months earlier, and had hoped against hope that she was wrong. "But you must understand that we are compelled to consider all options at present."

But the real Annie—the fierce, strong, capable Annie of before yesterday—had returned. Her hazel eyes burned with decision.

"I understand, my lady. And I will accept whatever is proven to be true. But I shall also like to help you discover that truth. What would you have me do to help you and Mr. Shawcross? Please give me an occupation, my lady, for I cannot stay one moment longer in this room with my thoughts." And before Petra could speak, she added, "And no matter what you ask me to do, I will bring you everything I find, whether it is gossip or something tangible. I shan't court your distrust ever again by not being completely truthful."

Hearing this, Petra felt as if she should do the same in return. She told Annie that she would be attempting to speak with Oliver again, and that she felt it best she go alone, or with Duncan.

The knowledge that her brother was about to be sent to a dungeon prison made worry course over Annie's face. But she understood why she could not go.

"I might spend the time either chastising my brother or crying over him, with how my emotions have been so out of hand. Yes, then it is right you go without me."

Petra nodded, and voiced an idea. "I know what would be immensely helpful. Sir Rufus worked here for fifteen years, and yet Oliver claims that he was not as well liked as it would appear."

"You would like me to go to the servants' hall and begin asking questions about Sir Rufus and what the servants have heard of him, and how they found him, yes?" Annie said, already looking like she was crafting ways in her mind to subtly introduce the conversation. When she saw Petra's smile, she grinned in return. "Then I shall do so, my lady. I shall go now and report back when I ready you for your first day as a patisserie judge."

When Annie had left, Petra wilted upon the sofa, the morning having been an exhausting one. She thought about ringing for a breakfast tray, but she knew going to the dining room itself would be the better option. It would be her first chance to do the same thing as Annie, to begin her interrogations. And it would likely be best to start them before any gossip that might arise began to spread.

There was a knock at the door, and Charles entered when bidden. By his slightly besotted smile, it was fairly clear he had seen Annie looking herself again. And by the flush upon his cheeks, Petra wagered herself that Annie had given Charles a kiss.

"I have done as you asked, my lady," he announced. "They are currently keeping Beecham in a locked room inside the Round Tower for his interrogations. It is a room within Colonel Wolston's apartments. Though as they are undergoing some renovations, he is kipping elsewhere on the grounds, leaving the entirety of the Tower otherwise empty."

"And how many guards are watching Mr. Beecham?" Petra asked.

"At present, there is but one guard on duty. He told me they are moving Beecham later to Curfew Tower. I'm told the dungeon has not been used as a prison since the Great Rebellion in 1651. Still, the current prison at the southwest end of the Lower Ward had a wall collapse, thereby reducing space, so the dungeon it is."

"Right, then," Petra said. "There is a covered staircase leading from the Edward the Third Tower to the Round Tower. It is only covered at the top, of course, but it should still allow me to make my way there with a smaller chance of being seen. Now, how to get the guard to allow me some time with Beecham . . ."

"I may have an idea, if I may," said Charles.

"Indeed?" Petra said. "Go on, then."

"Well, the guard was quite hungry, he was. He'd been assigned the sentry duty as a punishment of sorts, for oversleeping this morning. He'd had neither food nor drink, and I could hear his stomach noises. And, well, if you brought him some bread, cheese, and something to drink, he might allow you the time you require, and keep it quiet."

"Foyle," she said with a smile, reverting to his surname again, "I could not be happier Mr. Shawcross was in need of a valet, and that he was intelligent enough to choose you."

THIRTEEN

FINDING THE NECESSARY ITEMS TO BRIBE THE GUARD WITH was easier than expected once Petra realized she already had food available in her own room.

The tray that Charles had sent up for Annie earlier had been hardly touched, and so Petra—after first slathering a piece of toast with black currant jam and eating it so quickly that she barely tasted it—slowed down enough to sip on some now-cold tea as she crafted a sandwich of toast and cheese for the guard. Wrapping it tightly in a linen napkin, she then filled a flask with more tea. All of it she was able to tuck into her arm and hide beneath her tartan shawl.

"Blast it all that I must wear my best dresses this week," she nevertheless muttered after attempting in vain to slide the napkin-cloaked sandwich into a pocket that did not exist in her silk dress. She always had them sewn into her other dresses—much to her tailor's constant dismay—but for her finest finery, she had agreed to forgo the useful additions.

So, with Charles as a sort of advance guard, she discreetly followed him at a distance through the south side of the castle, ready to step into another hallway or hide somehow should she hear Charles greet someone.

It still being considered early for most after the previous evening's festivities, she only had to hide twice, and not from anyone she would consider suspicious. Neither could have won a race against a turtle due to their advanced age, much less choked Sir Rufus to death, of that she was certain.

Then came a third time she was compelled to hide, however. And when she did, she spied something that made her pause.

They had just entered the Edward III Tower. Charles, well in front of her, called out cheerfully, "Good morning, your lordship," and Petra slid behind the conveniently wide jousting armor of King Henry VIII, her stomach just touching the back faulds that angled outward and would have protected the monarch's waist and hips.

Thanking the heavens she wasn't pressed up against the Tudor king's massive codpiece—especially knowing His Majesty's manhood had been rumored to be riddled with the pox—Petra felt the need to giggle until movement outside the nearby window caught her eye.

She looked out and down onto the South Terrace, the pretty walkway running between the castle and the rectangular building generally known as the Queen's Lodge, where Queen Charlotte and King George often lived in the early days of their marriage, before his illness took over. Farther to the left, though Petra had to crane her neck to see it, was a portion of the Long Walk, which led through the beautiful parklands.

It was in the direction of the Long Walk that a woman was stepping quickly. Petra recognized her aunt Ophelia, despite her aunt's face being shielded by a bonnet and her dove-gray dress being mostly covered with a demi-length pelisse in a lilac hue.

It was the coat's luminous, lemon-hued satin lining that appeared when her aunt whirled to look behind her that gave her away. Some six months earlier, Petra had been with her aunt when she had commissioned that particular coat, teasing that she could see the lining from halfway across Buckfields—and she had not been wholly wrong.

Petra watched as Aunt Ophelia considered something, or someone, in the distance, then turned back and resumed walking in the direction she had initially been heading.

As her aunt always moved at an energetic pace and her expression was hidden by the bonnet, Petra could not discern if Aunt Ophelia were distressed, or merely surprised by a noise she had not expected. Regardless, no one appeared; Petra stayed where she was for several seconds to be certain her aunt was not followed.

Nevertheless, she frowned. She had never known her aunt to forgo her rejuvenating sleep after a dinner party that went into the wee hours. So where was Aunt Ophelia going? Was she just on a walk, or was she meeting someone? And, for that matter, where had she been early this morning when Sir Rufus was murdered?

Unbidden, a memory came to mind. Along with Lady Ophelia Throckmorton's bantam sense of style, she also had a temper that, much like her pelisse, stayed calm and sedate for the most part, until something made the searingly bright flash of lining that was her ire appear.

While the appearance of it was a rarity, Petra had occasionally known her aunt, when her patience had been lost, to do anything from snapping at her servants or loved ones to, once or twice, throwing a cup across the room, where it smashed into dozens of pieces.

Truly, Aunt Ophelia's bad humor would briefly burn hot, usually when she was under undue stress—and more often when she had not eaten properly—and then it would fade just as quickly. Petra could not say without guilt that her own temperament was any different. She was certainly never impressed with herself when she lost her control, and knew her aunt to be the same.

But there had been one night, when Petra was nearing her seventeenth birthday. As a treat, the earl had sent Petra and Annie to Morningside, the beautiful Yorkshire estate where Aunt Ophelia continued to live after the passing of her viscount husband. They had spent a most enjoyable three months in each other's company, and Petra and her aunt continued thereafter to be almost as close as sisters.

Or thick as thieves, as the earl was often wont to say, always with an affectionate smile.

But in this memory, it had been well over a year since Lord Throckmorton's death and her aunt was only truly coming out of mourning. For Ophelia and her viscount—whom Petra had called Uncle Albie— had been very much a love match, and the strength had only deepened despite their never being blessed with a child of their own.

During that particular stay at Morningside, one evening Petra had crept downstairs, long after she had been sent to bed, to find the house still and quiet. Much like Forsyth House in London, Morningside ran on a small number of servants, and the number had further decreased after the viscount's passing. There was not even a hall maid awake to ask if she needed some hot milk to help her sleep.

Thus, Petra had planned to collect her aunt's wolfhounds and take a turn about the safe confines of the walled-in knot garden, which had a trellis overflowing with night-scented jasmine and made for a delightfully calming walk. It was also positioned on the side of the house that had once held Uncle Albie's study and billiards room, making for a place to amble where she would not wake anyone.

But she had not been the first to have the idea.

Through the windows of the billiards room, two wolfhounds nearly as tall as she at her side, Petra watched her aunt Ophelia pacing the knot garden. On a stone bench, an oil lamp was burning brightly, easily lighting a wide swath of the garden. Thinking she would walk outside and join her aunt, Petra had blown out her own candle, and was about to open the doors when a man came into view.

He was a gentleman of some wealth by his clothing and polished boots, and looked to be in his mid-thirties. He also had a rakish quality to him, and after he stepped closer to the lamplight, she recognized him as Mr. Barwick, who owned the estate adjacent to the Morningside lands. Petra had met him several times, and had even danced with him once, but only because the hostess had put them together as partners.

As she watched from the billiards room, Mr. Barwick had seemed to be speaking mildly to Aunt Ophelia, a smile playing about his handsome face, his hands clasped in a relaxed manner behind his back.

Then, without warning, Aunt Ophelia rushed at Barwick and slapped him. Not just once, but twice. And then she leapt at him, her hands clamping around his neck, fingernails digging into his skin as she attempted to throttle him.

Barwick had managed to fend her off, stumbling backward with a shocked expression. Petra, too, had been shaken. She had never seen her aunt act in such a way. Blinded with rage seemingly from nowhere. And it was only the wolfhounds barking and lunging at the door that brought Aunt Ophelia and Petra both to their senses.

Hastily, Petra had retreated into the darkness of the room, but the last thing she saw was Barwick striding away and her aunt's face, still contorted in rage, as she peered toward the doors.

The next morning, however, Aunt Ophelia welcomed her in the breakfast room with her arms flung out and her usual "Petra, my love!" Her aunt had seemed entirely herself again, and no mention of a visit from a gentleman the night before was made by either aunt or niece.

It had been a scene quickly relegated to the safe confines of Petra's memory, but now it leapt forth in an undesirable manner. As much as she did not wish to admit it, there was a truth she did not like. Aunt Ophelia could, on occasion, fly into a rage so intense that she was capable of not just hurting another person, but potentially taking their life.

A polite cough now sounded. Petra gave her head a little clearing shake. Charles was giving the signal that the hallways were once again empty. She slid out from behind the suit of armor and they were soon walking through the tower named for the fourteenth-century king who increased the military might of England. As she took the covered steps upward, Petra kept glancing about. She saw no one on the grounds, but as the morning breeze whipped at her hair, she could not ignore the feeling she was being watched.

FOURTEEN

Charles had been quite correct. The guard was famished, and in gratitude for the food, agreed for Petra to have five minutes alone with his prisoner. She poured tea from the flask into a cup as he nevertheless cautioned her.

"Though not a minute longer, my lady, if you please. I do not wish to end up in Curfew Tower alongside Beecham for disobeying Colonel Wolston's orders. He or one of the other guards could arrive at any moment."

"I shall be brief," Petra assured him, recorking the flask. From one more napkin she had tucked under her shawl, she pulled out two pieces of shortbread. Offering them to the guard, she said, "But I expect you to go in the hall to give me those minutes in privacy when speaking with Mr. Beecham."

After a moment, the guard nodded, unlocked the door in question, growling at his prisoner to sit upon the floor and not move. When he left, closing the door to the main bedroom behind him, Petra drew in a breath and then entered Oliver Beecham's temporary cell.

Oliver stood when he saw her. He looked terrible, with his auburn hair disheveled and the bruises she had given him on his face fully blackened, plus a new cut upon his lip. By the way he winced as he stood, Petra felt it likely he had been beaten in an attempt to enact a confession.

"My lady, you should not be here."

Petra gave him a stern look, which enticed him into silence. She handed him the flask of tea, then held out the last piece of shortbread and a small hunk of cheese, both of which she'd managed to hide in the napkin to make it look empty. Oliver all but swooned at the sight of sustenance.

As he gratefully gulped down some of the tea, Petra looked about.

For the time being, his prison was not so terrible. It was a small dressing room that had been cleared of its belongings—Wolston's no doubt—in preparation for enlarging the space. A small window, not wide enough for even a person's head, was on one end to let in light. Nothing but a bucket was in the room, but at least the space was neither cold nor dirty at present. Still, if he were moved by the end of the day as expected, this relative nicety would not last long.

"May I ask—why are you here, my lady?" Oliver asked around his last mouthful of shortbread. "And Annie? Please, how is my sister?"

"Beecham," she replied, "this is probably the one time I shall have to speak with you, and we have no more than five minutes. Four, since I wanted to make certain you had food in you first. Thus, we must use the time wisely. No blustering, no undue questions. You must answer my queries so that Mr. Shawcross and I may best help you. Do you agree?"

He nodded, slowly, seemingly nonplussed.

"Though first, Annie is well, and most determined to help you be cleared. She is your sister, and she loves you dearly. Do not forget that." Seeing a wash of emotion in his eyes, she returned to the business at hand. "Now, let me see the palms of your hands."

Obediently, if curiously, he tucked the flask under his arm and turned his hands over. She looked at them closely, including the spaces between his fingers.

It had now been over an hour since he had been hauled away by Wolston's guards, but it did not matter. While there were a couple of old calluses, likely from his time working at the dockyards, or even from his recent training as a cook, there were no cuts, abrasions, or any residual redness on his hands. She then indicated he should turn his palms down, and frowned with what she saw.

The knuckles on his right hand were reddened, and two bore fresh, shallow cuts.

"How did this happen?"

"I got two good punches in to that guard from earlier, my lady," he said with some pride. Then his lips twisted in dismay as one hand went to his ribs. "When they took me to the King's Guard Chamber to interrogate me. Though he got me twice as good in return. I am well, though. Nothing I haven't experienced before. Wolston stopped him, but I don't think he would have if His Royal Highness hadn't arrived."

"The Prince Regent came to the Guard Chamber?"

Oliver shrugged, and uncorked the flask again, taking the last two gulps. "It seems so, my lady. I only heard him call out for Wolston—in that slightly high voice of his, it is quite recognizable. Wolston ordered them to stop and walked out to speak with the Prince. When Wolston came back in, he looked right smug and ordered me escorted here."

Petra wanted to add that the Prince's voice always sounded like a whiny little boy's, and that Wolston reminded her of an unmannered bully, but she said none of it. It would be most untoward for many reasons. Thus, she moved on.

"Tell me about the key they found on your person."

"It was not mine, my lady," Oliver said, his eyes looking a bit wild with the need to be believed. "I think the guard had it in his hand and pretended to find it in my waistcoat. I swear to you I have never seen it, nor did I know that Sir Rufus had the use of a safe in the castle."

"Mm, I admit I believe you," Petra said, recalling how the guard had the rather nimble fingers of a streetwise pickpocket. "I think he did plant it on you, but I felt I must ask."

Then she held up a hand to silence whatever diatribe on the subject seemed to be on Oliver's lips, for there were other, more important questions to be asked.

"Before Mr. Shawcross and the guards came," she said, "you told me you heard Sir Rufus laughing with an unknown person, and that he claimed to have hidden something others might want within the castle. Did you hear anything else? Did he give any clue as to who he was discussing, or where he had hidden whatever it is?"

Oliver ran his unblemished hand through his hair, pushing it back off his forehead. "It is all I have been thinking of since I was locked in here, my lady. But I do not know if I can offer you any other information than I already did."

"We are short on time," Petra said. "Let us try this—close your eyes and recollect exactly what happened, from the moment you first heard Sir Rufus talking to someone."

Squaring his shoulders, Oliver did as she instructed, his brows intermittently coming together as he thought back, searching for details in his mind.

"The Green Drawing Room was where I went in search of Sir Rufus. We arrived here at Windsor last week, of course, and he'd spent much time both there and in the drawing room of the Edward the Third Tower. I went to ask if he required my assistance before I went to the undercroft for the servants' meal. I stopped just outside the room when I heard his voice, see? It was quite clear he was speaking to someone and I did not wish to interrupt. He was laughing, and said . . ."

Oliver squeezed his eyes shut tighter and spoke the words with deliberate slowness, as if making certain he was repeating them exactly.

"He said: 'But I shall have the last say. For that which is being demanded—so much that I am being threatened over it—is now hidden in the castle, and I dare anyone to discover its location.'"

"And he used those particular words? 'Demanded,' 'threatened,' and so on?" Petra asked.

Oliver nodded, then opened his eyes, sighing with consternation.

"I wanted to have a look inside the room to see who his companion was, but then I heard the door being opened from farther down the hall. I'm afraid I did recognize that voice. It was the parlormaid with whom I had a . . . Well, if you'll pardon me, my lady, I felt it better that I should be elsewhere, so I left. I intended to ask Sir Rufus about those he rowed with earlier, and who he was talking to in the Green Drawing Room, but there was no time before the dinner."

"How do you mean?" Petra asked. "Were you not in his chambers as a valet would be?"

"I was, but though I always readied his clothing, occasionally helped him with his cravat, and gave his clothes a final brush before he would leave, he preferred to dress himself. Thus, I only saw him for a brief few minutes. And I must say, he was in rather a foul mood, and snapped at me when I momentarily laid the clothes brush on top of his recipes."

"What about when he returned after the fireworks?"

"It was half two in the morning when I heard him come in, though he remained uninterested in conversation. Told me to take his clothes, clean the smell and whisky from them, and leave him be so that he could ready his recipes for the last bit of sorting in the morning. And, as you know, I overslept, and the next time I saw him . . . he was dead."

Oliver's voice had quieted with his last memory of Sir Rufus, but then he met Petra's eyes and his voice became insistent.

"No matter my recent frustrations with him, my lady, he gave me employment when I most needed it. And then he trained me as a cook, allowing me to hone the skills that I found I enjoyed in my brief time in the navy. I am most indebted to him—I often told him as much. And even though I was angry that he had not given me credit for recipes I had devised, or that I had not been paid, I would never have wished him dead. Especially not like that. Not . . . *strangled*. But it was at another person's hand, my lady. I swear I only tried to save him."

Petra nodded. Again, she believed him. But there was no time to discuss it.

"Was there anyone else he quarreled with in recent weeks or months?" she asked, glancing toward the door, one ear half listening for the guard. "Did he receive any angry letters? To whom was he indebted?"

Oliver just shook his head helplessly.

"I know not, my lady. As I said earlier, Sir Rufus never allowed me anywhere near his correspondence, except to receive letters, pay any delivery costs, and leave them for him to read. And he received rather a lot, too. Letters praising his recipes and cookery books arrived from all over England—from both fine houses and those who could ill afford the cost of paper alike."

"And debts?"

"The same went for debts," Oliver replied. "I knew he had them, but I could not tell you with whom. I know the butcher, the greengrocer, and his tailor were three, but that is the extent of my knowledge."

Oliver then wryly, gently touched the bruised eye Petra had given him.

"Though a fortnight ago, he came home with an eye like mine and sore ribs. He would not tell me who was responsible for it. But the next day, I saw the butcher with a heavily bandaged hand—and a very cross wife telling anyone who asked that her husband had brawled with someone." His voice deepened with frustration. "Sir Rufus was still healing when we arrived here, and Wolston believes it was I who gave my employer his injuries, despite the fact that

Sir Rufus told Mrs. Daley, amongst others, something akin to the truth, that the injuries had come from a boxing match."

"Regarding the other arguments—how did you manage to overhear them?" she asked, glad at least that he had addressed Sir Rufus's black eye without her having to make the query.

"Sir Rufus had me regularly fetching items and bringing them to him in the Green Drawing Room. More ink, his extra spectacles, that kind of thing, even if he didn't need them. I reckon it made him feel quite the nib. Showing the real swells he had his own servant now." Oliver's shrug was surprisingly philosophical. "It meant I easily heard the quarrels, though, for I was in and out quite a bit."

"And no one else heard these interactions?" Petra asked with narrowed eyes.

"Not that I witnessed, my lady," he replied. "Those whose voices I did not recognize—including the sixth person whom I never heard speak—all were with Sir Rufus before the bulk of the guests were fully in residence for the celebrations, when the servants were busy tending to the line of arriving carriages and unloading trunks and so forth."

"And what of those with the Prince and Lady Ophelia?" Petra asked.

"When Sir Rufus came back from the fencing venue, his button having been lost, I took his coat to do the mending. He said he would wait in the drawing room. I then realized I'd dropped the button. When I discovered it not far from the drawing room door, I heard him arguing with Lady Ophelia. He said her name, so I was certain. I hid as she exited the room."

Oliver looked down at his toes for a moment.

"I made the mistake of asking Sir Rufus about my wages afterward, when he was still angry, and that is when he chose to wait with Mr. Shawcross. I was upset that he had put me off, yet again, which made me behave badly in front of you in the library. I do apologize, my lady."

"And I accept," she said. "But do continue. What of the Prince?"

"It happened when everyone else was out on the East Terrace watching fireworks. Sir Rufus had briefly returned to his bedchamber to drink a stomach tonic I always leave for him after a large meal. It seems His Royal Highness followed him. Upon my own return to the hallway, I heard the shouting and left again with some haste. You could not have paid me double my back wages to have the Prince discover me listening, especially after hearing him threatening Sir Rufus's life."

Petra could not blame him. "And when did the Prince leave?"

"Not long after, my lady, and Sir Rufus followed a minute or so later. As I said before, I did not see him again until half two this morning."

Petra could not think of anything else to ask, except to inquire about the exact village in Buckinghamshire where Sir Rufus's house was located, saying that possibly Mr. Shawcross could send one of his men there to search for anything that might point toward a motive for murder.

Oliver, his face darkening with frustration, said that he had already heard the guards being told to search his and Sir Rufus's bedchambers. Then he wryly added that they would not find the key to the house that was located in the village of Chesham, as the chef routinely hid it.

"He once bragged that a disgruntled former lover sent her servant to break into his house and rob it. Nevertheless, Sir Rufus became rather insistent on security, and to easily breach his house, one does need the key. You will find it tied to the back of the canopy of his bed, where the hangings begin, on the southwest corner."

Petra nodded. She heard a knock on the door to the main room. Their five minutes were up.

"My lady?" It was Charles. "We must away, and quickly. I believe Wolston is heading toward the Round Tower. There is little time to leave without being seen."

Petra looked at Oliver, watching his eyes grow fearful again.

"So long as you have been truthful with me, I will do everything in my power to save you, Mr. Beecham," she said. "And so will Annie and Mr. Shawcross. You have my word."

Oliver swallowed hard, bowed at the neck, and then met her eyes. "I may have been untruthful to others in the past, it is true. But I have never lied to you since meeting you today, my lady, nor will I in future. Everything I have said is the truth. I am innocent."

Petra was about to leave, but something was niggling at her brain after Charles had warned of their need to make haste. Then the guard was approaching, the key to lock Oliver's temporary cell in hand, just as the clock chimed the three-quarter hour, increasing the odd feeling. What was important about the time?

Then it came to her. Yet it was not just one recollection, but two, and both with few moments to spare.

"Beecham, you attested that Sir Rufus arrived back in his chambers at half two this morning. But I was part of one of the last groups of people to return to our rooms, and that was at half one. Where was he for another hour thereafter?"

But Oliver could only shake his head with a look of misery.

"I could not say, my lady. Sir Rufus returned in a temper and his clothes smelling of whisky—though it was plain he had not consumed much of it, for his head was clear and the whisky was mostly on his trouser legs. I assumed that he merely had a mishap whilst partaking of a nightcap, and spilt his drink upon his clothes."

She added this to her list of things to unravel, but there was one last thing she must ask.

"Beecham, did you know Sir Rufus was ill?"

"Ill?" he repeated, sounding confused. "He often complained he could no longer take rich food, but he never confessed to anything more." His voice went to a whisper. "Is it true? He was in bad health?"

Petra told him the truth, and Oliver sighed deeply.

"He should not have had that time taken from him, my lady."

"I would have to agree with you," she said. Then she took her leave.

Rushing out of the tower, she and Charles slipped through a passage door to stand with breaths held as they heard Wolston and two other guards tramping up the stairs toward the rooms where Oliver Beecham was being kept. Her eyes then met Charles's with measured relief when Wolston was heard to say that it would be better to leave Beecham to sit and starve for a while. That they would question him again later, at Curfew Tower.

For the time being, Oliver would likely be left alone in his cell.

"Will it not look suspicious if we are seen hurrying, my lady?" Charles asked as he followed behind Petra, who was stepping quickly back down the covered stairs. "Wolston will not be able to see us, I do not think," he added.

"I am hoping that is the case," Petra responded. "However, it is nearly eleven o'clock. Her Majesty asked me to be present at a kitchen demonstration that poor Sir Rufus had scheduled. I had nearly forgotten about it, and now there will be a group of ladies waiting in the Green Drawing Room for him. I must be the one to tell them the official story of Sir Rufus's death before anyone else can tell them the truth."

FIFTEEN

"Good morning, your ladyships," Petra said to the small group of women who had trickled into the drawing room. The first of whom was the imposingly tall Lady Norworthy, who eyed her through a lorgnette and said, "Why are you panting like one of your papa's racehorses after the two miles at Ascot, Lady Petra?"

After that, Petra had poured herself a glass of barley water from the sideboard and willed herself to look composed. For she had all but galloped through the castle to reach the drawing room on time.

She found Major Carlson sitting in an armchair near the drinks table, reading Lord Byron's tale in verse, *The Corsair*. Upon seeing Petra, he closed his book and stood quickly to greet her, a slight grimace crossing his features when he put pressure on his right leg.

"I say, if it is not my fellow excellent holder of architectural drawings," he said, recovering quickly to offer a smile. "Good morning, Lady Petra."

She laughed in return. "We were rather good at our job, weren't we, Major? Would you consider resigning your position as the Prince's solicitor to be known as the best drawings-holder in England, I wonder?"

Major Carlson rubbed his chin at her teasing, feigning deep consideration of the matter.

"Now that is quite the thought, for I have been thinking on what new occupation I could pursue in the future, should my life as the solicitor to the Prince Regent not work out."

Mimicking his playfully serious tone, she said, "Have you gone off the idea of continuing to rear pigs on your lands, then? I suppose I could not fault you, for I expect not having a cook like Chef Carême in residence would make the joy of having your own hand-reared pork about the house lessened."

Yet as soon as she said it, another spasm crossed the major's face, this time a pain of the emotional kind. Belatedly, she recalled that he had inherited his lands due to the deaths of his father and brother, and how he had not fully recovered from both tragedies.

"Oh, that was badly done of me! I do apologize, Major . . ." she began, but he waved her off.

"No need, Lady Petra," he said. "And from your reaction, I must surmise you have learned of why I now own my father's lands." He straightened like the soldier he once was, though his gray-blue eyes and his voice both seemed to harden. "It has been more than two years now since my father's death, which should *never* have happened. The same could be said for my mother and brother, of course, but for different reasons." He paused, then his tone eased considerably. "Nevertheless, I must learn to be better when someone makes a wholly innocent comment. Please forgive me."

"Very few of us are unmarked by tragedy, Major," Petra said, thinking of those sadnesses in her own past, "but the heart does not understand this. In my opinion, there is no timeline you must follow in your recovery."

The major's jaw tensed. He turned away, slipping *The Corsair* into a space on the shelf, leaving Petra concerned he had taken offense this time. But when he turned back, his lips were hitching upward. "Thank you, Lady Petra. I was thinking on such things yesterday as I sat here reading Byron. It indeed helps that you understand."

Petra smiled in return, then a thought struck her. "Major, did you happen to see Sir Rufus here in the drawing room yesterday?"

Now the major frowned a bit, clearly finding the change in subject a bit abrupt, but he answered in genial fashion.

"Certainly I saw Sir Rufus, yes. He is quite fond of spending time here in the drawing room. He arrived a few days earlier than the other guests to work on his recipe collection, you know, and Mrs. Daley teases him that this room has become his personal study." With a brief shrug of one shoulder, the major looked toward the desk at one side of the room. "We exchanged a 'good day,' he sat over there, working, and I was in my chair, right here, reading—and feeling the aforementioned pity for myself. The next time I lifted my eyes from my book, he had taken his leave."

Major Carlson then raised a quizzical eyebrow, too polite to ask Petra's reasons for wanting to know, or query her for why she was nodding thoughtfully.

"I'm afraid I have some rather sad news to impart about Sir Rufus," she said in an undertone, then tilted her head toward the group of women nearby. "However, I should like to tell everyone present at once, as it will be simpler. Will you stay to hear it?"

His eyes searched hers, alert for what news she had to impart, but nodded.

"Of course. I can see the news has distressed you. Please let me know if there is anything I may do to help."

"Thank you, Major," she said, and added with a brief smile, "If someone should swoon, I would be grateful if you might attempt to break their fall. It shall not, however, be me."

When Lady Norworthy, the two baronesses, three viscountesses, one countess, and two wives of baronets had all turned her way, Petra counted nine in attendance, not including herself.

"May I ask, does anyone know who the tenth—"

"It is I, Lady Petra," a voice gaily called out before she could finish her query.

Petra met the blue eyes of her aunt Ophelia as she sailed in, still in her gown of dove gray, though now made even more outwardly colorful with a shawl the color of a fresh orange.

"Lady Ophelia, how wonderful to see you this morning," Petra said with a smile. She held out a hand and her aunt crossed the room to her side, where they bussed each other on each cheek. Instead of stepping back, though, Petra felt her aunt pause, then speak under her breath.

"Darling, why is Major Carlson standing at the back of the room, watching us? Do not misunderstand me, he is quite handsome . . . goodness, he is not attempting to vie for your hand, is he? I would rather think Duncan—"

Petra gave a tsk, and then whispered in return before her aunt could complete her thought, "No, Aunt, he is not. I simply have an announcement to make, and since it will behoove everyone to hear it, I asked him to stay."

"Ah, well, one must ask, mustn't one?" Aunt Ophelia said merrily, then joined the small throng of ladies with the same expectant look as the others.

"Where is Sir Rufus, Lady Petra?" asked one of the baronesses, glancing over her shoulder to the door. "I have been looking forward to this since it was announced last evening. It is not often that one sees food actually being prepared, is it?"

"Quite so," said one of the baronets' wives.

"I must agree it is exciting," said the countess. Nearly everyone nodded their agreement.

Petra then explained that she must be the bearer of sad news, before relating the story that Duncan and Wolston had agreed upon.

"I am afraid that Sir Rufus Pomeroy took ill sometime late last night or early this morning. Or, as I was told, more ill than he already had been—though he did not let on."

Petra clasped her hands together, her eyes roaming all ten faces before her, trying not to read anything untoward in her aunt's widened blue eyes, or watch her more than would be acceptable.

"Sir Rufus has sadly passed away," she continued. "He was only discovered early this morning, so few know. I was asked by Her

Majesty to explain this lamentable news. Nevertheless, it has been decided to continue with the tour, if all of you would still enjoy such an event, despite the sadness of the occasion."

There was shocked silence for a full two heartbeats. Then calls of "Dreadful news!" and "Terribly, terribly sad!" and "My cook will be quite devastated indeed! She rather idolized him," amongst other exhortations, were heard.

Petra had been ready to jump forward to help any who needed an arm, or direct them to the nearest sofa, and from the corner of her eye, she saw the major doing the same, but it seemed there was no need. Aunt Ophelia looked as dumbstruck as the others, but not any more or less so. At least, as far as Petra could tell, because the statuesque Lady Norworthy shifted sideways, enough to block her aunt from view, in order to announce her opinions to the group.

"A sad day, to be sure. But I cannot claim to be much surprised by the news," drawled her ladyship. "Sir Rufus looked shockingly pinched in the cheeks yesterday, much less healthy than when I saw him recently in Yorkshire. Too thin all over, to be sure. He had lost a full stone, I would wager."

"He most definitely seemed to have some sort of digestion issue," agreed another, and Petra noted her aunt nodding vigorously at this. Yet was her aunt's complexion not paler than it had been a moment earlier? Petra felt it was.

Briefly, she glanced over to find Major Carlson. His face was grim at the news, but he gave her a brief bow at the neck before quietly exiting the drawing room.

Petra listened to the ladies around her discussing Sir Rufus's fate. No one seemed to question it for a moment.

Still, the ladies all clamored for their tour, with the countess saying, "I believe Sir Rufus would have wished us to continue. Thus, lead on, Lady Petra. Her Majesty told me that the handsome cook from France—Chef Carême, is it not?—has quite the passionate temper, but that you handled him quite easily. I am certain you can convince him to give us a demonstration once we are there, yes?"

It seemed the question was rhetorical as the ladies—Aunt Ophelia seemingly deep in conversation with the countess—walked smartly out of the drawing room without even waiting for a reply. With a sigh, Petra hurried from the room in their wake.

Sixteen

Chef Antonin Carême's dark eyes snapped with anger when Petra and the ten ladies entered the cavernous Great Kitchen of Windsor Castle. Several ovens lined one side, and a large fireplace was on the other, with copper pots, pans, and other instruments of cooking hanging from nearly every available space along the walls.

In the middle of the room were five long wooden tables. Standing six to a table were cooks, male and female alike, all busily working at their stations.

Some were stirring ingredients in large bowls. Others were kneading bread dough. Petra saw others basting some sort of fowl on a spit, chopping vegetables, or ladling various liquids into other copper pots. Some of the pots were large enough she felt a child could use one for a bathing tub.

At the far end were tables containing dishes fully prepared and arranged on silver platters. And not far from where they walked in were two men solemnly but handily using the sharpest of knives to slice raw meat from the bones of a pig. Part of her hoped the women would decide they did not wish to be here at the sight, thereby giving her reason to usher them all back to the drawing room for a soothing cup of tea she herself badly needed. Yet each one of the ladies in her charge seemed quite interested.

And when their presence was finally noted, every cook and kitchen maid in the room stopped what they were doing and hastily bowed or bobbed their curtsies. Their eyes were agog with the interruption, with some even looking a touch irritated, but no one said a word.

Except, that was, Chef Carême.

"What is this? Why are these ladies in my kitchen when my team and I are preparing the meal for later?" he asked, stalking over, as lithe as a gazelle. His white tunic was pristine, though the apron tied about his waist was stained from wiping his hands upon it.

A cloth was thrown over one shoulder, and he whisked it off and used it to grasp the handle of a copper pan that was boiling over, moving it swiftly off the flame.

The cook who had stopped watching the food he was preparing in order to stare at Petra's group now hung his head as he hurried to stir the contents with his spoon. His face was reddened from the heat and beaded with sweat.

The handsome Frenchman, however, with his swept-back dark hair and full lips, looked as if he had been standing outside in the refreshing morning air instead of near a hot flame. Nearby, a large piece of meat sizzled and sent a waft of heavenly scent into the air, mixing well with all the other scents currently flowing over Petra and her group of kitchen newcomers.

She stepped forward and spoke in French, knowing all the ladies present would understand most, if not all, of what she said.

She offered her apologies, explaining that their ladyships were here to better understand what happened in their own kitchens. That they were truly interested in the work that Chef Carême and his talented cooks did in these kitchens. And would he be so kind as to give a brief demonstration? Possibly on how he would make the sauce that would accompany either the beef or the fowl that was cooking?

"Oh, and how bread is made," breathed one viscountess, but in English.

"Please, Chef Carême, do show us," urged another, looking entirely hopeful.

Lady Norworthy used her lorgnette to peer over at one cook who was chopping vegetables at a high rate of speed.

"Astounding," she announced.

"I would have to agree," Aunt Ophelia said with one long, appreciative look at the Frenchman. Petra took another step forward, hastily saying the first thing that came to mind.

"And I would be indebted to your kindness, Chef Carême, as it is very clear that we are interrupting your day. We promise to stay no more than a quarter of an hour. You have my word."

Petra had noted that the chef's temper had already dissipated a notch. When his brown eyes shifted to Petra, his lips curved into a smile that seemed just for her. And when he spoke, his French-accented voice was like the warmed honey Petra would sometimes drizzle over a piece of toasted bread.

"Ah, yes, I do recall now. Sir Rufus, he asked me if he could bring a group to my kitchens for a little tour, no? I did not wish to disrupt my kitchens, but the Prince Regent, he says I must, so..." His lips turned down and his shoulders lifted up in that particular French way. "But where is Chef? Why did he not bring the ladyships himself?"

"*Il est mort*," replied Lady Norworthy succinctly in badly accented French. She was intently watching a cook dipping a rounded mold briefly into hot water and then turning it over onto a porcelain platter. It was a vegetable aspic, with orange carrots, green courgettes, red beetroot, and others, all chopped into small pieces to make for a beautifully colored presentation.

Without asking if it would be acceptable, the other women, including Aunt Ophelia, moved over to the table. The cook, a woman of no more than twenty with fair hair curling out from beneath her mob cap, looked rather startled. But when the countess asked her politely to explain what she had done, the girl began describing her process with admirable confidence.

Chef Carême, however, was looking to Petra, astounded at

what he had heard. She nodded, then confirmed in his mother tongue the half-truth that she had promised to repeat until further notice. That Sir Rufus had died early this morning after becoming ill.

Oddly, she felt grateful to see his reaction. It was clear he'd been none the wiser.

"But he came to the kitchens this morning." He began waving one hand in circles, as if to think back. "It was, ah, I think it was just before *sept*—seven, yes? He asked for some toast and café au lait. Plain toast—bah! Would not even take some of my *confiture de framboises*. The preserves of raspberry. Most delicious, Lady Petra. I should like you to try them sometime with me. On some of my *pain ordinaire*, perhaps? Or possibly with a lovely type of brioche bread I had in Austria, that I have begun to perfect with a lighter dough made with the yeast and with many flaky layers? The Austrians, they call it the *kipferl*, but I call mine *le croissant*, for it is in the shape of the new moon."

He used one hand to make a crescent shape even as his voice lowered seductively.

"I would happily have you try my *confiture de framboises* on whatever you desire."

Heavens was all her mind could say, again. Though she was also fascinated by how this Frenchman could go from showing shock at the death of Sir Rufus one moment to all but offering to take her to his bed the next.

If it had been anyone else, Petra might have found his attitude suspicious. However, she had never suspected the Frenchman in the first place.

Indeed, during the previous night's festivities, Petra had heard a few bits of information regarding both the current royal chef and Sir Rufus, the former one. While everyone expected the two to detest each other, it had not proven to be the case. They had respected one another on the whole, even if they had not attempted to spend time in each other's company. It was the prevailing thought that Sir Rufus enjoyed being retired and had no desire to assert any of his former power in the kitchen at Chef Carême's expense.

Plus, the Frenchman was too busy in the kitchens, and any number of his staff would have noticed if he had left for more than a few minutes. It seemed he was simply being what he was: focused on his food, somewhat self-centered, aware of his handsomeness, and very French.

Somehow, though, her mouth managed to emit the right words to stay on track.

"I thank you, Chef Carême. But—"

"Please, if you would call me Antonin, I would be most honored," he cut in, and Petra felt a tiny flutter in her belly nonetheless.

"I thank you for the kind offer, Chef Antonin," she repeated, using his title to better keep a distance. "But I must ask you about poor Sir Rufus. Did he say anything when he came to ask for toast and coffee? Or did he seem out of sorts in any way?" And when he looked as if he did not quite understand her questions, she repeated them in French.

"No, no. He looked like he has for the past week. How do you say—out of temper? Though he told one of my cooks that he would be meeting someone in the small library."

"I think he was referring to me," Petra said, then explained that she had planned to meet him as he finished sorting the recipes that would go in Her Majesty's collection.

The chef only cocked one of his dark eyebrows. "I do not think so, Lady Petra. Unless you were to have other relations with Sir Rufus?"

"I beg your pardon. '*Other relations*'?" Petra repeated frostily.

But he only smiled apologetically, and said, "Do forgive me, my lady. What I mean to say is that this person that Chef was to meet... he spoke of... how do you say... wishing to complete a debt... that he wished to be rid of this person."

A little thrill of apprehension went through Petra. This person had to be Sir Rufus's killer. "Was he referring to a man, perhaps? Did he mention a name?"

Chef Carême held up his hands as if to slow her rapid questions. "I do not know, Lady Petra. I never heard a name mentioned. Nor did I hear Chef confirm he was talking of a man, or a woman. Let me call over my cook who prepared his coffee and toast."

He called out a name and an older woman with a round face and a welcoming smile stepped over and curtsied to Petra. When Carême told the cook what had happened to Sir Rufus, she put her hand to her heart and had to steady herself for a moment. It was agreed that the chef's fate—even if they only knew the partially correct version—was quite sad. The cook then said that she had always admired Sir Rufus.

"Trained me, he did, my lady," she said. "I'm one of the few still here who can say that. I arrived for work here during his final years in Their Majesties' employ, when he were often off writing the first of his cookbooks. He were kind enough to sign mine last week. 'Tis a shame, it is. I mean, Sir Rufus were clearly not in the peak of health, but still. 'Tis a shame, isn't it, my lady?"

"Sir Rufus worked at my papa's house, Buckfields, when I was quite young," Petra said solemnly. "He was always kind to me, too, so I agree it is truly a sad thing. He will be missed."

She then went on to ask the cook about the conversation she had had with Sir Rufus that morning. The cook nodded, but then glanced at Petra with curiosity.

"I ain't opposed to telling you, my lady, especially as there's not much to say, but if Sir Rufus is dead, why does it matter? If your ladyship will pardon my asking . . ."

"It is a quite logical question," Petra said calmly, but inside she was in a panic.

As a naturally truthful person, she was finding it difficult to constantly remember to make inquiries in such a way that did not inspire suspicion. Especially as the Prince Regent had insisted upon it. She groped for a reason, and just when she felt the cook might become suspicious, a plausible one arrived on her tongue.

"I understand that it sounded as if Sir Rufus might have been in debt to someone. Should that still be the case, I should like to inform them of his passing and attempt to help work something out with his estate to settle the debt. Now, what did Chef tell you when you prepared his toast and coffee?"

The cook hand found this explanation satisfactory, it seemed, yet she still shrugged.

"But little, I'm afraid, my lady. I wished him a good morning and asked if he still liked his toast on the lighter side. He did, and when I were putting the bread on the toasting fork, we talked of the old days for a moment." She glanced worriedly toward Chef Carême, adding, "Nothing of importance, you understand. Just recollecting about how sometimes things are right funny in the kitchens, like His Royal Highness once gracing us with his presence—a red carpet were put down and everything—and asking that his favorite beef stew be made before him."

She stopped, wide-eyed, as if recalling too late that she was speaking with an earl's daughter, and a favorite of both the Queen and the Duchess of Hillmorton.

"Do not concern yourself," Petra said. "You may speak freely about His Royal Highness, so long as it is not to speak ill of him. I promise I will not fault you for an entertaining story."

The cook seemed relieved and promised it was agreeable.

"I have heard this story," said Chef Carême, "and it is most amusing."

"Well, he got quite cross, His Royal Highness did," the cook then continued, "when Sir Rufus said he could not make the beef, kidney bean, and pumpkin stew without accidentally making the Prince ill. Had to explain to His Royal Highness what every cook learns right quick—that red kidney beans, if they aren't first soaked and boiled proper like, can make even a man with the strongest constitution cast up his accounts, as it were, if not worse."

Petra had to suppress a smile. Just thinking of the Prince forcing the cooks to make his favorite stew, only to become ill from it—possibly to the point of vomiting and racing to his chamber pot—was indeed a diverting thought.

"And what did Sir Rufus say of the person with whom he was to meet?" she asked the cook, who had returned to looking a bit forlorn after remembering that her former mentor was gone. "Did he tell you what the person might have done to bother him? Or what his debts were?"

"He didn't, my lady," she replied. "He just complained a bit about his stomach, saying it acted up time and time again. Considering I hadn't heard of him having any other issues—he said his valet, Beecham, took good care of him, and I had to agree, though the valet can be too cheeky for his own good—I didn't feel as if something else were wrong."

It was gratifying to hear this about Oliver, especially as the valet had known nothing about Sir Rufus's cancer, but Petra gently pressed the cook about what she heard of the person Sir Rufus had met.

"He only said that he were meeting someone before the rest of the castle came to life," replied the cook. "No indeed, my lady, he never said whether it were a lady or gentleman he were meeting, and I cannot recall any other details. By this time, his toast were done and I was needed elsewhere. Sir Rufus took a tray with his toast and coffee, and I saw him no more."

Petra thanked her and the cook returned to her station, where she quickly spoke to the other chefs. They all looked varying levels of shocked.

Petra turned back to the Frenchman. She had him right here, and in private. It would be a very good time to discuss his staying in the Prince Regent's employ. But then again, she was also realizing just how hungry she was, for she had not yet had a proper breakfast.

Taking in the delicious smells of the Windsor Castle kitchens, she felt her stomach rumble. She longed to go to the dining room and make herself a plate.

Yet she had work to do, and she did not know if there would be another opportunity to speak with the chef—especially when he was seemingly so open to anything she might say.

"Chef Antonin," she said, and was about to switch to French and explain her task of convincing him to remain in England, when a realization hit her.

"*Oui*, Lady Petra?" he replied, his chocolate-brown eyes giving her a look that should have been quite unlawful. She felt her cheeks burn, just a bit.

"Where did Sir Rufus take his toast and coffee this morning?"

The Frenchman blinked once, clearly unused to having his powers of seduction go awry. Then he shrugged.

"To the small library, of course, on a tray. He planned to eat his plain toast there. He only made more work for my cooks, though, for his valet arrived later, requesting another tray of the toast and coffee." He threw up his hands in frustration toward the British palate. "*Les Anglais*! Bah! They have no appreciation for *les raffinements de la vie*!"

While Petra would disagree that the British knew nothing of the finer things in life, there was one thing she finally knew for certain. There had only been one tray in the library this morning—the one brought by Oliver Beecham. He had not mentioned seeing another, or that Sir Rufus might have already eaten.

That meant the killer had cleared away the breakfast tray after strangling Sir Rufus. But why?

Instinctively, Petra turned to look for her aunt, wanting to ask her opinion on the matter as much as she needed to ask about her whereabouts early this morning. She counted the ladies of rank in the kitchen, all enthusing over the food preparation they were witnessing. There were nine, not ten.

Aunt Ophelia, it seemed, had used the opportunity to her advantage and slipped away.

SEVENTEEN

"My lords, ladies, and gentlemen, welcome to the first day of Her Majesty Queen Charlotte's patisserie contest!"

There was clapping mixed with excited murmurs from the crowd as the Queen's steward, in his liveried finest, made this announcement.

He seemed to relish his role, and added a certain level of theatrics to the occasion, which even made the Queen and the Prince Regent look amused as they relaxed in ornately carved chairs on the North Terrace, in the shade of the castle walls. The rest of the guests sat on long benches and fanned themselves in the afternoon sun—though no one seemed to mind, especially with autumn and colder, shorter days quickly approaching.

Petra and her three fellow judges faced the guests while sitting at a huge mahogany table some twelve feet long and carved every bit as beautifully as the royal chairs. The low wall that marked the boundary of the terrace was mere steps away to their right, and a beautiful prospect was to be seen when looking over the wall and the chalk cliff on which the castle sat, including a view of the winding River Thames and bits of the village of Windsor.

Each had an individual teapot full of tea before them, plus a crystal carafe of water. They also had a fresh quill, its tip expertly sharpened, and a pot of ink. Lastly, they were provided with a quarto sheet of paper that had already been neatly labeled with the words *Round One: Shrewsbury Cake* at the top, and then numbered down the left side with numerals one through ten, giving ample space for notes.

Sitting to her right was Lord Wadley-Bates, looking both proud and nervous. He kept taking sips of his water, and a bit of sweat had formed upon his hairline. To her left was Lady Caroline, looking a bit like a little girl who was allowed to eat her pudding before dinner. And then in the leftmost chair, farthest from Petra, was Sir Franklin Haverstock. He kept his eyes on the paper before him, his occasional swallows noticeable due to the Adam's apple bobbing in his rather thin neck.

A few minutes earlier, before they walked out to their table, Petra had informed her fellow judges of Sir Rufus's passing using only the royally approved reasons for his death. All three had been shocked, but Petra could not help but feel as if Sir Franklin and Lord Wadley-Bates were not quite as surprised as they should have been. Though she could not praise her skills of observation too much, for she might not have noticed if it were not for what Annie had discovered.

As the Queen's steward began enthusing on Her Majesty's brilliance at devising such a contest, Petra thought back over the few short hours after she had escorted the nine remaining ladies back from the royal kitchens.

Finding she could no longer ignore her hunger, she had made her way to the dining room in hopes of both finding a proper breakfast and guests who, with properly delicate questioning, might reveal knowledge of anyone who might have wished Sir Rufus dead.

Officially called the King's Public Dining Room, the room overlooked the North Terrace and was decorated in a palette of blues and citron yellow. Petra expected it to be full of guests, but instead it seemed that nearly everyone had called for a breakfast tray to their room after the long night before. She sat across from an elderly viscount with her boiled egg, toast, marmalade, and a cup of milky coffee and attempted to make conversation, but his lordship proceeded to thoroughly ignore her presence as he made his way through a plate of eggs and cold pork slathered with mustard.

Afterward, Petra returned to her bedchamber, and laid down for a few moments of peace, wanting to begin sorting through her thoughts. The next thing she knew, Annie was once again gently shaking her awake.

"It is past one o'clock, my lady. We must ready you for your first day as a patisserie judge."

Though no sooner had Petra levered herself off the bed did Annie ask after her brother, her eyes huge with worry.

"I am certain he is innocent," Petra replied, before quickly adding, "No, you must not wilt with relief now. I must be dressed for the contest first."

Annie swiftly collected herself and became full of vigor.

"I saw Mr. Shawcross outside the servants' hall," she said. "It is beneath St. George's Hall and called the undercroft. Did you know it was a medieval wine cellar that was built by Edward the Third in the middle of the fourteenth century? Lovely vaulted ceilings, it has. Nevertheless, Mr. Shawcross told me he believed in Oliver's innocence as well, but he was called away before I could tell him what I discovered."

"Do not keep me in suspense a moment longer," Petra said.

As she tidied Petra's hair, Annie explained that she had discreetly questioned the servants regarding who they had witnessed walking through the castle that morning. With the festivities the night before, it seemed so few guests were up at an early hour that discovering their names was quite simple. Annie then said there were thirteen in all who were a possibility: nine gentlemen and four ladies.

She named three women, one of whom could easily be ruled out due to being both very petite and waddling about the castle due to being with child. The second was a young widowed countess who happened to be one of Caroline's many cousins, and the third was Lady Norworthy.

"Hmm," Petra mused. "Whilst no longer young, it must be admitted Lady Norworthy is tall and known to be an amateur sculptor of marble busts. Granted, her sculptures are not known for looking... well, like any person one might recognize, but working marble is not for the weak. It means Lady Norworthy is much stronger than she looks."

Annie nodded, then seemed to hesitate before continuing.

"I shall hazard a guess and say that Lady Ophelia is the fourth woman seen in the halls, thus confirming what Oliver had told us earlier, yes?" Petra asked dryly. And then explained that she had not only been told this by Tilly the hall maid, but had then witnessed Aunt Ophelia acting peculiar no less than two more times before the clock struck the noon hour.

Annie, who was fond of Aunt Ophelia too, could only breathe, "What will you do, my lady?"

Petra sighed. "I would like to turn a blind eye, but I cannot. I must be fair and agree that my aunt, like Lady Norworthy and Caroline's cousin, I suppose, has the strength and height needed to have strangled Sir Rufus, and that means I must investigate her." She lifted her chin, made her tone determinedly brisk. "Well, then, we must move on. Who were the nine gentlemen?"

Annie rattled off the first four men straightaway, all of whom Petra doubted could be the killer as they were some of the most elderly and frail guests at Windsor.

That left five gentlemen. One was the architect Jeffry Wyatt. Next was the royal solicitor Major Carlson—who had an infirmity, of course, but could still move with relative ease. The third was the Duke of Hillmorton—who was not young, but had the Shawcross vitality that made him look and act ten years younger. And then the fourth was the Prince Regent himself, once more confirming Oliver's story.

"The fifth gentleman, it seems, is either Sir Franklin or Lord Wadley-Bates," Annie said, "but I know not which."

She explained the judge in question had been seen by Tilly, but the girl had only seen the back of him, and only for a moment as he came out of a corridor.

Annie's exasperation was evident in her face in the dressing-table looking glass.

"And I said, 'Tilly, one man is all but bald and the other has a full head of hair! One is thin and the other quite substantial about the stomach. How could you not tell them apart?' All Tilly could say was that she only saw half of his back through the doorway, so telling whether he was slim or portly was difficult. And he was passing behind a large palm tree in a pot, thereby obscuring most of his head."

Annie heaved a sigh as she inserted the final pin into Petra's hair.

"I am vexed to say it, my lady, but it is possible Tilly could truly not determine which judge it was. For that matter, I could not gain any more intelligence regarding the men or women who were seen this morning, so I am not certain how much I have helped."

"You have done very well, Annie," Petra said, giving her a reassuring smile. "I know where to find Duncan before the contest begins, and no doubt he will agree that those we have just named should be questioned." She held Annie's eyes in the looking glass, her lips twisting in a show of conflicted feelings. "Though I should still like to question Aunt Ophelia on my own first, so I suppose I shall wait to tell him every name. Just for a bit longer. Nevertheless, I promise you I will quickly narrow down our list."

Now, as Petra glanced around at the assembled guests out on the North Terrace for the first day of the baking contest, she hoped she wasn't too hasty in making such a pledge. For those guests who were her most likely suspects—both the men and women alike—were in the audience, with two more sitting with her at the judges' table. All were listening intently to the steward, looking relaxed, almost sanguine, and thoroughly innocent.

EIGHTEEN

"Is this not capital, Lady Petra?" said Lord Wadley-Bates, leaning sideways to look at her with shining eyes. He then patted his stomach. "I ate very little at breakfast so I could be in fighting form to eat ten Shrewsbury cakes." He chuckled, making his eyes squint in the process. "Though I daresay I am always in form for eating sweet things, or so says my wife."

Petra could not help but respond coolly. Lord Wadley-Bates had just lost his most prolific author of cookery books, and he was acting almost as if nothing had happened.

"Indeed, my lord. Though I believe we should only eat a bite or two of each to keep from feeling ill from too much sweetness, would you not agree?"

The publisher blinked in confusion at her tone, then straightened in his chair.

"Yes. Yes, you are quite right, Lady Petra. We would not wish to ruin the last bake we taste by eating too much of the first."

Her Majesty's steward, emanating bonhomie, gestured toward the side of the castle, where ten cooks were lined up in a row. "Now, I should like to introduce to you our contestants, all of which are the most renowned cooks from the best houses in England."

He began calling out the cooks by name and house, in reverse order of precedence, beginning with a cook called Mrs. Taylor from Lawson Hall, which was the house of Sir William McEntire of Longhorsley, Northumberland. The names continued, with Petra recognizing nearly all the houses, including Norworthy Manor, the house of the dowager Lady Norworthy in Dunstable, Bedfordshire.

The cooks stepped forward when their names were called and bobbed a curtsy. Some looked terrified, some were blushing several shades of red, and some, like Petra's own Mrs. Bing, were smiling widely and confidently.

Petra momentarily forgot her troubles and felt a surge of pride when "Mrs. Bing, of Forsyth House, the London home of his lordship, the fifth Earl of Holbrook" was announced, and clapped harder than anyone. Except possibly Duncan, who also let out a sharp whistle that added an enchanting blush to Mrs. Bing's smile. The tenth cook was a Mrs. Tenney of Chatsworth House, home of His Grace, the sixth Duke of Devonshire, near Bakewell, Derbyshire.

Once the introductions had been made, a young baron called out, "I say, is it fair for one of the cooks to be in the employ of one of the judges?"

Her Majesty's steward gave an amiable laugh.

"Excellent question, my lord, but we have made certain it is quite fair, for this is a *blind* competition. Our judges will not know which bake—that is, which cake or biscuit or shortbread—comes from which cook. The bakes are all presented at the same time to the table just beyond where our judges sit, and then the cooks are taken back to a room where they cannot peek at the next process. The bakes from each of the cooks are then assigned a number, from one to ten, at random."

The steward gestured to the cooks to further explain.

"This makes certain that, for instance, if baker number three manages to tell one of the judges that the plate containing her Queen Anne biscuit would be labeled as number three, the order of the plates is then changed around enough that baker number three's plates might actually be labeled as plate number eight. Thus our judges will never know which cook produced which bake."

The crowd all looked as if this was acceptable and the steward went on, showing all his teeth in a laughing grin.

"Our own Mrs. Daley is supervising this process as well, so we know there shall be no acts of nonsense."

He gestured to Mrs. Daley, who was standing near the cooks as if guarding them against said nonsense, though she did give a little curtsy when there was clapping in her honor.

As such, the steward held out an arm toward the judges table, saying, "And with that, may I introduce our esteemed judges. From your left, we have Lord Wadley-Bates, Lady Petra Forsyth, Lady Caroline Markingham-Smythe, and Sir Franklin Haverstock."

More clapping ensued, and then the steward's smile left him and his voice grew solemn.

"However, as every guest here today knows, it was intended to have five judges. Her Majesty and His Royal Highness, the Prince Regent, have therefore bade me to announce the sad passing early this morning of former royal chef Sir Rufus Pomeroy."

While most of the guests nodded solemnly, indicating that they had already heard the news, a few did gasp, and the petite countess from the day before looked stricken. At her side, the Duchess of Hillmorton patted her hand.

The steward then nodded to one of his underlings and, almost out of nowhere, some twenty footmen stepped forward, all holding silver trays containing glasses of red wine.

"If you will," said the steward, "please take a glass and we will toast to Sir Rufus and all that he has given Their Majesties, and indeed the entirety of England, in his time as one of the most talented of chefs. Sir Rufus; we will remember him!"

"Sir Rufus, we will remember him!" chanted the crowd, and drank their wine.

Over the rim of her own glass, Petra could see Lady Norworthy and Aunt Ophelia, but both merely drank their wine, giving nothing of their feelings away.

Her gaze then roamed over the other men in the audience that Annie had confirmed had been seen in the castle early this morning. The Duke of Hillmorton, Mr. Wyatt, and Major Carlson all looked equally as solemn as those around them. The Prince, however—well, he simply looked a bit bored, which was hardly unusual.

Drat, Petra thought.

After one more somber moment, the steward's smile had returned.

"And now, Her Majesty's patisserie contest works like so: It shall last for five days in total. Today and for the next three days, two cooks shall be eliminated each round, leaving only two cooks on the fifth and final day of the contest. Our two finalists will then compete against one another for the honor of Her Majesty recognizing her as the best baker in England."

Everyone clapped for this, but Petra suddenly realized that, until now, she had not been nervous that she might inadvertently choose other cooks as a better baker than Mrs. Bing. As the ten cooks were ushered back inside the castle, she was a bit relieved none of them would be watching her as she tested and judged each bake.

The steward raised a small suspended gong, and spoke once more.

"And now our judges will commence their first tasting. Each cook was asked to bake their best Shrewsbury cakes and arrive with them to the castle. You will see that each judge has a platter containing ten plates, each with one biscuit apiece atop a napkin embroidered with a number. They will have one hour to taste all ten and make their selections for the top eight cooks to advance."

He went on to explain that no judge was allowed to speak to their fellow judges, or to anyone else, while they were tasting each biscuit.

"And thus, our honored guests, Her Majesty encourages you all to enjoy the terrace and walk about the castle and return for the results. The gong will sound again at ten minutes to the hour."

He then turned toward the judges' table with an expression of anticipation. He raised the golden stick wrapped thickly with silk at one end that formed the gong beater.

"Ready, my lord and lady judges? Yes? Then please begin!"

And with that, he rather enthusiastically swung the beater onto the gong, causing those guests nearest to him to hold their hands to their ears.

The guests did not immediately rise and leave, however. They all seemed curious to watch the judges take their first bites of the biscuit known as the Shrewsbury cake, and to see all that each judge did in determining its taste. Yet by the time Petra and her fellow judges had moved to their second plate, they lost interest and left.

For her part, Petra was only able to concentrate because Duncan had vowed to keep his eyes on those men and women on her list of suspects—save for Aunt Ophelia, the one person he did not yet know Oliver had identified. Otherwise, for the next hour, she was intent on nothing more than honoring Sir Rufus by doing her best to choose the most delicious eight of ten Shrewsbury cakes in the contest.

For each bake, she performed the same ritual, at first feeling a pang with a long-ago memory of Sir Rufus. Specifically, during his time at Buckfields when he'd been merely Chef Rufus, and how he had taught her to enjoy a freshly baked biscuit.

She recalled it with clarity not truly from the day, but because she had been doing the same routine—with only slight differences allowing for the type of baked good—for the past twenty years, every time her cook presented her with a new sweet creation.

Thus, from the silver platter with ten small plates, Petra chose a biscuit and first looked it over for the perfect pale gold color. She then tapped it with a knife that had been provided so that she could ascertain the sound.

She was looking to hear the noises of a crisp bake that was somehow not too crisp, which was the hallmark of a Shrewsbury cake. A good one, of course, should have a give to the teeth when one bit in, making almost no noise as one chewed and enjoyed.

She then held the biscuit to her nose, breathing in the scent of cinnamon and nutmeg, and that particularly sweet and heady scent of fresh butter, eggs, and flour that was the very foundation of the Shrewsbury cake.

And only then did she take her first bite. She chewed slowly and carefully, letting the flavors burst upon her tongue. On some, she noted the presence of caraway seeds, others not. Some had a dusting of cinnamon and sugar on the top, others were quite plain.

What was evident, however, was that all were delicious in their own right, and therefore she had to narrow them down by being quite picky about their looks, crispness, and spices.

Throughout it all, she did not look toward her fellow judges—and felt that Sir Franklin, Lady Caroline, and Lord Wadley-Bates were making just as much effort to take the contest seriously as she was. Until Sir Franklin began coughing.

Petra looked over in concern and saw Sir Franklin, his fist held to his mouth, as he hacked and looked across the terrace to the entrance to the stairs known as the Queen Elizabeth Steps. She followed his gaze, and thought she saw a shadow of a retreating person, but no one was there.

Moments later, despite going quite red in the face from embarrassment, Sir Franklin was able to rasp out, "I am well. Yes, I assure you, my ladies. There is no need to continue fussing—though I must admit that, at my age, having a pretty woman ask how I am with such concern is quite a delight."

Caroline poured Sir Franklin some tea, urging him to drink something warm to soothe his throat. Petra, however, could not help but wonder as she picked up her last Shrewsbury cake. Had whoever Sir Franklin saw caused him enough shock or fear to nearly choke on his biscuit? Or had it been a mere coincidence?

When Mrs. Bing's name was called out as one of the eight cooks to continue to the next round, Petra almost leapt to her feet with happiness. She did not, however, for it would be seen as favoritism, but she could not stop herself from grinning all the same.

"Congratulations to the cooks moving forward," said the steward after the two sobbing cooks who had lost were gently led away by Mrs. Daley. "And now I have the honor of announcing your next bake for tomorrow. Whilst the Shrewsbury cake is, in fact, a biscuit, this next challenge is called a cake but is, in fact, closer to a sweetened bread—and it is a favorite of both His Majesty, King George, and His Royal Highness, Prince George."

He turned to look directly at the remaining eight cooks.

"Ladies, for tomorrow, you are asked to make an *apple cake*. It must have a thin icing and must be made in the pans provided to you by Chef Carême. There shall be no decoration on your cake otherwise. Thank you, and we wish you luck in your baking endeavors."

Mrs. Bing and her fellow cooks all looked to one another with excitement as they went back into the castle. The steward then announced that the guests should proceed to the Quadrangle for a falconry demonstration that would officially open the week's events to the public.

"Outside the castle walls, the fair will be beginning with amusements for all. And inside shall be the same!" He went on to give reminders of two different lectures taking place in the afternoon—including one on the latest fashions for ladies, given by a tailor and a seamstress, then another talk on new flavors of snuff from a famous tobacconist—and then encouraged all guests to find tea and cakes in the second library.

As soon as the crowd began to disperse, Sir Franklin had crossed to speak with the steward. Lord Wadley-Bates, however, quickly joined the throng before Petra could privately ask him if it was he who had been walking about the castle this morning—and why he seemed to care little that his most famous author had died only hours earlier.

Petra searched for Duncan in the crowd, thinking maybe he might be able to speak with Lord Wadley-Bates. Instead, she watched him stealthily moving off with a look on his face that might seem relaxed to others, but Petra recognized as being focused on his pursuit.

Then she frowned, for following Duncan at a distance was Colonel Wolston.

She started a bit when Caroline called out, "Lady Ophelia!," but Petra watched as her aunt seemed engrossed in speaking with a group of ladies. Petra, however, knew her aunt was feigning interest in whatever the ladies were saying.

"She is avoiding me," she muttered.

"What was that?" Caroline asked as she rose from her judge's chair and smoothed out her skirts, which today were in silk damask the color of dark pumpkin.

Yet she failed to notice when Petra did not immediately answer. Nor did she seem to pick up on Petra's expression indicating she had news to impart. Instead, Caroline's mind was still on the contest.

"Were you able to tell which Shrewsbury cake was Mrs. Bing's? I kept thinking I would know as I have had so many over the years, but it was more difficult than I expected. But there were two I felt the most likely candidates."

Petra replied she felt it was the fourth Shrewsbury cake she tried, but she could not be certain. Each cook was instructed to make their bakes in the shape of a rectangle so that they all looked the same, but as Mrs. Bing usually made hers into rounds, it truly was impossible to tell.

"My Mrs. Bing always has that little crunchy bit of cinnamon and sugar at the top, which has quite made hers famous. But the seventh bake also had it, and was delicious as well, so I could not wager for certain which was which, especially as I felt both number four and seven were worthy of continuing on."

Caroline said that she had suspected the same two as well.

"And I accidentally saw Sir Franklin's ballot as he was folding it—truly, dearest, I did not plan it; he was quite slow at doing so, for it looked as if one of his fingers had a cut on it—but he also chose seven and four to move forward. On number four, he'd written 'exceptional' in his notes, so I am hoping the fourth one was indeed Mrs. Bing's."

"And I hope for that as well," Petra said, then realized exactly what she had heard. "Caro, did you say that Sir Franklin had a cut on his finger? Where?"

Caroline pointed to the space between her third and pinkie fingers. "Just there. Where I always get a cut when I am holding my horse's reins and he decides to misbehave."

"Did Sir Franklin have one on his other hand?" Petra asked.

Shrugging, Caroline said, "I do not know. Why is it important?"

By now they were nearly the last two guests out on the terrace. Petra put her arm through Caroline's and sighed.

"After eating all those biscuits, let us take a turn or two about the terrace, for I have much to tell you."

NINETEEN

It seemed that once the festivities had begun, Petra found there to be little or no time for the kind of investigation she was now used to conducting.

She considered the occasional stint of "bloodhounding," as Caroline often called it, that she had done over the years for her godmother, the Duchess of Hillmorton. Most of these tasks had involved simply making certain she listened to gossip and then passed the information along to the duchess.

The most interesting assignment she had performed in recent years had been to follow a baroness who, as it turned out, had been secretly making money to pay her husband's debts by sewing some of the finest gowns in London. In fact, Petra's dress for the upcoming ball to celebrate Their Majesties' anniversary had been made by Baroness Olney, and it was truly lovely. But thinking on her dress would not get her anywhere at present.

When telling Caroline about the shocking events surrounding Sir Rufus's death, Petra decided that if she was not ready to tell Duncan that Aunt Ophelia was named as someone who had crossed swords with Sir Rufus, then she should not yet tell Caroline either. As they walked back through the castle, her friend had immediately offered her assistance regarding her cousin, however. "Prinny will not suspect I wish to question him, and we may clear up this matter quickly."

"I thank you," Petra replied, giving Caroline's arm a grateful squeeze, "but I do not wish you to put yourself in the Prince's crosshairs in any way, relative or not." She grinned. "We shall let Duncan do those honors, for he is used to being the target of royal ire."

"Very true," Caroline said with a laugh, and had just begun relating a diverting bit of gossip when Mrs. Daley came bustling up.

"Lady Caroline, Lady Petra, there you are. Her Majesty would like the both of you to further assist her with certain aspects of the celebrations."

Petra and Caroline had looked at each other, then said in tandem, "Now, Mrs. Daley?"

The housekeeper nodded. "Yes, indeed, she would like you both to change, if needed, and make your way out to the Long Walk at once. It seems more of the citizens of Windsor have paid to enter the fair on the grounds than originally expected and, thus, Her Majesty has determined that they deserve more than just a few small attractions."

She addressed Caroline. "The royal archers will do a demonstration, and Her Majesty wishes for you to show your skills as an archeress."

Caroline lifted an eyebrow. "Did Her Majesty say how skilled I was to pretend to be?"

"How odd that you should ask. I was told you are to be as skilled as you feel you need to be, but Her Majesty would prefer if you did not overshadow all of her archers."

When Caroline's throaty laugh died down, she said, "I believe I can do that."

Looking a bit as if she knew she had missed an important fact, Mrs. Daley nevertheless smiled and looked to Petra.

"There is a gentleman here with a string of horses, all of whom do tricks on command and I know not what. He asked if there was an exceptionally good lady rider who would not be averse to riding one of the horses and staying aboard as it does some tricks. Her Majesty offered you. The military review grounds are just down the slope from the castle. That is where you should go."

"I do not think anyone needs to ask Lady Petra twice," Caroline drawled in amusement.

She was right and, once more, Petra found it a little too easy to push aside what she needed to concentrate on in order to do something infinitely more diverting.

For the next hour, she rode a beautiful gray stallion while wearing her new riding habit—which the horse trainer had dubbed "ingenious" when, because he was worried that she might expose her legs during one of the horse's tricks, she showed him the hidden breeches underneath.

Though she was indeed forced to ride sidesaddle, it did not matter. The gray was the most well-trained horse she had ever been on. And via verbal commands from the trainer on the ground, plus a few leg or rein commands that he had taught her before they began, she felt as if the horse under her was dancing over the green grass of the review grounds.

Afterward, the trainer had been so impressed that he had allowed her to ride another of his horses, a lovely mare, in the privacy of the training ring within the Windsor Castle stable yard. And he had not batted an eye when she had unbuttoned her skirt in order to ride astride.

It was when she was walking the horse to cool her off, leaning over the mare's neck to give her lots of well-earned pats, that Duncan arrived. Petra's wide smile upon seeing him lessened when, after he gave a brief grin and an appreciative once-over of several aspects of her figure, the pulsing muscle in his clenched jaw told her something was amiss.

"I must away," he said bitterly when she walked the mare up to him, whereby he gently stroked the horse's nose. "Or, I should say, I am being sent away. It is Wolston's doing, though it was the Prince who has issued the directive."

"What?" Petra said, swinging off the horse to land on the ground.

She spoke quietly, though they were quite alone. Only the low murmur of voices in the distance and the clip-clop of horse hooves on stone could be heard.

"When? And will you be returning?"

"I am to leave at first light tomorrow," he said. "I am being sent to Sir Rufus's house, at Chesham in Buckinghamshire, to determine the nature of his debts, as well as the whereabouts of his will. Charles—Foyle, that is—is to accompany me. Unless I wish to tax my horse, which I do not, the ride will take nearly every hour of daylight."

As Petra pulled the reins over the mare's head, Duncan ran his hand through his hair in irritation.

"I am told they found no evidence of a house key in either Sir Rufus's or Beecham's rooms, and therefore I will have to break a window. That will leave the house open to devious types intent on snabbling items from the house. I may have to leave Foyle there to protect it until a glazier can come, and I do not wish to do so."

He reached out to one of her curls that always seemed to come loose, right in front of her ear, and gently wound it about his finger.

"Whilst I did not lie when I told Her Majesty that you are most capable of taking care of yourself, I do not like the idea of leaving you at the castle when there is a murderer amongst us. And the same goes for Annie, Caroline, and your aunt Ophelia—not to mention my grandmama." His lips quirked for a moment. "Though, as an aside, I have learned this morning to never underestimate the power of love at any age."

"How do you mean?" Petra asked, who had felt herself pinken guiltily when he mentioned her aunt. Luckily, Duncan did not notice.

"Well, before coming across the housemaid, Marta, I had just returned from my ride and went to check on my grandfather, as His Grace was supposed to ride out with me, but did not appear. I was concerned enough that I rather barged into his chambers.

And what I found instead was, well . . . evidence that Shawcross men continue to be virile far longer than most. And though my own father was known to stray, the rumors that my grandpapa gave up his rakehell ways for his wife might very well be true. And before you ask, yes, I am certain it was both my grandparents."

Petra's eyes had flown open when she realized what he was saying. "*No.*"

"*Yes*," Duncan said, though he was rubbing a hand over his eyes as though he wished he could wipe the view from his mind. "It was only luck that neither of Their Graces saw or heard me, so I am saved that particular hell."

For a moment, they both laughed, equally delighted and horrified.

"Well, that rules out His Grace as someone I must investigate further," Petra said, grinning. "Not that I truly thought he would wish to strangle Sir Rufus, of course."

Her smile then faded, her own words having a sobering effect. Duncan took her shoulders in his hands and used his thumbs to make gentle rubbing motions along her collarbone.

"I mean it, my lady. I do not like the idea of leaving any of you when someone is cunning enough to commit a strangling and then walk about the castle without anyone the wiser."

"I cannot say I like it either," Petra admitted, "but at least I have strength in numbers. We shall all look out for one another."

When he brought her to his chest, she bit her lower lip, the guilt increasing that she still had not told him that Aunt Ophelia was another suspect. In truth, she thought he might have deduced it from his own interviews of various servants. But it seemed that had not been the case.

Duncan and Aunt Ophelia adored one another, it was true, but if he honestly felt concerned that her aunt might be dangerous, he might attempt to disobey the order from the Prince. He would want to stay in order to ascertain whether Aunt Ophelia was innocent or guilty without Petra having to do so.

And that would not do. Aunt Ophelia was *her* family, and Petra wanted to determine on her own whether her beloved aunt had committed such a horrid crime or not. Petra was willing to accept help in this endeavor, yes, but decided she could never let another prove or disprove her aunt's innocence. Not even Duncan.

Thus, she said not a word.

Duncan, however, seemed to still be fuming over being forced to leave. He issued a few swear words in Gaelic that had the mare pricking her ears, as if she might have heard them before. This made Duncan smile wryly and reach out to stroke her nose again. And then one of his eyebrows cocked when he saw Petra's face.

"Would you like to tell me why you are looking so happy at the news of my leaving, my lady?" he said, humor returning to his voice. "Is it because I shall not be in the castle, and therefore you may flirt with a certain French chef in my absence? The way he propositioned you in the kitchens was the talk of the servants' hall in the undercroft, you understand. I could not help but hear the gossip when I went there in search of Foyle."

Petra tsked, for even though he remained relaxed and smiling, she could see the questions remaining in his eyes.

With the mare conveniently blocking anyone's view of them, she took hold of Duncan's shirt and brought his lips down to hers. She let her hand go up into his hair, and pressed every bit of her she could against him, knowing certain parts of her anatomy—even ensconced in yards of woolen fabric—would fit at just the right parts of him to make that little groan issue from the back of his throat. She felt the same little thrill she always did when his arms came about her, one broad hand gently caressing the back of her head, the other snaking onto her bum with much more delicious insistence.

It was only when she felt she might lose her own head to the moment and pull him on top of her to the riding arena floor that she made herself take a step back. Then she tried for a stern look as his glazed-over green eyes watched her mouth intently.

"And if your sources spoke the truth, you would have heard that I gave no indication of returning the flirtation. But if you keep teasing me, Duncan Shawcross, maybe I shall."

When he issued another couple of oaths, she laughed and put her hands on his chest.

"Nevertheless, I was smiling before because I know where Sir Rufus kept the key to his house in Chesham. It is tied to the hangings on his bed. Oliver said as much."

"He did? When?"

Petra bit back an unladylike swear. Of course, she had forgotten that she had not yet told him about her visit with Oliver Beecham in his temporary prison in the Round Tower. But she also felt she could not be faulted for this. Until now, she had only been in Duncan's presence for two minutes put together since they stood next to each other in the Queen's Audience Chamber.

"The risk that you ran of Wolston seeing you . . ." Duncan began, following it with, "not only for you, but also for Beecham."

From beneath the mare's neck, who had been standing quite calmly during the whole conversation, Petra spied a stable lad coming to collect her. She showered the mare with grateful pats and a kiss on her soft nose before turning her reins over to the lad. Then she checked the time on her watch before doing the scandalous thing of grabbing Duncan's hand in public.

"Do come on, and hurry, if you please. It is still teatime in the library, which means there will likely be few in the halls. Let us sneak into Sir Rufus's chambers and get you that key. And whilst we are there, we can see if there might be anything else the former royal chef might have been hiding."

They were walking beneath a tree, its leaves already beginning to turn yellow, when Duncan swore again and released her hand.

"That right sod Wolston is heading this way and we cannot be seen together." He stepped behind another tree. "Go on. I will meet you in Sir Rufus's chambers as soon as I can."

TWENTY

From the pocket in her riding habit's breeches, Petra pulled out the thin leather roll of peacock green and was soon selecting the correct lockpick for Sir Rufus's door.

Excepting Wolston—and a few people sitting in the Green Drawing Room, chatting amiably with one another—she had not seen anyone as she navigated her way to Sir Rufus's rooms in the farthest corridor of the gentlemen's half of the south wing.

The lock gave with little noise, and she quickly turned the knob and entered, and then uttered a yelp at the same time as someone else.

"Lord Wadley-Bates!" she gasped. "What are you doing in here?"

The big man had started in surprise, and brought the piece of paper he was holding to his heart.

"Lady Petra, my dear, you frightened me." He then narrowed one eye as he peered at her. "And however did you get in? I ensured the door was locked behind me."

"I picked the lock, your lordship." She held up her picks and lifted her chin. Though Lord Wadley-Bates was indeed one of her suspects, for some reason she did not feel threatened by him. "Now, I would like an answer in return. How were you able to enter this room?"

Lord Wadley-Bates held up a key.

"I asked the royal butler, who happens to be my wife's cousin. Told him I'd have it back inside of a quarter of an hour, that I just needed to collect the manuscript Sir Rufus left for me. I am his publisher, you recall. His latest cookery book was due to me a fortnight ago. He claimed it was here, and I would like to still publish it if I can."

Petra put away her picks and then crossed her arms over her chest.

"Somehow I find that suspicious, your lordship. Especially as I took note of you as we did our first round of judging. You acted as if Sir Rufus's tragic demise meant little to you. Quite surprising, if you ask me. You are indeed the publisher of his very popular and lucrative cookery books. One would think you would be saddened by the death of your best-known author, and yet you appeared almost sanguine, as if it were merely another Tuesday."

She just stopped herself at the last minute from accusing him of murder, having only just recalled that everyone believed Sir Rufus's death to be tragic, but natural.

Lord Wadley-Bates, his second chin quivering, looked indignant for a long moment, and then his face crumpled with guilt. He laid the paper he was holding back on the desk.

"I am embarrassed, Lady Petra. Truly I am. Sir Rufus was a brilliant chef and his first three cookery books were a boon to my publishing house and me. I cannot tell you how much I admired him, and for a long while I was honored to call him my friend."

"Was?" she repeated. "Why is it that you two were no longer friendly?"

There was a sofa at the foot of the bed and his lordship sat down heavily onto it. He looked as if he had been wanting to confide in someone for quite some time as the words tumbled out of him.

"First, I must ask something of you, Lady Petra—though I have not mentioned it to anyone else." He looked up at her, the bags beneath his eyes and his full face giving him the look of a worried hound. "But I have heard a rumor—through my wife's cousin, you understand—that Sir Rufus did not die naturally. And that you were the one to discover him in the library. Is this true?"

With an inward curse that someone—likely Marta, the young housemaid—had talked, Petra uncrossed her arms.

"It is indeed true, my lord. Someone took Sir Rufus's life, and I would like to know who that blackguard was. And it is important that you not perpetuate this rumor, despite it being the truth. The Prince himself has insisted that we not worry his guests unless there seems to be a good reason to do so, which there is not at present."

Lord Wadley-Bates nodded wearily and put his head in his hands. "Lawks, the poor man." He once more met her eyes. "I am terribly sad that such a thing happened to him, but I do not know that I can claim the type of surprise that would be expected of me."

Petra went and sat next to the older man. "How do you mean?"

"Sir Rufus, he was a humble man—in general, you understand," said Lord Wadley-Bates. "At least, he was when he retired from service in the royal kitchens. Oh, he knew he was a brilliant chef, but he had remained mindful of himself otherwise. But success soon went directly to his head, as it often does with some."

He sighed, and went on to confirm what Oliver Beecham had said about his time as the chef's valet. That Sir Rufus was not as well liked as one would think.

"It was all because of his damned knighthood, in my opinion," he groused. "He insisted on being called *Sir* Rufus, chastising anyone who slipped and called him Chef—even calling out the Duke of Grafton to His Grace's face." Flinging up an exasperated hand, he said, "What was more, the last two cookery books Sir Rufus published were only mildly successful. And we had many letters from cooks all over the country saying that the recipes were simply rehashed from his earlier books. Sir Rufus begged me, and I agreed to another cookbook—just one more, you understand. Yet he never turned in any pages to me, though he claimed it was nearing completion. Our contract states it is mine to publish, if I can find it—and I expect it will be a success due to Sir Rufus's death."

"That is a quite cruel sentiment, my lord," Petra said coolly.

Now, Lord Wadley-Bates merely shrugged.

"Being a publisher of cookery and gardening books does not make one rich, Lady Petra. I am a man with seven children, four of them girls. I must do what I can to make money, for I wish for my girls to have an excellent dowry. I was only able to give them a minimal education, despite my title, and I would wish them to have something to live on should they not succeed in finding happy marriages."

On this, Petra could not fault him. And while she did not feel in her gut that Lord Wadley-Bates was the killer of Sir Rufus Pomeroy, she felt she must ask.

"My lord, would you please tell me why you were awake and out of your chambers early this morning—between seven and half past. For you were seen, and that is undoubtedly the time frame in which Sir Rufus's life was taken."

"Christ, do you mean it?" he replied. "I heard it was this morning, but not that—"

"If you would, sir. Please tell me where you were."

Lord Wadley-Bates blinked at Petra, surprised at her tone, which was soft, but commanding. It was clear he had not expected that level of strength from her, and he gave the impression of having mixed emotions at hearing it.

"I was speaking with Chef Carême in his personal sitting room, above the kitchens, on the first floor," he replied tightly. Then a flicker of guilt passed over his face. "I have put forth an offer to the Frenchman about doing his own cookery book. He was cautious when I first approached him with the idea. He said he wished to further speak with me, but early this morning—well before seven—was the only time he could meet me and speak freely."

Now a spark of irritation came into his eyes at having to explain himself to someone half his age—and a woman.

"So, yes, Lady Petra, I was out of my rooms, but Chef Carême can verify I was with him in his sitting room for almost three-quarters of an hour, beginning at six o'clock. Whilst he then left for the kitchens, he invited me to remain there, looking at some of his recipes for as long as I wished. I left his rooms at a quarter after seven. I was nowhere near the small library, to be sure."

"I hope you understand that I must check for myself, my lord," she replied evenly. She wished Chef Carême had mentioned meeting Lord Wadley-Bates this morning, but she was not surprised he wished not to speak of it until he had made a decision on writing a cookery book or not.

His lordship stood, the side of him that did not like answering to a younger woman winning out.

"Do as you please, Lady Petra. You will uncover that I rowed with Sir Rufus yesterday in the Green Drawing Room for not adhering to the deadline I set. We shouted in each other's faces, yes, but that is all. Thus, do not ever act as if you are accusing me again. Now, I must return this key to the butler. If you find Sir Rufus's manuscript, I expect you to hand it over. He and I had a binding contract, and thus it belongs to *me*. The only recipe I found in the minutes before you broke in was this one, on his desk."

He handed over the sheet of paper. On it was a recipe that Petra recognized. It was for the decadent chocolate cake known as the La Bella Contessa—the recipe that Sir Rufus had promised he would never publish.

Damn and blast.

There was a light knock at the door. Three short raps, a pause, and then a fourth. Duncan had arrived. She went and opened the door, whispering as he entered the room, "Lord Wadley-Bates was here first, looking for Sir Rufus's latest cookery manuscript. He has an alibi, and is not our man."

After Duncan entered the room, Petra then stood back and held the door open for her fellow judge, looking the older man directly in the eyes.

"I shall see you tomorrow on the North Terrace for our second day of judging, my lord. And if I find the pages you are looking for, I shall bring them to you so long as we can find no reason that it might have been a motive for Sir Rufus's death. However, if we do find the pages, and if Sir Rufus would have had payment coming to him, I will expect you to pay his estate. For I know Sir Rufus left this earth with debts, as well as a valet who deserves his wages."

"If you find it, I shall of course pay what is owed," Lord Wadley-Bates said, looking irritated that she would suggest otherwise.

"Excellent. And I shall remind you again to keep your counsel concerning the nature of Sir Rufus's death, by the order of the Prince Regent."

He nodded and went to walk out the door, before stopping and turning back.

"But I will tell you this, my lady. After I finally left Chef Carême's rooms, I saw two people heading away from the area near the library. One was your aunt, Lady Ophelia Throckmorton, and the other was our fellow judge, Sir Franklin."

"You look as if you have more to say, my lord," Petra said dryly, weary of hearing her aunt's name in connection with Sir Rufus's death. She was also finding it difficult to think of Sir Franklin as someone with a reason to kill the former royal chef. Though what she heard next changed her mind on that score.

"Only this," said his lordship. "And I take no pleasure in relating it, but Sir Franklin has been jealous of Sir Rufus for years. The former is actually quite a good cook, but was never properly trained. Nevertheless, he has long pestered me to allow him to write a cookery book. When he found out that Sir Rufus was going to be here, and be one of our judges, he was incensed, to say the least."

"And Lady Ophelia?" asked Duncan, after a quick glance at Petra.

"All I know is that her ladyship detested Sir Rufus. I know not why, but recently Lady Ophelia and I both attended a musicale at Chatsworth House in Derbyshire. When I mentioned Sir Rufus, I felt as if she might like to . . . Well, I shall use the words her ladyship did: She said she would happily claw his eyes out if given the chance."

With that, he gave a slight bow in Petra and Duncan's direction, and was gone.

Twenty-One

"My lady," Duncan said mildly as he watched Petra clamber up onto Sir Rufus's bed, "are we going to discuss what his lordship told you?"

Petra, however, leapt off the bed, one hand triumphantly in the air.

"I have found it!" she said. Then explained that Sir Rufus always hid his key after once having it stolen, which allowed his house to be easily robbed. "At least, that is what Oliver claims," she said when she held it out to Duncan.

He did not take it, but continued to stand with his hands on his hips.

"Very well." She stepped toward him and slipped the key into the pocket of his waistcoat.

"Petra..."

"I do not wish to discuss it at the moment," she returned finally. "I wish to confront my aunt on my own."

"You know I love Aunt Ophelia, too. I should like to help," Duncan said.

"And I would prefer to speak with her by myself," Petra said, her voice as tight as her shoulders were feeling. She rolled them back, hearing the muscles make popping noises in protest.

Duncan came around behind her, and began kneading his thumbs into her tense muscles. She groaned, and she could hear a hint of a satisfied smile in his voice as he thankfully changed the subject.

"I actually remember hearing a story about that incident with Sir Rufus being robbed. There was a rumor a lady of rank had a flirtation, or possibly more, with Sir Rufus. She wrote him a love letter and then later, when her affections were not returned, instructed her footman to retrieve it. Only the footman went too far and stole other items as well."

"I wonder who the lady was," Petra mused.

"I'm sure Grandmama would know."

"True, there is very little gossip Her Grace does not hear," she said.

"Indeed," Duncan said with a chuckle. He bent and gave Petra's neck a kiss, and then moved to the nearby desk to carefully go through the other papers that remained on it. They were all merely proposed supper menus for various well-known ladies of the ton.

Petra was briefly amused at seeing menus for the ever-competitive sisters Lady Elizabeth and Lady Sloan. Each had crossed out items that were in any way similar to her sister's suggested dishes and then requested a revised menu.

"Do you see any markings beneath the menus that would indicate something else of note being written?" Duncan asked. "We both know from experience that it has happened."

Petra used her quizzing glass, then reported, "They are exactly what they appear to be, which is no doubt why they were left here by Wolston's men. Duncan?"

"Yes?" he replied as he lay down on the floor next to the bed to look beneath it.

"Do you think there really is a safe that Sir Rufus was using? One that the Prince Regent had allowed him to borrow? You do know that the guard only pretended to find a key on Oliver's person, yes?"

"If Teddy had been here, he would have laughed," Duncan said as he stood again. "Nothing under the bed that I could find. But to answer your question, I asked, of course, but that sod Wolston merely told me that it was castle business. That whatever Sir Rufus had in the safe had been taken by his valet." He sighed and began to move the desk away from the wall to check behind it. "I said I did not believe a safe existed, but Wolston gave no reply. And when I pointed out that nothing had been found on Beecham, or in his quarters, Wolston claimed that Beecham must have already sold it to pay the money he owes. And it seems Beecham did manage to pay some of his gambling debts, at least, if not those from Wolston's men. For I spoke with one undergardener and a footman, both of whom said that he was able to pay them back yesterday evening, whilst we were at supper."

It was Petra's turn to sigh, having an immediate hunch as to where Oliver obtained his blunt.

"Annie," she said, kneeling down beside the wardrobe and beginning to feel about. "She must have given him the money. It only makes sense—at least if I am to continue to believe him innocent of theft as well as murder. And if that is the case, I am determined that he pay her back. You may have to give Oliver a job, however. For though I think him quite charming, I will not have Annie continually worried that he will misbehave."

"Ah, but first we have to keep him from being hanged for a crime he did not commit," Duncan said.

Petra was listening as she reached beneath the wardrobe—and hoping not to encounter a spider or a mouse at the same time—when her fingers touched on something that felt like leather. She pulled it out, finding it to be a leather case secured by straps. Duncan's dark eyebrows rose in curiosity.

"Oliver said that Sir Rufus normally put his recipes in a leather case," Petra explained. "Yet last night—or, rather, early this morning, after Sir Rufus returned here to his room, Oliver said it could not be found. Instead, it seems Sir Rufus rolled up his recipes and secured them with a length of black silk ribbon."

"As in the ribbon he was strangled with?" Duncan asked with narrowed eyes.

Petra nodded. "Oliver claims to have never seen the ribbon

before, too. But this case, it was underneath the wardrobe. Do you think Sir Rufus placed it there and only claimed not to know where it was? Or possibly Oliver did?"

Duncan encouraged her to see if anything was inside. Petra unbuckled the leather straps and lifted the top half of the case.

"I think we have found the missing cookery book," Petra said, then her brows knitted when she read one of the pages. "Or maybe not."

Inside was what looked to be part of a manuscript, yes, but there were no recipes. Even with writing on the front and back of each piece of paper, there were only a handful of pages. She looked over the first few and gave Duncan the rest to peruse.

"Why, I believe it is a book Sir Rufus was writing—a memoir, to be exact. There is an introduction where he explains who he is and . . . yes, here is the title page. He called it *My Life as Chef to the Aristocracy: Secrets Obtained over Thirty Years of Cooking for the Royal Family and the Ton*." She looked up at Duncan, incredulous. "Secrets? Of the royal family and the aristocracy? Surely he was not expecting to print this?"

That muscle in Duncan's jaw was jumping again. "I think he was. And unless he habitually stopped writing in mid-thought, I think this is only a small part of what he left behind."

After a pause, Duncan turned one sheet around and handed it to Petra, indicating a couple of different paragraphs.

She read the page, and then read it again. It contained quite a few sentences where a word or phrase was crossed out and then rewritten, all in the same hand, leaving no doubt that it was still Sir Rufus's work. Each time, the newer version took a sentence that contained interesting anecdotes and made it into something that read as scandalous or libelous, or both. One paragraph fairly leapt out at her when her father's name was referenced.

During the ten years I worked for the fifth Earl of Holbrook at Buckfields, his grand estate in Newmarket, County Suffolk, I found his lordship to be so lacking in intelligence that it was rather excruciating each time I was compelled to be in his presence.

Indeed, the only time he showed any level of acumen was when it came to his horses, and in choosing a wife. For if you are unaware, dear reader, if it were not for the beautiful countess and her expansive dowry, the earldom of Holbrook would surely be on its way to extinction.

"What a spiteful thing to write," she breathed, almost unable to take it in.

While Petra could not claim that her father was a scholar, he was, in her opinion, one of the smartest and kindest men she knew—even if he was as imperfect as any other person on the whole.

Firstly, he did not feel threatened by an intelligent woman—for it was he who encouraged Petra in all her endeavors when she was young. And secondly, he would admit when he was wrong and do his best to correct his mistakes. All of this she knew now more than ever. Those such as the earl were few and far between, both as men and as fathers.

She went to hand the page back to Duncan, but he indicated she should look again.

"Read on, my lady," he said grimly. "The part at the bottom of the page."

Petra did, and her lips parted in shock.

It was a recollection of a small dinner party at St. James's Palace in 1799, four years into Sir Rufus's tenure as the royal chef. It had been cheekily termed in the scandal sheets "The Night of a Thousand Their Graces," as every single duke and duchess in England had been in attendance, including those of Hillmorton, Richmond, Devonshire, Grafton, Rutland, and Carlingford, who were Caroline's own parents.

Sir Rufus went on to tease "rather horrid behavior of one of the illustrious duchesses in attendance" that included speaking so ill of her young, and only, daughter that it even shocked the Queen. Who, as Sir Rufus put it, "whilst devoted to her own children, was known to express little affection for those belonging to others."

Sir Rufus went on to write that determining the identity of the duchess would hardly be difficult for anyone who paid attention, for within two years the Her Grace in question was living in "the family's most opulent manor in Bath, and has rarely been seen in London since."

Petra was agog. "He is talking about Caroline's mama. I am certain of it. When the Duke of Carlingford had finally had enough of his wife's behavior toward Caroline, she was sent to live at Opal Hill Manor, in Bath, in 1801."

"I surmised it was the Duchess of Carlingford," Duncan said. "Caroline has told me a bit of her upbringing. But also, the timing does not fit any of the other duchesses."

Petra was shaking her head slowly as if stupefied.

"I did not know Sir Rufus was such a man—to smile in one's face and then write such terrible things behind one's back. It makes me truly sad to find this out now, after holding him in such high esteem for so long."

Duncan took one of her hands and held it up to his chest. "Your willingness to see the good in people is one of the many reasons I am honored to have your heart, my lady."

For this, he received another kiss, but they did not allow it to distract them from returning to the matter at hand.

"In my speaking with others today," Duncan said, "it seems that Oliver Beecham might have been correct in that Sir Rufus was no longer well liked, maybe more than we realized."

"Yes, and I can now see why," Petra said. "Were there any more like this in the other pages?" she asked, skimming the others she held. "Mine only go into Sir Rufus's background and his first years training at the house of Lord and Lady Cruikshank from 1778 until 1785, after which he first came to Buckfields."

Duncan handed her one more page.

"I found this one of interest. Read the last two paragraphs at the bottom."

Taking it, Petra did as he instructed, and found not gossip, but more of a treatise on his time working for the Prince Regent, plus something that read almost like a warning.

My first two years in the employ of His Royal Highness were nothing short of stupendous, I must say. My cooking was enjoyed to its fullest, with the Prince's already substantial girth growing by inches due to his love of my cuisine. Their Majesties showered me with compliments as well, so much so that I was regularly invited to the dining room to hear their praises.

Yet if His Royal Highness or Her Majesty happen to read this, I would advise them to remember not to have such private conversations when a chef of exceptional intelligence is nearby. They should most definitely refrain of speaking of acts that might be considered

Petra flipped the page over, looking for the rest of the sentence. There was only a blank page.

"Where is the rest of it?" she asked, looking to Duncan and the other pages he held in his hand.

"That is the last page we have. There are not even any other pieces of paper to show that he was intending to write more."

He cocked an eyebrow and waited, and Petra knew what that meant. He was allowing her to test her mind and come up with a theory. It was becoming one of her favorite things to do when working alongside him, the bandying about of ideas.

She chewed on her lip, and thought on it. Then she looked

through the other pages as well. It seemed to be little parts of a manuscript, rather than, say, the entire first chapter.

She did not know many authors of books, for knowing Lord Byron was not truly the same as wishing to have discussions with him about his writings. Or wishing to speak with him at all.

But she reasoned that, while authors likely did not all write the same way, it was probable that some might write parts of their books—whether it be a few lines or a few paragraphs—when a particularly good way of expressing their thoughts came about. And those words or paragraphs would then be inserted into the place the author would best like them to be once they had the whole story—or memoir, as it were—written.

Yet these pages belonging to Sir Rufus seemed more . . . chaotic. As if there was indeed more of the memoir to be read, but only these pages had been left. She found another page that ended in mid-sentence, which strengthened this idea.

"I would like to say that I believe these papers were left specifically for us. For it does seem a bit too much of a coincidence that the book's title page"—she then selected the one mentioning the earl—"and this one with the rather scurrilous mentions of my papa, and then Caroline's parents, were left in the leather case. Yet at the same time, I think it much too far-fetched that anyone was to know that I would be the one to discover Sir Rufus's murder, or that I would be willing to look further into it. Especially as, the more I think on it, Sir Rufus's murder seemed . . . as if it happened on the spur of the moment."

"I agree," murmured Duncan, though he encouraged her to continue. She indicated the leather case again.

"No, I feel as if Sir Rufus lied to Oliver about not knowing where his case was. If he was more unkind and scheming than I ever realized, he probably told many—or at least hinted to them—that he would be writing such a memoir. And thus, he likely knew that one of them would come looking for these pages. I told you, did

I not, about how I saw him turn pale when he saw certain people yesterday in the library?"

Duncan nodded, and she continued, pacing around the room a bit as she thought.

"And last night, when Caroline and I were reading out the list of events happening at the castle today, when I said Sir Rufus's name, he was staring mournfully into the distance. He also seemed quite insistent when he bade me not to be late in meeting him in the library this morning." She stopped pacing. "Duncan, I think Sir Rufus knew that his cruelty toward others in the mining of gossip was coming back to hurt him." Her voice became quiet. "I wonder if he planned to ask for my help."

"I cannot disagree that he may have known something might happen because of his actions," Duncan said, rubbing his chin thoughtfully. Then he reached for her hand. "But if it means anything, when Sir Rufus and I were at the fencing venue, we talked about you at length and he seemed to know nothing of your recent adventures, nor did I offer up any stories. If Sir Rufus were planning on asking for your help, he would have been deliberately planning on putting you in danger, not knowing anything more than your innately intrepid qualities." He smiled wryly, then kissed the back of her hand. "And yes, my lady, I am saying that you should not take on any guilt, even though I know you will to one extent or another."

Petra thought on this for a moment, sighed, then gave him a similar grin in return. "You are correct—on all counts." She laid the manuscript pages she held on top of the case.

"Nevertheless, I think Sir Rufus himself left these pages to tantalize whoever found them. Possibly to entice the reader, for they would know there was much more gossip to be had."

"Or enrage said reader," Duncan said. "And I would have to agree with you there, too." He grinned, touching his thumb to the corner of her lips, which had parted with a sudden intake of breath. "You have an alternate theory?"

"Not alternate, no. Duncan, I think the rest of this memoir is what Sir Rufus claimed to have hidden in the castle. And our killer is determined to find it."

Twenty-Two

Not long thereafter, Petra learned a valuable lesson regarding her bloodhounding. To wit, it was almost comical how quickly her investigative plans could go awry. Especially when no one was to know she was investigating.

It had begun mere moments after she and Duncan had snuck out of Sir Rufus's room and quickly separated down different corridors, with Petra dashing down the stairs to the Quadrangle, allowing herself to mingle with the crowd enjoying the late-afternoon sun and watching the funambulists once more entertaining the crowd.

She had intended to walk around just long enough to be seen, and then go in search of Aunt Ophelia, for she felt it more important than ever to confront her aunt and obtain the truth as soon as possible.

Instead, Petra was found by the Duchess of Hillmorton, who took her arm and said, "Come with me, my dear," in a voice that brooked no argument. She then directed a narrow stare toward a group of six ladies all around Petra's age, sipping lemonade and looking about with varying levels of haughtiness.

"Ahh, it is all six patronesses of Almack's, in one tight group," she said, then gave a sniff. "They serve to remind me that most ladies of your generation are impudent chits, despite their family names and influence over society."

"I admit I find most of them to be quite pleasant when taken individually," Petra said, "but they all seem to grow much higher in the instep when they flock together."

"Indeed they do," said the duchess with a chuckle, but Petra gave them one speculative glance before turning away.

The patronesses, despite their relative youth, held the keys to London society in the form of vouchers allowing admittance to the coveted balls held in the Almack's assembly rooms. As such, Petra had occasionally wondered if these ladies might be responsible for some of the coolness she had recently experienced within society, despite the significant number of invitations that sat upon her mantel at Forsyth House.

But the patronesses were soon forgotten as she walked alongside the duchess into the Queen's Drawing Room to attend another, longer lecture given by architect Jeffry Wyatt.

"He does excellent work and shall be knighted in future, mark my words," Her Grace said as they entered the beautiful room with its white walls and goldenrod accents, adding, "and when I told him as much, he said that, should that honor be bestowed upon him, he intends to change his surname to Wyatville—only with one *t* instead of two. It seems he wishes to set himself more easily apart from his uncle James Wyatt, who was appointed by His Majesty twenty years ago to renovate the castle's exterior to the gloriously Gothic look we have today. Mr. Jeffry Wyatt was up quite early this morning, in fact, making drawings of the eastern façade. His Grace and I saw him ourselves."

Petra watched as a tiny, satisfied smile came over her godmother's face and suppressed a grin. For she knew exactly why Their Graces would have been awake and together at such an early hour. Little did Her Grace know, her morning enjoyment of the duke, and vice versa, had also inadvertently given Mr. Wyatt an alibi for Sir Rufus's murder.

The duchess chose them seats in the middle of the room, almost directly beneath the glittering cut-glass chandelier. Petra did try once to engage her in a discussion about Sir Rufus while the other ladies and gentlemen were not listening. Upon hearing his name, though, Her Grace simply murmured, "Quite sad. Quite sad indeed. A talent he was."

Petra at first meant to ask if Her Grace knew that the former royal chef was writing a memoir full of gossip regarding the ton. Yet with so many people about—including Major Carlson, who nodded politely as he chose a seat two rows behind—her fortitude on that particular line disappeared. Instead she asked if Her Grace recalled hearing gossip that Sir Rufus's house had once been robbed by a footman.

"Hmm?" said the duchess as Mr. Wyatt walked to the front of the room. "Oh yes, my dear. Some three years ago. And quite the scandal that was for . . ." She tilted her head to her left. Petra looked to find a half dozen ladies of rank settling into their seats.

"Who do you mean, Your Grace?" she whispered, only to have the duchess flap her hand in a shushing way when Mr. Wyatt politely cleared his voice to begin what would be a quite interesting lecture. And when it was over, the duchess all but sprang from her seat to speak with the architect, saying, "The duke and I wish to remodel the south wing of Hillmorton House, and I think this Mr. Wyatt—or Wyatville, whichever he prefers—would be just the man."

And by the time Petra had risen from her seat, all the ladies in question who, three years earlier, might have sent their footman to retrieve a letter from Sir Rufus's house were gone.

Was it coincidence that Lady Norworthy was in the group, or had the duchess meant one of the others who were sitting around her? One of whom was the young dowager countess and cousin to the Prince and Caroline.

Petra left the ballroom intending to find Lady Norworthy and at least discover her reasons for being awake and roaming the castle at such an early hour that morning. Yet, despite her ladyship being quite tall, she managed to vanish into the crowd rather easily.

Thwarted in accomplishing this particular interview, in the end Petra found the lively atmosphere of the castle's evening activities easier to enjoy than to ignore.

As the clock's hours marched forward into the night, there was no shortage of diverting things to do—everything from a watercolor class to more lectures, lawn bowling on the terraces, and a tour of the private royal apartments. There was even an artist who would paint small portraits and a poet who would craft a personalized humorous poem for any guest who wanted one.

Some of the men also had a friendly boxing match outside in the Quadrangle, and the Prince announced a progressive game of whist in the Queen's Ballroom that would last over the next four nights, with the winning team being awarded the two beautiful card tables that were inlaid with mother-of-pearl and made to be easily transported.

And, of course, there was dancing, with an orchestra playing in Horn Court and guests choosing partners however they pleased instead of by traditional ballroom protocol.

Caroline had tried to tempt Petra into joining her for the dancing, but Petra declined. She had caught glimpses of every one of her suspects and she was determined to follow them and see if she could engage them in conversation.

It proved harder than she thought, for she spent her time rushing about, trying to find each one, only to see no way of easily speaking with them without causing undue attention.

Lady Norworthy, she saw, eagerly attended the tour of the royal apartments. Sir Franklin enjoyed the lawn bowling. Even Lord Wadley-Bates—now considered innocent but his movements noted nonetheless—entered the boxing arena against Duncan, and then quickly gave up, laughing, less than five minutes later. Duncan then won a round handily against one of the Coldstream Guards while, off in a corner, Colonel Wolston watched everything with a dark expression.

Then the Prince Regent mostly sat about in one of the ornate chairs reserved for him, eating and drinking every plate of food and glass of wine offered by various footmen.

As for the other women on her list, Petra spied her aunt Ophelia—tonight in a shawl the red of a cardinal's wing—having a conversation with the young, widowed countess Petra had seen earlier. They stood talking near the statue of King Charles II until the pretty countess, looking distressed, pulled out a handkerchief and blew her nose while Aunt Ophelia hurried off with a determined look upon her face.

Petra, some lengths behind, followed her aunt into the castle, only to find herself in the ballroom where the whist tournament was beginning.

Aunt Ophelia quickly partnered with the Duchess of Hillmorton and they shooed away two other women so that they could sit across from Major Carlson and a baron. Petra attempted to draw her aunt away and speak with her before the game began, but the duchess said, "Whatever it is can wait, Lady Petra. I should like to win, and no one is a better whist player than Lady Ophelia. She wins tricks as if by magic."

The major, expertly shuffling a deck of cards, raised one fair eyebrow as a competitive gleam came into his eyes.

"Mm, yes, I heard somewhere that whist is best played by those with a significant *calculating power*. Is that true, Lady Ophelia? Are the tricks you collect due to your ability to be that type of person?"

Petra could not help but be amused when her aunt, bracelets clacking and red shawl slipping off her shoulders in an accidentally seductive manner, collected her cards and gave a bold retort.

"I will be the last to deny it, Major. When one regularly plays with men, she must first learn *all the tricks*. And then one utilizes them to her advantage to win the game." She looked at him over her cards, her blue eyes steely. "And win I shall."

This was met by delighted laughs from the women and loud

guffaws from the men until the duchess thumped her fist on the table and said, "Are we playing, or are we laughing?"

It was then that Petra had turned to see the young countess standing off to one side, still looking out of sorts. Petra fetched two glasses of wine from a tray and went to stand by her, offering up a glass with a smile.

"Thank you, Lady Petra. I normally do not drink wine, except with my dinner, you understand. As cousin to His Majesty, I feel it is best to comport myself with decorum should I be called upon to represent the royal family in some endeavor. But at this moment, it is welcomed."

Petra wryly thought back to how glassy-eyed the Prince had already become—and it was not yet eight o'clock—and decided not to comment upon the royal family and decorum.

Instead, she gently explained that she had seen her ladyship looking out of sorts and wished to help, if she could. After the briefest of pauses, she added, "And though poor Sir Rufus was taken from this earth today, he once worked for my papa at Buckfields, and I recall him saying that a small glass of wine is always helpful in putting what is out of sorts back into line."

Actually, Sir Rufus had said nothing of the sort—at least, not that she knew of—but Petra was rather proud of herself for finding a way to mention the chef. Especially when the countess nodded, her nose reddening with emotion as she stared forlornly at the whist players, watching as Major Carlson shifted his bad leg before he smirked and threw out a card.

Petra turned to her companion and found the countess had fled. She hastened to follow, but Caroline appeared, stopping Petra in her tracks.

Standing on her toes to look over Caroline's shoulder, Petra quickly explained that the countess was one of the women seen walking the castle halls at the time of Sir Rufus's death. "She seemed quite distressed when I mentioned him. I must interview her—hopefully to rule her out."

Caroline gave a mildly derisive huff.

"Believe me, dearest, you do not want to engage with my cousin unless you wish to be subjected to a long-winded story of some sort. Usually including five very silly reasons why she must not do something she wishes to do because she might be called upon to act in some vague royal duty, and she must be ready when the moment comes."

Then at seeing Petra's expression, she relented.

"Oh, all right. Wait here. I will go after her in your stead and discover her reasons for being up so early this morning, for I may do so in much quicker fashion."

With only slight impatience, Petra sipped her wine and watched as her aunt and her godmother won the next round of whist handily against the major and the baron. And true to her word, Caroline glided back to her side, a triumphant look on her face.

"First of all, when my cousin felt I was insinuating that she was upset over 'a former chef—someone who was all but a tradesman,' I thought she might report me as a traitor to Their Majesties." Caroline's brown eyes rolled heavenward.

Petra frowned. "Then what was making her so distressed?"

Caroline angled her chin toward the whist table, where they could just see the Duchess of Hillmorton dealing out cards with a wicked smile, and Major Carlson glowering.

"It seems my exceedingly proper cousin—who has only been a widow since January—has been having a liaison with Prinny's personal solicitor. It began some weeks ago when she visited Windsor, and became quite torrid. And whilst she worried things had cooled, last night at supper she was seated next to him, and he was quite flirty."

"You jest. The major?" Petra returned.

Caroline smirked. "A handsome gentleman with a tragic past who shows an unexpectedly diverting side? Dearest, they barely have to flirt to do their wooing. Especially in my cousin's case, for before she knew it, she was agreeing to come to his room at the end of the evening. She felt the major was sure to propose, and thus fueled her fires, as it were."

Caroline's lips then briefly turned down, causing one of Petra's eyebrows to rise upward.

"I shall wager a guess," Petra said dryly, "the major did not propose?"

Shaking her head, Caroline's voice softened in sympathy for her cousin.

"No, he did not. He accepted her favors last night, and when she tried to take leave of him earlier this morning, he seduced her again, causing her to be forced to walk the castle's halls at seven o'clock and be seen."

"That was indeed cruel of him," Petra said. "Though as he was seen, too, I assume he at least escorted her away from his quarters. Did she know where he went?"

"For his morning walk, it seems." Caroline shrugged as she stared darkly at the major. "My cousin may be rather silly at times, but I daresay she did not deserve such treatment."

Petra agreed as she glanced over to the major, then the crowd briefly parted and she could see Aunt Ophelia, staring daggers at the fair-headed, handsome royal solicitor, who either did not notice or was doing a fine job ignoring her. Petra felt as if she now understood what she had seen earlier between her aunt and the young countess.

"I think Aunt Ophelia is already determined to make the major understand he has been a rakehell, and she will not tolerate it," said Petra in admiration. They both watched the major's cheeks reddening at something Lady Ophelia said, which she followed with a win at another round of whist, causing the duchess to let out a satisfied cackle.

Caroline took Petra's arm in hers.

"Then I think we have seen enough. My cousin is being defended by a true tigress and I am glad of it. You will now come dance, Lady Petra Forsyth."

And when she added in a whisper, "I have made certain Shawcross will be there, too, and looking for a partner," Petra could not, and did not, resist.

TWENTY-THREE

Wednesday, 6 September 1815
Day three of the royal celebrations

IN THE EARLIEST HOURS OF THE MORNING, WELL BEFORE THE cock crowed, Petra gave Duncan one last, long kiss before he slipped from her bed, dressed, and left her room. He had done so with such a lack of sound that if it were not for the candle glowing on the side table allowing her to bear witness, she might have believed he could disappear at will.

"I must learn how to do that," she mumbled as sleep overtook her again. It was nine o'clock before Annie woke her for the day.

Sipping a strong cup of tea, Petra nibbled on toast with butter and marmalade until she finally felt awake and turned her mind to implementing three endeavors. One was to discover who killed Sir Rufus, of course. Another was to find the hiding place for the rest of his no-doubt-scandalous memoir. And at some point, she would attempt a third: to convince the talented Chef Carême to remain in England for another two years.

Then she soon had a fourth goal when Annie was brushing her hair and lamented, "Oh, I am longing to see my brother to make certain he is well, but Charles told me it would be best that I not."

"I will see if I can bribe a guard or a servant to check on him," Petra promised her. "It will save you from having to explain why you wish to know and giving away your connection to Oliver. But if we find he is poorly, I shall then go to the Queen."

Annie pressed her lips together, but her eyes shone bright with emotion. "Thank you, my lady."

Once dressed in a damask-striped gown the color of thyme leaves, though, Petra decided she must wait no longer to speak with Aunt Ophelia. As soon as Annie left for the servants' hall, Petra marched over to her aunt's door and rapped briskly. It was Geraldine who answered.

"My Lady Ophelia? I am afraid she is already out, Lady Petra."

Resisting the urge to make a frustrated noise, Petra asked, "Did you tell my aunt I wish to speak with her?"

Geraldine replied placidly that she had, but Petra decided she would leave a note for her aunt this time and asked to borrow a quill and paper.

Over the back of the desk chair, Petra found her aunt's silk robe with the feather trim. Geraldine hastily snatched it up and began walking off, making a silk ribbon in a lavender hue that had been trapped beneath flutter toward the floor. Instinctively, Petra grabbed it before it landed, managing to catch one edge. She then held it out to Geraldine, who took it and began winding it around two of her fingers.

"My lady likes a ribbon to hold back her hair in the nighttime," she said. "I am forever redoing it in the morning to have it lay in the fashionable Titus look. These ribbons, I have *cinquante* of them— fifty, no? One in every possible color. I must, because my lady is always losing them."

She gave a very French-sounding *pfft* noise that equated to an admonishing tut before striding back to the dressing room, muttering the whole way in French about the time it takes to craft beautiful hair every morning as Petra sat at the desk and wrote a short missive to her aunt. After folding it and leaving it propped against the inkwell, she stood, and then went still.

Something about Geraldine rolling that ribbon around her fingers made her recall with a shudder the black ribbon around Sir

Rufus's neck, tightened into an unending stranglehold. Then she realized the lavender one looked to be the exact width, length, and silk material as the murder weapon.

Her mind's eye saw the ribbon she'd handed to Geraldine. It had carefully sewn edges to stave off unraveling, did it not? This was nothing novel, of course. Annie sewed the edges of her ribbons, too, neatly but simply. Yet the edge of this ribbon had been beautifully worked, with straight, even overcast stitches all the way across, but probably double the amount strictly needed. And it looked exactly like the needlework edge of the black ribbon she'd seen when Wolston had cut it away from Sir Rufus's neck.

The question formed in her mind before she could stop it: Could the black ribbon then belong to Aunt Ophelia? Hastily, she called out to Geraldine.

"Does Lady Ophelia have a black ribbon, by chance? I, ah, should like to borrow it—to accent my dress for the ball on Saturday."

"Of course, Lady Petra," Geraldine replied. "I shall bring it." And several moments later, she walked out of Aunt Ophelia's dressing room, holding out a dark ribbon.

"I apologize, my lady, but I cannot find the black one. Lady Ophelia, she wore it two nights ago, after Her Majesty's supper. I put it in her hair myself, before she poured the whiskies. She dismissed me before I could pin it in place. She must have lost the ribbon when she slept. But I have this one. Your Annie, she said your gown is darkest blue. This color would look better in your hair, no?"

Petra took the blue ribbon like an automaton, noting the perfectly stitched edges.

"Is this your excellent needlework?" she asked, wondering if Geraldine's tendency toward laziness might mean she routinely asked one of Aunt Ophelia's other servants to do such work. But when Geraldine confirmed it was, her eyes shining with pride, Petra said, "Well done, then," even as she mentally scrambled for a reason the black ribbon would be missing. Recalling Tilly mentioning whisky as well, she asked if it were possible Lady Ophelia had gifted the ribbon to her.

"Give it to the little hall maid?" responded Geraldine. "She is a sweet girl, but no."

"Then look under the bed for the black one, please, Geraldine. Yes, now."

She received a scandalized look, yet Geraldine did as asked. Petra's heart skipped when a small sound of triumph was heard, but when Geraldine got to her feet, it was not the black ribbon she held, but a ring instead. Specifically the gold ring Aunt Ophelia had worn the night of the supper, with its huge lapis-lazuli cabochon.

"Oh la la, I thought my lady had lost this when she could not find it yesterday morning. It was hidden behind the bedpost. Do you know what this is, my lady? It once belonged to the second Countess of Holbrook—your great-great-grandmother, *n'est-ce pas?* I believe she was named Louisa, no? Like my lady's middle name."

Petra watched as Geraldine, using her thumb and first finger, then pulled up on one side of the cabochon, showing it to be on a hinge.

"You are correct," Petra said, fascination briefly diverting her thoughts. "Louisa, the second Countess of Holbrook, commissioned it during her disastrous first marriage, before marrying the earl. Aunt Ophelia has told me the story many times, about how Louisa managed to escape her first husband, but I never knew the ring opened."

Geraldine pointed to the space beneath the lapis-lazuli stone.

"See? It has a place inside to conceal. Lady Ophelia once used it for a love note written by her husband, Lord Throckmorton." Holding the ring to her breast in supreme relief, Geraldine then wrinkled her nose. "Ooh, but there is a scent on it. Like the *amandes*. I shall clean it and present it to my lady when she returns. She will be so happy!"

Geraldine rushed off, humming merrily at finding a lost ring of such importance. She had clearly forgotten all about looking for the black ribbon.

Petra, however, could not. Leaving the dark blue ribbon on the desk, she rushed to peer under the bed again, checking behind all the bedposts, then frantically searched under her aunt's pillows and in the bed linens.

She found nothing, all the while trying to remind herself that it was likely half the ladies here at Windsor had at least one black silk ribbon in their possession. That it could have belonged to anyone.

But was it *likely*? She picked up the blue one again, running her fingers over one sewn edge, and knew it was not. The black ribbon used to strangle Sir Rufus almost assuredly belonged to Aunt Ophelia.

Theories as to how Sir Rufus came by the ribbon began springing to mind. Could he have stolen it for some strange reason of his own? Or maybe it was possible he had asked Aunt Ophelia for a ribbon to tie up his recipes—or to use as a bookmark when sorting his pages—and she had agreed to give him one. Or could the two have been the most secret of lovers, and he accepted the ribbon from Aunt Ophelia as a small remembrance of her affection?

Petra quickly rejected this last idea as ridiculous, but otherwise, no other good suppositions were coming to mind.

Nevertheless, it does not mean she is guilty of anything, she thought fiercely, but fearful thoughts instantly chipped away at her bravado. It could not be denied that Aunt Ophelia had a temper. She had not only been seen in the castle's halls at the time of Sir Rufus's murder, but she had also been heard arguing with the former chef the evening before. And if that were not enough, she had also declared herself to Lord Wadley-Bates as wishing to harm Sir Rufus.

Petra had a sudden vision of Aunt Ophelia going to the small library that morning to confront Sir Rufus for some unknown reason. The two began to argue. Possibly Sir Rufus said something so cutting that Aunt Ophelia lost her head. Then she spied her own black ribbon, sitting next to his recipes. She snatched it up and, her mind clouded with anger and her height putting her nearly even with Sir Rufus, snaked it around his neck and tightened it. Then she pulled, harder and harder, until she took his life.

Petra's heart was beating wildly with the unwelcome thoughts. Breathing in a shuddering breath, she quietly exited her aunt's room, clutching the blue ribbon she'd been given in her fist, worry gripping her heart as she hurried back into her own chambers.

For the time being, she no longer wished to find Aunt Ophelia and speak with her. For when she did, she might have to learn an awful truth, and she could not bear the idea of it.

Aunt Ophelia had been just as much of an older sister—loving and warm—as she had been a caring secondary parent and a delightfully diverting aunt. After Petra had tragically lost her fiancé three years ago, Aunt Ophelia had been the person whose strength she emulated. For her aunt had shown great perseverance after not only losing her husband, but also previously losing two children in the womb. She had been Petra's very model on how to hold her head high and walk with one foot in front of the other until life began to be bearable once more.

Petra stopped at the looking glass and saw her pale, stricken face, causing the smattering of freckles across her nose to stand out even more. It was not just from the realization that Aunt Ophelia could possibly have murdered Sir Rufus, but also because that, if it turned out her worst fears were true, she knew what she would have to do. She might allow her aunt to walk free for another few days, but in the end, she could not live with herself unless she did what was right.

"Though if I must, I do not know how I shall do it, or how I shall bear it," she whispered to her reflection.

Twenty-Four

For a while, Petra tried to sit quietly in her room and think over everything she knew, but was soon feeling like she might climb the floral-wallpapered walls. The only thing to do was to freshen her face, dab her favorite Floris night-scented jasmine to her pulse points, and go to the library for some coffee and a look at the schedule of events.

There were a few lectures scheduled to start at eleven, but since most aristocrats were loath to rise before ten in the morning on any regular day, most events would begin at one o'clock. The fair on the grounds began around the same time to give the Windsor townspeople time to do their morning chores and enjoy the events in the afternoons.

Thusly finding two discussions she would like to attend, as well as her own duties as a patisserie judge at three, Petra had what was left of the morning hours to do as she pleased.

She decided it should begin with attempting to find Colonel Wolston and ask after Oliver. And then she would attempt to speak with Chef Carême.

Only she found herself on the ground floor, near the servants' hall first, and Chef Carême's handsome visage appeared quickly when she asked a kitchen maid to fetch him.

The Frenchman, however, rebuffed her attempts to have a conversation, and in the most elegant way. He had kissed her hand and looked into her eyes with his own gorgeous brown ones that reminded her somehow of Mrs. Bing's best spiced hot chocolate.

Then he told her in his beautiful mother tongue that he was quite busy, but he would be delighted to meet with her on the morrow. Would early in the morning suit? Yes? Splendid! He would have coffee ready and he would make her some of his croissants, which he was certain she would enjoy, for they were flaky and buttery and truly exceptional, if he could say so himself.

A smile came into his dark eyes as he switched to English and said in low, deep tones, "And I shall make certain you taste my *confiture de framboises* as well, Lady Petra."

Petra left feeling a little stunned, and wondering if she would ever be able to see or taste raspberry jam without thinking very naughty thoughts about handsome men.

After which, she wandered the halls of the castle on the ground and first floors, avoiding anyone likely to be more talkative than she was willing to endure. Which, at present, was most people.

She found a bit of privacy in the middle of the north wing and relished the silence as she walked up the Queen's Great Staircase. As she neared the first floor, she realized the Queen's Guard Chamber would be just behind her, in a position to look out over the Quadrangle.

Slowing her pace, she heard men's voices seemingly coming from the Guard Chamber. They were kept low, yet she could hear what they were saying. One—the Prince Regent—sounded angry, and the other—Colonel Wolston—sounded as if he was controlling his emotions.

Taking two more steps up, she was able to peek through the railing and look to her right without being seen, though her view was partially obstructed.

She could see the Prince's form—and more clearly hear his unique way of speaking. He shifted, and she then saw Colonel Wolston. He looked as if he was making a point while trying very hard to be obsequious to the Prince.

"Have you found it?" the Prince snapped.

"Not yet, Your Highness," replied Wolston. "But if I may suggest—the valet—I do not think we should—"

"I do not require your suggestions. Where is the major? I must speak with him."

"I will send someone to his room posthaste, Sir."

"No, *you* will find him, and send him to *me*."

Briefly, Petra saw the figure of the Prince Regent step into view again. He pointed a finger at Wolston and jabbed the colonel in the chest. Once, then twice, as he made his point.

"I must be certain of the law. You will locate it, and the major," said the Prince. "And deal with the valet. You may then find me in the Quadrangle."

Wolston looked as if he were using every bit of his soldierly training to not react, but she could see his jaw was tight and angry spots of red had appeared on his cheeks when the Prince turned away.

Petra turned, hitched up her skirts, and dashed back down the staircase. Lucky for her, there was a sudden spate of violin playing from outside, no doubt a warm-up from the musicians who produced jaunty tunes throughout the day, that hid her footsteps.

Once on the ground floor, she hurried into Horn Court, where a lecture was happening on famous British artists of the seventeenth and eighteenth centuries. She chose a chair at the back of the room and thought on what she had just heard from the Prince and his constable.

Her hand was at her heart as she thought on the Prince's words, even as the lecturer was discussing Thomas Gainsborough. It caused the man to smile kindly at her and exclaim to all in attendance that Gainsborough did often elicit such swooning in females from his work.

But Petra did not care. She was realizing that when the Prince was asking if Wolston had found something that clearly made His Royal Highness vexed, it had to be Sir Rufus's manuscript.

Yet what did the Prince mean by "deal with the valet"? There was no doubt he was talking about Oliver Beecham. What did he expect Wolston to do? Was Oliver attempting to break out of his cell, or being disruptive to the point that the Prince was concerned a particularly inquisitive guest exploring the grounds near the Lower Ward might hear him?

She did not even know if this were possible considering Oliver was in the dungeon, but reasoned there was a possibility. The dungeon would have to have access to air, would it not? And if so, it would be possible for Oliver to yell loud enough to be heard by someone.

Yet when the lecturer began discussing royal portraits and mentioned Mary, Queen of Scots, it led Petra to think on Lady Jane Grey. She had been named Edward VI's successor—not either of his sisters, the then-princesses Mary and Elizabeth.

Yet Lady Jane had only ruled England for nine days due to Princess Mary usurping the crown and having poor Jane beheaded.

This, of course, then made Petra think on Prince George and his order to have Oliver Beecham hanged without a trial. Each, in Petra's eyes, an utterly senseless act. Lady Jane could have been sent away with her handsome husband to live out their days in exile. And Oliver was likely innocent, making the directive much worse.

Petra waited until the lecturer turned his back and slipped out of the room. She did not wish to think on the cruelty of royal sons and daughters, thank you very much.

For I already must think on duplicitous aunts, she thought with a sigh.

Twenty-Five

Deciding fresh air was warranted for such thoughts—and gave her a greater chance of not having to speak with others—Petra crossed to the south side of the castle and exited out at the stairs that would deposit her onto the Long Walk.

As expected, she found herself able to think with a bit more clarity as she walked the gentle downward slope of the wide path lined with a glorious double row of elm trees. And when she felt the desire, she would turn, walk under the leafy canopy and into the parkland, where she passed by oaks that were ancient enough to have witnessed the first royal hunts led by William I of Normandy.

She spent the entire time thinking and wandering, without much of a direction, knowing she could not truly get lost—at least, not for long. Not only was it fairly easy to turn in a northerly direction and see a part of the castle's outline, but from the moment she stepped out, she was not truly alone. For there were also guests walking all over the park, eager to take in the sunny day and temperate weather.

She saw all of her fellow judges at one point or another, with Lord Wadley-Bates striding out as if attempting to work off some of the Shrewsbury cakes he had consumed the day before. Then, later, she saw Caroline walking with two of the Queen's ladies-in-waiting, who were also her distant cousins.

Sir Franklin, too, was out, strolling with hands behind his back alongside the Duchess of Hillmorton, who seemed to be quite animated as she spoke. Then she made a gesture as if throwing a ball and Petra laughed upon realizing the two were discussing lawn bowling.

The humor died in her throat, however, at seeing her aunt Ophelia. She wore yet another shawl—this one daffodil yellow with pink edging—over her shoulders, and Petra spotted her from a distance before hiding behind a tree like a bit of a coward. The tables had turned, it seemed. She knew she couldn't avoid talking to her aunt for long, but at the moment, she simply could not face it.

Her worries were unfounded, though, for she watched as Aunt Ophelia looked about before walking off in the opposite direction.

Then for some time thereafter, Petra was gloriously by herself. She heard the sounds of others around her—people talking and laughing as they moved around the trees within the parkland, some of whom she could see, others just voices drifting over the breeze. At one point, she heard running somewhere off to her right, heading in the same northwestern direction as she, but the sound soon faded and only birdsong was in her ears.

She then found herself nearing Frogmore House, the white palatial home about a half mile south of the castle that had recently been updated by the Queen and so named for the abundance of frogs that lived in the nearby waters.

"Hallo?" gasped a voice. "Could you help, please?"

Petra turned in the direction of the voice as it called out again, moving into a stand of trees, and nearly stumbled over the legs of a man.

Or, rather, she stumbled over one leg, as he was holding the other and grimacing.

It was Major Carlson—and though she felt he had used the young countess in a terrible manner, it was clear he was hurting quite badly.

She knelt on the grass beside him. "Major? What has happened?"

His handsome face was in a grimace, almost looking as if he were baring his teeth at her.

"I thought I would test my leg by doing what I enjoyed as a boy, and I tried to climb that tree," he gasped out, tilting his head toward a beautiful elm. "My blasted leg failed me, as it has for years now. I landed wrongly, and I am hurt."

"I can see that," Petra said. "Can you stand, do you think? Is anything broken?"

After a moment more of palpating his leg, he said, "No, I do not think it is broken. I think I have simply made my old injury worse."

"I am glad I came along, then," Petra said. She held out a hand to him. "Come on, up you get. Though I am not certain you deserve my help."

She had to leverage all her strength to pull him to his feet, as his bad leg could bear little weight. Still, at her words, the major released her hand to lean up against the tree. There was a sheen of sweat over his forehead from the exertion, dampening his fair hair. The skin beneath his eyes seemed to tighten.

"How do you mean?" he asked.

Petra put her hands to her hips. "Do not take that growling tone with me, sir, even if it is because you are hurt. I thought you an honorable man, and a gentleman."

"Ah, I wondered if she might tell you." He shrugged, some of the pain lessening from his face now that he was upright. "It was a risk on my part, I suppose."

Petra was aghast. "A risk? That is what you call doing your part in the ruination of a gently bred woman, and a widow to boot? One who, yes, can be a bit silly. And she has been married and has children, so she cannot be wholly a simpleton in such matters." She narrowed her eyes into a fierce glare. "Yet that is not the point, sir. You treated the countess very ill indeed. Seducing her *twice*? I hope you are not proud of yourself for proving to be a rake of the first order."

The major had listened to her rant, almost looking surprised, but then a small smile played at his lips.

"I agree it was badly done of me," he said. "I shall apologize to her ladyship with great ceremony if you will simply help me back to the Long Walk, where I might find a gentleman to assist me back to the castle."

"You must promise me that you will apologize to the countess, first thing after you are seen by the royal physician," she said as the major massaged his leg. Then she tilted her head. "Well, His Royal Highness is looking for you, so you shall have to find him first."

"The Prince?" the major said, his eyes narrowing as he abruptly stopped kneading his leg. "Did he send you to find me?"

"No," she said, silently cursing herself for saying such a thing. For if he repeated it, saying that it had come from her, then the Prince would know she had been listening to his conversation with Wolston, and he would not be pleased. Thinking quickly, she added, "I overheard Colonel Wolston asking someone if they had seen you, that is all."

The major nodded thoughtfully, then a bit of his charming smile appeared.

"I shall get my leg checked forthwith, then go directly to see His Royal Highness. But I shall promise you I will have apologized to the lovely countess by the end of the evening." He dipped his chin, and looked at Petra with a pitiable expression. "Now, will you help me, Lady Petra?"

Petra rolled her eyes and sighed with some dramatics. "Yes, fine. Put your arm about my shoulder."

The major did as she directed, all but slinging his arm around her neck as he was standing mostly on one leg. She took hold of his wrist, as he leaned all his weight on her, grunting as he tried to move his injured leg. They took one step and he jerked with a hiss, his forearm reflexively coming up under her throat.

"Major? Can you not hold any more of your own weight?" she

said on a cough. She tried to bring his wrist down, but it held fast at her neck. "Major?"

For a moment, she worried he had passed out from the pain, for he did not respond, and she found herself trapped in the crook of his arm, which was tightening rapidly, the wool of his coat rising up and covering her mouth... She began to hear panic pounding in her head as she used both hands, struggling to pull his arm down... And then he seemed to steady himself.

"My apologies, Lady Petra," he panted, lessening his hold. "I had to get my sea legs, as it were." And then he lifted his arm off of her as he gave an embarrassed chuckle. "I suppose I should have chosen someone taller."

Petra continued to cough, her eyes watering, yet she said, "Yes, I think you are right, Major."

"I think so as well, Major Carlson," came a deep, rough-sounding voice.

Petra blinked, a scarlet coat of the Coldstream Guards coming into view. Colonel Wolston was standing before her. His eyes roamed over her face in narrowed fashion, and then he switched his gaze to the major.

"Yes, you should have known better than to ask a woman to do a job that requires a man's strength. You should have asked Lady Petra to simply fetch help."

"I do apologize, my lady," said the major, looking quite distraught now.

But Petra just glared at Wolston. Duncan was right; he was a sod.

Wolston seemed to relish her seething. With a smirk, he walked over to give the major his shoulder. "His Royal Highness would like to see you. Thus, we must get on. Good day, Lady Petra."

And when the major had hobbled off—the height and broad shoulders of Colonel Wolston such that even when he leaned his weight on the colonel, it was not an issue—Petra was left scowling.

She turned back to the tree that had been the major's downfall. Then she looked around her to see if anyone else was nearby. She saw and heard no one. Then with two running steps, she launched herself up to grab the lowest limb, her walking boots scraping small pieces of bark from the tree trunk as they found purchase. A moment later, she was sitting on the tree limb, her feet swinging in the air.

"I would wager Colonel Wolston couldn't have done this in a silk dress," she said aloud with some triumph.

And there she stayed for the next quarter of an hour, simply thinking and letting her feet dangle, not caring if anyone should come along and tell her it was unladylike. No one did, however, and that suited her just fine.

Then her feet stilled with a thought so fleeting, she could not grasp it in time. She stayed sitting on the tree branch, observing the tree and her surroundings, waiting for the thought to return, but it did not. Finally, she gripped the tree limb with both hands on her left side before swinging herself off. She dangled for a moment, and then dropped, landing softly on the earth next to the tree trunk.

With her feet on the ground again, a thought did actually spring to mind, but it was about how she might keep her promise to Annie and check on Oliver. After a cup of tea, that was. Shaking out her skirts and dislodging a leaf or two, Petra began striding back toward the Long Walk, heading to the castle and the second library. Though when she reached the Quadrangle, what she saw stopped her in her tracks.

It was the six Lady Patronesses of Almack's again, all taking the air together, and looking about with a familiar expression—as if they were beautiful hawks searching for a bright-eyed rabbit into whom they could sink their talons.

Petra's eyes darted left, then right, looking for a way out. Then one spied her and thrust out an arm, giving away Petra's position.

Heart quickening, Petra fell into step beside a tall footman carrying a serving platter filled with glasses of lemonade, hoping he would obscure her from view. That she could make it across the expanse of the Quadrangle without having to succumb to making polite conversation.

The footman looked down, startled, and she whispered, "Keep moving, do!"

"Yes, my lady," he replied hastily, just as she heard a voice ringing out, "Why, I thought I saw Lady Petra. How strange indeed!"

Scurrying under the archway of the state entrance, she peeked back around the corner, still able to make out the six patronesses.

"Zounds, that was close," Petra breathed, a giggle of relief escaping as she made her way into the north wing.

TWENTY-SIX

Since she was already on the ground floor, she strolled into the main library in search of a cup of tea and did not mind at all when no one else was there except for two elderly, and rather deaf, ladies of rank. As they shouted gossip at each other from the recent scandal sheets, recounting the details wrong as often as right, they seemed completely unaware of Petra, who poured herself some hyson tea and sipped it, savoring the pale green freshness, as she went to sit on a chair by the windows.

"The terms they use today, Lady Ethelridge!" shouted one, a dowager countess, in a quavering voice. "Whatever do you think is meant by 'they were playing at the rantum-scantum'? Does it have anything to do with rats?"

"No, no, Lady Biddlecombe," replied the other, a dowager viscountess, at equal levels. "It means to make the beast with two backs, as one often said in our day. Only the scandal sheet I read said there were two gentlemen and one lady. Or was it two ladies and one gentleman? Thus, three backs?"

"Ah, yes," shouted the countess, nodding. "I did that once with Lord Buzbee and Lady Prudey—who was not a prude at all. Quite misnamed, that one. Enjoyed myself immensely with both of them. But then one marries an earl ten years one's senior and ends up in the wilds of Lincolnshire. Rather lessens one's opportunities!"

"Indeed!" returned the viscountess, adding, "I preferred the two gentlemen, myself, you know."

"Yes, I do, dear," said the countess, and they both broke into cackling laughs.

Pressing her lips together keep from laughing, Petra rose and hastily exited the library, passing the footman whose face had turned several shades of pink. Still, she could not help but think that it was just these types of stories that Sir Rufus had been planning on incorporating into his memoir. And such things would indeed scandalize the entire aristocracy, and titillate all of London.

It would sell more books for Lord Wadley-Bates than he could ever imagine, too, Petra mused as she moved quickly through the picture gallery, heading vaguely eastward, *Enough to provide ample dowries for all his daughters, would it not?*

Still, though she considered returning his lordship's name to her suspects list, there was something that made her think Lord Wadley-Bates really did believe the manuscript he sought was a cookery book. Duncan had felt the same, in fact, she recalled. Then her lips had made a little upward curve. He had told her when she lay entwined in his arms and legs last night, after a rather energetic bit of two-person rantum-scantum themselves.

Petra found the quiet halls calming as she strolled down a hallway with only an occasional niche holding a small bronze or marble statue. Realizing she was heading in the direction of the kitchens—where she was not allowed while Mrs. Bing was competing—she hastily turned a corner and found Mrs. Daley checking a windowsill for dust and tutting at one of her hall maids.

"Go fetch your cleaning rags and do these sills again, my girl," the housekeeper was saying, not unkindly. Turning and spying Petra, who had come to a hesitant stop, Mrs. Daley curtsied with a smile, as if it were a common occurrence to find guests wandering aimlessly in this section of the castle.

"How has your stay at Windsor been thus far, my lady?" she asked, to which Petra replied with very truthful praise for the Queen's hospitality, as well as Mrs. Daley and all her staff.

Mrs. Daley accepted this with a gracious nod, her eyes continuing to search Petra's countenance.

"If I may be so bold, my lady," she began, "I cannot fail to miss it when one of Her Majesty's guests has that particular look I can see on your face. It always tells me that something is required that said guest might find uncomfortable to request. Please know, you may ask me anything, and I shall hold it in the strictest confidence."

Petra realized she must appear somewhat worried, but in reality, she had simply realized she had been gifted an opportunity and was wondering how best to go about framing her question.

Just then, the hall maid returned with her cleaning rags and Mrs. Daley showed Petra back down the hall the way she had come, and into a small room.

It was a simple room with upholstered benches on each side, plus iron clothes hooks on the walls. There was one window overlooking the North Terrace, with two chairs and footstools positioned so that the sitter might enjoy the view.

"This is the former Pages' Room, my lady, but whilst they have accommodation elsewhere in the castle, we still call it that," explained Mrs. Daley. "It is now a place of quiet refuge for myself and the head butler, when needed. We will not be disturbed here, I assure you."

As they each took a chair, Petra rather blurted out her question.

"Mrs. Daley, might you know of an excellent hiding place for something small—about the size of a book?"

Quickly recovering her aplomb, Mrs. Daley confidently replied.

"My lady, I have been housekeeper here for twenty years, and I was every type of maid before that. I can say without question that there are hundreds of places in this castle where one might hide something the size of which you are discussing. And, as there are around a thousand rooms in this castle, and each one might have several places of concealment, well, the number would be quite high."

"I see," said Petra.

"Did you know that last year, one of my parlormaids accidentally knocked a painting down that had not been moved since before I came here?" said Mrs. Daley. "And behind it we found a loose piece of stone. Removing that stone, we found a drawing made by King Charles I in 1648, right before his execution early the next year. You know the castle was briefly used as a prison during that time by the Parliamentarians for those loyal to the crown, yes? The drawing was of the King's view from his window just two days before Christmas—he signed it, dated it, and wrote a few words about how much he loved England. He must have put it behind that loose stone, and there it stayed, completely hidden, for over a hundred and sixty-five years."

"Goodness," Petra said, feeling suddenly overwhelmed. She had but four days left to look—and that was only if someone else did not find Sir Rufus's memoir before her. It seemed she would never be able to discover it at this rate. She found her shoulders slumping, and after a pause, Mrs. Daley spoke in a cautious tone.

"May I be so bold as to ask . . ." she said. "Would this have anything to do with what Sir Rufus was writing? Well, one does hear things, my lady. Including the valet for Lord Wadley-Bates being late for his breakfast because his master had him up half the night searching the castle for a manuscript written by the late royal chef, rest his soul."

"You are correct, Mrs. Daley," Petra replied. "I am referring to Sir Rufus's papers. Lord Wadley-Bates, as his publisher, asked me to help recover them. It seems Sir Rufus hid them for reasons unknown, but it is most important that they be recovered."

"I expected as much," Mrs. Daley replied, and her particular expression told Petra she might know the papers were not simply a collection of recipes for another cookery book, but instead something much less wholesome.

Yet Petra felt it best not to provide confirmation. Though she trusted the Windsor Castle housekeeper, on the chance that Mrs. Daley was unsure of the contents, it was best to keep her own counsel.

"I'm afraid I could not tell you where Sir Rufus hid his papers, my lady," said Mrs. Daley finally. "But I can tell you that Lord Wadley-Bates and his valet were thorough in searching the gentlemen's quarters and the Green Drawing Room. I also know it could not be in the royal apartments, as they are guarded day and night by footmen."

"So that leaves how many rooms to search?"

Mrs. Daley chuckled. "Somewhere in excess of eight hundred, my lady."

"Heavens," Petra said faintly.

Mrs. Daley considered her for a long moment. Then she seemed to come to some decision.

"Would you like some assistance with your endeavor, my lady?" She lowered her voice, despite the fact that they could not be heard. "Only Her Majesty knows this, but I keep a team of trusted, experienced maids of all positions who are enlisted when I require something done... of a sensitive nature. If you should like us to help you search the castle, we would be honored."

Petra hesitated. What if one of these housemaids found the manuscript and read it? Naturally, though, Mrs. Daley seemed to already know her thoughts.

"I can assure you that none of my girls will do anything beyond locating the hiding place and then alerting me."

"I must confess I would greatly appreciate the help, Mrs. Daley," Petra said with a smile.

"It was one of my girls who told Colonel Wolston where to find the small safe Sir Rufus had been using and for which the colonel had been searching, in fact," said the housekeeper proudly.

"Truly?" Petra said. "Where was it?"

"It was in the Green Drawing Room, in one of the cabinets. My parlormaid had seen Sir Rufus opening it several times. She said she never saw anything in it other than quills and writing paper. But then she heard Sir Rufus tell someone that the key had been stolen—"

Mrs. Daley stopped abruptly. She looked uncomfortable and fiddled with one of the items on her chatelaine. Petra gave her a mild version of the cutty-eye.

"Mrs. Daley? I know you are aware of all that happened in the library yesterday morning. That Sir Rufus did not die in a natural way, but instead was murdered. And that his valet, Mr. Beecham, is said to have committed the crime."

A bit of pink tinged Mrs. Daley's cheeks. Petra continued on.

"Not only that, but Beecham is said to have stolen the key to a safe, and then all the items from within it. I admit I wondered how the key was found." She paused, then added, "Since I doubt one of your girls stole the key, might I be correct in thinking the parlormaid *found* the key and gave it to Colonel Wolston to implicate Mr. Beecham? If so, would she happen to be the same parlormaid that Mr. Beecham seduced?"

Mrs. Daley nodded with a sigh.

"Yes, my lady. And I do apologize on her behalf. Mr. Beecham used her quite ill, I'm afraid. I have already spoken to the girl and set her straight. Explained that the truth is always preferable to a lie, even when it hurts to say it. I took her to Colonel Wolston, where she confessed that the key was dropped by Sir Rufus, and she picked it up and . . . used the opportunity in quite the wrong manner. She explained Mr. Beecham did not steal from Sir Rufus."

"And?" Petra prompted, though she felt she already knew.

"The colonel was interested in what she had to say, but admitted that it does nothing to help his fate."

"I cannot claim surprise," Petra said darkly. Then she decided to take a chance. "Mrs. Daley, if I may continue to have your strictest confidence, both Mr. Shawcross and I do not believe that Mr. Beecham is guilty of killing Sir Rufus at all."

"Yes? Well, I confess that is good news to my ears," replied Mrs.

Daley. "As much of a rake as Mr. Beecham is, I did rather find his cheekiness endearing."

"I am worried that Mr. Beecham is being used quite ill himself, though," Petra continued. "That he is being set up to be a victim of some deception. I am attempting to discover who truly killed Sir Rufus as best I can, but I need to make certain there will be a Mr. Beecham, alive and well, to set free when I do. Will you help?"

A gleam came into Mrs. Daley's eyes. "I shall see what I can do, my lady. Do you simply wish to know his condition? Or are you hoping to lay eyes on Mr. Beecham yourself?"

Petra thought about Annie, and knew the answer straightaway.

"I would prefer to see him myself. Or have my lady's maid, Annie, go in my stead if time is of the essence and I am not available."

Mrs. Daley nodded, and it seemed her clever mind was already making plans.

"I have an idea brewing, my lady. I shall send word to you as soon as I can."

"My lords, ladies, and gentlemen, welcome to the second day of Her Majesty's patisserie contest! Eight cooks remain in the contest, and today we have the tasting of eight, no doubt delicious *apple cakes*."

The steward was in fine form again, and Petra idly wondered if he did indeed have a performer's background. He managed to have the crowd of aristocrats smiling, as well as the eight cooks, who were all lined up once more just outside the castle.

She glanced over at Mrs. Bing and was relieved to see her cook looking confident even though apple cake was rarely on Petra's menus. For while she enjoyed a slice every now and again, she had so many others she preferred and, thus, she did not know how much experience Mrs. Bing would bring to this particular bake.

She recalled that Sir Rufus used to make the cake in the Buckfields kitchens, though, for the earl would often send Petra in to beg some of the apples for whatever retired racehorse he had let live out its days in the beautiful paddock outside his study.

Once in the kitchens, she invariably would attempt to take as many apples as she could hold in the skirt of her dress, and recalled Sir Rufus playfully acting confused as he asked, "But how will I ever make my famous apple cake if you steal all the apples, Lady Petra?" To this, she would giggle and give all back but one. And then Sir Rufus would bow and present her with a second, as if he were offering her a crown.

Indeed, discovering your childhood idols were not who you thought they were did make a rather large lump form in one's throat. Hastily, Petra poured herself a cup of tea from the pot in front of her and sipped on it, letting the warmth calm her.

"Dearest, are you all right?" Caroline hissed from the corner of her mouth, looking at her worriedly.

Petra nodded, flashing her friend a quick smile. She then shifted her attention back to the steward, who was expounding on the attributes of an apple cake, or rather reading from an explanation written by Sir Franklin, who was nodding along with every word while the steward explained that the cake's dough should be spiced with coffee, sugar, and nutmeg or allspice.

"And, of course, butter!" the steward said merrily. "Then it is rolled out and spread over apples that have been pared, cored, and chopped into quite small bits—which are often combined with more butter. Afterward, there is much working of the dough, a process I am told is called folding, before rolling it out, and letting it sit about so that it doubles in size. Only then is it popped into an oven. After baking, it is given a thin icing made of confectioner's sugar and water, and should look something like this!"

The steward flung his arm out and it was then that two footmen removed a decorative linen from the table full of bakes to reveal eight silver cake stands. Each held a single apple cake, which looked to be more akin to a beautifully made loaf of bread, with dark swirls from the coffee and spices, as well as little bits of apples poking out here and there. Each cake seemed to have a different amount of the icing, from one with just drizzles to another that was nearly all coated in the glistening white mixture.

The crowd let out appreciative noises, which made the steward grin and the cooks give each other excitedly nervous glances.

The steward then told the crowd that the judges would be given three-quarters of an hour to do their taste testing. The cooks were escorted out just as he urged everyone to enjoy the lovely afternoon, but return with haste upon hearing the gong.

"Ready, my lord and lady judges? Yes? Then please begin!" he said, and gave an enthusiastic beat onto said gong before the crowd began milling away.

For this bake, each cook made only one apple cake, and a maid from the Windsor kitchens was cutting each of the eight loaves. Four slices from the middle of each cake were then taken and placed on plates for the judges, one slice per judge.

Using her fork, Petra cut her first bite of her first apple cake of the contest. She chose to take a bite from the center of the piece, and then a second that would contain part of the iced top.

She bit into the soft, bread-like dough, getting a delicious burst of bitter coffee sweetened with sugar and spiced with a bit of nutmeg. Then came the pieces of apple, giving a different kind of sweetness, plus a good texture as the fruit had not gone entirely soft.

The entirety of it was delicious, and she made notes on everything important about the slice of apple cake, and continued doing so until she had tasted every one.

And though her eighth, and last, slice of apple cake had been the best of the bunch—perfectly sweetened and tender, with the slightest hint of cinnamon mixed into the ideal amount of icing—she put her quill down slowly, and folded her page of notes listing her top six choices, feeling a touch out of sorts.

She poured one last cup of tea, and drank it down, watching the sunlight changing the color of the castle's exterior walls as a cloud drifted by. True, her spirits had returned to their normal state, as did her confidence in herself. Yet with them came the feeling of something in the air, like that charge before a storm that makes the hair on one's arms stand on end. She was worried something might happen if she didn't discover Sir Rufus's murderer soon.

She blinked and came back to herself when the steward's gong sounded, and soon the guests wandered their way back to hear the results. As the six remaining cooks all stepped forward when their names were called—huzzah, Mrs. Bing was one of them!—Petra clapped heartily, but her eyes kept glancing out into the crowd.

She watched Colonel Wolston standing with his arms crossed at the back of the crowd, his eyes flicking to meet hers. Lady Norworthy, holding her lorgnette spectacles up to her eyes as she peered at something in her hand, her frown growing deeper by the moment.

She noted Major Carlson, who inclined his head to her and then toward his left, where she could see he was seated next to the beautiful young countess, who looked quite happy with the arrangement. And Aunt Ophelia, who offered a wide smile... seconds before she was borne away by the Duchess of Hillmorton.

Then she turned to note Sir Franklin, who clapped and looked happier than she had ever seen him—especially when the next bake was announced as fairy cakes, which he could be heard telling Caroline were one of his favorites.

And lastly, there was the Prince Regent, who had barely clapped for the talented cooks—unlike the Queen, who had been effusive—before he launched himself out of his chair, motioned irritably toward Wolston, and returned to the castle.

Which of them was a murderer? And why did she now have the strange feeling there might be more than one?

TWENTY-SEVEN

"Dearest, when I pulled you aside after our judging duties were complete and demanded to know what was amiss with you, I did not expect you would have so bloody much to say. Or that you would be convincing me to forgo a lesson on the latest way to perform the Viennese waltz to help you search the castle."

Petra, who had told Caroline about all her latest findings—save for her worries about Aunt Ophelia and the true relationship between Annie and Oliver—nevertheless grinned.

"Grumble all you like, Caroline, but I recall that every time you visited Buckfields when we were girls, Papa would devise a treasure hunt for you, Duncan, and me, all due to your begging him to do so. And when you did not locate the treasure first, you would pout for hours afterward."

"It is unfair of you to call out my competitive side, for you know I cannot now give in," Caroline retorted. "And I only had to pout that one year, I must remind you. When we were all of eight years of age. Every other time, I discovered the treasure long before you and Duncan."

"That is only because Duncan and I worked so hard to thwart each other's progress in the beginning that we lost valuable searching time," Petra said.

Caroline gave her a mock look of pity.

"And to think it took you until you were four and twenty years old to realize how you felt about him." One dark eyebrow then arched high. "Oh, is this why you require my assistance? Because you cannot see what is right in front of you without my pointing it out?" She turned to the third person in Petra's bedchamber. "Would you not agree I have discovered the truth of this matter, Annie?"

Annie's hands went up as she took two steps backward with a laugh that was half amused, half nervous.

"Oh, no, Lady Caroline. You will not pit me between the two of you again on this count. I have learned my lesson."

"Spoilsport," Caroline said, pushing out her lower lip in an exaggerated pout and eliciting grins from Petra and Annie. Then the clock on Petra's mantel sounded six bright chimes, and she cleared her throat.

"All right," Petra said. "We know the manuscript cannot be in the royal apartments, and it was not found in any of the gentlemen's chambers. Mrs. Daley will be having her housemaids go through rooms in the north wing of the castle once the guests retire to their beds tonight. But they likely can only search a handful before they, too, need to be sent to their beds in anticipation of their early-morning duties. Thus, I have asked Mrs. Daley to give us a section of the castle to search where Sir Rufus was known to spend time. We are going to the Edward the Third Tower. Specifically, the drawing room. She told me that, before the celebrations started, Sir Rufus often spent time reading there in the evenings, as it is smaller and warmer than the Green Drawing Room."

"I have never known a cannier housekeeper than Mrs. Daley," Caroline mused, clearly impressed.

"Now, it is six o'clock, and the servants are at their evening meal belowstairs," Petra continued. "Mrs. Daley has arranged to make certain there will be no lady's maids or footmen in the tower for this one hour. And those guests staying in the rooms are all confirmed to be at various lectures." She looked to Annie. "Also, there is a wardrobe on the ground floor that is locked. If you will take the wardrobe, Caroline and I will begin going through the drawing room."

The three crept out into the corridor, until Annie reminded them that they need not do so, for there was no one about, and they were not, in fact, doing anything wrong.

"Right. Thank you, Annie," Petra said on a laugh, and they hurried to the tower, where Annie went down the circular staircase and Caroline and Petra climbed up to the next floor.

"Are you certain we should not go through some of the bedchambers?" Caroline asked as they surveyed the large drawing room, which was, as hoped, quite empty. "I would rather love to break in and have a look about. This is where the former queen's maids of honor lived, you know, and the intriguing stories one heard of their exploits . . ."

"And you think there would be proof of such from more than fifty years ago, do you?" Petra said, chuckling. "What, a love letter stuck behind the wardrobe or similar?"

Caroline shrugged, undeterred as she looked beneath sofa cushions. "It is possible. I was never allowed to go in during my childhood visits, so it would be such fun."

Petra, recalling Mrs. Daley's story of loose bricks behind paintings, was already looking behind each one she encountered on the wall. She also thought on Caroline's unbothered response when she gently broke the news that Sir Rufus's memoir contained scandalous references to her own parents, the Duke and Duchess of Carlingford. Petra remained a touch concerned that her friend was hiding her true feelings on the matter, even if she was not saying so.

"It would be quite fun to see where those exploits took place. If we have time, I think we should do just that."

Not long thereafter, Annie arrived. The wardrobe contained nothing but fresh linens and extra pillows. She then took the far side of the drawing room and joined the search. With the use of one of Petra's skeleton keys, she opened a locked *bureau à cylindre* desk at the far end of the room. Beneath the tambour door were the usual writing materials, quills, and ink.

Upon examination, Petra found nothing unusual except a crumpled piece of paper in the very back of one of the compartments. Caroline eagerly snatched it from her fingers, clearly expecting it to be one of the aforementioned naughty missives left over from a former lady-in-waiting. A moment later and with a disappointed sigh, she gave it back.

"It looks like something Frances would write when she dispenses a tincture for an ailing customer. It says 'Administer no more than one spoonful for desired effect.' It's written to Prinny, though. Of course I'm certain—look there, it reads, 'My Dear YRH.' My cousin allows those he knows well to use that abbreviation for Your Royal Highness. It was probably written by his physician."

Petra smoothed it out, noting it had yellowed, as if it had not been written recently. There was no date or signature, but the hand did seem a bit familiar. She noted that the words "no more" in the directive had been underlined twice. Whatever the Prince Regent had been prescribed, it was a potent mixture.

"Strange to have it be left here," Petra said. "Especially since it was clearly written long ago."

"Well, the desk was locked," Caroline said. "And Prinny is rather known for carrying bits and bobs in his pockets and then disposing of them whenever it pleases him. I expect he found it in his pocket ages ago, crumpled it, and threw it in the desk. No one noticed, and then the desk was locked. Oh, hello, Mrs. Daley. Would you agree?"

Petra looked up to find the housekeeper bobbing a curtsy in the doorway.

"If you'll pardon my overhearing, my ladies," she said, "Lady Caroline has the gist of it, for I have seen that very piece of paper. Last week, I was supervising the airing out of the guest rooms, and noted His Royal Highness looking at it as he and Sir Rufus related some diverting memory regarding the late Lord Carlson. Oh, no, I did not hear much of the story itself, Lady Petra, for I was too busy, but the two did enjoy a laugh about it. Yet when Major Carlson arrived, the Prince crumpled the paper with some haste, threw it into the desk, and locked it." She frowned. "Later, the major did ask if I had a key to the desk, and I said I would not open it without the permission of the Prince. It was curious, but whilst the major seemed cross, he then began laughing gaily, saying he already felt certain of what was on the page."

"How odd," Caroline said vaguely. "Do you have any other informative news for us, Mrs. Daley?"

"I'm afraid I do not bring word of the manuscript, my lady." Her eyes twinkled with satisfaction. "But I do bring a possible way to see Mr. Beecham."

"Truly?" Petra said, her focus shifting. Annie and Caroline both moved closer. "What is your plan?"

"One of the guards at Curfew Tower is rather sweet on one of my girls. He told her that between ten o'clock and ten minutes past, there is only one guard watching the dungeons—he himself. If you go down to the Lower Ward just after ten o'clock, my lady, the guard said he would allow you in to see Mr. Beecham. He warns that, with the time it takes to descend the stairs to the dungeon, and return, you will have no more than a minute or two with Mr. Beecham. But it will allow you to see him nonetheless."

"Mrs. Daley, I am indebted to you," Petra said with audible relief. "And I am quite fast at taking stairs, even in a dress, if I may say so. Now, where exactly do I go, and how can I be sure I am speaking with the correct guard?"

It was explained that the tower was behind a series of apartments used by the clerks, canons, and organist of St. George's Chapel.

"The lodgings are shaped like a horseshoe, so the area is referred to as the Horseshoe Cloister. Near the end of the Lower Ward, there is an entrance into the cloister that curves around the gardens to another passageway at the northwest side, and to Curfew Tower. The door at the far right is where the guard will be. I am not to tell you his name, but he has a quite visible scar across his cheekbone." She ran her finger in vertical fashion from just below her eye, almost to her lip. "Others have scars, but not like his. He is rather impossible to miss."

For a moment, the housekeeper wrung her hands.

"I must impress upon you, my lady, that you will have only enough time to see Mr. Beecham and ascertain his health. Then you *must* leave. If it is helpful, the guard claims Mr. Beecham is quite well. Thus, if you should not like to risk it, I have his word on the matter."

Petra managed a glance at Annie and saw her pleading eyes.

"I will go, Mrs. Daley, and if anything goes awry, I will ensure that no mention of your name or your very helpful housemaids will come about. I am hoping Mr. Beecham might have recalled something that would help us find the manuscript, or point us toward the person who killed poor Sir Rufus. Thus, I believe it is worth taking the risk."

TWENTY-EIGHT

As it turned out, the lesson regarding the latest steps in the Viennese waltz was so popular that the instructor offered a second class later that evening. Petra and Caroline, both having donned their evening dresses, rushed to Horn Court as soon as it was announced. And, it appeared, so did a good number of other ladies.

"We shall have to share the available men and dance with our fellow women, it seems," Caroline said, then called out, "Lady Ophelia, do come over and stand with us!"

"Darlings!" cried Aunt Ophelia, clasping hands tightly with first Petra, then Caroline, to give them kisses on the cheek. "I feel as if I have hardly seen either of you in the past two days. We must rectify that."

She turned, her silk dress the color of rosewood offset by a shawl of brightest magenta, making a swirl of color like the hottest part of a flame, and proceeded to tell two nearby ladies with great expansiveness how proud she was of her niece and Lady Caroline.

Petra felt a little odd hearing this after feeling her aunt had been evading her, not to mention several hours of determinedly avoiding her aunt all on her own. But as Caroline was as yet none the wiser of Petra's feelings on this particular score, all she could do was be as blithe as her aunt until the waltz instructor took to the floor and began his teachings.

"I do not care if Lord Byron decried this type of close dancing so much that he wrote an awful poem about it," whispered Caroline as the instructor explained the steps. "Being able to dance all but held in my Whitfield's strong arms is the way I should always like it to be."

The mention of Byron made Petra look around the room for Major Carlson, for she thought she had seen his stoic countenance and fair hair standing near Lady Norworthy, but he was nowhere to be seen as the instructor announced they would soon be pairing off to try the new steps.

"What if you do not enjoy being so close to your dance partner?" Petra asked as she discreetly nodded to a couple of men in the crowd, both of whom she and Caroline never particularly cared to have on their dance cards.

"Then I shall simply suggest a country dance," Caroline replied. "Oh, good, it is time for us to practice."

And within seconds, a handsome gentleman had borne Caroline to the dance floor. Petra saw one of the more odious men striding her way and muttered, "Bollocks."

"Darling, dance the waltz with me?" Aunt Ophelia said, holding out her hand as she glanced quickly toward the approaching gentleman.

"I would be honored," Petra replied hastily and the two moved quickly onto the dance floor, much to the gentleman's chagrin. "Thank you," she whispered.

"Petra my love, you know I will always do my best to protect you," her aunt replied with a smile. Before Petra could form a reply, the instructor was calling out reminders on how the dancers should begin.

As instructed, Petra and her aunt put their right arms about each other's waists, and then clasped their left hands before raising them high in a graceful arc above their heads. The orchestra played the lively music at a slower pace to allow everyone to learn the movements as the instructor called out the steps.

"All right, my lords, ladies, and gentlemen. Now, if you and your partner will turn in a small circle, just as I showed you. Up slightly on your toes. That's it. *One*, two, three, *one*, two, three. Keep turning, if you will!"

Possibly it was the music relaxing her, but Petra felt the return of her usual courage to do what was needed. "Aunt Ophelia," she began as they spun easily to the rhythm. "I really must speak with you."

"About what, darling?" she asked, smiling. Petra, however, did not return the gesture as they continued to dance in a circle.

"About Sir Rufus. It is important."

The instructor then called for the partners to switch arms, clasping their right hands before raising them in an arc.

Her aunt fumbled, tripping a bit over her own feet, and she laughed at herself before saying, "Sir Rufus? Well, I cannot think why. But whatever it is, it must wait as I am determined to concentrate on this. I promised to teach my handsome vicar upon my return home."

Almost as if her aunt had wished it, the orchestra began to speed up to the normal tempo and the instructor was loudly counting, "*One*, two, three, *one*, two, three," over and over, clapping to emphasize the steps. There was laughter all around as partners tried to master the quicker steps, with some being better than others.

And just as Petra was about to insist again to her aunt that they speak, the instructor called out, "Now, let us all change partners and practice with someone else!"

Before she could do anything, her aunt had given her a peck on the cheek, saying, "Darling, you are a wonderful dancer. Thank you for partnering me!" even as she was being led off by an enthusiastic-looking viscount.

Sighing, Petra spied Lady Norworthy looking about for a partner. "Excellent," she said under her breath, and aimed in her ladyship's direction, only to be stopped in her tracks by Sir Franklin.

"Would you be so kind as to partner me, Lady Petra?" he said with a little bow. "For I should like to speak with you in some semblance of privacy. It is regarding a matter of great importance." He gave a little half smile that was almost shy, and a fine sheen of sweat had broken out upon his forehead. "To both of us."

"Oh?" Petra said, a bit flummoxed.

Much belatedly, she vaguely recalled seeing Sir Franklin casting glances toward her before their second day of judging had begun. He was a widower fifteen years her senior, though he seemed quite a bit older, with his thin, hunched shoulders, balding pate, and hooked nose. He had proven to be a kind man, and quite knowledgeable of baking practices, as evidenced by the description of apple cakes he had written out for the steward to read to the audience.

But, lawks, she now remembered overhearing gossip that Sir Franklin was wishing to marry again. Was he thinking that her kindness to him was a willingness to consider a courtship? Or even a proposal?

Oh, this cannot happen, she thought wildly as she looked about for an escape.

And then she spied the tall, stern form of Lady Norworthy striding toward her.

"I must offer my apologies, Sir Franklin," Petra said with a smile, "but I promised to partner with—"

Then Lady Norworthy was standing there. "Sir Franklin, you are tall enough to dance with me. Will you allow me to practice the waltz with you?" She turned to Petra. "If you do not mind, of course, Lady Petra."

Feeling both relieved and as if her plans to speak with Lady Norworthy had been foiled again, Petra backed away with a smile, pretending not to notice as Sir Franklin's eyes went wide with surprise and his mouth opened and closed, but no sound emerged.

She stayed long enough to see Lady Norworthy all but yank a stunned-looking Sir Franklin's arm up and over his head as the music started again. She looked around for Aunt Ophelia, and found her viscount partner dancing with someone new.

Petra hurried out of the courtyard, her eyes searching for that bright magenta shawl. Once again, her attempt was thwarted as she made her way into the Quadrangle in search of her aunt, only to find the grounds had become as lively as the night before, if not more so.

Torches burned everywhere, lighting up the open space that, later in the week, would be the site of the tilting tournament. Jaunty tunes were being played by five violin players. As Petra wended her way through throngs of gentlemen laughing, playing cards, and watching more friendly boxing matches in the makeshift ring, she spied the Prince Regent sitting once more in his opulent chair as others—even the much older gentlemen—sat upon wooden benches. They all were eating legs of chicken and hunks of bread off pewter plates and listening to some story that one of them was telling, all nodding sagely as their teeth tore at their meal.

"If I were you," drawled the Prince, loud enough for Petra to hear as she passed by, "I would bring them back to heel *tout de suite*. Would you not agree, Wolston?"

Petra glanced sideways to see that the colonel was standing just behind the Prince, feet slightly apart and arms behind his back, like a guard dog on two feet. He met Petra's eyes as he replied, loud enough to be heard above the din.

"Indeed I would, Your Royal Highness."

Though she kept walking as if she had not heard, Petra shivered involuntarily. Not at Wolston's steely gaze—despite knowing she would soon be encouraging one of his guards to disobey orders at Curfew Tower—but instead at the Prince Regent.

Petra had not grown up idolizing the royal family, truth be known. Respecting them, yes, but not revering them. She behaved with the decorum expected of her when she was around one or more of the royals, but she did not see them as having a divine right to anything, much less to rule England.

Yet they were her monarchs, her Prince Regent, and her princes and princesses. She felt loyalty to them nonetheless, and was proud to be one of their subjects, especially when they supported charities that helped improve the lives of her fellow English men and women, whether that be groups providing assistance to the poorest members of society or groups that helped advance the sciences.

But loyalty to the royal family did not make Petra remotely blind to the unsavory aspects she occasionally witnessed.

Nor would it make her accepting of a prince regent who might have taken the life of one of his subjects, if that were the case.

Frustratingly, while Aunt Ophelia's continued avoidance of her was not making Petra more confident in her innocence, she could not shake the feeling that her aunt might not be the only person who could be considered at fault. Though whether another culprit's malfeasance was regarding the death of Sir Rufus, or something else entirely, she was not quite certain.

Feeling as if she'd had quite enough for one day—with more still to come in less than an hour when she attempted to see Oliver in Curfew Tower—Petra collected a lit candle from a hall maid and made her way back to the south wing and her bedchamber, thinking a lie-down might be in order, just for a bit.

Though when she turned in to her corridor, she stopped. In the darkness of the end of the hall, something was there. Standing stock-still, like a predator might, making no noise at all.

She blinked, and then it began sprinting toward her. She cried out when it was a halfway to her—but her cry was one of joy.

"Sable!" she gasped. Placing the candle on a nearby chest, she crouched down to greet the pointing dog who was galloping her way, her rope lead still affixed to her collar. "Oh, my darling! How are you here?"

Then her hound was wiggling with supreme happiness, circling her, coming in for kisses and ear scratches, only to move out again, panting ecstatically as her tail wagged furiously. And at the same time, Petra could hear sounds of exclamation.

She looked up and saw one familiar face, then a second. Both belonged to humans, and were quite dear. And one of them was holding the lead of another dog.

"Lottie! Frances! You are here early! Oh, I am delighted! But how is this so?"

And then the door to her own chamber opened, with Annie first poking her head out before opening the door wide to let everyone into the room, which was cheerfully lit by a bright fire and two candelabras.

Petra and her friends were clasping hands and giving each other kisses on each cheek as everyone spoke at once.

"We both received a letter," said Lottie Reed, her light green eyes bright with merriment and her white-blond curls springing out from under a pink bonnet. Fitz, the terrier on a lead, was standing on his hind feet, begging Petra to pet him. She happily obliged.

"From Her Majesty's steward," added Frances Bardwell, her own bonnet flung back to reveal her pin-straight dark fringe and a wide smile that fully reached her brown eyes.

"We were asked to come early, as the fair was larger than expected."

"We thought we would be at Frogmore House, so that's where we directed the carriage."

"But our things were being taken here, to the castle. We just arrived, and shall be next to you and Caroline."

"Did I hear my name?" Caroline said, coming into Petra's room.

"Look who's here," Petra said.

With happy exclamations, Caroline rushed over to greet their friends.

"Excellent," she said, picking up Fitz and cuddling him to her cheek. "Now I shall not have to wait outside the dungeon on my own."

Frances and Lottie both stilled, their eyes going wide at hearing the word "dungeon." Smiling, Annie said, "I shall fetch some tea and food, my lady."

"And I shall explain," Petra said.

Less than an hour later, the dogs were left in the care of Caroline's lady's maid as Petra, Lottie, Frances, Caroline, and Annie made their way down to the Lower Ward, chatting amiably.

There were small groups of ladies here and there walking about, seemingly more than willing to be out in a safe place in the still-pleasant night air and leave the men to their carousing back in the Quadrangle. The occasional gentleman walking with a lady on his arm could be seen as well.

Yet when Petra and her friends entered the passageway to the Horseshoe Cloister, it was peacefully empty. They saw two other guardsmen striding off in the distance in the direction of the castle, one clapping the other on the back, but no one else. Moving through the second passageway, the others hung back while Petra and Annie approached the guard with the scar over his cheekbone.

He held the lead of a harrier, the breed of hound favored by His Majesty, the King, for rabbit hunting. While Petra knew most harriers were friendly, this one clearly took his guarding duties seriously, emitting a brief woof of warning as the bells of St. George's Chapel struck ten o'clock. The guard with the scar frowned, clearly recognizing Petra.

"I don't know if you should go in, my lady," he said, his eyes darting about.

"And why is that, guard?" she replied. And when he did not answer, Petra said, "Though you will not stop me, I take it?"

He worked his jaw for a moment, then shook his head. "But if you have not returned in under ten minutes, my lady . . . And it will take you some of that simply to make it down to the dungeons . . ."

"My lady's maid and I will take the chance," Petra said firmly. "Now, please open the door."

The inside of Curfew Tower was dark and a bit spooky on the ground floor, even with torches burning brightly in various brackets. Two lamps, already lit, were near the staircase leading down to the dungeons. She and Annie each took one and together rushed down the stairs.

The dungeon was nearly pitch-black, and the smell of an earthen floor mixed with the sharp stench of urine assaulted her nose. Annie found a torch on the wall and lit it for extra light.

There were a series of cells built into the round room, all with iron gates. Rusted iron shackles set into the stone walls—left over from the time of the English Civil War—hung ominously still. Yet with the flickering of the torchlight, they also seemed like they might move on their own at any moment, as if ghosts of prisoners past were still restrained by their wrists and ankles and had been stunned into temporary stillness by the sight of two women.

"Oliver?" Annie called out.

There was no answer.

Petra pointed across the room. "Annie, take that side and look into each cell, I will take this side."

Using her lantern, Petra peered into the first cell. It was barely large enough for a grown man to lie down in, and she nearly let out a yelp as a rat scurried across the floor, slipping through a hole in the wall. The next was the same, only thankfully without vermin. In the third cell, she saw him.

"Oliver!" she exclaimed.

He was in a heap on the ground, unconscious, his face a bloody mess. She could not tell if he was dead or alive.

Petra had her lockpicks out before Annie had even run across the dungeon. Annie called her brother's name as she gripped the iron bars, but there was no answer.

Already working her picks, Petra stopped and turned to Annie, who had let out a whimper of fear.

"Go back upstairs and get Frances. She noted some herbs in the cloister gardens that were excellent for healing. Tell her we may need them."

"Please do not let my brother die, my lady," Annie said, her hazel eyes huge with worry.

"I will do everything in my power. Now go."

And as Annie's boots made rapid taps up the stairs, Petra resumed working her picks. Then she was swinging the iron gate wide and rushed inside, dropping to her knees beside Oliver.

She felt for a pulse—it was there. Then she could see Oliver's chest rise and fall.

From her reticule she produced a small flask of barley water and her handkerchief. Wetting the soft linen, she used it to wipe blood from Oliver's mouth and nose, feeling relief when his eyes fluttered open and he winced.

"You will be all right," she said, as he spit out some blood with a groan. "Help is coming."

Indeed, there were sounds of boots on the stairs, and Petra concentrated on giving Oliver a drink of the barley water as she shouted, "Frances! Hurry, do!"

The voice that came from outside the cell, however, was entirely too deep.

"Your friend shall not be coming, Lady Petra. And you should not be here, with my prisoner."

As she was already bent over him, Petra whispered three words into Oliver's ear. "Do. Not. Move." Then she stood and turned to see three red uniforms the color of darkest blood in the dim light, with Colonel Wolston advancing slowly toward her.

Twenty-Nine

"What is this?" Petra snapped, glaring imperiously at each of the three guards; the one with the scar, who had allowed her entry, noticeably absent. Then she took in the bayonets being held by the two flanking Wolston and a shot of fear sliced her belly even as she shifted to stand between Oliver and these soldiers.

Wolston came to the open cell door, and held out a gloved hand.

"Come, Lady Petra. I shall take you aboveground again, and I shall not tell the Prince Regent you violated his orders if you leave quietly."

Petra did not acquiesce, though it was briefly tempting. Instead, she flung out her hand, gesturing to Oliver, who had wisely gone still, his eyes closed and bloodied mouth slack.

"What have you done to this man? He has been beaten."

Wolston shrugged. "We should like a confession before he is hanged, my lady."

"And?" she demanded, when he did not continue.

"And Beecham has not given us one."

Petra gaped for a moment, and then said, "Are you bloody well in earnest?"

This caused the two bayonet-wielding guards to glance at each other in a mixture of shock and humor, and one side of Wolston's mouth tick upward, which only made her pique rise.

"So, Colonel Wolston, you are telling me that you intend to beat this man into a confession, when no one has yet proven him guilty, much less you?"

She saw a flash of anger come into the colonel's eyes, but it did not make her back down.

"For if you had done your job, as the guardsmen of Windsor should, you would have investigated this crime properly, as I have. And if you had so much as asked a few housemaids, or even Mrs. Daley, you would have been able to determine that there are several people in this castle who could have killed Sir Rufus."

"Does that include Beecham here, my lady?" Wolston said lazily, but she could hear the thread of steel behind his words.

"Do you know what, Colonel?" she said, taking one minute step forward, but not enough that he could easily reach out and yank her from the cell and Oliver's side. Not without her having the leverage to do something hurtful to him first. "It actually does not. Would you care to know why?"

Wolston seemed amused by her anger now and crossed his arms over his chest.

"Do tell, Lady Petra. I am all aquiver to know."

This made the other guards chuckle, of course. And though she wished to yell the words, she bit them back, and straightened her spine. She spoke calmly—and only a bit through gritted teeth, for men who insulted her intelligence would never cease to infuriate her.

"Because Mr. Beecham here, as a valet, was not wearing gloves, and there is no way he could have choked a fully grown man with a very slippery silk ribbon without so much as reddened hands, or a cut, or a blister. And yet he had none of those things. Mr. Shawcross and I both realized this after you had taken Beecham away, and we will testify as such."

Wolston scoffed at this. "He could have worn gloves to do the deed, and then hidden them when he heard that housemaid coming."

"And yet Mr. Shawcross searched the library afterward and found no gloves," Petra shot back. "Also, regarding the safe key you claimed to have found on Mr. Beecham. I watched as your nimble-fingered guard searched him. I know that it was placed on Mr. Beecham's person."

"Then why did you not say so at the time, my lady? It is not as if I did not give you ample opportunity," Wolston said, arching one eyebrow.

"I wished to make certain of what I saw," she replied a touch lamely, knowing it sounded like something a silly woman who could not make decisions on her own would say. Which was exactly what Wolston expected to hear.

"You could have come to speak with me after you talked with Shawcross," he returned. "I am certain he would have granted you permission to do so."

Petra, in her embarrassed frustration, had looked to the floor. But upon hearing him claim that Duncan held control over her, she stilled, her head still tilted down.

Then slowly, she raised just her eyes to Wolston's. And when she held his gaze, only then did she lift her chin to level.

She was focused on Wolston, but she saw the two guards behind him shift slightly. A maddened woman who screeches and flails and yells, that was what he was expecting to incur with his comment. It was not what he saw, and she could tell when his eyes widened a fraction.

"Do you not agree," she said evenly, though her eyes never left his, "that a citizen is presumed innocent until they are *proven* guilty? And a person who cannot be proven to be as such should not be beaten until he confesses to something he did not do?"

Her voice, while it did not grow louder, did grow stronger as she bent and lifted her lantern by its wire handle.

"And do you not agree, that a citizen whose guilt cannot be established, and who is wholly beaten until half dead, deserves to have the same respect and care that is owed to all of us?"

Wolston did not reply, but he glanced down at Oliver. Petra had held the lantern over the valet's face, allowing the light to illuminate the extent of his injuries. Oddly, for a moment she felt as if Wolston seemed surprised at what he saw. And by the way a muscle briefly throbbed in his jaw, he seemed angered as well, before his expression smoothed into a mask as still as Oliver's own form.

"Now, you will allow me to call my friend, Miss Bardwell, down, as well as my lady's maid. Miss Bardwell is an apothecarist, and a damned brilliant one at that," she said, eliciting another twitch from the guards at her use of unladylike language. "You will allow us to care for Mr. Beecham and ensure that he is not in danger of taking a turn for the worse. You will bring us whatever it is that we require, and that includes food and water for Mr. Beecham."

"And if I refuse?" Wolston asked, his slight smirk back in place.

Petra took another step forward.

"Then I shall use every bit of influence at my disposal to make certain that my logical and reasonable requests are granted. And you should not underestimate my influence, Colonel Wolston, for I have quite a bit."

She tilted her head just a bit to the side, and batted her eyes with a charming baring of her teeth.

"Thus, Colonel, you have two choices. You can either do as I ask, and the royal family shall never know. Or I can go to the Prince Regent, and Her Majesty, the Queen, and you can see just how much you like your job once I have swayed them to see my point of view."

Behind him, the two guards cast their eyes down, just in case Wolston had turned to see if they were laughing at his expense.

"Do it," he said to his men without looking anywhere but at Petra. "One of you bring the two ladies. The other, fetch supplies and food. Go. Now."

The two men turned and dashed up the stairs. Petra did not move from her position, however. She had not ceased boring her gaze into Wolston's face, and did not stop now.

"Thank you," she said crisply nonetheless.

Wolston changed his stance, resting his weight on one of his legs, the other bent slightly at the knee and turned out. One of his thumbs hooked into the belt about his scarlet coat.

"So you are the one," he said.

"I am the one, what?" she asked, feeling her hackles start to rise again.

"The woman responsible for saving Prince Frederick, and indeed our entire nation, from the threats of radicals." A little smile came onto his lips. And for once, it was not mocking. "You are the one who saved those women from the asylum."

Petra lifted her chin again, unwilling to trust he was being truly complimentary.

"And if I am?"

He didn't speak for a moment, just regarded her.

"Well done," he finally said, and gave her a brief bow at the neck.

There came the sound of feet on stairs again. When he turned to walk away, she took a chance and called out, "Colonel Wolston. Why do I have the feeling that you did not, in fact, order the extensive beating of this man?" She pointed down to Oliver, who had slightly moved his head, grimacing as he did.

"Because I did not, Lady Petra. Now, you are welcome to tend to my prisoner. Yet I have my orders for the present. You must do as you see fit, but I shall continue to keep him here until my own general says otherwise."

Annie and Frances were flying down the last few steps, torches in hand, their eyes already on Oliver. But Wolston's own looked into Petra's with meaning.

It was what she already knew, but he was giving it further impact.

Wolston was saying that His Royal Highness, the Prince Regent, was giving the orders. And he was telling Petra that he, too, knew they were dead wrong.

THIRTY

Thursday, 7 September 1815
Day four of the royal celebrations

"Wake up, my lady. We must ready you to meet with Chef Carême."

Petra tried to swat Annie's hands away as they gently shook her shoulders, but she was on her stomach, making her sleep-weakened flapping the very definition of ineffectual.

"What was that, my lady?" Annie said in a singsong voice, knowing full well that Petra had said nothing other than incoherent mumbling. "You wish for Sable to fetch a stick? Why, I feel as if she would be happy to. Let me throw one. Oh dear, it has landed directly on your ladyship's bum."

And before Petra could say "I am awake!" she was being pushed deeper into the soft bed by three stone's worth of happy dog lying across her lower back.

"Blast," muttered Petra, her curse sounding as weak as her one-eyed glare at Annie, who was still standing at the side of the bed.

"Whilst you are pinned down, my lady, I have something to say."

"And you cannot say it when I am on my feet, making my way to the chamber pot?" Petra asked with a yawn.

"I should like you to stay where you are, just for a moment, so that you cannot pretend as if you do not need to hear my words."

Petra opened both eyes. Annie's voice had gone quite serious.

Was she wishing to leave her employ? Had Oliver's near death the night before made her feel as if being a part of Petra's world was too dangerous?

"What is it, Annie?" she said in a near whisper. Even Sable stopped chewing her stick long enough to perk up her ears and look curiously between the two women.

Annie's hazel eyes were filled with emotion. "Oliver told me what you did for him last night, my lady. What you said to Colonel Wolston—and what you threatened as well. How you put your own influence with the royal family on the line for him, and thus for me. I wish for you to know how much it means to me. I am more indebted to you than you can know. And so is Oliver. We both now have hope that he will be exonerated, and I am so very, very grateful."

Gently pushing Sable off her, Petra sat up, swung her legs over the side of the bed, and took Annie's hands.

"You owe me nothing, Annie, for I would not be half the woman I am without your patience and kindness and ability to push me in the right direction year after year. I am indebted to you as well, and always will be."

There was a bit of sniffling from each, which had Sable coming over and licking both their faces, bringing laughter back to the room.

"But we must remember that we cannot sit on our laurels as far as Oliver is concerned. There is still much to determine."

Indeed, Frances told them later that, had Oliver not received attention for his wounds when he did, he would have been a lot worse off. Between Frances and Annie, they were able to clean and dress his cuts, and get some food and water in him—plus one of Frances's concoctions for pain.

Petra and Caroline, working their charms in tandem, were able to then convince the guards to obtain permission from Wolston for a pallet for Oliver to lie upon, and a blanket—albeit a thin one—to cover him. And Lottie did her part by delighting the guards with her ability to teach the harrier a trick to offer his paw to shake.

In all, they stayed, tending to Oliver, for nearly two hours, and only agreed to leave when Wolston sent word consenting Annie or Frances to come every night at ten o'clock to see to Oliver and check his wounds, making the guard with the scar—who only had to endure a dressing-down from Wolston, and not anything worse—say with something like awe, "Cor, my lady. I ain't never heard Colonel Wolston give in to no one. Hat's off to you."

Now, Petra ruffled Sable's silky ears and said, "Oh, how I wish Duncan would return, just because I wish to see his face. But for now, I must see another handsome man and fulfill my obligation to the Prince, whether I wish to help His Royal Highness or not."

Giving her hound a kiss on the head, she went off to make her ablutions and meet Chef Antonin Carême in hopes of convincing him to stay in England for another two years.

"No!"

Even with a French accent, that word did not sound any better to Petra's ears.

Especially when the handsome chef threw a towel over his shoulder and turned to stalk out of the vaulted undercroft, which was empty at present except for the two of them, a tray with expertly made coffee in a silver pot, two cups and saucers, and then a plate holding three delicious-looking flaky pastries he called his croissants, with two pots on the side. One containing fresh butter, the other filled with his raspberry preserves. Petra, in explaining her reasons for wishing to talk with the chef on behalf of the Prince, had not even had the time to try any of it before he uttered that one syllable and turned to leave the room.

"But Chef Antonin," she said, hurrying after him. "The Prince believes you to be the best chef in the world, and he wishes to honor you by asking you to stay for another two years complete."

"Bah," said Carême, stopping and turning back to face her. "The Prince, he does not honor me." He switched into French, adding, "He wishes nothing more than to parade me around as a symbol of how the English conquered my country. And then he demands I cook what he likes, and yet most people at his table prefer—how do you English call it—the nursery food. Such simple, stodgy food with no flavor or flair! No, I will not stay, Lady Petra, even for one as beautiful and delightful as you."

As quickly as it had come on, his temper softened, and those lovely dark eyes of his roamed over her face, lingering on her lips.

"For you will be gone come Monday, and I will be left in this dreary, gray country without your light and beauty to make it better."

Oh, heavens, she thought helplessly. She felt rather lost in his gaze for a moment, but the back of her mind was registering that her knees were not in danger of feeling weak, nor were there butterflies erupting low in her belly. Not the way they did when Duncan Shawcross so much as came within six feet of her. Not the way they did when Duncan showed her how he loved her intelligence, her humor, and her strength of character as much as he did her body.

Yet she let herself enjoy the feeling of being adored by another handsome man, just for a moment. Quite a long moment, in fact.

"What would it take for you to stay here for another two years, and train eight chefs to take over for you when you return to your country?"

She put her hands behind her back and walked a slow circle around him, knowing he would follow her every move, especially because she knew her cornflower-blue silk dress brought out her eyes, and her bosom would look to be about to burst forth from the top of her bodice when she adjusted the grip of her hands at her back. To emphasize her points, as it were, she, too, switched to French.

"What if you asked for a salary that would enable you to return to France with enough money to open your own restaurant?" She blinked up at him innocently. "Or if you obtained it in writing that you have final say over every menu for a state dinner?" Pulling her lower lip briefly into her mouth and then releasing it, she asked, "Or if you asked for both?"

The chef's eyes did not leave her lips. "You are quite persuasive, Lady Petra."

She stopped and smiled broadly. "But did it work, Chef Antonin?"

He glared at her with appreciation for her tactics while muttering a few mild curses, and then tilted his head back toward the tray of coffee and croissants.

"I shall think about it, yes? Now, come try my croissants and *confiture de framboises*, and tell me what you think. For I expect you, *mon cherie*, have much more appreciation for delicious food than the Prince who has sent you here to charm me."

He took two steps then stopped abruptly.

"But, I will never agree to training eight chefs!" He held up one splayed hand, plus the thumb of his other. "Six, at most!"

THIRTY-ONE

FEELING AS IF SHE HAD ACCOMPLISHED AT LEAST ONE THING properly in convincing Chef Carême to stay in the Prince's employ, Petra gave herself over to enjoying the day.

She spent part of her morning assisting Frances as she led a demonstration about household apothecary needs. Frances didn't truly need an assistant, but as she was never comfortable in crowds and some forty women arrived in Brick Court to hear her speak, Petra simply stood by her friend and held up ingredients until Frances became so lost in her explanations that she overcame her anxieties.

Afterward, Petra helped Lottie as she displayed her exceptional dog-training skills out in the Quadrangle. Though Fitz and Sable had been allowed in the castle, Lottie had also brought another three dogs with her, all in various stages of their training. They were being looked after by the Master of Hounds in the dog kennels when not performing their tricks, obedience, or agility in leaping over a series of small obstacles put in their path.

Then, later in the afternoon, Caroline would be displaying her archery skills again. This time alongside three other lady archers, and Petra was looking forward to watching her friend's talents shine.

But first, she and Petra had the important task of judging the next bake in the patisserie contest—the fairy cake.

As they arrived at the judging table, Lord Wadley-Bates immediately engaged Caroline in conversation about the technical aspects of archery. Petra listened on, distracted enough that she did not notice when Sir Franklin hurried over.

"Lady Petra," he said in an undertone, moving slightly too close, "I must speak with you. Might you promise me a few moments of your time after we complete our judging duties today? It truly is important that we speak. I must confess something from my very soul."

Petra took a slight step back, noting that he looked a bit disheveled and wild-eyed, as if he were filled with nervous energy at doing something that required his fortitude. It rather reminded her of one of her past suitors who asked for her hand.

Could Sir Franklin truly be thinking that she might accept a proposal? Surely not, and she felt a firm deterrent might be best. Yet since guests were beginning to arrive to observe the start of the judging, she walked him over to the low wall forming the edge of the North Terrace.

"Sir Franklin," she said kindly, "I am mindful of the honor you are attempting to bestow, but I am afraid I do not wish to ever—"

His eyes flew wide, then his brows slammed together as he lowered his voice to a hissing whisper.

"What? I do beg your pardon, Lady Petra, but I had no intention of asking for your hand. No, my confession is about something else entirely. Something infinitely more important to my well-being."

He stared into her eyes, as if wishing her to read his mind. When she did not, he hissed, "It is in regard to Sir Rufus."

Petra's gasp was lost within the low rumble from the crowd. Could it be? Was Sir Franklin about to confess to killing Sir Rufus?

"Judges, would you please take your places?" said Her Majesty's steward with a smile and a bow.

Petra gave Sir Franklin a nod. "After the judging," she said as they made their way to the table.

Lord Wadley-Bates took his seat next to Petra with the same hopeful look he had given her each time they crossed paths since the night she had found him in Sir Rufus's bedchamber. But of his lordship's look, she had no confusion; he was hoping she had found the missing manuscript.

"I am afraid not yet," she said quietly. "But I am looking diligently."

"I can only hope it will be found, for the money is sorely needed," he said, his expression turned downcast.

Petra put the question to Lord Wadley-Bates that she had been wanting to for two days now. "My lord, is that all the manuscript is? Simply another book of Sir Rufus's recipes?"

Lord Wadley-Bates blinked at her. "Of course, Lady Petra. That is what my publishing house does—cookery books and gardening books. That is all. What else would he have written?"

"Nothing, my lord," she said. "It was but a silly question, I assure you."

This seemed an acceptable answer to him, and then they both looked around to see that Caroline had taken her seat to the left of Petra but was frowning at the linen tablecloth. Due to the efforts of some unknown passing bird, it now required a cleaning.

Sir Franklin gallantly offered to switch places with Caroline as one of the footmen arrived with their individual pots of tea, along with cups and saucers. In the crowd, Petra spotted Lottie and Frances and gave them a little wave.

"My lords, ladies, and gentlemen!" sang out the steward, with his usual flair. "There are six bakers left in Her Majesty's patisserie contest, and six amazing cooks they are! Their Shrewsbury cakes shone, their apple cakes inspired awe, and today they shall endeavor to show us how festive they can be in not only the baking of, but also the decorating of, *fairy cakes*."

The crowd all glanced at one another with excitement. Thus far, the bakes had featured little in the way of adornment. This time was different. It was not just about how the small round cakes about the size of a fist tasted and were baked, but also how they enticed the eye.

Petra gave the smallest of glances over to the six cooks. She was happy to see they all looked excited and nervous, but determined, including Mrs. Bing.

"Each cook was asked to make a fairy cake of simple vanilla sponge. Delicious in and of itself, as we all know," continued the steward, smiling and nodding at the crowd, who chuckled in return and nodded their agreement. Fairy cakes in any form were always welcomed at everyone's table, it was clear.

The steward checked the piece of paper Sir Franklin had given him with notes on what to say.

"Our six cooks are being judged on how their fairy cakes look and taste, first and foremost. But, there is more! Our cooks were to choose whatever decoration they so pleased, but they must make all four in the exact same manner. It could be simple and elegant, or elaborate and fanciful. But . . ."

He paused for effect, and grinned when some in the crowd leaned forward in anticipation.

"The decoration must taste as good as the fairy cake, and complement the vanilla sponge." When the audience looked suitably impressed at the difficulty, the steward added, "And thus, our honored judges must score the bakes on several different attributes. This will be as much as a challenge for them as it was for the cooks."

Like before, he gestured to the footmen who had a cloth over the table full of bakes. They lifted the cloth and the audience oohed and aahed. Petra, too, felt excitement coming on once more.

The fairy cakes looked like small works of art. One was topped with spun sugar formed into an upside-down cone, which sparkled like gold dust. Another had an icing crafted to look like a bed of white and pink roses.

Yet another contained miniature marzipan figures in the shape of fruit all nestled into a cornucopia made of some sort of biscuit.

The next had an icing somehow tinted a pale green with a small bouquet of sugared, edible flowers.

Of the final two, one had a coating of shiny chocolate topped with dozens of sugar pearls in varying hues of pastel colors. And the other had a thin white icing before being topped with glistening glacé cherries made brighter with small triangles of candied lemon.

"How wonderful," Petra whispered.

Truly, they were all incredible. And Petra could say with complete honesty that she knew not which one had been decorated by Mrs. Bing. For while she had seen her cook make some beautiful embellishments to her desserts, she had never seen her do anything quite at this level.

Similar to the previous two days, all four judges received platters, this time with six plates. Each had a napkin embroidered with a number, and on top was one of the beautiful fairy cakes. All the judges were smiling when the steward said, "Ready, my lord and lady judges? Yes? Then please begin!"

This time a good number of the guests stayed to watch, including Frances, Lottie, and Aunt Ophelia, who had instantly become a favorite of Petra's newest friends. It had been Caroline who introduced them, however, as Aunt Ophelia, today in a shawl of sky blue, seemed to only be willing to come within shouting distance of her niece. Hastily, Petra glanced through the rest of the crowd so that she would not frown at her aunt looking so carefree.

Colonel Wolston was standing at the back of the crowd as usual, though his jaw seemed less clenched when he fleetingly met her eyes. The Duchess of Hillmorton was talking with Lady Norworthy, who looked distracted—though it could have been by the stunning bakes. Major Carlson had also been in the crowd, but was one of the many who wandered away from the North Terrace as soon as the first gong was sounded.

The Prince and the Queen both sat on their chairs, and this

time the Prince seemed slightly more interested in the goings-on—though when she looked up again a few minutes later, he, too, had left.

Midway through, a footman brought fresh pots for all four judges. The tea was darker and more bitter than Petra was used to, but she felt it was somewhat needed due to the extra sweetness of the decorated fairy cakes, delicious as they were.

Petra had found the one with the marzipan fruits to be so sweet that she nearly felt her teeth hurt. The cake itself was a bit dry, too, though the taste was excellent. The cake with the spun sugar added a delightful crunch, but was a bit hard to eat in a ladylike manner. The next one, with the roses made from icing, was rather messy, with all that icing coating Petra's fingers and fork. Yet the look and taste were delicious.

But her three favorites were the fairy cake with the chocolate icing and sugar pearls, the one with the sugared flowers, and the one with the glacé cherries. All three were magnificent, with a lovely crumb to their cakes and the perfect balance of the sponge and the decoration. Yet on the last bake, the little hint of candied lemon brought a lovely brightness to the cherries and to the outstanding vanilla sponge itself.

As Mrs. Bing knew how much she loved chocolate, Petra wondered if that fairy cake might have been hers. But in the end, if she had to wager herself, she felt it might have been a different one.

"I wonder if I could get yet another pot of tea?" Sir Franklin said, just loud enough for Petra to hear. She slid her pot over to him. "I have only had one cup, and I do believe the tea is still quite warm."

"I thank you, Lady Petra," he said, pouring a full cup and drinking it as the steward once again came to the front to address the crowd.

"My lords, ladies, and gentlemen!" he called out, his gong having sounded a few minutes earlier to call the judging to an end and the guests back to the North Terrace. "I have the names of the cooks who will advance to the round of four! That is, our next-to-last round. I shall name them along with the fairy cake that earned them their advancement. And their names and houses, in order of precedence, are..."

This time a drummer had come onto the terrace and gave a drumroll that made the cooks lined up outside the castle grab each other's hands and look on with excitement.

"Mrs. Tenney of Chatsworth, with the lovely field of roses on her fairy cake! Mrs. Bing of Forsyth House, who topped hers with glorious candied cherries and lemons! Mrs. Davis of Norworthy Manor, who complemented hers with the prettiest sugared flowers! And Mrs. Taylor of Lawson Hall, who used chocolate and sugar pearls to a most excellent effect!"

Petra's heart went out to the two cooks whose faces crumpled with their elimination, but it soared again upon seeing Mrs. Bing, her hands to her pinkened cheeks with sheer delight. Her bake had deserved to push her through. Even her fellow three judges agreed.

"And she has never made you anything of the like?" asked Sir Franklin, using his fork to spear a leftover glacé cherry.

"Not like this, but I certainly will ask her for it in future," Petra said.

The guests, including the Queen—who looked entirely pleased at the way the contest was progressing and attracting an excellent crowd—left the terrace on the arm of the Prince. Soon all that was left were the footmen who were beginning to clear away the plates, Petra and her fellow judges, and a handful of guests milling about, including Aunt Ophelia, Lottie, and Frances. Lord Wadley-Bates, having been quite impressed by both Petra's friends, strode over to speak with them.

"Come, dearest, and let us hear what our friends think of our judging," Caroline said.

"I will be there in one moment," she replied, groping for a suitable excuse. "I, ah, wish to ask Sir Franklin about the explanations he writes out for the steward."

Caroline floated off and was soon laughing with her friends and Aunt Ophelia.

The footmen came to take away the pots of tea, but Sir Franklin told them to return later. He poured himself another cup, and Petra could see his eyes darting about. He had become nervous-looking once more.

"I do not think we have much time," Petra said. Aware that she had jumped to conclusions with Sir Franklin earlier, she wanted to be certain before she accused him of Sir Rufus's death, so she chose her words with more care. "You indicated you wish to confess to me something about Sir Rufus. I am willing to hear whatever it is you have to say. After that, however, I shall insist we speak with Colonel Wolston, for he is in charge of investigating the death—"

Sir Franklin's eyes snapped to her face, shock showing plainly. "'*Investigating*'?" He blinked. "Lady Petra, how did you know I believe Sir Rufus's death was not a natural one?"

Petra stared at him, at the utter lack of guile in his features. It was clear that Sir Franklin, along with the rest of the guests, still had no idea that anyone felt the former royal chef had not died of natural causes.

Damn. And blast.

"I can only say that it is a possibility," she said hastily in low tones, keeping an eye on her friends in case they looked her way. She countered his question: "Then why did you tell me you wished *to confess* something about Sir Rufus?"

Sir Franklin held up a hand of acquiescence with a brief, embarrassed chuckle.

"I must apologize. I do realize now how that might have sounded when I said it."

Then his thin lips twisted for a moment. He shifted in his chair, and when he spoke, his voice became increasingly petulant.

"Though I did not care for Sir Rufus. No, indeed, I did not. Most of the recipes in his last cookery book were mine, Lady Petra, did you know? He stole them from me after finding them in my study during a visit he made to Northumberland at my behest. I was hoping to write a cookery book of my own, and I invited him to my home in hopes that he would see my recipes as worthy of trying, and then delicious enough to belong in their own book. I had hoped he would vouch for my talents with Lord Wadley-Bates. Instead, he stole from me, changed my recipes ever so slightly, and published them as his own."

Petra was shocked to hear this, even if it veered off the original topic. Yet she recalled Oliver Beecham saying that Sir Rufus had not created recipes in some time, and that he took credit for some of Oliver's, so she could not say she found the accusation all that hard to believe.

"Does Lord Wadley-Bates know?" Petra found it odd that the two would be judging together if there was an animosity over Sir Franklin's recipes.

But then, when she thought on it, she realized the two men tended to stay as far away from each other as possible. In fact, she had rarely ever seen the two speak—and when they did, it was only for the briefest of moments.

"He does know," said Sir Franklin, taking a sip of his tea, even as he glared in the direction of their fellow judge. "He claims Sir Rufus presented my recipes as his own, and he had no reason to believe otherwise. Tosh, I say! When I went to his lordship's publishing house to complain, I saw the original pages of recipes. On one— that of a delicious rump roast with a coating of rosemary and other herbs mixed with butter, and then served with potatoes and winter squash that have been roasted to perfection—his instructions still bear the aside I had written of 'my darling wife's favorite.' Sir Rufus never took a wife! He simply forgot to remove my words when he presented them to his lordship for publishing. There simply is no denying the truth."

"I see," Petra said. "And I think it horrible that Sir Rufus stole from you."

"Yes, well, Lord Wadley-Bates has offered to add my name onto the cookery book when it is printed again," he said. "I accepted, but said it was only a start. I wish to write a book of recipes of my own. I believe they would be highly regarded. Now if I can only convince his lordship to agree with me and publish it."

Petra did not mention that Lord Wadley-Bates was currently rather short on money. The offer of a new cookery book was something the two men must simply determine on their own.

"But what does all of this have to do with what you wanted to confess, Sir Franklin?" she asked, her impatience showing as she glanced out to her friends and then back to her fellow judge.

He had briefly put his hand over his abdomen with a slight grimace, but then he poured more tea and drained his cup, making a face at the over-brewed bitterness and smacking his lips after as if he might be judging the tea the way he did the bakes. Putting the teacup down, he looked into Petra's eyes.

"I have wondered whether to say this or not. I was even warned not to—"

"Warned off? By whom?" Petra asked.

He lowered his voice to a whisper, his eyes darting around. "By Lady Norworthy. She told me not to say who I saw that morning."

"Who you saw the morning of Sir Rufus's murder?" Petra asked, and he nodded.

"Though I believe Lady Norworthy was only the messenger. I cannot understand why she of all people would have been chosen . . ."

Petra recalled the night before, in Horn Court, when learning the Viennese waltz. How Sir Franklin had requested to partner her in a dance so he could speak with her, only for Lady Norworthy to stride over and cut in.

Had it been then that her ladyship had issued her warning to Sir Franklin? Petra asked the question, and he confirmed her hunch. Digesting this, she encouraged him to continue. Sir Franklin was perspiring again, but was all willingness otherwise.

"The morning of his death, I was going to confront Sir Rufus about stealing my recipes, you see. I had not thus far, and did not know if I had the nerve to do so. After all, though I know the recipes he stole were mine, I do recognize that all one must do is change an ingredient or two just slightly—or write a cooking direction differently—and the recipe becomes someone else's. There are very few that can be solely attributed to one person, you understand, Lady Petra."

She nodded. "Of course. And then?"

"I came to the picture gallery," he said, "and saw Sir Rufus, entering the library carrying a breakfast tray, his recipes on top, tied with a bow. The ones he would present to the Queen as his, which would be preserved in the royal collections forevermore under the name Sir Rufus Pomeroy."

"A black bow, did you say? Made of silk ribbon?" Petra asked.

He shrugged. "I know little of such things, but it was most certainly a black ribbon. Nevertheless, I knew some of those recipes were mine, and I was suddenly enraged. Enough, I daresay, to have taken his life. But I quickly calmed myself, you understand."

"Of course," Petra said. "As anyone with a respect for others' lives does."

"Indeed," Sir Franklin said, and he stuck a finger between his neck and cravat and pulled at the fabric a bit, as if he were overheated, and then reached for the pot of tea again.

This time, Petra calmly poured him another cup, and one for herself. He was about to drink, but he lowered his cup, seemingly lost in the memory of that day.

"I was in the picture gallery, and once I had calmed my anger, I still wanted to go in and speak with him. If I had, I would have pleaded with him to at least put my name on the recipes he took from me. I would have shared credit with him, I swear it."

"I have no doubt, Sir Franklin," she said soothingly.

Once more, he pulled at his cravat, making another wincing face. "I think it is possible all that sugar from the fairy cakes has been a bit too much. I feel rather . . . odd."

"It was quite a lot of sugar, I agree. But please continue, Sir Franklin. And then my friend Frances, who is an apothecarist, will tell you what might make your stomach feel better. What happened to make you not go into the library?"

"Sir Rufus had closed the library doors. Yet I was close enough that I heard a brief shout directed at him from someone else who must have already been in the room. A man, I think." He shrugged. "Or possibly a woman. Then I heard what sounded like a table falling over and porcelain breaking."

Once more, he shifted uncomfortably, his speech becoming raspy.

"I went to knock upon the door, but all seemed quiet. I left the gallery in haste, heading back to my rooms . . . then felt it best to return . . . to confirm Sir Rufus was . . . unhurt. That's when I saw someone else . . . and they saw me."

Sir Franklin made a little sound, as if he were clearing his throat. He put the teacup and saucer down and held his abdomen. His face was turning pale and his face was screwed up.

Petra's brows came together. "Sir Franklin, are you well?"

"Help me, Lady Petra," he gasped.

And then Sir Franklin made a gagging noise before falling off his chair and onto the stone of the North Terrace, writhing in agony.

THIRTY-TWO

"I am certain it was arsenic," Frances said. "And Petra, I believe you were the intended victim."

Those words continued to ring in Petra's ears as she lay in bed sometime later.

If Frances had not been just steps away, and so knowledgeable, Sir Franklin would have died—and Petra would have likely been quite a bit more ill at present.

After Frances took in Sir Franklin's symptoms—and Petra whispering in her ear that he had been threatened—Frances had first asked if she had smelled the scent of bitter almonds.

"No, not even in any of the fairy cakes. Why?"

But Frances did not answer. She ordered a footman to make haste to the kitchens and fetch some charcoal. While they waited for him to return, Lottie and Aunt Ophelia gamely helped Sir Franklin over to the terrace wall. Then Frances induced him to vomit over the side by instructing him to stick two of his fingers to the back of his own throat.

As there was a kitchen entrance just down the side of the North Terrace, the footman had thankfully returned quickly, and Frances had then helped Sir Franklin to ingest the charcoal.

Petra, thoroughly shocked, was about to do what was natural to her and take a drink of her tea when Frances had yelled, "Petra, stop!"

"I think the tea was how it was administered," Frances said gravely. "Caroline said the second pots of tea were brewed incredibly strong, and that bitterness, combined with the sweetness of the fairy cakes, would have masked the worst of the taste."

Within minutes thereafter, Petra had felt a cramping in her abdomen as well, and Frances hauled her to her feet. "Come on, my friend. We must make you vomit."

At this, Aunt Ophelia—who had looked more stunned than everyone—had leapt forward to hold Petra's hand, saying, "I will be right by your side, my love. Do not worry."

If Petra had felt any better at that point, she might have commented that it was the first time her aunt had willingly remained in her presence for any length of time since the murder. But she loathed being physically ill, and it was worse as she was forced to make herself do so over the side of Windsor Castle.

"I heard Queen Elizabeth herself once became ill over the side of the terrace and found it quite interesting to note how far down it all went," said Aunt Ophelia, in an attempt at humor as she gently rubbed circles onto Petra's back. "So I would say that you are in excellent company, my love."

After that somewhat humiliating, if potentially lifesaving, exercise, Petra was then subjected to a disgusting dose of charcoal as well.

Caroline and Lord Wadley-Bates stood, looking fearful they would be next, but Frances was quick to reassure them.

"If either of you had a tea laced with arsenic, you would be experiencing symptoms of stomach cramps by now, at the very least. Do not force me to be indelicate and tell you the other symptoms. Are either of you experiencing any pain?"

They both shook their heads. And then Caroline snapped out of her reverie and took charge in the way she did best.

She dispatched three of the five footmen to make certain no one came out onto the terrace, citing a wish not to allow Her Majesty's wonderful patisserie contest to become the subject of gossip or fearmongering. Two more footmen were sent to fetch a litter for transporting Sir Franklin to a bedchamber. He had resumed a position of being curled up in a ball, moaning with misery, on the stone terrace, though somewhat hidden by the judges' table.

"We shall let Colonel Wolston decide where best to keep him safe," Caroline announced, then proceeded to send Lord Wadley-Bates in search of the colonel.

When his lordship asked where he should look first, Aunt Ophelia said, "Come, my lord. I expect I can find him," and marched off, her blue shawl catching air and bellowing out behind her.

"And I shall seek out the Windsor housekeeper," Caroline said. "If there is anyone who can determine who put poison in the pots of tea—and can do so without fuss and without announcing it to the entire castle—it is Mrs. Daley."

It was then that Frances had explained her theory that Petra was meant to have the full effect of the poison.

"If the arsenic had been in the first pots of tea, the symptoms would have shown much earlier. I think it was put in the second pots—and only in yours. You took one cup from that pot, but gave the rest to Sir Franklin. He drank a good bit of the pot as the judging was concluding, and a quarter of an hour later, the symptoms had started."

She left Sir Franklin's side to check Petra's pulse and search her eyes for signs of, well, Petra did not know and did not wish to ask.

"This is why you only have mild symptoms. I expect you will be quite well very quickly, but I wish you to take to your bed and rest for a while."

Wolston came running soon after, and with the help of his guards, Sir Franklin was carried on a litter back to his bedchamber. Mrs. Daley looked the remaining guard up and down, then decided it wouldn't do to have him standing sentry in his distinctive Coldstreamer tunics. Instead, she decreed he would be dressed as a footman before being placed in Sir Franklin's corridor.

"Wouldn't do to worry our guests by having a frightening-looking guard pacing about," she said as she bore the guard away to find him the suitable livery of a footman.

Not long after, Mrs. Daley had returned, a frightened, crying housemaid who looked no more than a girl of fifteen following in her wake.

"Did *she* add the poison?" Caroline asked, looking as surprised as everyone.

"No, this one is not to blame, my lady," Mrs. Daley said, glaring at the girl nonetheless. "It was one of the newer footmen, been here only a fortnight. He scarpered as soon as he realized what he had wrought. He is gone, I'm afraid." She turned to the young housemaid. "Go on, girl, tell Lady Petra and Lady Caroline and all of these fine ladies here what you told me."

The girl went on to say through her tears that the now-former footman bragged to her that he had been given five bob to do nothing more than pour a paper twist containing white powder into the teapot destined for Lady Petra. That he had been told it was merely a health tonic as Lady Petra had complained of stomach upset after yesterday's apple cake tasting.

"Did he say who asked him to add the poison to my tea?" Petra had asked. "Was it a gentleman, perhaps?" She did not wish to, but she added, "Or a lady?"

Yet she had a feeling the housemaid would not know, and she was not wrong. The conversation between the girl and the footman had been brief, taking place just before he had walked out to the North Terrace with the four fresh pots of tea. Mrs. Daley could confirm that the girl was kept busy and was nowhere near the footman prior to a few moments before he left with the tea.

Mrs. Daley had then pledged with her life that no one would have to watch themselves when they ate or drank from there on out.

"You have my word, my ladies," she said before making her curtsy and chivvying the young housemaid back into the castle.

Frances, who had listened to all of this with quiet patience, did not mince her words.

"Are we certain Mrs. Daley is someone to be trusted?"

Caroline was about to defend the Windsor housekeeper, but it was Colonel Wolston who stepped forward.

"She is indeed to be trusted, Miss Bardwell. I give you my word, and that of Her Majesty, the Queen."

This satisfied all. Yet when no one was looking, Petra had cut her eyes to Wolston. He met hers briefly, soberly, before giving her a small nod and turning to follow Mrs. Daley.

He had invoked the Queen, but not the Prince. What was more, he seemed glad that Petra had noticed.

It was as if he were offering her an unspoken truce. Not only that, but possibly an invitation to a conversation as well.

Petra, however, was recalling Sir Franklin's tale. Not only had he seen another person, but prior to that he'd heard someone already inside the small library, and an angry shout at Sir Rufus. And then something—or someone—had fallen to the ground.

It had to be Sir Rufus who fell. But she had to wonder, did his killer enter not from the picture gallery, but from the main library instead?

Petra did not wish to fall asleep. It was barely half past seven—much too early. Indeed, when she had agreed to take to her bed after Frances was satisfied both she and Sir Franklin were out of danger, she had every intention of simply resting and thinking through the intertwined ribbons that were all the facts in her mind.

Silk ribbons, they were. In royal purple, vibrant scarlet, the brightest green, a muted charcoal gray, and black as a polished jet bead. They undulated and swirled, turning themselves into the links of a necklace's fine chain, until the colors blurred from one into the next before twisting themselves about the black ribbon. It had then tied itself into a pretty bow, allowing the colorful chain to rest about her neck.

In the looking glass, she admired the necklace against her skin, shimmering slightly in the candlelight. Then frowned as the gray ribbon looked frayed and weak. She plucked it from the necklace, but it held fast on one end to the black ribbon for one long moment before dropping soundlessly away.

The remaining necklace was bright and strong. She smiled as she picked up a glass tumbler engraved with a hunting scene, swirling the amber liquid inside.

She went to drink it, then stopped, for there was something in her glass. It was a ring, the lapis-lazuli cabochon looking nearly black beneath the whisky. She could see the little compartment inside. She went to fish out the ring, but it proved too slippery. When her fingers finally touched the stone, it had turned to an almond.

Then she felt the need to pull at her cravat. No, it was a necklace, was it not? Purple and red and brightest green. It had tightened suddenly about her neck.

She dropped the glass of whisky as she felt her breathing labor. It landed softly upon the ground, next to a beautiful Wedgwood cake stand. Atop it was a cake, the chocolate shiny and smooth and topped with a line of crushed walnuts that had been first glazed with honey, cinnamon, and sugar.

La Bella Contessa, hiding layer upon layer beneath its icing.

Then she stumbled back, jerking at the necklace, for it had tightened. In the mirror, the loops of the black bow became larger and larger as the necklace of ribbons dug into her neck. The purple would be the color of her bruises. The red of her blood.

And the green, it was the vibrant color of someone's eyes.

Duncan. His name was echoing in her mind as she grabbed hold of the silken necklace and pulled with all her might. The black bow came undone and the ribbons loosened, then fell in inexorable slowness to the ground, one by one.

She looked about for them, panting, her hand to her sore neck. The black ribbon had turned to dust. The tattered gray one lay off to one side, never really a part of the necklace. The bright green and the scarlet ribbons were somewhere, yes. She could sense them, yet she could not see them.

Once more, she looked down. The whisky glass had turned into a rat. It ignored the cake, and took the purple ribbon in its mouth. She bent to retrieve it, but the rat dashed away, slipping silently through a hole in the wall.

THIRTY-THREE

Friday, 8 September 1815
Day five of the royal celebrations

LADY PETRA SAT UP IN BED, GASPING FOR AIR. SHE COULD FEEL the perspiration running down her face as her shaking hand went to her throat.

And then came a brief noise. A soft whine. After a moment, the whine came again. It was closer, and then there was a snuffling sound. *Sable.*

Throwing off her counterpane, Petra stumbled over to her dressing table, where Annie had left a thumb lamp burning. Sable followed, ears perked and concern making the little brows above her eyes dance as she watched Petra's every move. A looking glass was above the table and Petra leaned close to it. Her neck was clean and unblemished.

"It was but a dream," she whispered, still feeling weakened. Sable leaned up against her legs, and she bent to rub her dog's silky ears, gratefully repeating, "It was only a dream."

She angled the thumb lamp over to the clock on the mantel. It was nearly two o'clock in the morning. It was likely some of the guests were still awake and enjoying themselves in the Quadrangle, most of them no doubt gentlemen who were gambling and drinking. But even with her door closed, she could tell her corridor was quiet.

The previous day had been a long one for everyone, even for her friends who had not been poisoned with arsenic. Before Petra had drifted off, they had all come by to check on her, with even Caroline expressing a wish for an early night. Frances, exhausted from an eventful day, and from playing nursemaid to poor Sir Franklin, had come to Petra's room with Lottie and the dogs for only a few minutes before they began yawning, saying they would both have an early supper and then heed the call of sleep.

Annie, who had been fussing over Petra, making her soak in a warm bath, had only agreed to leave when Petra reminded her that she must be at Curfew Tower at ten o'clock to make certain Oliver was healing from the beating he had received.

The beating Petra knew the Prince Regent had authorized—and seemingly behind Colonel Wolston's back, though for reasons Petra still did not understand.

"Afterward, I wish you to go to your own room and rest as well," she had told Annie. "For I am in no danger any longer. And there is much to think on for our last two days here at Windsor. I think we both could use some sleep to ensure our minds are not weary."

Still, she could tell Annie had been back to check on her. For one, there had not been a thumb lamp burning earlier. Nor had Sable been in the room. However, as grateful as she was for Annie, she was glad her lady's maid had not been here to witness her nightmare. Being fussed over for a second time in a handful of hours would have been more than she could bear.

Petra eyed her bed. She did not wish to try and sleep again, not yet. Plus, now that the peculiar heaviness in body and sluggishness of mind that came from awakening from such a horrid dream was lifting, she was no longer tired.

"Let us go for a walk," she told Sable. "For I am certain some air will do us both good—and I think best when I am perambulating, do I not?"

By the time she found her cheerful pink long-sleeved dress in a heavy cotton, pulled on her stockings, tied her garters, laced up her half boots, and slipped on a spencer in a quilted dark green that offered extra warmth, nearly another half hour had passed, as well as the last of her dream-induced shakiness.

Though just before she left her bedchamber, she went back into her dressing room and added to her ensemble, fastening below each of her knees a strap of leather. Both buckled instead of tied, yet they were each quite different.

She had commissioned them recently, based on a pair of garters she had modified a couple of months earlier. The left held leather slots for her most useful lockpicks, and ensured the picks would not poke her skin or damage her stockings.

The right, however, held a small leather scabbard, which she inserted the blade of the new dagger Duncan had gifted her. It was larger than the little one with the jeweled hilt she had often carried before.

But this new dagger was also the right size for her hand, and the blade was neither too long to be held against her leg without getting caught on her dress as she walked, nor too short to properly be of use, should she need it.

In truth, she did not enjoy carrying a knife about, and hoped she would never have to do more than wield it about threateningly—and only if necessary at that. Since she had recently learned to defend herself with her own body, arms, and legs—and the occasional broom, it seemed—she had felt stronger, more in control of her own safety. So much so that she rarely carried her dagger anymore.

But as of the incident where she was poisoned, she once more felt it wise to have it on her person. The memory of her terrible dream made her touch her throat, the ghost of a tightening necklace made of silk ribbons still quite vivid. Yes, she would wear her dagger, for one never knew when it could be useful, did one?

With a lamp in her hand and candelabras or torches in brackets every so often, the halls and corridors of Windsor Castle were still lit, even if very quiet, as she walked Sable out and onto the South Terrace.

The evening was even cooler than the night before had been, heralding the coming of autumn. She picked up her pace, wishing she had worn her demi-length walking coat instead of simply a spencer.

When she reached the steps that would take her down to the torchlit gardens below the East Terrace, she was about to let Sable off her lead when she caught sight of a tall woman wearing a blue walking coat, a hood covering her head. The woman was walking the structured gardens, seemingly not noticing the cheeky statue of a water nymph as she stared at the ground as if in deep concentration.

For a moment, Petra thought it was her aunt Ophelia, but then the woman turned, and Petra saw it was Lady Norworthy. When her ladyship noted Petra stepping quickly toward her, she removed her hood, her gray hair almost moon-bright in the absence of the planet itself.

"I have felt that you might wish to speak with me, Lady Petra," she said, her usual blunt delivery quite intact, even though her voice lacked its usual strength. Her lorgnette was in one hand, seemingly an extension of her arm, but she did not hold it up to her eyes, almost as if she rather decided it best that she not be able to see Petra's expression clearly.

"Why is that, Lady Norworthy?" Petra asked, gesturing to a nearby stone bench and waiting until they were both settled.

"Because I went to speak with Sir Franklin tonight, when I heard he was poorly. He was being tended to, but not up to conversation, and I was sent away. However, I rather felt he was being guarded."

"You would be correct," Petra replied, but offered no more explanations.

"It is because I threatened him, I'm afraid," said Lady Norworthy, her mouth turning down in a frown that expressed deep disappointment—in herself.

Petra released the lead from Sable's collar and let her enjoy the gardens.

"Did you? Or did you merely pass along a threat from someone else?" She raised one eyebrow slightly. "Possibly from someone who was blackmailing you? Regarding your relationship with Sir Rufus Pomeroy from three or so years ago, and a certain love letter that was stolen, along with other items, by an unscrupulous footman?"

Now Lady Norworthy brought her lorgnette up, and her eyes seemed twice their usual size due to the spectacles as well as her surprise.

"How would you know such a thing?" she asked. "How would you know any of it? I am, of course, aware that I caused a scandal in my little part of Bedfordshire, but the next time I was in London, I realized that almost nobody had even heard of my shameful actions. Thus, how would you know . . . about the—" She lowered her voice to a whisper, despite the fact that they were quite alone under the pitch-black, star-strewn sky, with the hulking outline of the castle looming like a peaceful giant some twenty yards away. "The *blackmail*."

"I think I would have guessed it eventually, but it was Sir Franklin who explained some of it, and I concluded the rest," Petra answered. "For he, too, knew that you were not the type to issue such threats. Not unless you were coerced into doing so to save yourself, or another."

Lady Norworthy hung her head.

"It was the former, Lady Petra. I was saving only myself."

Petra turned slightly toward the older woman. "I think if you explained, your ladyship, I might better understand."

There was a long pause, but then Lady Norworthy nodded and spoke.

"It began in the summer of 1812. I had been a widow for some time and I invited Sir Rufus to a house party to both cook and be a guest. A radical view, I know, but I did find him fascinating—and so did my invitees. He remained at Norworthy Manor for some weeks afterward, ostensibly to train my own cook, but in reality we had begun a love affair."

She looked up at the night sky for a moment before speaking again.

"It lasted six glorious weeks, and then we parted amicably. Yes, indeed we did, Lady Petra. However, when loneliness overtook me one night, I wrote him a love letter that was, well, it was more than I ever thought I would express on paper, much less speak to another person. And I foolishly posted it before I could think on the implications. I expected Sir Rufus to reply in kind, and for our love to continue in the form of letters, and the occasional visit to one another. That would have been enough for me. Instead, I never heard from him."

"I'm sorry," Petra said quietly.

"It was heartbreaking, yes. But I did not stop there. Not long thereafter, I learned he would be attending a nearby village fete and was staying at the inn. I then made the further mistake of sending a footman I knew had questionable morals to locate Sir Rufus's key at the inn and then ride the fifteen miles to Chesham to retrieve my letter. Only Sir Rufus returned home early, and caught my footman in the act of stealing from him. I was made infamous in a most terrible way."

This time, Petra stayed quiet, for there was nothing she could say.

"And then, last year, I was visiting a friend in Bath," Lady Norworthy continued. "Said friend—in whom I had confided my embarrassing truth—told me that Sir Rufus was planning on writing a memoir that would scandalize society, and that he was planning on printing my letter! I had loved him, and he was willing to lay bare my innermost thoughts for people to read and laugh at!"

Lady Norworthy's voice finally cracked, and she pulled a handkerchief from within her sleeve.

"Do forgive me, Lady Petra. I cannot believe a woman of my age would act so silly."

"When it comes to our heart, age makes no difference on how it breaks," Petra said, and saw by the way Lady Norworthy's lips gave a trembling half smile that she had heard Petra's sincerity.

"When I received my invitation to Her Majesty's week of celebrations here at Windsor, well, I was elated," she continued. "I so rarely go to London anymore, and my one child is long married and emigrated to Canada with her husband and children. Whilst my late husband was once the highest-ranking serjeant-at-law in His Majesty's court, I am, quite simply, of no use to the Crown. Thus, this was a treat, until I arrived and saw Sir Rufus Pomeroy again."

Then her expression became positively glowering, which appeared to intensify when she shifted toward Petra and the lamplight flickered up into her ladyship's face, emphasizing every emotion-filled crease and line.

"I was humiliated. Upon my first encounter with Sir Rufus, he refused to shake hands with me! I could have throttled the man. I cornered him in the Green Drawing Room and told him what I thought of his behavior. He was cruelly dismissive in return, and I left in a huff. I recollected the experience to Lady Ophelia, and she was shocked, I tell you. Then I overheard Sir Rufus asking you to meet him in the small library on Tuesday morning. I thus awoke early that day and intended to confront him again before you arrived to look at his recipes."

"Did you?" Petra asked quietly. "Confront him, I mean?"

"Oh, I would have, Lady Petra, if I had not gone to the dining room first," she replied. "My emotions were running too high, and I did not wish for Sir Rufus to find me in any other way but controlled this time. Thus, I drank some tea and ate some kedgeree. And by the time I finished, I felt myself again. I realized I am not to blame for his rakish, unfeeling behavior, nor should I allow him to make me feel small."

"Hear, hear," Petra said.

Lady Norworthy smiled briefly. "But to ensure I remained

strong, I chose to walk out on the North Terrace a bit to further clear my head."

"What time was this?" Petra asked sharply.

Lady Norworthy was most definitely feeling like herself again, for she held up her lorgnette and gave a briefly searing look.

"You are quite impertinent, Lady Petra." But she lowered the spectacles and said, "It was a quarter past seven by the time I made my way across the Quadrangle back to my room. No, I did not go back to the library. For I had come across Sir Franklin and he informed me Sir Rufus already had a visitor in the library. He did not tell me who it was." Up came her lorgnette again. "I assumed it was you. And then during the waltzing lessons, when I was, shall we say, *encouraged* to impress upon Sir Franklin that he not confess to seeing who he saw, I felt certain that it was you, and he was protecting you from further scandal."

Petra was already blinking stupidly at Lady Norworthy's comment about Sir Franklin being ordered not to identify who Sir Rufus had been with in the library, but then she blurted out, "Protect me from scandal? From what scandal?"

Lady Norworthy gave her a sideways look.

"From your behavior, Lady Petra. From the fact that you and Mr. Shawcross so willingly engage in amorous activities outside of the bounds of marriage that he now keeps a room in Forsyth House. From the way you agreed to meet a bachelor man, even if one more than three decades your senior, in the morning hours and did not bring a lady's maid. And from the way you run about, involving yourself in men's work—or so others might say. I do not take issue with any of your choices, you understand, but others do. There are some, I was told, who do not like how you are behaving at all."

Petra was about to ask who, but Lady Norworthy once more put her spectacles up to her eyes.

"I was told you have a dagger fastened about your thigh. Is this true?"

Lady Norworthy seemed more fascinated than offended. And when Petra responded, "It is about my calf," and then lifted her skirts on the right side to show the dagger, she still could not believe what she had heard.

"Fascinating," said Lady Norworthy, approval in her voice. "Though why you are wearing it here, at Windsor, when we are amongst our own and quite safe, I do not understand."

Petra opened her mouth, then closed it again. It was clear from Lady Norworthy's tone and everything she had just confessed that she was not only innocent of Sir Rufus's murder, but also supremely unaware of the dangers lurking within the castle walls. It was also evident that Sir Franklin had been frightened enough by the threat Lady Norworthy had conveyed that he did not correct her when she thought Petra was the person he had seen the morning Sir Rufus died.

Lady Norworthy stifled a yawn. It seemed that after unburdening herself, her troubles had disappeared. Now, she declared, standing up and dusting off her skirts, she could go inside and finally sleep.

"Will you walk with me, Lady Petra?" she asked.

"I think I may take another moment to myself," Petra said, still feeling stupefied by what she had heard. "May I ask one other question, though? Who asked you to tell Sir Franklin that he should not admit to what he saw?"

Now, Lady Norworthy looked uncomfortable.

"I am not certain I should say."

Petra stood up. The night when they had learned the Viennese waltz, she had not seen Lady Norworthy speaking with any men, so she could only guess.

"Was it Colonel Wolston, by chance? Or possibly Major Carlson?"

At hearing the major's name, Lady Norworthy worked her jaw as if she were attempting to keep her mouth closed.

"I am correct. It was Major Carlson," Petra said.

"Well, no," said Lady Norworthy. "Not exactly. He was acting on behalf of someone else who knew of my scandal and said I must pass along the message, or else my past transgressions would be dredged up again for all the ton to know."

For one moment, Petra simply blinked, thoroughly nonplussed. And then her eyes flew wide.

"Do you mean . . . the Prince?"

This time, Lady Petra did not use her lorgnette, but steadily, meaningfully held Petra's gaze.

"Good night, Lady Petra," she said, and began walking back toward the castle.

Sable came trotting up as Petra simply stood in the gardens, staring into the black night, faint bits of pale color coming from dahlias, Michaelmas daisies, and autumn crocus flowers.

Petra recalled Frances mentioning the seeds of the crocus were used by the Prince as a treatment for his gout, and how ingesting too much could be poisonous. The flowers themselves were deadly, too.

It was not hard to then believe the man who would be the next king of England would know how to poison someone, then, was it?

Lamp in hand, Petra hardly noticed the cold night air as she and Sable made their way back into the castle. Her mind was simply overburdened with too many theories and questions to count. And yet, tiredness had stolen over her again. She yawned as she opened her door and went in, placing the lamp on the bedside table.

She was yawning again as a soft knock came at her door and vaguely noted Sable's ears perking up. She opened it again, and Sable leapt sideways. Petra herself was not so quick, however.

A ghostly white figure that seemed blurred at the edges rushed at her, something shiny throwing off a glint as the light from Petra's lamp struck it.

And then the wraith was upon her, its arms stretched out, lunging for her throat with a silver blade.

THIRTY-FOUR

"Oh, my darling Petra! You are safe!"

Petra spit out a white feather from the masses of them that had engulfed her when the spirit—her aunt Ophelia, that was—had thrown her arms about her neck. A sob that comes from abject fear was in Petra's ear as her aunt, wearing only her night chemise and her white silk robe, feathered trim and all, held her tight, her shoulders shaking.

Petra returned the embrace, suddenly needing it as much as her aunt did.

"Whatever is the matter?" she asked once her door was closed again and she had hastily lit a candelabra. She looked up to find tears running down her aunt's face, her short, stylish hair pushed back from her forehead by a silk ribbon of salmon pink. In her hand was the glinting steel blade. It was a butter knife.

Gently taking her aunt's hand, she took the knife from her fingers and pulled her over to the sofa before retrieving the candelabra and placing it on the low table.

"I was so frightened something had happened to you," said Aunt Ophelia as Petra poured them both a glass of water. "I went to bed, but I could scarcely sleep. I woke up but a half hour ago. I simply knew I had to speak with you, and tell you everything. I came and knocked on your door, but you did not answer. I tried the door, and it was unlocked. When I came in, your bed was in disarray, your chemise on the floor, and you were gone. I felt certain someone had abducted you. And after what you went through today? How you were poisoned? Oh, my darling love, I thought I was going to lose you..."

She put her hand over her mouth and cried for several long seconds, squeezing her eyes shut as she shuddered. When she opened them, they glowed in the candlelight like blue topaz, her dark eyelashes, wet with tears, only serving to prettily enhance her Forsyth eyes.

Petra reached out and took her aunt's hand again, squeezing her fingers.

"I am well, Aunt. I simply could not sleep, like you, and so I took Sable out for a walk." She smiled and nodded to the knife, now on the table and still winking in the candlelight. "But what were you planning on doing with that butter knife?"

"I was going to rescue you, of course," her aunt said, dabbing at her eyes with a handkerchief Petra handed her. "I was going to go after that blackguard—both of them—and I would have fought for you tooth and nail." She held up the tumbler full of water. It was etched like the one in Petra's dream, only this set had a quaint pastoral scene with cows, horses, sheep, and one donkey. "Might you have any whisky to go with this? I am afraid my nerves are still in a muddle and a nip would be quite helpful."

Petra rose from the sofa with both their glasses, wanting to ask so many questions. As she poured, her eyes fell onto the donkey etched onto her glass. It wore a head-collar, and a child was pulling ineffectually on the lead as the donkey set back on his heels, refusing to budge.

She and her aunt had always been quite similar in that, when someone tried to force them to do something, both were apt to refuse to comply in much the same manner.

Yet when they were ready to do whatever had been asked of them? Well, that was a whole different matter. Now it was up to

Petra to simply wait until her aunt started to speak, and then she was sure the dam would break.

At the same time, however, ideas were falling into place. Beginning when she held out one glass and recalled Tilly, their hall maid, saying she had removed whisky glasses from Aunt Ophelia's room. Not simply one glass, but *glasses*. More than one.

Even when quite out of sorts, Petra's aunt rarely drank very much. So why would the housemaid have removed two glasses?

The second thing that Petra recalled was from her nightmare. She had seen the ring Geraldine found—the gold one with the large lapis-lazuli cabochon that concealed a hidden space.

In my dream, when I touched the stone, it turned into an almond, she thought. *And did not Frances ask me if I smelled almonds yesterday when she was attempting to determine which poison had been put in my teapot?*

Then she recalled Geraldine's words when she located the ring. She had smelled a scent upon it, saying, *"Like the* amandes.*"*

Thoughts came quickly, jostling for space in her brain. An almond scent had been emanating from the ring. Two whisky glasses could only mean Aunt Ophelia had a guest in her room after Monday's supper. She'd been wearing a black silk ribbon in her hair. The next day, that very ribbon had been used to strangle Sir Rufus Pomeroy.

As Petra had walked back along the terraces after speaking with Lady Norworthy, though, she had begun to wonder if everything that pointed to Aunt Ophelia as the guilty party had been but circumstance. But then why had she dreamt about almonds?

Petra reclaimed her seat on the couch, but then she stood up again like a shot. The words tumbled out of her mouth, sounding as appalled as she was.

"Bloody hell, Aunt Ophelia, did you attempt to poison Sir Rufus with *cyanide*?"

The glass tumbler her aunt had taken dropped to the rug when her hand went slack, whisky and water splashing out everywhere.

"How did you know?" she whispered.

"Petra, darling, you must let me explain," Aunt Ophelia said, following Petra about the bedchamber as she paced, her hands on top of her head in a shocked, dumbfounded manner.

When Petra did not stop, her aunt stood in the middle of the room and began speaking, her voice radiating a desperation to be heard.

"I was being forced to, Petra, but I simply could not go through with it at the last minute. I could not take a life! I could not take *Sir Rufus's* life, no matter what he had done."

Petra did not miss the truth in her aunt's voice, yet it was not quite enough to assuage the idea that Aunt Ophelia had, for a short while, been willing to murder him with poison.

"I was to invite Sir Rufus to my bedchamber after Her Majesty's supper, hinting to him that I would be willing to assist him with his debts," Aunt Ophelia was saying. "My purpose was to ask about a manuscript, for it seemed he was to write a new cookery book—only that is not what it truly is. And by the look on your countenance, I feel as if this part you already know."

"It is to be a memoir, filled with defamatory gossip that he has obtained during his years cooking for and visiting the best houses in England. Duncan and I found a few pages from it, but the rest of it is hidden somewhere in the castle. I have been searching for it since then."

Her aunt nodded, yet thankfully it did not stop her confession.

"Well, that night, if Sir Rufus refused to tell me where the pages could be found, I was to put the cyanide in his drink and send him on his way. I was told the dose would allow him enough time to walk back to his room before dying of its effects, but I am not so certain now. I overheard Frances telling Lottie that even a small amount is lethal quite quickly." She visibly blanched at the thought. "Yet, the man was too stubborn by half and would not tell me where his pages were hidden."

Reaching up, she touched the pink bow that pushed the hair off her face.

"We argued about it, to the point that I yanked out the ribbon that was in my hair in frustration. And yet, he still did not acquiesce, even though he did not seem to even want the blasted manuscript!"

Petra's brows knitted at this, but Aunt Ophelia did not notice.

"I had poured us both a glass of whisky for a nightcap and I put the cyanide I had concealed on my person in one glass—"

"Concealed in our ancestor's ring, yes?" Petra cut in. "Within its hinged compartment."

"Yes," replied Aunt Ophelia, her eyes filled with painful guilt. Then they flashed with something akin to determination. "Yet when I continued to press Sir Rufus for what I needed—and he became angrier that I would not lend him money for his debts—he reached for one of the whiskies. It was the untainted glass, but I slapped his hand away as he lifted it anyway, causing the drink to spill all over his trousers. He left in high dudgeon only moments later."

Ahh, thought Petra. *This is how Sir Rufus arrived back in his own quarters soaked in whisky, but not drunk.*

"Nevertheless," said Aunt Ophelia, "I was so angry at myself for having considered such a cruel deed that, after Sir Rufus left, I removed my great-grandmother's ring and flung it under the bed. For I could not bear to look at it, or myself. I felt unworthy of our ancestor's legacy of strength."

Aunt Ophelia looked to the windows. One curtain was partially pulled back, and the blackness of the night outside combined with the candlelit room had created the effect of a looking glass. She stared unhappily at her reflection for a moment before returning her gaze to Petra.

"And then Tuesday morning, I woke up early. I could not sleep, so I went out for a walk. I thought of you, my beautiful, headstrong, clever niece, whom I love more than life itself. I could not bear the thought of you knowing what I had nearly done. I have met many odious men—and a few women—in my life. And no matter how much I loathed them, I never once considered such a heinous act."

"Then why did you?" Petra asked.

"Because something I did nearly eight years earlier was being used against me, and for a time, the threat made me forget the person I have always been."

Petra walked closer, her eyes narrowed suspiciously.

"What did you do eight years ago, Aunt Ophelia?"

She took a deep breath and reached for Petra's hand.

"To understand, you must first know facts from even farther back."

"All right. Tell me what I need to know, then."

With a squeeze of Petra's fingers, she then picked up the fallen whisky glass and placed it on the table. Petra sat, and waited.

"When your dear uncle Albie passed, he left me quite wealthy, but he had not informed me of *all* his business dealings. Most have been no issue, and even have added further to my coffers. But there has been one difficulty."

Nervous energy seemed to be flowing through her, so much that the feathers upon her silk robe fluttered as if there were a slight breeze in the room.

"I have no doubt you recall that the Throckmorton lands on which Morningside sits border those of an exceedingly wealthy and handsome gentleman of about my age. A Mr. Barwick, who was one of the most notorious rakes in Yorkshire."

"I remember," Petra said. She once more recalled that night so many years ago when she had witnessed her aunt losing control of her senses, attacking Mr. Barwick seemingly without warning.

"Well, after my Albie's death, I discovered he had entered into a business scheme with Mr. Barwick, whom I knew but little at the time. After my mourning period, however, Mr. Barwick and I became . . . more acquainted."

Aunt Ophelia then flapped a hand in irritated fashion.

"Oh, I do not know why I am being so careful. It is simply not in my nature." She sat down, looking into Petra's eyes. "Petra, my love, Barwick was charming and handsome and he and I entered into an amorous affair. With some abandon, I might add, on both our parts."

She paused, then shook her head as if disappointed.

"Yet I quickly found his interests in that matter often veered toward the unusual, shall we say." She then lifted her chin, unashamed. "Done correctly, and with agreement by both parties as to the limitations, those acts can often be rather pleasurable, yes. Barwick learned I was amenable to some of his whims, and not to most of them. Our liaisons became infrequent, but enough to slake our respective desires."

She exhaled a dark sigh.

"Soon, though, he felt it time to take a wife. And it was very soon thereafter that you came for a much-anticipated visit. You were nearing your seventeenth year and arrived looking every inch a gorgeous young woman—and Mr. Barwick noticed."

Petra felt herself tense even as she watched her aunt's beautiful face cloud over with anger at the memory.

"During your visit, we attended several parties, you may recall, and Mr. Barwick was at many of them. You played whist alongside him once, and even partnered with him on a dance, all of which displayed your wit and charm and beauty to their fullest extent, without you even attempting to try. Indeed, I was so proud of the woman you had become."

Briefly, her smile appeared before it fell as she related the rest of the story.

"That night in question, however, Barwick came to Morningside. He and I met outside in the knot garden, after you had gone to bed.

He was his usual charming self and I thought he was going to ask me to marry him. I would have said no, of course, but please do not disapprove of my ego too much if I say I did enjoy the thought of being asked."

Aunt Ophelia paced back and forth for a few steps, and then reclaimed her seat next to Petra.

"Instead, Barwick said that he was going to ask for *your* hand. He quite calmly began explaining to me that I was too old to become his wife and bear him children. That he needed someone young and . . . trainable to his whims."

Aunt Ophelia's jaw tightened.

"Oh, I knew he was trying to belittle me, to make me feel like an old crone though I was hardly past the age of thirty. I did not care, however, and can claim no bruised feelings on that account. All I cared about was protecting you. And when he so easily began telling me in horrid detail the things he would do to you—on your wedding night, no less—I am afraid I lost all my senses. There is no other way to say it: I attacked him."

"You slapped him," Petra said, recalling that night. "Twice. And then you went for his throat. I saw it, but I hid before you could see me. Oh, Aunt Ophelia . . . I am grateful you protected me."

This time she reached for her aunt's hands, finding them cold and clenched tight with anger. Petra warmed them with her own, and Aunt Ophelia began to relax.

"Still, you must understand how this all fits in, Petra," she insisted, tensing again. It was clear her aunt needed to say everything that had been on her mind.

"I am listening," she said.

"Barwick did leave that night, yes," said her aunt. "And he never attempted to ask for your hand. But he promised he would ruin me. Yet as time passed and nothing happened, I thought that was the end of it. We remained civil in public, and our solicitors handled anything pertaining to the business. He married a lovely young woman, who sadly no longer resembles the friendly, confident lass I first met, though she has managed to give him two sons."

"I am sorry, Aunt," Petra said soberly. "For you and for Barwick's poor wife and sons."

"I am as well, my darling," Aunt Ophelia said. "Yet my circumstances do become worse. And once more, I must go briefly back in time to tell you how Sir Rufus came into my life as more than simply my dear brother's chef—or the royal chef, for that matter."

When her aunt looked weary, Petra rose from the sofa and went to pour her another glass of whisky, adding in a good amount of water along with it. Aunt Ophelia took a long gulp, coughed once, and then resumed her story.

"In August of last year, I commissioned Sir Rufus to come to Yorkshire and speak about his cookery books, where he stayed at Morningside for a fortnight. He met all my friends and acquaintances, and was greatly admired. Prinny even came to one of the suppers, and was delighted to have Sir Rufus's excellent food once more. And in the interest of continuing to have good business dealings, I invited Mr. Barwick and his wife as well."

Petra nodded; it only made sense.

"Then about a month ago, a solicitor arrived at Morningside with news. Mr. Barwick, I was told, had suddenly fled the country, abandoning his wife and children and leaving behind debts that would take his wife three lifetimes to pay. And the business scheme he and my late Albie had entered into? Barwick had run it into the ground, incurring great debts—and legally, they are now mine to pay."

"You cannot be serious," Petra breathed when her aunt named the amount.

"I am afraid I am, darling. And here is where all of my stories come together. The business scheme had, unbeknownst to me, recently acquired some influential investors—all quite secret, you understand. The most important one, who had invested quite a large amount of money, was Prinny—though he could ill afford to do so." Aunt Ophelia bit her lip for a moment, then said, "He had heard of the venture whilst at my own house party... through Sir Rufus."

"Of course," Petra said on a sigh before taking a gulp of her whisky, too. "The former royal chef who kept his ears constantly open to gossip, and used it when it pleased him. I have sadly discovered this over the last couple of days. And should I surmise that Sir Rufus heard of the venture through Mr. Barwick?"

"Indeed you should," her aunt replied darkly. "Nevertheless, though Prinny understood I was not to blame, I was told he wanted his funds returned with haste, especially now that the public is more outraged than ever at the royal family's rather flagrant spending. I received this demand all but straight from his royal mouth, too. For you see, the solicitor in question on my doorstep was Major Carlson."

She held up a finger as Petra's lips parted.

"It seems Major Carlson did not become the royal solicitor for no reason. Who I saw as an upright, handsome gentleman with a limp from his time protecting our country belied a man who was quite ruthless in the name of the Crown. The major explained to me that the Prince had recently become aware that Sir Rufus had been writing a memoir, and that it contained scandalous information he had overheard throughout the years. That the Prince's best men had tried to find the manuscript, but to no avail. All they found was another cookery book Sir Rufus was crafting."

"He had become rather paranoid after having his house broken into some three years ago," Petra mused. "I have a feeling he has been keeping his manuscript well hidden, even when he arrived here earlier than the other guests—ostensibly to work on that very cookery book."

"It seems so," agreed Aunt Ophelia. "And I expect the major knew this, for he put forward two choices to me. If I came to Windsor and obtained the manuscript that threatened such scandal, I could either have my debts from the business scheme Barwick had run into the ground forgiven in their entirety, or I could have that equal amount forgiven for Barwick's wife and her sons, one of whom has never been in good health and requires constant care."

"What?" Petra exclaimed. "You could either save yourself or save another? That is hardly a fair option for a debt you had no part in incurring."

Her aunt gave a bitter shrug.

"And is this the real reason why you arrived here with no notice to me?"

She nodded. "I was told that to fail in finding the manuscript would be considered unacceptable, for the stories supposedly in the memoir not only could cause many high-ranking peers to be the laughingstock of England, but also would likely disgrace the monarchy itself. That finding it was almost as important as returning the Prince's investment monies."

Aunt Ophelia's brow furrowed briefly with a memory.

"The major's insistence was, dare I say, almost . . . frenzied. He seemed to abandon his usual control for a moment, and seemed to deliberately misquote the Bible."

"Deliberately?" Petra repeated. "How do you mean?"

"He said, 'And they shall know the truth, and the truth shall make him free.' Yes, that is correct—he said, 'The truth shall make *him* free.' I asked if he were referring to the Prince, but he just laughed. In a way that unnerved me, I must say."

"Is that so?" Petra said, a thought forming. Could there be something in the manuscript about the major himself?

But Aunt Ophelia was using her fingers to rub the space between her eyes, still intent on her explanations.

"Nevertheless, upon telling the major that I doubted Sir Rufus would give me anything, especially as he had already asked to borrow money from me to pay his own debts—and when I had refused, he had become quite rude—the major then offered me another two choices. One was that I could administer a poison to Sir Rufus, which I happened to know would end his life sooner than expected.

Seeing the question on Petra's face, she smiled thinly.

"Yes, he had confided that he was afflicted with cancer. I cannot deny that, in the moment of my greatest stress and worry, the idea that I might be poisoning someone who would not live much longer anyway did make it briefly seem somewhat logical."

Aunt and niece both simply looked at each other for a long moment. Then Aunt Ophelia spoke with soft finality laced with fury.

"The other option was that both Mrs. Barwick and I would lose our houses and our lands. It was emphasized that she and her sons would be thrown out of their house immediately, and that *the Crown*, meaning the Prince himself, whilst sympathetic in general, would not grant Mrs. Barwick clemency simply because one of the children is sickly."

The anger in her voice took on a further edge of acid.

"Oh, and while it matters to me little, I would be stripped of my title as Viscountess Throckmorton and be exiled to the Orkney Islands. Though I could still be called Lady Ophelia, of course, having been born an earl's daughter. Lucky me."

Petra was seething, both for her aunt and for a woman and children she did not even know. For the lengths the Prince Regent would go to protect himself, even at the expense of the innocent.

"But you did not succeed in killing Sir Rufus."

It was a statement with the edge of a question.

"No, indeed. I neither poisoned him, nor did I strangle him."

She chuckled briefly at Petra's look of surprise.

"Do not think you alone gained information, my love. I overheard Lottie and Frances talking about Sir Rufus being strangled with a black silk ribbon. I realized you likely thought I did it, and I could not blame you, but it was not I. Though Sir Rufus, when leaving my bedchamber smelling of whisky, did snatch up the ribbon I had pulled from my hair. It was a petty act of a disgruntled man, but I did not stop him." She sighed again. "Though I wish I had."

Petra did, too. Briefly, she wondered why Sir Rufus had then used the ribbon to secure his recipes. A further act of pettiness? No, it was likely a convenience. One that allowed him to leave the defamatory memoir pages to be discovered in his usual leather case.

Thinking on the truth, Petra explained about Oliver, Annie's connection to him, and how he had heard five people arguing with Sir Rufus in the Green Drawing Room. How she knew two for certain—Aunt Ophelia herself and the Prince Regent—who Oliver said threatened the former royal chef. Then she explained that, after learning the names of every person walking the halls the morning of the murder—and via both some bloodhounding and some trial and error—she had been able to narrow her list and begin ruling people out. This included Lady Norworthy, Lord Wadley-Bates, and even Sir Franklin Haverstock, who had not argued with Sir Rufus in the drawing room, but seemingly had motive to want him dead.

"Then since you are innocent, too, Aunt, there are only two other possibilities," Petra said. "Major Carlson, and the Prince Regent." She screwed up her face for a moment. "Though I somehow feel as if they are both guilty of wrongdoings, yet one is truly a murderer."

"What about Colonel Wolston?" asked her aunt, adding, "I also heard your friends saying that you suspected him, as did Duncan."

"I think the colonel is doing the same thing in his position as the Windsor Castle constable as Major Carlson is as the royal solicitor. They are both obeying orders. But whilst I first saw Major Carlson as a sympathetic gentleman with hurt in his past and Colonel Wolston as, well . . . as quite the bully—one who enjoyed underestimating women and throwing suspects who had not been proven guilty into a dungeon, no less—I have since revised my opinions on both. For my good opinion can indeed be lost. Though once lost, it may be recovered again when someone shows me the goodness within their true selves."

Aunt Ophelia took both of Petra's hands in hers.

"That is both a Forsyth trait, and one you received from your mama. She, like me and your papa, would be so proud of you."

After a sniffle that had Sable tilting her head in silent curiosity, Petra returned to the matter at hand.

"We must determine if it was the major or the Prince who killed Sir Rufus. And we must find that manuscript."

She went to rise, but her aunt gently kept hold of her hands, keeping her in place. Then she spoke in low tones.

"Darling Petra, I am loath to say this, but you do understand that, whether or not we find the manuscript, if the Prince Regent is found to be the guilty party, there is nothing we can do to rectify the situation, yes? If we speak out, we will be called liars, and rebels, and insane. Especially because we are women. If we go to the newspapers, we might be the next in prison—and that is if we live to even see outside the castle walls again. And if we simply confront him, the Prince will never again believe he can trust us to keep our silence. We will have to look over our shoulders every moment of every day because there might be someone wishing to silence us with the utmost permanence."

Petra swallowed. Of course, she knew this, but hearing it put so calmly was sobering.

"The Prince *will* become king," Aunt Ophelia continued, "and whether we find the scandal-filled memoir or it is never found, the story of a former royal chef who might have known some silly gossip will fade away into legend. We, however, will be branded traitors to our King and nation, no matter what you might have done in the past to help the royal family. Your papa, your brother Alexander, and all your friends will suffer the same fate. I am not attempting to deter you, my dearest girl. I simply wish for you to truly realize what it means to take our next steps. Are you certain you wish to proceed?"

"You would take those steps with me?" Petra asked, for she had only heard "us" or "we" or "our," never simply "you."

"I would never leave your side," Aunt Ophelia replied without hesitation.

They spoke of their plans until exhaustion overcame both of them, but they did not sleep for long. The sun was just cresting the horizon and the clock hands showed it to be half five when Petra and her aunt left her bedchamber, determination fueling their steps. Moments later, Petra was shaking someone awake. One brown eye opened just enough to glare at her. Petra grinned.

"Caroline, dearest, you must wake up and get dressed, for we require you show us all the secret passages in the castle. We will need them if we are to trap a killer."

THIRTY-FIVE

"There are only four secret passageways? That is all?"

"Dearest, you asked me to show you the ones I knew," Caroline said grumpily. "I know of four, and now you have seen them. One in the guest wing that will take you from the Green Drawing Room to the South Terrace. A second that will take you from St. George's Hall into the kitchen larder. A third that will take you beneath the Great Staircase, giving access to both Brick Court and Horn Court. And the last—the one we just went through—from King John's Tower into the Queen's Ballroom."

She turned with pleading eyes toward Petra while Frances, Lottie, and Aunt Ophelia, the latter two holding the leads of both dogs, all walked around the quiet library, looking at books.

"Now may I go to bed again? Whitfield arrives today to do the swimming contest in Virginia Water Lake and I should like to look my best for him."

Petra looped her arm through Caroline's. "You know you look stunning even on five minutes of sleep. And since that is the case, I need all of us to help me with one more task here in the north wing whilst it is still too early for guests, or indeed the servants."

Caroline groaned. "You wish us to look for the manuscript. Did Mrs. Daley not already have her team of maids look here?"

"She was going to have them search the libraries this morning. But I had Annie tell her we would do so."

Annie, carrying a breakfast tray and still worried for Petra's health after the poisoning, had arrived early to Petra's bedchamber just as Aunt Ophelia left to change into a suitable dress. Petra, too, had changed, and she used the time to eat a piece of toast and tell Annie their plans.

"What will you have me do, my lady?" she had asked when all had been said.

"It is important that you stay near Curfew Tower to be on the lookout for any strange situations that might affect Oliver's life or health. I am glad to know you found him much improved, though. And that he is receiving proper food and drink. I am hoping we will have him released soon."

Nodding, Annie insisted on tidying Petra's hair before leaving once more to play her part in keeping Oliver safe.

Now, Caroline drew in a deep breath and stood tall, looking commandingly about the room. "All right, then, ladies. We are to search. The sooner we do so, the quicker I can return to my warm bed."

Some twenty minutes later, Lottie, Aunt Ophelia, and Fitz came hurrying back into the main library. "We have found another secret door," Lottie said excitedly. "Come, look."

Everyone followed to the edge of the main library, and a bookcase.

"I noticed some of the books looked like they needed straightening," Lottie said. "And then I noticed Fitz sniffing at where the bookcase meets the wall. I nearly tripped over his lead and put my hand on this book"—she pointed to a leather-bound copy of *Plants and Fauna of Northern Ireland*—"and I accidentally pulled it toward me."

She put a finger at the top of the book, angling it toward her. They heard a muffled click, and then part of the bookcase became a door.

"Where does it lead to?" asked Frances.

"We must explore and see," said Aunt Ophelia with a merry shrug. "There have been many changes to Windsor Castle since

1066, of course. These rooms likely used to be something else before they became libraries. No doubt they will change again in the future, for I hear Prinny is rather desperate to make renovations once he becomes King. He would like to now, but Her Majesty says he must wait."

Lottie said she would take Fitz and see where the corridor led, and Caroline went with her in case they ran into someone.

"I think this was how the killer escaped without detection," Petra said as they went inside, to which her aunt and Frances both agreed.

In one corner, Petra spied a breakfast tray with a coffeepot, an empty toast rack, and the broken shards of a cup, saucer, and plate. She felt sure this was the tray Sir Rufus brought from the kitchens. But if his killer took it, why was it here?

A short time later, Caroline and Lottie returned. The passageway led to Brick Court, but connected to another secret door into the small library.

"An excellent escape route indeed," Petra said.

Caroline, though, said that there was, in fact, one more secret door she had forgotten. However, it was more of a servants' door that was rarely used, so she hadn't counted it. Thus, they all trooped toward the end of the main library, near where it connected to the Queen's Ballroom. Caroline pushed open a door, which led to a series of steps.

"They go down, and out to the Quadrangle," she said. "But a servant can more easily reach the kitchens by this path if they are in a particular hurry. Or, they can cross the Quadrangle without having to wend their way through rooms."

It was decided the killer could have taken either exit, but that did not get Petra and her friends any closer to finding the manuscript. So they went back to looking for possible hiding places, or books that looked like they had been recently stuffed with extra pages. Lottie and Frances then moved with Petra into the small library, and the search began anew.

A night without much sleep had suddenly caught up to Petra. She looked through the main doors of the small library and saw the beautiful picture gallery.

"I will begin to check behind the portraits," she said—but in reality, she simply wished to sit on one of the benches and breathe for a few moments.

She had seen the room each day as she went through it to get to the libraries, of course, but she had barely stopped to look at any of the paintings. Famous artists such as Sir Anthony van Dyck, Sir Peter Lely, William Wissing, Joshua Reynolds, and Thomas Gainsborough were all represented. There were even a Titian and a Caravaggio, this one titled *Boy Peeling Fruit*.

But the bulk were portraits. King James I, King Henry VIII, Sir William Berkeley, the Duke of Albemarle, and many more, including some of whose subjects were once known as King Charles II's "Beauties." Petra walked slowly by seventeenth-century paintings of the Lady Sunderland, the Duchess of Somerset, and the Countess of Northumberland, amongst others.

Now, she was at the farthest corner, near the window that overlooked the North Terrace, and saw two benches.

She twirled around, deciding upon which one she would sit, and looked up. And she saw herself.

But it was not. She took three quick steps up to the large painting that was nearly her own height. With a background of lush green trees, recognizable as a small stand of oaks on the eastern side of Buckfields, a beautiful woman leaned slightly against the large stone column of a house.

In a Grecian-inspired silk dress of the lightest blue and a silhouette that was more reminiscent of the new, sleeker column styles that Petra and her friends wore, she was luminous. Her reddish-blond curls were piled high on her head and were not powdered as was the fashion. She wore a diaphanous shawl that curved into her elbows and flowed down like a waterfall to be caught in her lovely, slender fingers. She looked out from the painting, directly at Petra.

The plaque read MARIA ELINOR, COUNTESS OF HOLBROOK (1781).

Petra stared at her mother, who would have been twenty at the time of the sitting. Just four years younger than she herself was.

She had never seen this portrait of her mother before, though she knew it existed. It was painted by the great Thomas Gainsborough and had been in the country house of her uncle Tobias, who had barely escaped England earlier this year. The last Petra and her papa had heard of him, he was living in America, somewhere in Boston. They had agreed they felt rather sorry for Boston.

She knew her uncle had incurred great debts, and his house and possessions had been quickly sold to satisfy those to whom he owed money. Petra's father had sent some of his men to the house to collect any family memorabilia, but the Gainsborough portrait, as it had been always called, had gone.

No doubt it had been given by her uncle to either the Prince or the Queen as an apology, or to satisfy some debt, for it was known that Gainsborough had told His Majesty, King George, that the countess had been one of his very favorite portraits to paint, and that made it more valuable.

Petra looked up into her mother's face, seeing the little smile, her beautiful eyes, and the golden-red curls that were just like Petra's own. She wished with every fiber of her being that she could see her mother smile at her like that, just once.

A tear slid down her cheek as she put out her hand, her fingertips gently touching her mother's hand. Then she absently traced the ornate carving of the gilded wood frame as she took in every inch of her mother on the canvas.

Her fingers noted something different before she did, and after a long moment, she looked down at the small rectangular bump amongst all the frame's graceful curves and swirls. It was almost invisible to the eye, it blended in so well, this small little rectangle. She bent to get a closer look, and her heart began to thud in her chest.

It was another little plaque, hidden in the frame, for only the earl—who had framed the portrait—and those who found the painting as special as Petra did to discover.

LA BELLA CONTESSA

It was the name of the cake Sir Rufus had created for her mother. He had taken the moniker from the very name the Earl of Holbrook affectionately called his wife, beginning from when the two had toured Italy on their honeymoon. Petra still had a love letter written from her father to her mother, and he had begun with the salutation *La Bella Contessa, My Beautiful Countess*. It was how he would begin every letter to her until her mother's passing.

Petra then recalled seeing the recipe for the La Bella Contessa cake when she searched Sir Rufus's bedchamber, and feeling like he had deliberately, cruelly, left it out for her to find. A way for her to know that he had gone back on his word to never publish the recipe.

But what if he had been in fear for his life? What if he had truly felt his life might end during this week in the castle, and what if he had left that recipe out as a clue to the location of where he hid his memoir? A clue only she would be likely to recognize.

Petra eyed the painting again, this time where it met the stone wall behind. She recalled the story Mrs. Daley had told her of the housemaid who, upon removing a painting that had not been moved for over a century, found a loose stone with a hiding place behind it. Could it be possible that the same thing could happen here?

Slowly, for she worried about damaging the painting, Petra pulled the lower corner to see if it would come loose from the wall. It did, and upon seeing the painting was securely hung at the top, she pulled the painting farther away, looking for a loose stone in the wall. They all looked firmly in place. She tapped a few she could reach, just to be certain. Nothing.

"Bollocks," she whispered, then pulled her head back around to grin sheepishly up at the countess. "My apologies for my language, Mama. You never should have left Papa and so many stable lads to raise me—though I think you already knew you were doing what was best for me."

She went to slowly lower the painting back onto the wall, and that was when her fingers touched something else.

Once more, she lifted the painting, but this time she peered at the actual back of the portrait. Behind the struts that supported the large canvas, slid between the pieces of wood and the painting of the beautiful countess herself, were several sheets of paper. Even higher were more, for a total of three sections. By standing on her toes and sticking her tongue between her teeth, she just managed to remove them all.

She had found it. In her hands was Sir Rufus's manuscript.

Petra sank to the floor and did a rough count. There were around five and seventy pages, written in small, careful script on front and back, using every available inch of space.

Petra riffled through the stack, for the first time really noting Sir Rufus's slanting hand, which occasionally became an untidy scrawl. It looked familiar—and the reason came to her on a brief intake of breath. The crumpled note found in the *bureau à cylindre* desk, the one that read like physician's instructions to the Prince. Sir Rufus had written it, just as he'd written this manuscript.

Then she came to another page. The handwriting was spikier and, upon no more than a glance, it looked to be written in a more formal manner.

Quickly, she skimmed the words. Then had to force herself to slow down, and manage her suddenly shallow breathing.

This was not a letter, it was a legal document—and a damning one. It was relating multiple conversations, in detail of how His

Royal Highness, Prince George, planned to have his father stripped of his crown so that he, the Prince, could be declared King.

Sirs, the document went on to read, *this is a deliberate act of treachery. The Prince Regent is a traitor to our country, and the royal family, and I recommend all charges relating to treason be brought against him.*

It was signed *Major H. F. Carlson, Royal Solicitor to His Royal Highness, Prince George.*

And the person who was listed as being able to confirm at least two of the conversations was the former royal chef, Sir Rufus Pomeroy.

"This is what the Prince truly sought," Petra said aloud, her hand going to her forehead in disbelief. "This could have him stripped of his title and banished from Great Britain at the least. Or worse, likely imprisoned, and hanged or beheaded."

A voice came from the doorway.

"Mm, yes, that is rather something I would wish to avoid."

THIRTY-SIX

Petra scrambled to her feet and curtsied, holding the paper behind her back.

"Your Royal Highness, I did not hear you come in."

"Evidently not," said the Prince, advancing slowly toward her.

Petra glanced at the door; no one was there to bear witness.

"Your friends and Lady Ophelia are in the small library," the Prince said, easily knowing her thoughts. "They shall not disturb us."

He came within two strides of her, and peered down at the pages scattered upon the floor.

"I see you have found what so many have been looking for, Lady Petra. And you have discovered it is not just a memoir filled with salacious gossip my former chef overheard and disrespectfully recorded on paper. It also contains a petition for my arrest penned by my royal solicitor, Major Carlson."

There was no sense in denying it. "Indeed, Sir," she replied. Then blinked in some confusion. "But I am afraid I do not understand. Why is Major Carlson still here at the castle? I have seen you speaking with him several times, and heard you once asking him where the manuscript is. How does he not . . . ?" She drew in a soft breath, and brought the petition from behind her back. "The major thinks you are unaware this exists."

The Prince gave a mirthless chuckle. "Yes, he thinks I am quite unwitting, the fool. It was Sir Rufus who told me the first afternoon of these celebrations. I spoke with the chef twice—he rather angered me both times—and I am afraid he had no other chance to tell the tale."

Petra was horrified, but she kept her expression as calm as she could, though another puzzle piece had slid into place. The sixth person Oliver Beecham had mentioned, but had never heard speak, was not a separate person at all. Instead, it was the Prince, who had confronted Sir Rufus twice, only to have Sir Rufus taunt him about having hidden the information he needed.

"Would you at least tell me what happened, Your Royal Highness?" she said. "For I know you must have entered the small library through the main library—and no servant saw you because you used the secret passageways. And I expected you exited in the same manner? But then how did you see Sir Franklin?"

The Prince had been looking as if her suppositions were simply a foregone conclusion, but now he sniffed dismissively.

"I never saw Sir Franklin, Lady Petra, and would no more worry if I had. But you are correct otherwise. I went to seek help from Colonel Wolston."

"To remove Sir Rufus's body from the library before anyone could see it?" Petra asked quietly.

While the Prince had never been her favorite in the royal family, it was truly horrid to hear him all but confess in such a cold manner to strangling someone. Citizens were supposed to be able to trust their leaders, were they not? The sinking feeling in her stomach almost made her feel as if she had been poisoned again.

Then she startled, taking a half step back, when the Prince all but bellowed his reply.

"*What?*" he said, his eyes bugging with her question. "Of course not, Lady Petra. I fetched the colonel to provide the chef with assistance. When I came through the secret doorway, well, Mama would say I was in high dudgeon. I shouted, "A word, you fiend!" and regrettably, it frightened Sir Rufus enough that he startled, just like you did. He tripped over his own feet, and fell, injuring his wrist. Broke one of Mama's Wedgwood coffee cups when he fell, plus a plate, too. In my haste, I even apologized to Sir Rufus, before telling him I would return *tout de suite*. I was so out of sorts, I took the tray with me and left it in the secret passageway."

Petra forgot herself for a moment, and gave the Prince Regent the cutty-eye.

"You are saying you did not strangle him? Sir?"

The Prince jutted his chin and literally rolled his royal eyes, making him rather look like an indignant boy of eight who had been falsely accused of stealing biscuits.

"If I had wished to kill Sir Rufus, I would have used the horseman's mace that was all but within arm's reach, Lady Petra. I would have bashed him on the head, and then used the spiked end to stab him in the neck, right at that rather large vein." With one pudgy, beringed finger, he stroked the side of his neck. "He would have been dead in seconds. I certainly would not have worked for minutes strangling him using some woman's hair ribbon. I was not even wearing my gloves!" He paused, adding silkily, "But Major Carlson was."

Seeing Petra's shocked face, her mouth dropping open when he identified the murderer—and that he had clearly known all along the major was the guilty man—the Prince tsked.

"Wolston and I returned by way of the main library and, unbeknownst to Major Carlson, who was off his head with rage, we witnessed him in the last seconds of strangling Sir Rufus. Oh, do not look at me in such a way, Lady Petra, the deed had sadly been done. There was nothing we could do."

He paced in front of her for a few steps. Petra, her head spinning with revelations, was just realizing it must have been the major himself who had seen Sir Franklin—and vice versa—when the Prince continued.

"Wolston wanted to arrest him, and I agreed, but then came a knock on the library doors—it was the valet calling out, startling

Major Carlson. Wolston and I barely made it to my secret door when the major came running through the main library. It was clear he used the hidden servant's door, which prevented him from being seen. Yes, of course there is a peephole, do not be a simpleton! One must be able to ensure one will not be seen before one exits a secret passageway, mustn't one, Lady Petra?"

For a moment, Petra could do nothing but stare at somewhere left of the Prince's ear, and then her eyes snapped to his face.

"You will have to forgive my impertinence, Your Royal Highness, but I must speak with some outrage. Why did you send Colonel Wolston to follow Mr. Shawcross to the library and be *absolutely beastly* to that innocent valet? Why did you not arrest Major Carlson immediately after you saw him kill Sir Rufus? Do you know the major also poisoned Sir Franklin? With arsenic in a pot of tea. But that pot was meant for *me*."

And then a memory from finding the major in the grove of trees within the Long Walk came to her mind. One that she had thought nothing of until now. The incident had suddenly been reshaped in her mind. The innocent becoming the sinister. She resisted the urge to feel her own neck.

"And after he had already tried to strangle me once on the Long Walk. Yes, indeed, Sir, he pretended to hurt his leg and asked me to assist him. Then he slung his arm about my shoulders and pretended to be so in pain that his arm went under my neck. And then he kept tightening his hold, choking me as I attempted to help him. If Colonel Wolston had not arrived, I would likely be strangled and dead, too!"

It was a sight she would unlikely see again, but the Prince Regent looked pale and horrified. His hand even went to his mouth for a moment. Then he gained command of himself and stood straight and still once more.

"I did not know, Lady Petra," he finally said. "I hope you will forgive me for letting Carlson remain at large."

Petra did not immediately speak, for she was recalling another innocent-seeming situation, this one involving the major and the young dowager countess whose affections he had been so determined to have the night of the supper. He had seduced her a second time the morning of Sir Rufus's murder. Petra now thought it possible that Major Carlson did so in order to give him an alibi if required.

Or was it possible he was simply that much of a cad? It was indeed hard to tell.

Yet Petra's silence had unnerved the Prince and he began rattling off his reasonings, looking shamefaced. Yet, the whiny thread in his voice made it difficult to give him any pity.

"I had to let the major go free, you understand. He had composed that petition you have in your hands right now. I had to find it before he was arrested so he could not shout about it for all and sundry to hear. For if I were in possession of the petition, he would have no proof."

"Especially after murdering Sir Rufus, the one other person who could testify to his claims," Petra said thoughtfully.

"Indeed, Lady Petra. The major's rooms and office were discreetly searched, and the petition could not be found. Wolston thought that the reason the major strangled Sir Rufus was because he had flown into a rage after Sir Rufus himself had stolen the evidence." The Prince nodded to the paper in Petra's hand, one side of his mouth briefly quirking up. "One of the major's flaws in being my royal solicitor is that he never makes copies of the documents he draws up at the same time as the original."

"So you were unaware Sir Rufus had stolen this petition?" Petra asked, and the Prince nodded.

"You are correct. I realized what must have happened, however, when the major began acting desperate to locate something. It seems he and Lord Wadley-Bates were both searching the Green Drawing Room at the same time—the major for the document you are holding, and Wadley-Bates for Sir Rufus's cookery book manuscript—unaware, I think, of what his author had truly written. It was postulated that Sir Rufus might have taken the petition and hidden it with the defamatory memoir he has managed to keep out of our hands for so long. And it seems he did."

Petra wanted to gather all the aforementioned memoir pages, roll them up, and give the Prince Regent a good whack with them. Or maybe a dozen good whacks. Instead, she stood there, looking at the petition again.

"Is this true, Sir?" she asked quietly. "All that Major Carlson has put forth?"

The Prince looked mulish for a moment, and then seemed to deflate a bit.

"It is, Lady Petra. To an extent. It seems the wording makes me willing to commit regicide in order to wear the crown. That part is not true. I love my papa, and I have the utmost respect for both the institution that is the Crown *and* my King. I merely believe Great Britain would be stronger if she were ruled by a king who could stand proudly in front of his people and give them confidence in both their monarch and their country.

"It has already been four years since I became the Prince Regent, and there were spates of time before this that I ruled as the regent as well. I have proven myself, and yet the title of King is not mine to have. My poor papa . . . His Majesty would never know if he were no longer on the throne. His mind is sadly gone. I simply think it is time, Lady Petra. But my wishes, and my words, were turned into something cruel and heinous by Major Carlson. I felt as if he understood them—at least in the beginning—so I cannot think as to why he would do such a thing."

Petra did not wish to, but she believed the Prince when he said he thought he was doing what was best for the country—not that she either agreed or disagreed. She felt he had a point, but did not especially feel the need to strip the crown from King George before his death. It was something to debate with her friends at some later point. If she were even allowed to, that was.

Yet she also felt the Prince was genuinely confused by the major's actions. He felt hurt and betrayed. And Petra, too, was surprised. In fact, she wondered if there might be another reason for Major Carlson's willingness to vilify the Prince. Choosing her words carefully and bracing herself for a heated reaction, she asked him just that, and was surprised when he seemed to think on it.

He turned his head to regard some of the magnificent portraits, his eyes landing on one of the famous Beauties. He admired her décolletage as he spoke musingly.

"He has never seemed to get over the sad death of his own papa, you know, and I expect the false idea that I might wish mine the same fate has made the major cease to think clearly. I suppose I could understand such a notion. His father, Lord Carlson, was my own dear friend—and oh, the pranks we used to play on one another! I recall one time fondly where he managed to detour my path so that I ended up ankle-deep in horse muck—I later 'accidentally' made him stumble directly into a pig trough." The Prince chuckled at this memory, but his voice soon quieted. "Lord Carlson took his own life, but the major has never truly seemed to wrap his mind about that fact. I suppose I could understand that as well. I witnessed the so-called black dog taking Lord Carlson in its grip many times over the years, each time seemingly dragging him deeper into his despairs. It did not just come from the tragedies of his eldest son and wife, you know, but from somewhere deep within him. I don't know that the major truly saw that."

The Prince pursed his lips thoughtfully, then turned back to fix his blue eyes onto Petra, his mind once more turned back to himself.

"It may interest you to know, that even before today, I had decided not to go through with any avenue that might force the issue of being crowned before my father's death."

She gave him a small smile. "I am happy to hear it, Sir."

"And may I trust that you will not repeat what you have read in this document?" he asked, one eyebrow raising.

Petra blinked. "Of course, Your Royal Highness. I would have no reason to repeat it. I swear it most faithfully."

"Good," he said, with a look of relief that quickly vanished into his normal, slightly bored countenance. "For I like you, Lady Petra, and I would not wish to be forced to make certain you uphold your promise."

He held out a hand, and Petra handed him the document. But she did not release it completely.

"Sir, if I may be so bold, what assurance do I have that you will not go back on your word?"

"Is not my word good enough?"

"Normally, I would say yes, Your Royal Highness. But I am afraid that, in this instance, I require something more."

The Prince looked as if he might give a snappish reply, then he realized this was not an unreasonable question.

"Call your friends, Lady Ophelia, and my cousin Lady Caroline in."

Petra went to the doors and did as she was asked. Moments later, her aunt and her friends all flowed silently inside, Sable and Fitz with their ears up and their tails down, as if unsure of the situation. She then returned to where she had previously stood, near the Prince.

Everyone curtsied. Lottie spoke a word in Gaelic and both Fitz and Sable sank down on their front paws in a very proper bow. Prince George stared at the dogs, and then nodded and murmured, "Capital, capital."

And then two more people entered the room, and Petra's heart did a joyful little flip when she saw Duncan.

He stepped slowly inside, bowing to the Prince, his face a calm but serious mask. Following him, with no trace of animosity on his countenance, was Colonel Wolston.

"Your Royal Highness, I come bearing information," Duncan said. "But it may wait if you would like Wolston and myself to leave."

"Indeed, Sir," Wolston said.

"No, Wolston. Remain here," said the Prince.

"May Mr. Shawcross stay as well, Sir?" Petra asked. She paused, then mustered her confidence. "For not only is he Her Majesty's and Her Grace's trusted intelligence officer, but I think you are already aware of the gossip surrounding Mr. Shawcross and me. It is true, I assure you. And thus, he is a most trusted confidant and friend."

Lottie and Frances looked on in awe. Caroline and Aunt Ophelia looked proud. Duncan looked prouder. Wolston looked inscrutable. The Prince looked exasperated, but waved her off.

"Yes, yes, Lady Petra. Shawcross may stay."

Silence reigned afterward for several moments. Petra briefly bit her lip, wondering if she had finally been too impertinent, and would be sent off to America on the next ship.

"Lady Petra has done me a great service," the Prince said suddenly, making everyone start slightly. He seemed not to notice as he regarded his fingernails for a moment. "She has risked everything for the truth. And there is a quite specific truth she now knows about me. Lady Petra has asked for assurance that the knowledge she has obtained will not put her life, or the lives of those she cares about, in danger. And she is right to ask for such assurance."

This caused the eyes of the women standing before her to widen. For that matter, so did Petra's. Even Duncan and Wolston briefly glanced at Petra, then back to the Prince.

"As such, I am giving Lady Petra the right to tell the five of you what she knows," the Prince continued. "For Wolston is already aware. Yet all of you will hear me as I give my word that no harm shall come to any of you with this knowledge. I shall trust that you will never speak of it, and you shall trust me to hold my counsel as well. So long as this is the case, there shall be no repercussions."

He looked at Petra and she curtsied. "Thank you, Your Royal Highness."

He inclined his head graciously.

When the Prince turned back to Petra, Duncan sent her a wink. She had to curl her toes not to grin, or return the wink, lest the Prince think it was for him. For Petra recalled her aunt Ophelia saying the Prince kissed rather like a gasping toad. She bit the inside of her cheek to keep from a burst of laughter that, knowing herself, would no doubt include an unladylike snort.

Instead, she used her voice again.

"Sir, if I may, I have one more request."

He raised an eyebrow and his nostrils flared, but he did not say no.

"I would like you to release Mr. Oliver Beecham, valet for Sir Rufus, from custody in the Curfew Tower dungeon. Especially as he is wholly innocent. And if there are any documents that have been drawn up falsely saying otherwise, they should be destroyed."

The Prince pursed his lips, but without much irritation.

"Yes, I suppose it is the right thing to do," he said on a sigh. He looked to Wolston. "See that it is done." He then looked to Duncan. "Shawcross, give the valet some coin for his troubles. And if he has any reasonable debts, pay them. But it should be impressed upon him to keep his counsel as to what happened. Also, I want him gone from the castle grounds by tonight."

"I will do so, Sir," Duncan said, and Wolston gave his pledge as well.

The Prince shook his hair back, making his chins wobble.

"We have just about one full day before over a thousand guests descend upon Windsor Castle for the ball, Lady Petra," he said. "This includes the tilting out on the Quadrangle, as well as the finale of the patisserie contest. I should like to enjoy every minute of it—including the tilt, where I have wagered my mama on who will win. Thus, what say you on how we should induce Major Carlson to confess?"

Petra grinned. For her mind had already been ruminating on just such an offer.

"I say that if you are amenable, Sir, I should like to use you as bait."

THIRTY-SEVEN

"My lords, ladies, and gentlemen!" called out the Queen's steward with as much aplomb as ever. "Welcome to the fourth day of Her Majesty's patisserie contest!"

By now the crowd had begun to look forward to the steward's antics and they clapped heartily. Petra did, too, even while using the moment to watch as Lottie, who was sitting next to Major Carlson on one of the long benches in the second row. She was holding Fitz, and used her bright, sweet smile to encourage the major to shift over. Then over some more, until he was positioned between Lottie and the terrace wall.

Realizing this, he tried to stand and move, but with a word in Fitz's ear from Lottie, the little terrier leapt into the major's lap like he wished for nothing more than to be petted. Lottie cooed, scratching Fitz behind the ear, even as Frances slipped onto the bench beside her, followed by Aunt Ophelia and the unwitting Duchess of Hillmorton. The major looked disgruntled, but there was nothing he could do. He was pinned in by four women—including one duchess—until the gong's first sounding.

While the steward was enthusing over the previous days of the contest, Petra then surreptitiously watched as Duncan, who had been standing at the back of the seating area, casually walked back into the castle.

"You will see, my lords and ladies, that we have a new judge for today," continued the steward with a wide smile. "Sir Franklin Haverstock unfortunately was taken slightly ill, but is expected to return for the finale tomorrow. Until then, please welcome the commanding officer of His Majesty's Coldstream Guards, Colonel Wolston!"

The colonel accepted the clapping with a smile, and Petra was left thinking he looked rather nice that way. And glancing over at the seats crowded with guests, she felt Lottie might be noticing as well.

Surprisingly, Petra found it was an attraction she did not mind watching as it unfolded.

For earlier, once everyone had left the picture gallery and Petra's plan to entrap Major Carlson had been laid out and refined, she found herself alone with Wolston, who silently helped her pick up and tidy the pages of Sir Rufus's memoir.

Taking the last few sheets she handed him, he said, "Because it is my job, my lady."

"I beg your pardon?" Petra said, confused.

"You are wondering why I followed the orders I was given."

"Why you allowed an innocent man to be treated poorly, thrown into a dungeon, beaten, and nearly hanged?" Petra asked, the false sweetness in her tone thicker than treacle.

"I did not order the beating. His Roy—" Wolston stopped himself. "No, you are correct. All of it was wrong. But it is my job to ensure that the royal family stays safe, even if that sometimes entails doing things I would rather not."

"Then it is a pitiable job, at least when you are required to do such things."

"I cannot disagree with you on that score, Lady Petra," he said, a brief half smile coming to his lips. "If it helps any, I would not have allowed Beecham to hang. I would have created false evidence of some unknown blackguard being seen if I had to, but I would not have let an innocent man lose his life."

"It does help, yes," Petra said, but only after several seconds of thinking this over.

"But I take protecting the royal family quite seriously," he said.

"Most days, it is the right and correct thing to do, and I sleep exceptionally well at night. There are only some days—like this past week—that I do not."

After another moment, Petra nodded. She could understand this. Duncan himself occasionally lived in what he called "the gray in-between" that ran down the middle of right and wrong. When he had to walk that line, Petra could see the strain it put on him. She was quite happy that most of the time, he was on the correct side.

"I must say that I rather enjoyed the verbal tilting contest you and I engaged in," Wolston said with another half smile, this one a bit longer in duration. "You are every bit as Shawcross described, Lady Petra." He chuckled at the look on her face. "Are you surprised that Shawcross and I have formed a truce? Or that I agree with his rather effusive praise of you."

"Both," she blurted out, then said, "but I am rather glad you and I are now comrades. Though I hope to never hear you speak that way to me again, unless you should like a good bash on the conker."

Wolston chuckled with his hands up in surrender, and then sketched a bow, saying he would see her at the patisserie judges' table.

"We are to meet in the Pages' Room, Major," Petra reminded him, "for Chef Carême to instruct us on what we should look for in today's bakes, as one is his own creation."

Wolston nodded and moved off. But before reaching the doors, however, he turned back and asked with a charmingly nervous look if her friend, Miss Lottie Reed, had an attachment with anyone in particular.

"She is quite unattached, Colonel," Petra said. She had felt free to give this information after Lottie had whispered much the same question in Petra's ear earlier. Wolston, his mind favorably engaged with thoughts of Lottie, had finally left the picture gallery, manuscript in hand, not noticing Petra had held back one page, or the troubled look that crossed her features.

It had caught her eye because it was simply a handful of notes in Sir Rufus's hand. Words he intended to turn into another tale, no doubt. Though little embellishment was required to make it scandalous, for it concerned the Prince Regent, his late comrade Lord Carlson, and—the word circled with such angry force that the paper had torn—poison. And to the side, Petra saw five words in the spiky hand belonging to the still-grieving son of the poisoned man: *He will die for this.*

Yet she could not help but wonder: Was the major referring to Sir Rufus, the Prince Regent, or both?

The crowd's gasp brought Petra's concentration smartly back to the North Terrace. The steward had just explained that the difficulty of the patisserie contest had increased significantly.

In both giddy anticipation and also nervous hopes for Mrs. Bing, Petra rubbed her perspiring palms on the skirts of her blue riding habit, which she had worn because it was the easiest outfit to get herself in and out of without Annie's help. For her lady's maid—after tearfully embracing Petra—had raced out to Curfew Tower to greet Oliver as he was being released. She had a small bag of money from Duncan, some supplies from Frances for Oliver's continued healing, and a set of clothes from Oliver's own trunks for him to change into.

"Once he's had a bath and a shave," Duncan had said with a chuckle. "For he smells worse than five pigs in a rotten pigsty, I can tell you that."

"Where will they stay?" Petra asked.

"The Horse and Groom, directly outside the castle walls," Duncan said. "Wolston himself spoke with the proprietor to make certain Annie and Beecham would be treated well. And tomorrow, they set off for London. They will go to my town house until you and I return after the contest."

Smiling at the thought of Annie and her brother having time together, Petra gave her attention to the steward as he explained the bakes.

"The four remaining cooks were asked to make two recipes each for this round!" he said grandly. "One is a pudding they have made likely many times at their respective houses—the blancmange! Each cook must use the same base ingredients: cream, sugar, almonds, and some isinglass, which provides the pudding its thickness. It should be in a decorative mold of the cook's choice. But it is at their discretion to add flavorings, or even color. It is served cold and, as Chef Antonin Carême tells me, the blancmange must be very smooth and very white to be at its most delicious."

The crowd made murmurs of excitement and the steward patiently waited for them to quieten.

"But then our cooks were also challenged to make a recipe they have never even seen before! This recipe, honored guests, is one Chef Carême invented himself and is called the fanchonette. I am told they are small tarts with a lemon custard and topped with a glistening meringue. And as I understand it, they are in equal parts sweet and bright to the tongue, and wholly delectable!"

Petra nodded her agreement. Catching this, the grinning steward explained that the four judges had been shown by Chef Carême exactly what his fanchonettes should look like, and been given a taste to know how best to judge those baked by the remaining cooks. He then reminded everyone to return when they heard his gong and then cried out his now-familiar refrain.

"Ready, my lord and lady judges? Yes? Then please begin!"

Petra was amused to note Lottie, Frances, and Aunt Ophelia standing as if to get a better look at the puddings, thereby continuing to block Major Carlson's exit. Then she and her fellow judges rose and walked to the main table, where they viewed the four blancmanges as whole desserts, each molded into a different shape to best show off the glistening, creamy pudding. Once they all were satisfied and had made notes to themselves, the blancmanges were each cut into four equal parts for the judges.

At the same time the judges received another set of four plates, each containing two small fanchonette tarts. For the first time, Petra could tell which cooks had a natural affinity for any recipe, and which did not.

Of the four plates of fanchonettes, one contained perfect-looking small tarts with glistening meringue tops and just a hint of lemony yellow custard peeking out of the pastry shell. A second plate of them looked quite nicely done, but not as pretty as the first. The third plate held tarts that were just shy of burnt or falling apart, and the fourth were clearly fanchonettes, but possibly how a first-time baker might make them.

Yet as these were experienced cooks, the bakes themselves all tasted delicious, despite their shortcomings. In all, Petra found it a much harder decision, for the cook with the beautiful fanchonettes had made a blancmange that was slightly less flavorful, and was studded with almonds in quite an odd way. And then the cook whose fanchonettes were quite simple-looking had made the silkiest blancmange flavored with lavender and rose essence, which made a whispered "delicious" escape Petra's lips.

When the guests were all gathered again, they looked on with bated breaths. Despite the gentle nature of the contest—for no one but Petra's friends and Major Carlson knew there had been a poisoning the day before—everyone had become invested in knowing which house would be home to the best baker in England.

"Oh, I cannot look!" Petra said quietly to her fellow judges as the steward rose to announce the two finalists. She put her hands up to half cover her eyes. "Caroline, how does Mrs. Bing seem?"

"Like she wishes to win, dearest," Caroline replied.

"Hmm, she does indeed," said Lord Wadley-Bates genially, and almost as if he were eyeing Petra's cook for being a potential authoress of a cookery book.

"And the two cooks moving forward to the finals are . . ." Once more, the drumroll came from one of the Coldstream Guards. "Mrs. Bing of Forsyth House and Mrs. Davis of Norworthy Manor!"

Petra wanted to jump up and down like Frances and Lottie—who had returned to their seats with Fitz. Instead, she clapped enthusiastically for her cook, with quick glances back at Lottie, who was holding up one of her dog's paws in what looked to be a wave.

In fact, Lottie was giving a signal. She was indicating that Duncan and Charles had begun to implement the agreed-upon trap for the major. Petra searched for the royal solicitor, and found him now sitting next to the widowed countess he had seduced. She was casting him glances, which he ignored as he clapped. When his eyes met Petra's, they narrowed, and she hastily looked away.

Touching her right earring, Petra then signaled back to Lottie that she was ready, and continued heartily clapping for the finalists. She did briefly catch Mrs. Bing's eyes, though, and gave her a smile and a nod, which made her cook grin ever wider.

The steward managed to quiet the clapping, his own delight obvious.

"And tomorrow, for our final day of the contest, our two finalists will cook their most difficult bake yet. It is another of Chef Carême's recipes, and he has created it specially to celebrate the lasting love between Their Majesties, our beloved King George and Queen Charlotte, on the occasion of four and fifty years of marriage.

"The recipe is called *vol-au-vents Puits d'Amour,* or the Fountain of Love vol-au-vents! They are light and airy pastries formed into a shape of the cook's choice and having a hollow middle. They are then dipped in caramel, and filled with a pastry crème, again of the cook's choice, and then decorated with various garnishes. They will be a delight to look at, and shall no doubt taste even better." When the crowd murmured their excitement, the steward added, "And remember, whilst our judges will submit their recommendations, Chef Carême himself has the honor of deciding the winner of Her Majesty's patisserie contest."

More enthusiastic clapping ensued, and then a team of liveried footmen arrived holding platters full of fanchonettes.

"My lords, ladies, and gentlemen, as a treat, Chef Carême would like for you all to try one of his fanchonettes," said the steward. "Then, if you will, there are carriages waiting to take all of you down to the south end of Windsor Great Park and Virginia Water Lake for an afternoon of thrilling swimming contests. Please, enjoy!"

There was lively chatter as the guests rose and descended on the platters, including the Queen. Enjoying their fanchonettes and none the wiser that a killer was about to be unmasked on the North Terrace, the crowd slowly dispersed in the direction of the waiting carriages.

But Petra had taken note of something even before the guests stood, and a dose of apprehension washed the lingering sweetness from her mouth. Hastily she waved her three friends over, and beckoned to Colonel Wolston, too.

"Where is Aunt Ophelia? And the major?" she asked. "The plan was to confront him here, on the terrace, but they seem to have disappeared."

"Not only that," Caroline said, looking about. "But so has the Prince."

THIRTY-EIGHT

Wolston answered first. "I noted His Royal Highness was called away by one of my men as the two finalists were announced. I shall go in search of him now."

He strode off and Lottie's voice lowered to a whisper. "Lady Ophelia said she required the *chamber pot*." A level of anguish came into her voice. "She hurried off after we heard Mrs. Bing's name, intent on being here to help with the trap. Then I became caught up cheering the finalists and failed to notice she hadn't returned."

"We do not even know if there is an issue yet," Petra said soothingly. "Did anyone see the major leave?"

"I did," replied Frances. "I heard him tell that poor countess he is treating so ill that he wished to stretch his bad leg. I saw him then speak first with Sir Franklin and then Lord Wadley-Bates. Then he was gone. Duncan is already attempting to locate him."

"Good," Petra said. "In the meantime, we shall stay here and wait. Once the Prince has returned, and the major can be lured back, our plan will go into motion."

"And it is a good one," said Lottie, "with the Prince pretending to accuse Lady Ophelia of murdering Sir Rufus, and you tearfully admitting all the ways she is guilty."

"I rather like the part where Lady Ophelia pretends to lose control of her senses, becoming so desperate that she blurts out to the major the information you found in Sir Rufus's memoir," Frances said.

"Adding kindling to the major's rage until he confesses or does something quite stupid, at which point Wolston and Shawcross will both jump out and apprehend him," added Caroline with some satisfaction. "Though I hoped my Whitfield would be able to add a third trusted bit of well-formed muscle to the mix. But the timing for the swimming contests was moved up in order to draw the attention of the guests away, and alas, he must compete. I suppose it is for the best."

Much to Caroline's delight, her paramour, Lord Whitfield, had arrived this morning, just after the events that had taken place in the picture gallery. He and Caroline had immediately gone out onto the Long Walk and had disappeared until an hour before the patisserie contest. Petra had picked a blade of grass from Caroline's rather untidy chignon just before they had sat down at the judges' table.

Though Caroline's mouth had curved upward like a cat with cream, her smile had not reached her eyes like usual. However, when Petra asked if anything was amiss, the response was a blithe "No, no, of course not."

"Why do you not go with the other guests down to the lake and watch Whitfield compete?" Petra now said. "We have this task in hand, do we not? And if you recall, there will be a team of Coldstream Guards standing by to help apprehend the major. Really, you should go."

Caroline's eyes brightened in a hopeful way. "All right. I think I shall, then," she said, and rushed off after kissing each of her friends on both cheeks, urging them all to be careful.

Soon, the crowds had thinned to nothing, and another team of footmen was swarming in to remove the judging tables and benches, leaving Petra, Lottie, Frances, and the dogs all standing on the North Terrace, not far from the Queen Elizabeth Steps.

Duncan and Colonel Wolston arrived together moments later, with Charles following close behind.

"We have had reports that Major Carlson has taken the Prince to St. George's Chapel. The Prince told the guards that he had business to discuss with the major, and they are to be left alone."

"Truly?" Petra asked. "Do you believe that he will attempt to convince the major to turn himself in? Or is he simply being foolish?"

"I take no pleasure in saying it, but with the Prince, it could be either," replied Wolston grimly. "One of my guards said that he heard the major say he had news for the Prince's daughter, the Princess Charlotte, who is currently residing in Dorset. His Royal Highness and the princess have recently reconciled from her refusal to marry the Prince of Orange of the Netherlands, and she has petitioned her father to contact the man she wishes to marry, Prince Leopold of Saxe-Coburg. He has done so through Major Carlson, and it is possible the major has news that will be difficult to explain to the princess."

"Then do you recommend we give them some time?" Petra asked. "What if the major intends to harm the Prince?"

"I had the same questions, Lady Petra. And I must say I do not like this at all. The guards who gave me this information . . . let us just say that I feel their loyalty could easily stray," Wolston said, before seeming to come to a decision. "Shawcross, will you accompany me to the chapel? I know a way in where we will be able to at least determine the safety of the Prince."

Duncan readily agreed and it was decided by all that Petra and her friends would be safer in some other part of the castle. Indicating Charles, he said, "I shall send Foyle back within the hour to meet you ladies in the Green Drawing Room. At that point, we can then revise our plan to entrap Major Carlson."

As the three of them walked across the Quadrangle, a footman came running up, looking to Frances.

"Miss Bardwell? I was asked by Chef Carême to see if you could come. One of our cooks has burned her hand quite badly."

"Yes, of course," Frances said. "I need my supplies, though."

"Lottie and I will bring them," Petra said. "Go and help that girl as best you can until then."

Frances hurried off with the footman toward the kitchens, while Petra and Lottie aimed toward the south wing and their corridor of rooms, where they collected Frances's apothecary bag. They had just left the dogs in the room enjoying bowls of water and a treat of dried pigs' ears when Tilly, their hall maid, arrived.

She curtsied and said, "I have a note for you, Lady Petra, from Lady Ophelia."

"Where did you see her? And when?" Petra demanded, taking the note.

"It were, oh, about ten minutes ago, my lady," Tilly said, uncertainty showing in her eyes at Petra's fierce look. "She came up to me, handed me the note, and told me to give it to you. She said nothing else, my lady. Lord Wadley-Bates were waitin' for her ladyship, though."

Petra felt herself relax. If Aunt Ophelia was with Lord Wadley-Bates, then she was not in any danger. Then she read the note, in her aunt's neat script.

My darling Petra. Come <u>alone</u> to the top of the Round Tower. Your loving aunt, Ophelia Louisa

Frowning, Petra turned the note over, but found nothing else. Come to the Round Tower, alone? It was a strange request, and nothing like any note she'd ever received from her spirited aunt. And why would Aunt Ophelia be with Lord Wadley-Bates to begin with? Was she indeed safe with the publisher?

Petra quickly thought back to finding Lord Wadley-Bates in Sir Rufus's bedchamber. To how he knew rather a lot of information concerning Sir Rufus's dealings, but seemed to be so innocent, and quite kind even when imparting unsavory details.

Gooseflesh popped up on her arms as she realized she might

have believed in the publisher's goodness when he did not deserve it. She read the note again. Could it be that Lord Wadley-Bates and Major Carlson had conspired together to kill the former royal chef? If so, it would no doubt be to publish the cookery book for profit—and possibly even the memoir, too.

Yes, if his lordship had indeed known about the memoir, he might have easily convinced the major that, with the right edits guaranteed to remove any mention of Major Carlson and the Prince Regent, the subsequent book would still be scandalously truthful in the extreme. And the type that would sell an extraordinary number of books, too.

Enough to give his lordship's four daughters an excellent dowry. And enough that Major Carlson could leave the Prince's employ and start a new life, one that possibly would have made his late father proud.

Something about this thought . . . about the truth . . . well, it felt almost like something inside of her was nudging her forward, as if attempting to guide her in the right direction.

But this feeling was soon superseded by thoughts of Aunt Ophelia. Had Major Carlson and Lord Wadley-Bates somehow figured out Petra's plan to capture the major, and then abducted Aunt Ophelia in order to force Petra's hand?

And what about the Prince? Was he indeed safe with Duncan and Wolston at St. George's Chapel? Or had he colluded with the major and the publisher as well? Fingers to her lips, Petra cursed softly. She would have to go to the Round Tower, by herself as directed, and find out.

Yet she would not allow herself to be alone there for long.

She turned to Lottie, who was checking Frances's apothecary bag and had not noticed anything amiss. When she spoke, Petra worked to keep her voice light.

"Lottie," she said, "my aunt would like my assistance with some matter. Why do you not take Tilly with you to the kitchens so that

Frances may help the girl who has burned herself? I shall meet you both in the Green Drawing Room afterward."

It took no more persuading. Lottie and the hall maid hurried off toward the kitchens, their arms laden with all the supplies Frances could need.

For a moment, Petra felt rather ridiculous, standing in her bedchamber, alone, with a cryptic and confusing note clenched in her hand, and it was a feeling she loathed.

But she rectified it by adding a few words to the note that her friends would soon see.

Finding the dark-blue ribbon Aunt Ophelia's lady's maid had given her, Petra returned to Lottie and Frances's room, rolling up her aunt's note with her own wording added, and affixing it to Sable's collar with the ribbon as her hound chewed happily on her treat. Then she rushed out of the room and dashed across the hall, knocking on her aunt's door.

"Geraldine?" she called.

When her aunt's lady's maid failed to answer, Petra did not hesitate, but pulled up the skirt of her riding habit to reveal the leather garters and extracted the right lockpicks.

Moments later, she was in her aunt's room, but it was empty.

Petra was about to leave when she thought again on the note her aunt had written.

It had been signed *Ophelia Louisa*—something her aunt never did, though she was proud to be named after her great-grandmother.

Why would she have invoked the name Louisa, then? What was she trying to say?

It came to Petra as she recalled the day when she'd asked Geraldine to look for the black silk ribbon, but all that had been found was . . .

"The ring," she whispered, and rushed into the dressing room, looking for her aunt's jewelry case. She soon found the ring, with its large cabochon of lapis lazuli. Carefully, she opened the hinge. Had her aunt refilled it with poison, to use against a foe as a last resort?

And yet, the space was empty. She slid the ring onto the middle finger of her right hand regardless. Why had Aunt Ophelia deliberately alluded to it, though?

"I cannot think on it now," Petra said aloud, with the sudden feeling that she was running out of time. She dashed out of her aunt's room—and nearly collided with Lady Norworthy.

"Why, Lady Petra. The very person for whom I was searching."

"Lady Norworthy, I am afraid I do not have—"

"Of course you have the time," her ladyship replied with a frown, and all but shooed Petra back into her own room. Closing the door and swiftly raising her lorgnette to her eyes, she said, "Your duties as patisserie judge are completed for the day, and I merely have a question to ask of you. I speak on behalf of Her Majesty, in fact. I came back early from the swimming contest in order to pose it to you."

"Indeed?" Petra said, impatiently pushing away a stray curl from her face, which was no doubt flushed.

"I was telling Her Majesty that the rumor is true—that you have been learning to protect yourself," said Lady Norworthy, seemingly oblivious to Petra's state. "Her Majesty believes you should give a lecture on the subject. To be kept very quiet, of course. Only those ladies we believe would be genuinely interested."

"Well—"

"We would hold the session in the Queen's private apartments, so any ladies wishing to participate may do so without fear of being seen. Shall I tell Her Majesty you are amenable?"

Petra was about to acquiesce, when a question all but sprang from her mind to her lips without her bidding it.

"Forgive me, Lady Norworthy, but I never asked—how exactly

did you learn about my taking instruction for my own self-defense? And who told you about the knife I keep on my garters?"

Her ladyship's lorgnette slowly lowered, and pink spots bloomed on her cheeks.

"Why, I..."

"Did you hear it from Sir Rufus?" Petra asked, not unkindly.

"Not exactly," she responded. "I did not tell an untruth when I said I had not *spoken* to Sir Rufus before confronting him this past Monday. But I did *see* him recently. At a dinner party in Yorkshire, at your aunt Ophelia's. Sir Rufus was there as well. Decorum made me pretend I did not care, but when I was walking past the billiards room and heard him talking, I could not forgo listening..." For a moment, she looked like a heartsick young girl. "... and hoping he said something favorable about me."

"I think that is only understandable," Petra said, valiantly hiding her impatience. She glanced at the clock on the mantel. A quarter of an hour had passed since she had been given the note Aunt Ophelia had written. "And it was then you heard Sir Rufus imparting gossip about me?"

"It was," Lady Norworthy responded, with a bit more of her usual confidence. "He was most impressed, I must tell you. But Major Carlson quickly cut him off."

Petra had been glancing at the clock again, thinking that she had little time to reach the Round Tower—along with a brief thought that Duncan had been wrong; Sir Rufus *had* known about her exploits—but then her gaze snapped to the older woman's face. "The major? What were they discussing?"

"I don't know if that is meaningful to—"

"Lady Norworthy, please. It may be important. Do tell me what was said."

The lorgnette made its appearance again.

"Yes, impertinent you are, even if impressive. Yet, I shall tell you, though it is not much. The major was demanding to know information about his late father. Sadly took his own life, you know, but it seems the major feels otherwise. And he claimed that Sir Rufus knew the truth, and that this truth would set him free—'him' being his father, and his reputation, or so he said." Her ladyship's lips pursed as if she almost felt embarrassed to say it, but she added, "Then Sir Rufus laughed and said something quite odd."

Petra raised her eyebrows in question.

"'It was only bean water.' That's what he said, albeit with much laughter. Strange, do you not agree, Lady Petra? Now I shall return to my own rooms to rest, but Her Majesty will be pleased you agreed to her idea."

Lady Norworthy exited before Petra could form any reply.

"Bean water?" she then repeated aloud, perplexed, before emitting a gasp.

Lifting the skirts of her riding habit, she raced into her dressing room and threw open her wardrobe. Colonel Wolston might have Sir Rufus's scandalous manuscript, but he did not know there was one page missing, containing one very interesting memory. She retrieved it, and hastily read it again, with Sir Rufus's words, and his laughter, in mind.

Everything that had happened . . . every bit of it . . . was about revenge.

As she hurried through the Edward III Tower, Petra checked her watch. If she was lucky, there would not be too much time from the moment she set foot into the Round Tower and when her friends found her note. Whether it would be enough time for them to arrive and help was another question entirely, however.

Once on the covered stairs, Petra paused for one more minute to adjust the buttons down the center of her riding-habit skirts to give her as much access to her dagger as she could without it being obvious. She wished she had an extra weapon, but she had not been able to think of anything that would not be visible, and therefore anger either Major Carlson or Lord Wadley-Bates—or both. She did not want to entice them to do anything she would regret.

"Why did I not see it?" Petra chastised herself under her breath as she hurried up the covered stairs. The two of them must have been working together somehow, plotting their retaliations. And because she had the proof, Aunt Ophelia was in danger.

Momentarily peeking out of the covered stairs over the Quadrangle, it was almost eerily quiet with all the guests off some four miles away at Virginia Water Lake for the swimming contests. Petra hesitated one more second to crane her head sideways, taking in the Round Tower. She let her eyes travel up the medieval tower that wasn't actually wholly round. It had been recently raised to its current height by order of the Prince Regent himself to form the archives, where books, papers, and treasures of all kinds relating to the history of Great Britain would be kept, including Sir Rufus's recipes. She had been told that, inside the tower, there were two hundred steps to the top, but climbing them was worth it for the incredible views of Windsor Great Park and County Berkshire.

Her eyes stopped when they reached the battlements at the top of the tower: toothlike merlons rising into the air before dipping into the spaces called crenels. Petra's gaze then met that of a woman who stood between two merlons. She had short, dark hair that came forward in the Titus fashion.

She was standing very still, her palms flat on the stone crenel, as if frightened to move a single muscle. And around her neck was a silk ribbon, its vibrant fuschia color causing it to stand out against her pale skin.

"Aunt Ophelia," whispered Petra.

Then a man could be seen at her aunt's back. As Aunt Ophelia was tall, it took Petra a moment to make out who it was, and then she watched in horror as Major Carlson looked down, searching until he found Petra's eyes. She saw the flash of his teeth as he grinned. And then he began tightening the ribbon around Aunt Ophelia's neck.

Thirty-Nine

Petra pushed through the doors to the ground floor of the Round Tower, panting after running up the last of the covered stairs and thankful she had loosened the bottom three buttons of her riding-habit skirt.

She found the stairwell that would take her up to the top of the tower, crying out as she fumbled with shaky fingers to loosen her skirt's remaining buttons. The topmost one refused to budge. With an angry noise, she ripped off the button, throwing it against the creamy stone walls before fastening each side of her skirts to the hooks hidden at the small of her back.

Her legs then freed, she began taking the stairs at a run.

Somehow, she made it up around half of the two hundred steps without feeling much the worse for wear except for a sheen of perspiration on her face. She exercised far more than most ladies of her station, rode horses every day, and was used to great numbers of stairs, of course. Yet nearly as soon as she mounted the next steps, everything within her started to burn, and she was forced to climb at a frustratingly slower pace.

By the time she neared the top, her lungs and legs were weak and on fire. She had a stitch in her chest, her heart was pounding through the embroidery on her riding jacket, and sweat was pouring down her temples. She was struggling to breathe, but it did not keep her from seeing that a heavy wooden door had been left cracked open, as if the major was intending to taunt her. No doubt he was expecting her to be much slower than she was. That she would arrive weak and unable to breathe, only to find her beloved aunt strangled at his hands.

I cannot let that happen, Petra thought wildly.

And yet, she was indeed weakened by the climb. She could do nothing but lean against the wall, taking heaving breaths, unable to move, her whole body feeling wobbly and unsure. She knew that with each second, she was losing time, and so was her aunt, but right now, struggling to catch her breath, she felt nothing but spent.

Would Aunt Ophelia be dead by now? If possible, Petra's heart beat faster, and her eyes grew blurry with angry tears. She had to move.

Then she felt her breathing ease, her strength returning, just a bit. But it would have to be enough.

She staggered the last few steps. There was no sense in being quiet, as Petra realized this situation had been designed specifically to make certain she would see her aunt in trouble and come running. Even if the major thought she would be slower, he still knew she was on her way.

The thought that he had wantonly underestimated her made her find a reserve of strength from somewhere deep inside. She tried to remember the things she had been taught recently. About when to fight, when to negotiate, and when to run. When to be quiet, and when to be loud.

Then she heard the gasps and whimpers of her aunt as she was being strangled. She was still alive.

Petra pulled her dagger from the garter on her leg. It was time to be as loud as she bloody well could.

Drawing in a breath, she gave a raspy yell, and kicked open the door.

It was not as heavy as it looked, and it swung back quickly. Petra heard an *oof* and then something bang against the battlements behind the door. She did not care, and did not hesitate. She ran headlong toward the man choking Aunt Ophelia, yanking her backward, pulling at the bright pink ribbon with a sinister smile upon his face.

Vaguely, she saw that her aunt had managed to get her fingers up under the ribbon. She was still struggling, using all her might.

And when her Forsyth blue eyes saw Petra hurtling toward her, dagger in hand, she managed to turn, taking Major Carlson with her, making him a larger target. But he saw Petra, too, and she could see the rage contorting his face. He had not been quick enough, and he knew it.

Then the major released his hold on the ribbon circling Aunt Ophelia's neck and lunged for Petra. As he did, Petra dropped into a crouch, and felt her curls ruffle as he swiped and only grabbed air.

Then she was turning sideways, putting all her weight on her left leg as she thrust outward her right heel, sharp and fast, just as she'd been made to practice, over and over. Her bootheel struck his kneecap with a dull crunch.

Major Carlson crumpled to the ground, howling, directly beside Aunt Ophelia, who had dropped down onto all fours, coughing and wheezing, one hand scrabbling to fully release the ribbon about her neck.

But the major's anger was enough that he saw his chance and grabbed for the ends of the ribbon again, yanking Aunt Ophelia fully to the ground, pulling with all his might, his face turning puce with exertion and pain.

Petra had stumbled with the impact of her kick and scrambled to right herself. She realized she had dropped her dagger, but there was no time to find it. As her aunt made a horrid gagging noise, Petra ran forward and jammed her boot down on the major's kneecap again, then added a second kick to his damaged thigh. With an enraged bellow, he released Aunt Ophelia for a second time, rolling onto his back.

"Sir Rufus deserved to die!" he yelled, spit flying from his mouth. "They both deserved to die for what they did to my father!"

"And what was that, Major?" Petra called out between ragged breaths. She already knew the answer, courtesy of Sir Rufus's memoir, but she wanted to be certain.

"They poisoned him! For no other reason than my father embarrassed him, our self-righteous Prince! Then they denigrated my father's good name by telling all of society he took his own life! The Prince killed a good man to assuage his own pitiful, wounded ego. It has been burning at me, at my mind and my soul like neverending flames ever since I have learned of what he did." The major put his hands to his head, grasping at his hair as if wishing to pull out his tortured thoughts, then he snarled, "I cannot let such a man live! He deserved to die too!"

With a cackling laugh coming from his throat despite his grimaces of pain, Major Carlson jerked his head over his shoulder. Petra looked across the battlements.

The Prince Regent lay on his side, completely still upon the stone of the Round Tower. Petra drew in a sharp, horrified breath. Then turned back to the major.

"You believe yourself to be seeking revenge, Major," she said. "But you are misguided. You are mourning the loss of your father, and it is understandable, but the Prince Regent did not poison him. At least, not fatally."

And then she relayed the information that she had come to understand from Sir Rufus's memoir.

"Your father and the Prince routinely played tricks on one another as longtime friends often do. He made your father briefly ill for embarrassing him, yes, but the Prince's retaliation was not meant to be sinister, but in line with past pranks. It was badly done, but that was it. I truly believe that if he understood how deep your father's despair had become, that he never would have played such a trick in the first place."

"You are a liar," he spat. "The Prince is willing to kill the King, just as he killed my father!"

"I have proof of what I say, Major!" she shouted back. "If you will allow me—if you will leave here with me, and leave Lady Ophelia in peace—I will show you."

Petra saw something for the first time in looking into Major Carlson's face, his once-handsome countenance now poisoned in its own way. For she saw a level of madness that only comes with a pure belief in an untruth, and an inability to rein in his hurt and pain enough to consider anything other than that which was fueling his rage.

For a moment, she felt genuine pity for him. And then he was hauling himself up on one knee and lunged forward again, his hands reaching for her leather garter and her lockpicks.

"Petra!" rasped Aunt Ophelia.

Leaping away from his grasp at the last second, Petra's arms pinwheeled so wildly that the blue stone of her ancestor's ring smacked her forehead as she steadied herself. But the major was undeterred. Before she could move another step, he had gathered himself and was suddenly flying toward her.

And in the space between heartbeats, Petra recalled why her great-great-grandmother had commissioned the ring with the lapis lazuli nearly the size of a quail egg. Why Aunt Ophelia had wanted Petra to think about their shared relative who had escaped her abusive first husband. The ring had not been used as a vessel for poison, no.

It had been used as a weapon.

And Petra brought her right hand back in a fist, and slammed the cabochon directly between the major's gray-blue eyes.

She felt the punch travel painfully up her entire arm. For one moment, the major teetered, still on one knee, before his eyes rolled up into his head and he fell, collapsing on the stone.

Seeing her dagger a few feet away, Petra rushed for it and then ran to release the ribbon from her aunt's neck, letting it fall away, harmless once more. Aunt Ophelia was still coughing and wheezing. "The Prince," she managed to say.

But Petra had heard the groan from behind the door she had kicked open. She stood, legs planted securely, dagger ready for Lord Wadley-Bates to come at her and her aunt.

She felt a hand on her leg. "No," Aunt Ophelia wheezed. "He was coerced . . . by the major into abducting me. He is not to blame."

Lord Wadley-Bates was stumbling from behind the door, looking dazed.

"Are you certain?" Petra asked, eyeing him as he rubbed the back of his head.

Aunt Ophelia nodded. "Prinny," she said. "Go."

Petra picked up the fuschia ribbon. "You must tie the major's hands."

When her aunt began crawling toward the unconscious Major Carlson, Petra dashed over to the Prince Regent, dropping down beside him on her knees.

Anxiously, she felt for a pulse. It was there, slow and strong. She put her hand on his shoulder.

"Your Royal Highness? Can you hear me?"

He gave a groan and his eyes fluttered open.

Petra sighed with relief. She then released another, longer breath, adding a smile when Duncan, Charles, and Colonel Wolston arrived, followed by Sable, who was seemingly leading half the Coldstream Guards as they flowed onto the battlements of the Round Tower.

Her friends had found her note, it seemed, and had sent an abundance of help.

FORTY

"You do realize we shall never be able to speak of this," Aunt Ophelia said in a low voice as she and Petra relaxed in their respective copper baths full of steaming, fragrant water and loads of bubbles. "Darling, the Prince *fainted*. We would face the rack if we told anyone."

They both erupted into giggles as Caroline, Lottie, and Frances came in, the latter bearing her supplies and already eyeing the red weal around Aunt Ophelia's neck.

"My, my," Caroline drawled, setting a vase full of freshly cut dahlias on the small table between the two tubs. "So this is what one must do to gain access to the Queen's very own bathing chamber, is it? Simply save the life of a prince who had been knocked unconscious by his own royal solicitor?"

Petra could not look at her aunt. For if she did, neither of them would be able to keep up the ruse that Petra herself had started when Colonel Wolston ran to assist the Prince and she hastily yelped out, "He was struck, upon the temple, by Major Carlson and lost consciousness!"

Wolston had raised an eyebrow after searching for a contusion and finding nothing but a scrape upon His Royal Highness's cheekbone from falling upon the stone. But Wolston did not contradict her story.

Lottie let Sable off her lead and Petra sat up a bit to give her hound a kiss on the snout when Sable sniffed at the bubbles, her tail wagging furiously. Lottie had not been able to close her mouth from the moment she walked in, taking in the frescoes on the ceiling and the gilt, well, everything.

"Lawks, it is rather opulent in here, is it not?"

"Darlings, when Her Majesty insists we bathe in her rooms, we bathe in her rooms, overabundance of gold leafing and painted cherubs ogling our bits and all," said Aunt Ophelia, her voice still a bit raspy from her terrible experience.

Lottie tipped her head back to survey the cherubs. "Oh, they are being a bit cheeky, aren't they?"

Everyone laughed, but Petra noticed that Caroline merely smiled. Which was quite unlike her. Normally her throaty laugh would be reverberating about the room. She met Petra's eyes and gave a mere shake of her head as if to say, *Do not ask, dearest.*

Petra really did not have to ask, however. She knew that Caroline and the man she loved, Lord Whitfield, were on borrowed time. Caroline was married to a kind, wonderful man, but one who was already in love with another man himself. But Caroline and her Captain Smythe were from two of the oldest and most powerful families in England, and thus divorce was not possible.

Whitfield, on the other hand, had come to the point in his life when he realized he needed a wife, and an heir—neither of which he could legally have with Caroline, though he was as in love with her as she was with him. Even Caroline's captain approved of the match, yet there was nothing to be done.

Petra could only assume that Whitfield had met a woman he could marry, and was willing to marry, and thus, the love of a lifetime was coming to an end.

Petra's heart went out to her friend. And she worried Duncan would feel that need someday himself, too. He continued to claim he was happy being a roguish, older cousin to his many younger ones, as well as an uncle to his brother James's impending child. Yet time could only tell. And she would handle it with as much grace as she could muster, if need be. Though it would bring her to her knees like nothing else.

"Dearest," Caroline said, bringing her out of her thoughts. "Shawcross and Wolston are scheduled to compete against each other at the tilting contest later today. He bade me tell you, for I think he is hoping you will be there to watch so that, as per tradition, he may kiss the maiden he wishes when he wins."

She grinned at Petra, who returned the gesture. Then she turned to Lottie, her eyebrows waggling.

"And, Miss Lottie Reed, I think a certain colonel might be hoping for a kiss from you if *he* should win."

Lottie flushed charmingly and Frances held out a small tin from her bag full of balms, tinctures, herbs, and other apothecarist items.

"They are pastilles of mint, for one's breath. I recently began making them and cannot keep them in stock."

Lottie at first could only stare at the tin, and then she took it with a shy grin.

"Hurrah!" sang out Aunt Ophelia, and everyone laughed. And Petra reminded herself to send word to Duncan to allow Wolston to win.

The Prince Regent and his mama sat side by side at a table in the Queen's Audience Chamber. But they were smiling as Petra and Aunt Ophelia walked in and made their curtsies.

When they were all seated and niceties exchanged, the Prince had some sobering news.

"I was just informed that Major Carlson had some poison hidden on his person. After he came to his senses long enough to realize he was in my dungeon at Curfew Tower, and that he would be unlikely to live much longer, he ingested it. I am told it was cyanide."

Petra and her aunt only nodded sadly, for there was little one could say.

Except, she did. "I believe the major was intending on using it to poison you, Your Royal Highness. Out of revenge. He would probably have done so by forcing it into your mouth whilst you were unconscious if he had first succeeded in killing Lady Ophelia." She glanced at her aunt, who touched her throat with a look of dismay.

"Do explain what you mean by 'revenge,' Lady Petra," demanded the Queen, and then reminded them they had little time before the tilting contest, so she should not be concerned with mincing her words. Petra nodded and met the eyes of the Prince Regent.

"Please forgive me for my bluntness, Sir, but when I read through Sir Rufus's memoir pages, I saw notes he'd put down, no doubt intending to form into another story. Though hastily written, the notes related how you sought him out at a house party in the spring of 1813. He wrote that you asked for a 'poison' in order to use it on Lord Carlson, the major's late father, because his lordship made the unfortunate mistake of embarrassing you."

The Prince shifted in his chair, but did not tell her to cease speaking, so she continued.

"What is also unfortunate is that, whilst Sir Rufus did indicate in his notes that you merely requested a concoction of kidney-bean water, he indeed first referred to it as a poison. Now, Major Carlson had also heard this whole story from Sir Rufus himself, but it was either not explained properly or the major's grief or anger made him willfully misunderstand. For the major did not accept that whilst you were indeed embarrassed by Lord Carlson, you did not take your friend's actions so wholly to heart. You did, however, wish to retaliate—in jest, of course."

"That was all it was meant to be," the Prince said, sounding half plaintive, and half belligerent. "Merely a reciprocal prank upon my friend. I put some of the kidney-bean water Sir Rufus gave me into his drink. He was to have excessive flatulence whilst at a small dinner party. Stink up the room a bit! Have everyone pinch their noses around him, laugh at him, that sort of thing." His expression turned puckish. "And that's all that happened, too. He was my friend; I certainly would never have wanted him dead."

Petra nodded. She truly felt the Prince believed this—and that the late Lord Carlson likely did too. *And if he had explained as much to his son, maybe the major would not have gone down the path he did*, she thought sadly. But then again, she realized, it was often a truth that with loved ones, sometimes not enough is ever said, each thinking they already know what is in the other's heart—and this often went treble for men.

"That is true, Sir," she said nonetheless. "You did not wish whatsoever to kill him, and we have three means of proof. For one, we found more notes—possibly unseen by the major—where Sir Rufus discussed the timing of this incident, including your exact words. It happened in late April of 1813, and was meant to cause Lord Carlson only discomfort."

From her reticule, Petra then removed the crumpled note that read like orders from a physician—*Administer no more than one spoonful for desired effect*—causing the Prince to blanch when he saw it.

He looked so distressed, in fact, that Petra did not have the heart to tell him that his laughing with Sir Rufus a few days earlier about the prank—and throwing the note into a desk in front of Major Carlson—was likely what sent the major on his final path to murder. Instead, she continued her explanations for the Queen.

"It seems you abided by this and gave just enough to give Lord Carlson minor stomach issues and nothing more. Then, sadly, the baron died by ingesting a lethal dose of laudanum in early May of 1813. I discreetly asked someone who would have known about the timing, and all of what I just said was confirmed."

The Prince said, "Who? Who else would have known the truth of this?"

"If I may, there is someone outside who can attest to it," Petra said.

The Queen nodded and the footmen opened the doors. In walked a handsome man, auburn hair neatly combed back, and hazel eyes, one of them blackened, that shone with nervousness behind a battered face. He stopped a few feet from the table and bowed.

"And who is this ruffian?" demanded the Prince, looking at him with distaste.

"This, Your Royal Highness, is Sir Rufus's valet, Mr. Oliver Beecham."

It took a moment for the realization to sink in, and then the Prince deflated.

"Ah" was all he said.

The Queen looked like she was holding back a roll of her eyes, and invited Oliver to speak.

"Your Royal Highness, Your Majesty, I had just come into Sir Rufus's employ in early 1813 when you sought out Sir Rufus to ask about the kidney beans. It was at a house party, where he had been invited to speak on cooking, and you were the honored guest. It was late, but Sir Rufus was kindly showing me some cooking techniques in the kitchen when you arrived. I was in the larder, fetching some ingredients, and I stayed put until you had gone. I heard you say you only wanted a bit of the kidney-bean water. Just enough to cause 'a good bit of flatulence,' is what you said, Sir, if you don't mind me repeating it."

"His Royal Highness does not, and we are grateful to you, Mr. Beecham," the Queen said graciously. The Prince then muttered, "Yes, quite grateful."

Oliver was smart enough to know when he should exit a room, but not before charmingly wishing Her Majesty congratulations on her anniversary, earning him a rare smile. He bowed, adding an extra one to Petra, and left. She then spoke once more.

"I believe that when the major discovered—forgive me, Sir, but what he felt was a cruel act upon his father fueled by nothing but an embarrassing moment—he could not abide by it, and it sent him into a rage. One that might have been building within him for some time for various reasons, such as his time in battle, or other losses that sadly worked on his mind, body, and his very soul. Nevertheless, it was a rage from which he could not recover. He therefore felt the need to seek vengeance."

Petra met the Prince's gaze, and did not add that he had been correct, that his attempts to take the crown from his own father, King George, had likely made it worse. By the way the Prince looked away in shame, he already knew. Yet the Queen insisted on further explanations, so Petra danced around the truth.

"And it seems that he first lost control of himself after an argument in the Green Drawing Room with Sir Rufus on the first day of the celebrations." She looked to her aunt. "But an hour ago, we learned that a hall maid overheard the argument. It was about the major finding Sir Rufus's memoir, including the notes regarding the prank played on Lord Carlson. Then Sir Rufus, using his belowstairs influence, obtained a key to the major's room and took back every piece of written proof the major had that made him feel justified in wanting revenge. The major was so incensed, it evidently brought him to tears, likely further fueling his anger."

Her eyes shifted briefly back to the Prince, who understood she was also referring to the petition the major had drawn up for his suspected treachery. He flushed, but said nothing.

"Regardless, after killing Sir Rufus, he then attempted to kill me because I was coming too close to the truth. But his ultimate target was you, Your Royal Highness."

The Queen then glanced to her son, who was staring at the table, and Petra felt he was likely realizing that his actions had caused far too much heartache. Thus, she and Aunt Ophelia were dismissed, but not without sincere gratitude from both mother and son.

Yet just before they left, the Queen's footmen opened the doors and announced that Mr. Shawcross and Colonel Wolston were there and asking for the briefest of audiences.

They were told to come in, and all four in the room looked curiously at one another when significant clanking could be heard.

But it was soon clear why, and Petra's smile quickly stretched wide at the sight.

Both men walked in wearing almost full suits of armor, except for the helmets, in preparation for the tilting contest. And far from looking silly, they both looked impossibly handsome, with Petra finding it hard to remove her eyes from Duncan's broad chest.

With a quick flash of a smile, he then walked forward and handed the Prince a piece of paper.

"I found this alongside Sir Rufus's will, Your Royal Highness. It seems that he wished everyone to know that he only wrote his memoir because he needed money for his debts that were incurred by investing in a scheme run by a Mr. Barwick of Yorkshire."

The Prince went slightly pale—again—and Petra and her aunt Ophelia exchanged discreet glances.

"Sir Rufus was quite ill, of course," Duncan continued, "and hoped that proceeds from the book could go to help those who lost all their funds in this scheme. In this letter, he expressed his wishes that if he died before it went to publication, that someone should revise the book to keep any names out of it. The scandals, he indicated, would sell the book. And people could speculate all they liked. But if the stories were turned vague, then the chances that anyone would truly be hurt would be minimal."

The Prince read Sir Rufus's letter, with the Queen looking over his shoulder. He glanced up at his mama and she nodded her approval.

"I think that is brilliant," said Aunt Ophelia. "Your Royal Highness, if you would permit me, I am quite the scribe, and I would love to transform this memoir into something that helps others whilst never truly hurting anyone. Would you allow me the chance?"

Finally, the Prince smiled.

"I think it a fine plan, Lady Ophelia. A fine plan indeed."

FORTY-ONE

Saturday, 9 September 1815
Day six of the royal celebrations

"My lords, ladies, and gentlemen!" cried the steward, throwing his arms out wide. "Welcome to the final bake of Her Majesty's patisserie contest!"

The clapping was wildly enthusiastic. Wagers had been made on who would win—Mrs. Bing of Forsyth House or Mrs. Davis of Norworthy Manor—and Lady Petra and Lady Norworthy made everyone laugh by playfully glaring at one another as if they would demand a duel if their respective cook did not win. Nevertheless, Petra was quite glad that Chef Carême would make the final decision as to which cook would earn the title.

Though Petra was not so certain the Prince would forgive her for telling the Frenchman to name his own terms for staying in England another two years. For he demanded two thousand pounds per annum—nearly ten times the amount any other chef would be paid—and full authority to revise any menus for state dinners.

Additionally, he would only train six chefs, no more, and insisted one of them would be Oliver Beecham. The Prince agreed. And Annie could not have been happier for or prouder of her brother, who finally seemed to understand that working hard and choosing the right path in life would take him further than any scheme could ever do.

"And now," the steward continued, "our judges will taste both *vol-au-vents Puits d'Amour* and make their selection as to which is the best bake. Then Chef Antonin Carême will decide the winner. Therefore, for the last time during these celebrations, are you ready, my lord and lady judges? Yes? Then please begin!"

Petra and Caroline both audibly oohed when the vol-au-vents were brought out. They were positively stunning. One had a pastry in the shape of a diamond and was filled with vanilla Chantilly cream with multiple spun-sugar intertwining hearts that were dusted with a touch of gold leaf, making them sparkle enchantingly every time the sun peeked out from behind the clouds.

The other was an octagon-shaped pastry filled with crème flavored with violets and a hint of lemon before being topped with tiny candied violets forming, and linking together, the letters G and C for King George and Queen Charlotte, creating an edible royal love cypher.

Petra was in a quandary immediately. Both had delightfully crisp pastries the perfect shade of light brown and had been dipped in luscious caramel before being dusted with chopped pistachios. One had given a bit of extra salt to their caramel, and the other had roasted their pistachios. Both added an extra layer of complexity that she adored.

And as for their fillings, the Chantilly cream was whipped and thickened to perfection, and then the violet crème had a deliciously light floral taste that was brightened by a bit of lemon. Their decorations were simple, but with a bit of whimsy.

In all, both bakes were just different enough to be their own, yet were clearly in the spirit of Chef Carême's own recipe, which the Frenchman had described to the judges in detail so they knew what to expect. And the problem was then that both were so exquisite that Petra could honestly not say which one she liked better.

And thus, she said as much on her judge's sheet.

Once all four judges had turned in their decisions, they left the table so that Chef Carême could stride out alone in his white uniform and hat he called a toque, giving a bow to the applause he received, before sitting down with his own plates of vol-au-vents.

Petra watched in fascination as he picked up the plates and looked at the bakes from all angles. He tapped the sides, broke off a bit of the pastry and crushed it between his fingers. He seemed to judge the amount of pistachios, and tasted the caramel on its own via his fingers. Then he tasted the fillings on their own as well.

And once he had done all of that, only then did he take a bite of each bake as a whole, chewing first slowly, then quickly. And throughout it all, he showed no emotion whatsoever.

When he had tried but two bites of each bake, he sat back in his chair, eyeing both, arms crossed over his chest, seemingly knowing the crowd of well-dressed guests was watching his every move—they loving it as much as he. Then he stood and walked over to speak with the Queen.

Petra saw her raise her eyebrows, and after a moment, she inclined her head.

A footman was signaled and Petra watched as Mrs. Bing and Mrs. Davis—both impeccably turned out in fresh dresses and crisp white aprons and caps—walked out, side by side, nervous but smiling. Petra crossed her fingers behind her back.

"My lords, ladies, and gentlemen," said Chef Carême to the crowd. "It is the rare thing when a talented cook can take a recipe they have never seen before and make a masterpiece. And tonight, I have seen not one, but two cooks do just that."

He turned and gestured to Petra, Caroline, Sir Franklin, and Lord Wadley-Bates.

"I noted that our esteemed judges could not decide which cook made the better vol-au-vent," he continued. "And I thought, 'Bah! I shall show them!' But instead, I have had the pleasure of trying two of the best adaptations of my recipe I have ever tasted."

He turned to Mrs. Bing and Mrs. Davis, who clutched each other's hands and held their respective breaths.

"Ladies, your bakes... *c'est magnifique*." He kissed the tips of his fingers in a show of deliciousness. "And therefore, with the permission of Her Majesty, I am declaring *both of you* the best cooks in England!"

Mrs. Bing and Mrs. Davis could not have been happier. They were applauded for some minutes—with Petra clapping the hardest and Duncan letting out a loud whoop. And then two lovely bouquets of flowers—in reality, one large bouquet, hastily divided—were presented to the cooks.

Later, Petra would send another bouquet to Mrs. Bing's room with a letter of congratulations, a directive to take a week off to go home to the Devon coast and see her family to celebrate, and a small purse with enough coin to travel well and possibly buy herself a present. She received a charming note from Mrs. Bing, stained with happy tears, in return.

And later still, after Petra had taught five brave women—Lady Norworthy amongst them—an introductory instruction on defending themselves, and when twilight had begun outside Petra's bedchamber windows, Annie held up a stunning gown. It was of midnight blue velvet embroidered heavily with iridescent beads over the bodice before lessening in number until they looked like a dozen or so shooting stars on the final yards of her skirt. Annie's eyes shone with delight, not least because Oliver's testimony meant she had been able to return to the castle for the final evening.

"Now, my lady. Let us ready you for the ball."

Everyone danced the Viennese waltz. Instead of in the Queen's ballroom, nearly a thousand guests milled about the Quadrangle, eating, drinking, and dancing through the night until it turned into early morning.

And between the glorious evening, the beautiful gowns, and

the incredible decorations that had been erected overnight by the extremely hardworking servants of Windsor Castle that made the open-air space look like a fairyland, the final night of Her Majesty's week of celebrations was more memorable than anyone could have imagined.

Colonel Wolston had won the tilt—earning the Prince the five shillings he had bet his mama—and earning Wolston a very public kiss from Miss Lottie Reed.

Petra, Frances, and Aunt Ophelia squealed when Wolston charmingly invited Lottie to dance, where the two stared into each other's eyes the entire time. Caroline and her dark-haired, blue-eyed Lord Whitfield were already showing off their skills at the latest dance steps. To anyone else, nothing seemed amiss. But to Petra, they both looked as if they were determined to enjoy themselves despite knowing their respective hearts would be breaking soon.

Lord Wadley-Bates then asked Aunt Ophelia if she might dance—still looking a bit boot-faced for having allowed Major Carlson to threaten him into forcing Lady Ophelia up into the Round Tower. She accepted, reminding him that he was forgiven, but warning him never to do it again or he would feel a large lapis-lazuli cabochon between his eyes.

Sir Franklin, having fully recovered from being poisoned, had taken a very kindly and paternal liking to Frances, and asked her to dance so that he might speak with her about her processes for concocting her balms and tinctures.

And then Duncan whisked Petra to the dance floor, much to her delight. Eschewing every rule of society, she stayed in his arms for three more dances, knowing her behavior was being watched by the Lady Patronesses of Almack's, amongst others, and not caring one jot. There would be a time and a place for facing the fact that her behavior was causing more talk than she wanted, but it would simply have to wait.

Afterward, he would walk her out to the North Terrace, where they blended into the darkness and shared several long kisses, with Duncan praising her for how she'd handled herself on the battlements of the Round Tower.

"*C'est magnifique*, my lady," he said, his smiling lips touching her ear.

"Heavens," she said on a happy sigh, as his attentions made her shiver and press herself more fully against him for another kiss.

Then, with her hand clasped in his, they walked up the steps named for a royal princess turned queen who bravely ruled on her own terms, and strolled back into the beautiful, celebratory evening.

AUTHOR'S HISTORICAL NOTE

I'M A SUCKER FOR USING REAL HISTORICAL PLACES AND NAMES in my books, so setting this book at Windsor Castle and using a few real names made me a bit giddy. And as a *Great British Bake Off* lover, the castle made for the perfect place for Queen Charlotte to hold her inaugural (if fictional) patisserie contest.

But writing about the castle and trying to get all the rooms straight was not as easy as I thought it would be. Windsor Castle has been in existence in some way since 1066 and it has evolved, been enlarged, and rooms moved around many times over. I was lucky enough to find two maps of the castle that helped immensely—one from 1760 of the entire castle grounds, and another of the ground floor of the Upper Ward from 1811—and combined them both in deciding where rooms were situated in my story. I also used the names of what the rooms or areas might have been called at the time (which may not be what they are called now, in case you've visited and are thinking, *Isn't it called the Grand Staircase, not the Great Staircase?*).

Then I worked in some artistic license after finding a map of the castle from 1898 that showed two adjoining ground-floor libraries that sat in the north wing between the picture gallery on the east side and Queen Elizabeth's Gallery on the west side. I loved the idea of utilizing those two libraries—with one being the site of the murder—and so I did.

I also found a painting of the royal kitchens, which fascinated me. And while I fictionalized the story, the Prince Regent (later

George IV), did once visit the royal kitchens, and a red carpet was laid down for his visit—but it happened at The Royal Pavilion at Brighton, not at Windsor Castle.

Speaking of kitchens, then there is Chef Marie-Antoine Carême, also known as Antonin Carême (ca. 1783–1833). He was a renowned French chef—and arguably the first true celebrity chef—and was responsible for some of the foods or sauces we still know today, such as vol-au-vents, profiteroles (choux à la crème), fanchonettes, elaborate sugar sculptures called pièces montées and the so-called mother sauces, including béchamel.

While he did, in fact, work for the Prince Regent, I did bring Chef Carême to England earlier than he was there in real life. He actually worked for Prinny from 1816 to 1817, both in London and in Brighton—earning two thousand pounds per year when most earned two hundred per annum—before deciding he'd had enough of England and returning to France. The Prince did attempt to entice him to stay, however, and reading that inspired me to put it into the story, with Lady Petra being the one who convinces him to remain for a little while longer.

While Chef Carême was called "the king of chefs, and the chef of kings," the one thing I gave him in this book that he is not actually credited with inventing was the croissant. Evolving from the Austrian kipferl, a crescent-shaped pastry, the croissant did not begin to emerge in Paris until the late 1830s. However, considering all Chef Carême gave to the culinary world, it would not surprise me if he had created something similar.

As for all the bakes that Lady Petra has the pleasure of tasting as one of the patisserie judges, I found recipes for all of them while looking through several delightful cookbooks of the Regency era. Without a doubt, I could have had the contest go on for three weeks or more with all the fun recipes I found for biscuits, cakes, candies, and so many other sweet treats!

ACKNOWLEDGMENTS

I can honestly say I've loved writing all my books, but this one was especially fun. I think I smiled my way through every chapter! And I continue to be grateful to my incredible editor at Minotaur Books, Hannah O'Grady, and my wonderful agents, Christina Hogrebe and Jess Errera at Jane Rotrosen Agency, for being a part of my life in a way that helps me to fulfill my dreams of writing books like this that make me so very happy.

Huge thanks also go to Madeline Alsup, Sara Beth Haring, and Sara LaCotti, whose help is always appreciated, and who always make me look good. And to David Baldeosingh Rotstein and Peyton Stark, for creating one heck of a gorgeous cover for Lady Petra's third adventure, and Meryl Levavi, who designed the interior. Special thanks also goes to Liane Payne, who brilliantly illustrated my two-page map of the Windsor Castle grounds.

As always, I send thanks and love to my amazing parents and friends for all their continued support. Writing may be a solitary endeavor (though I love every second of creating these worlds from my own research and imagination), but with my friends and family cheering me on, I never feel alone.

And big, huge thanks go out to readers, reviewers, and librarians, who make every bit of an author's world that much brighter.

ABOUT THE AUTHOR

Annie Hewitt Photography

Celeste Connally is the *USA Today* bestselling author of the Lady Petra Inquires series, an Agatha Award nominee, and a former freelance writer and editor. Her mysteries are set in Regency-era England and feature a headstrong heroine and as many equestrian scenes as her plots and editor will allow. She delights in giving her mysteries a good dose of romance, too, and a few research facts she hopes you'll find as interesting as she does. Passionate about history and slightly obsessed with period dramas, what Celeste loves most is reading and writing about women who don't always do as they are told.